# THE IMPORT

## A MATTHEW RIKER NOVEL

J.T. BAIER

# PROLOGUE

It had been a night for violence.

Blood ran freely from the knife wound on Matthew Riker's leg and from the cut over his eye. The bullet hole in his shoulder ached, and his left eye swelled more with each passing minute. Corpses lay outside the small airfield's gate and around the hangar. Several more bodies kept him company on the rooftop. In the distance, a plane was burning.

He'd made a promise to leave his life of violence behind, and for six years, he'd kept that vow. Breaking it would almost certainly result in his death. But that was a problem for tomorrow. Today, all that mattered was a small girl. She was close by and she needed his help. Everything that he had done would be for nothing if he couldn't save her.

A man stood on the roof across from Riker. The moonlight cast a long shadow from his enormous frame. Hatred came off him like waves off a mirage. He stalked toward Riker with one goal—murder. If he was successful, the world would pay a great price.

But Riker didn't care about that right now. He only cared about protecting the girl.

He and the other man were alone on that roof, two warriors facing off with only stars to bear witness. The other man was hurt too. The bandages around his head proved that. But was he as hurt as Riker?

"Let's finish this," the man said, his voice a low growl that somehow carried across the space between them.

Riker leaned forward, shifting his weight onto the balls of his feet, preparing for battle. This would be his final proving ground.

He was hurt. He was beyond exhausted. He was ready.

"Yeah," he said to the hulking killer shuffling toward him. "Let's finish it."

# 1

*FIVE DAYS earlier*

RIKER LIFTED the crate out of the back of his truck and started toward the entrance to the fairgrounds. The wood felt rough against his calloused hands as he moved through the nearly empty parking lot. The people around him were taking it slow, enjoying the relatively cool August morning. Riker was glad the crowd was still light. The Henderson County Fair would be packed in a few hours, and he wasn't one for crowds. He much preferred the solitude of his farm. It was safer for him there.

Still, Henry Garrett was one of his oldest customers. When he'd called an hour ago asking for an emergency resupply, Riker couldn't turn him down. Besides, Riker genuinely liked the guy. Not so much that he wouldn't give him hell for dragging him out to the fairgrounds on a Friday morning, but enough that he'd let the matter drop in a month or two.

Riker moved his six-foot-one frame at an easy pace, eyes scanning for Henry's booth. Many of the vendors were still setting up for the day, warming up their fryers or organizing the prizes that would never be won in their rigged games. He spotted Henry up ahead, hard at work arranging the crafts on his table. The older man broke out in a wide grin when he spotted Riker.

"That's what I call service," he said.

Riker set his crate on the table. "Don't think you're going to avoid the ten percent delivery fee just by being friendly."

"I wouldn't dream of it. But I assume I'll be getting my usual ten percent 'Favorite Customer' discount."

"Tell you what. Buy me a beer next time I see you at the Wagon Wheel and we'll call it even."

Henry grinned again. "This is why I like you, Riker. You're one of the last reasonable humans."

Riker went to work removing jars of honey from the crate and lining them up on Henry's table. "You want to settle up today or should I bill you?"

Henry didn't answer. His eyes were fixed on something behind Riker. Henry's serious expression along with the sounds of feet striking the packed dirt and labored, panicked breathing caused Riker to turn.

A woman was running through the fairgrounds. She was moving at a good clip, headed directly toward Riker. Her hair was a tangled mess. She had an angry red welt under her left eye that would soon resolve itself into a nasty bruise, and blood seeped from a busted lower lip. She clutched a little girl to her chest. The girl hugged her tightly, her face buried in the woman's neck.

Riker took a step back to give the woman room. She passed by close enough that the dust she kicked up settled on his shoes. He only had a moment to ponder the strangeness of a woman and child sprinting through a fairground before he saw the people pursuing her.

The two men were perhaps a bit overdressed for a county fair with their polo shirts tucked into their dress slacks and their loafers slapping against the ground as they ran. One of the men was heavier than the other, and as he lumbered past, Riker could make out the distinct bulge of a gun under his windbreaker.

Riker watched for a long moment, taking it all in.

"What do you suppose that was all about?" Henry asked.

"Don't know." Riker stared at the woman disappearing into the distance and the men chasing her. It was none of his business, and it certainly wasn't his responsibility. His job was to keep his head down, stay out of trouble, and sell local honey to people like Henry Garrett.

He glanced at Henry and saw a drawn, concerned expression on the man's face.

"Was she carrying a child?"

"Yeah, I think she was." He set another jar of honey on the table.

Henry pulled out a cell phone. "Think I should call somebody?"

Before Riker could answer, a piercing cry cut through the air. Somewhere nearby, a child was screaming. The sound ran through him like a jolt from a live wire.

Henry fumbled with the touchscreen on his phone. "I'm calling 9-1-1."

Riker stared at the phone. The fairgrounds were on the outskirts of Flat Rock, North Carolina, population just a hair over three thousand. The town had only ten police officers. Riker had spotted one of them outside the fairgrounds, but

Frank Jacobs was pushing seventy, and his failing eyesight was a frequent subject of local humor. The thought of that man in a shootout with the two hard-looking individuals who'd ran past Riker didn't fill him with confidence. The other cops would take at least fifteen minutes to arrive from town. Plenty of time for the men to do whatever they wanted with the woman and child.

The child screamed again.

Riker instinctively clocked the source of that scream. It was coming from somewhere near the Ferris wheel. Before he could talk himself out of it, he set the crate down and started in that direction.

The main thoroughfare cut a lazy circle around the perimeter of the fairgrounds. The woman and her attackers had followed that route. Riker took a straighter path, heading through the center of the fair. He didn't run hard, instead favoring a steady jog that allowed him to take in his surroundings and assess the situation. All the while a little voice in his head was whispering to him.

*Don't get involved. The price is too high. Whatever's happening here, it's not worth the consequences.*

Back in the old days, that voice had been his constant companion. It had helped him get through BUD/S and helped him survive countless missions with the SEALs. And after his time in the military was through and he'd moved on to his covert position with the organization known as QS-4, the voice had become even more a part of his everyday life.

But all that was six years in the past. He was a civilian now.

He didn't ignore the voice; it had a valid point, after all. But he didn't give in to it either. He just kept moving toward the direction of the scream.

He squeezed between two booths, one that sold balloons and another featuring a game with plastic ducks. He paused when he spotted the woman, her back against a small outbuilding that housed bathrooms and storage. The little girl was still clutched to her chest, but her head was no longer buried in the woman's neck. Her eyes were wide as she stared at the two men stalking toward her, guns drawn.

The thinner man was closest to the woman. He held his gun in a two-handed grip, and he spoke in a quiet voice. "We're going to go back to the car now. No more trouble, understand? Play nice and you might just live through this."

"We both know that's not true," the woman said.

The child let out a soft whimper as the bigger man inched slowly to the side, trying to flank the woman.

Riker reached into the booth next to him and grabbed a helium tank. As he waited for the big man to move into the perfect position, he let the voice in his head have one last say.

*Don't do this, Riker. You made a promise.*

He glanced at the child's tear-streaked face and quieted the voice.

The big man moved another few inches. When he was standing directly in front of the bathroom door, Riker surged forward. He swung the helium tank hard, driving the cold metal into the man's ample stomach. The air rushed out of the man's lungs with an audible *whoosh* as he careened backward. He hit the door and it swung open. Somehow, he managed to keep his feet under him for three more steps, then he collapsed and landed hard.

Riker was on him before the door swung shut. The man started to raise his gun, but Riker brought his foot down, stomping on the man's wrist. The hand went limp and the pistol clattered to the concrete floor.

Dropping to one knee, Riker let gravity do the work. His knee landed on the man's upper diaphragm, once again forcing all the air out of his lungs in a hoarse wheeze. Panic filled the large man's eyes. Riker took a deep breath and held it as he cranked open the valve of the helium tank. He shoved the nozzle into the man's mouth as he let the pressure off of his stomach. The man gasped, taking in a deep lungful of helium. His arms flailed, hitting the walls and floor. Riker clamped a hand over his nose. The man took one more breath of helium and went limp.

Riker waited, turning to the door of the small bathroom as the hiss of the helium filled his ears. He moved his body flush to the entrance wall. The second man rushed in, pushing the woman in front of him, one arm around her neck. He held his gun out straight, pointed into the bathroom. Riker brought the metal tank down hard on his wrist. There was a crack and the gun flew out of his hand. The man let go of the woman and instinctively grabbed his broken wrist. Riker brought the tank around into the man's stomach. The move worked just as well as it had the first time. The man doubled over, wheezing for air. Riker knocked him to the floor and forced the gas from the tank into his mouth. Moments later, he too was limp on the ground.

After shutting the helium tank's valve, Riker grabbed both guns off the floor. He slipped them into the pocket of his hoodie and walked out of the bathroom. The woman followed him, clutching the child.

"Thank you." Her voice squeaked from helium. She took in a large breath of fresh air. Her voice was closer to normal when she spoke again. "Those men... Are they dead?"

"They'll be fine." Both men had been breathing evenly when Riker left the bathroom. People required air with a twenty-one percent mix of oxygen. What he'd done with the helium was the equivalent of choking them out. He didn't know how long they'd be unconscious, but he wasn't about to stick around to find out.

Riker expected to see a crowd gathered, or maybe a few people trying to capture the incident on their cellphones. Instead, he found the same sparsely populated thoroughfare as before. The entire encounter had lasted less than a minute, most of it in the bathroom, and apparently it had gone unnoticed.

He turned and started back toward Henry Garrett's booth.

The woman hesitated only a moment before hurrying after him. "Why didn't you just hit them over the head with the helium tank?"

"Because life's not a cartoon." Riker knew from experience that smashing a hard metal object into a skull was unpredictable. If you went too soft or hit the head at the wrong angle, it caused nothing more than pain and anger. If you hit too hard, you could crack the skull, possibly killing your enemy. He stopped and turned to the woman. "Listen, the police are going to be here soon. My friend already called them. When they get here, I'd appreciate it if you could leave me out of the story."

The woman let out a laugh. "Should I tell them I took out two armed men with a helium tank?"

Riker shrugged. "Tell them whatever you want. Just don't mention me."

"Are you wanted or something?"

"No. Quite the opposite. And I'd prefer to stay that way."

The woman took a step toward him. "Listen, I appreciate your help, I really do. But those guys weren't alone. I saw at least two others. They're probably looking for us now."

"Like I said, the police—"

"How long until they get here? Are we just supposed to hope they find us before those other men do? Or before the ones in the bathroom wake up?"

The little girl turned her head, peeking shyly at Riker. She was Chinese, and though Riker was no expert when it came to kids, he would have put her age at about three. She wasn't crying anymore, but tears still streaked her face. Her small hands clutched at the fabric of the woman's shirt.

The woman was Caucasian, and there was the slightest hint of a French accent in her voice. She'd probably worked hard to rid herself of it, but Riker's ears still picked it up. She looked to be in her late thirties, a few years older than Riker. Her eyes were desperate, wide with fear. Riker didn't know how she'd gotten herself into this mess, and he hoped he'd never have to find out. But one thing was clear. These two needed help.

The little voice in Riker's head spoke again.

*You don't owe these people anything. You've done enough.*

The woman took another step toward him. "I'm Helen Wilborn. This is my daughter, Li."

Riker hesitated. Every piece of information he learned took him another step into these dangerous waters. "Matthew Riker."

The woman smiled weakly. "Nice to meet you, Matthew."

Riker looked over the fairgrounds. People moved slowly across dusty fields filled with tents and booths. Some held large plastic cups of overpriced domestic beer. A few families pushed strollers. Everything looked like it should.

He walked a few feet from the woman to a line of fifty-gallon trash barrels and pulled the guns out of his pockets. They were both Glock 19s, one of the most popular handguns in the United States. They were compact, reliable, and easy to maintain. Was it a coincidence that these two were carrying matching pistols? Or did it mean they were part of some organization that assigned the same weapon to all its men?

He forced his mind to stop following that line of thought. It still came naturally to him, observing the situation and drawing conclusions. Evaluating possible threats based on all the available information. But he didn't need to investigate this. He needed to get out of there.

He ejected the magazine from the first weapon and popped the round out of the chamber. He wiped them down with his sleeve and tossed them in the trash can. He did the same with the magazine from the other weapon. Next, he wiped down the guns themselves.

"What are you doing?" Helen asked. "Shouldn't we hold on to those? What if the other guys show up?"

Riker finished wiping down the first weapon and threw it into another trash can, a few barrels down from where he'd discarded the magazines. "Guns are great if you want to shoot someone. Since I don't plan on killing anybody today, they're not going to do us a lot of good."

"So you'll help us?" Helen asked. There was something in her voice that hadn't been there before. Hope.

Riker didn't answer. His gaze drifted over Helen's shoulder. A hundred yards down the thoroughfare, he saw two men dressed in polo shirts and windbreakers headed their way.

*It's not too late*, the voice in his head said. *Don't get more involved than you already are.*

The little girl whispered something to her mother. Riker didn't catch it, but he recognized the language. Mandarin. He looked at her tear-streaked face for a long moment.

He'd give this woman and child ten minutes of his time, he promised himself. Just until the police arrived. Then he'd go home and forget all about this. He wasn't breaking a promise. It was a momentary lapse, nothing more.

He grabbed the woman's arm and pulled her between two booths. "Come with me."

## 2

Riker led Helen and Li through the maze of cables, trailers, and trash cans behind the booths. This was the part of the fair the customers weren't meant to see, the messy reality behind the flashy façade. They weaved their way through the narrow walkway and came out in a smaller area featuring the less popular booths. They were far away from the land of the Tilt-a-Whirl and the Gravitron; this was a province of deep-fried Oreos and airbrushed T-shirts. The stink of the animals was thicker in the air here. The barn where the 4-H kids showed off their livestock wasn't far away.

Helen quickened her pace, stepping alongside Riker. "What are we doing?"

He shot her a glance. "We're getting you to safety."

She cast a skeptical look toward the long, narrow pole barn up ahead where horses neighed and whinnied in their stalls. "With the animals?"

"Not exactly." Riker kept moving until they reached another, smaller building. He cocked his thumb at one of the doors. "In here."

Helen stared at it for a long moment. The old faded sign read "Women." She didn't look pleased. "Another restroom? You gotta be kidding me. We go in there, we're trapped."

"Only if they find you." He nodded toward the door again. "Look, we don't have to fend them off all day. Just until the police get here. I'm not spending that time running around the fair trying to avoid them. It's too risky. You two hide in here and lock the door."

"Pretty sure the flimsy lock on the bathroom door isn't going to stop those guys."

"I'll be close by, watching. In the unlikely event they do start busting into random ladies' restrooms, I'll make sure they don't get in this one."

For a moment, it looked like Helen was going to do as Riker suggested. Then she looked back in the direction they'd come. "These guys? They're serious business. You don't want to get on their bad sides."

"A little late for that."

Helen met his gaze. Her eyes were a vibrant shade of green Riker wasn't sure he'd ever seen before, and they seemed to be searching for something. She turned the small child in her arms so he could see the girl's face. "Please don't abandon us."

Riker had no doubt Helen's emerald eyes had commanded the obedience of many men. He looked at Li. Her cheeks were still wet with tears, but much of the fear was gone now, replaced with wonder as she looked around at the fair. To any adult who'd spent time in a town larger than Flat Rock, this county fair was a small-time affair, bordering on cheesy. But to Li, it was clearly a marvel. Her eyes darted from one sight to the next, never settling anywhere for long. There was so much she wanted to see.

Riker turned back to Helen.

He nodded toward the restroom. "Go. Before they find us."

This time, Helen did so.

Riker caught the door just before it swung shut. "Keep the door locked. When it's time to open it, I'll knock five times, fast. Got it?"

"Five fast knocks. Got it. And Matthew? Thank you."

He swallowed hard. It had been a long time since anyone had given him that sincere of a thank you for anything. He waited until he heard the restroom lock click shut before he wandered away, not moving fast. Just a man enjoying a lazy afternoon at the fair, trying his best not to appear hurried. All the while, his mind was working.

What had Helen gotten herself wrapped up in? It was clear these men were out to capture her rather than kill her. But why? Did she have information they needed? Was it something about the kid? Or maybe she was on the run from a bad relationship, the kind of guy with enough money to hire goons like these and not enough sense to realize when things were over with his woman.

In the end, it didn't matter. Soon enough, the cops would show up and Helen and Li would be their problem.

No sooner had the thought crossed his mind than the skeptical, overly cautious voice in his head spoke up again. *You really think a small-town cop or two is going to be able to handle four of these guys?*

Maybe not if the men were serious. But Riker had been around the block enough to know that most criminals avoided crossing law enforcement. Maybe they'd win in a straight-up battle with a cop, but were a woman and small child worth the hell that would rain down on them afterward? Local, state, federal...they'd have every police officer in North Carolina gunning for them. And Riker was willing to bet that guys like these had their fingers in more than one illegal pie. Would they risk all that to get one woman? Riker doubted it. So all he had to do was wait and keep one eye on the restroom door.

Riker's phone buzzed, and he fished it out of his pocket. It was a text from Henry.

*Everything alright? You took off fast.*

*Yeah*, Riker typed in reply. He hesitated a moment, then added more. *I'm with the woman and the kid. Let me know the moment the cops arrive.*

*Will do.*

Riker slid the phone back into his pocket and made his way to one of the nearby booths. He wanted to look inconspicuous and non-threatening, and nothing looked less conspicuous and threatening than a man eating cheesecake-on-a-stick. He was about to order when he caught something out of the corner of his eye. Two men in polo shirts.

He turned so he was perpendicular to the approaching men. He could see them out of his periphery, but he didn't appear to be watching them.

The kid at the booth leaned forward expectantly. If he was of legal working age, it was a close thing. "Help you?"

"I'm still looking." Riker had his head angled toward the menu, but his attention was focused on the men. They were moving slow, checking every shadow and corner before moving on, and they were almost to the bathroom. "How's the cheesecake-on-a-stick?"

The kid looked at him blankly for a long moment before answering. "It's a piece of deep-fried-cheesecake-on-a-stick. It's pretty much what you'd expect."

Riker stood in silence, waiting as the men drew parallel to the restroom. Every muscle was tense. They were twenty feet away. If they tried the door, he intended to be in motion before they had a chance to break the lock.

But they didn't. They moved past the restroom, not even glancing at it. Riker let out his breath in a relieved sigh.

They were only ten feet away from Riker when someone else appeared, shouting to them. The big man Riker had asphyxiated with the helium. He was cradling his injured right wrist in his left hand, but he was moving fast. Riker started to turn, intending to walk in the other direction, but the big man's eyes locked on him. He let out an angry shout and ran toward his friends.

Riker did the mental math in an instant. Three of them, two probably armed, against one of him. Out here in the open, there was no way he'd win that fight. Not without killing them. On the plus side, he had their attention. Every moment they were focused on him was one moment they weren't busting down that restroom door.

He scanned the surroundings with his eyes, and it didn't take him long to find the best venue for what was about to happen—the pole barn up ahead. He risked one glance back as he made his way to the building. The big man was frantically gesturing toward Riker and trying to explain to the others, but they had yet to take action. Riker took a deep breath and stepped into the barn.

Horses stood in tight stalls side by side along the length of the building. Their harnesses held their faces near their feed against the wall. They were fenced in on two sides, with their rears toward the center of the barn. The air was thick with their musk and hay particles. Riker scanned the barn, looking for anything that might give him an advantage. He noticed one horse stomping its feet, pulling against its harness. He hustled over to the stall with the rambunctious horse and slid inside, crouching down in front of it. He took the horse's reins in one hand and patted it with the other, calming it. Then he waited.

His heart quickened when he heard the men enter the building. Their feet crunched the gravel. Though he couldn't see them from his position, he could tell they were walking slowly, checking each stall. He kept his breathing steady and resisted the instinct to run or attack. He knew he would have to time this perfectly. If he rushed things, he'd end up with a bullet in his head. He listened to the approaching footsteps and watched the sliver of space between the horse and the stall.

The moment Riker saw the first foot come into view, he let go of the reins and clapped his hands in front of the horse's eyes. The horse bucked, throwing back its legs in a powerful kick. Riker heard the man's ribs crack as he was lifted off the ground and slammed into the man next to him.

Riker sprang to his feet and squeezed past the horse. The two men were on the ground, and it was clear that the one who'd been kicked was no longer a threat. He gasped for air, and even through his shirt, Riker could see the misshapen form of his broken ribs. The man he'd knocked over was another story. He'd be back on his feet in a moment.

Riker saw movement out of the corner of his eye and turned just in time to see the big guy with the broken wrist rushing at him. Riker silently cursed. He'd have to make short work of this guy so he could focus on his armed friends. As the big man reached him, Riker spun, slamming an elbow into the man's back. The force of Riker's blow and his own momentum sent him sprawling into the horse. The animal kicked again, but its hoof didn't connect as solidly this time. The glancing blow knocked the big man to the side.

The other man, still on the ground, fumbled his gun out of his shoulder holster and raised it, but Riker was already in motion. He could see from the bend in the man's arm that his shot would go right, so Riker dove left as the gun went off. The bullet passed close enough that he could feel it next to his right ear. He landed on his stomach a few feet to the man's right. The guy tried to move his arm to get a second shot off, but Riker was ready. He grabbed the wrist and spun his legs around, putting one on top of the man's chest and the other over his neck. He arched his back and pulled as hard as he could on the arm. He could feel the tendons tearing from the hyper extension. The man screamed and the gun fell from his hand. Riker let go of the arm and the man rolled to his side. This was all Riker needed. He quickly wrapped an arm under his neck.

The big man was back up now, going for the gun on the ground. Riker kept his arm tight around the first man's neck as he lashed out with his foot, kicking the gun deep into the stall. The big man hesitated, reluctant to approach the horse that had already kicked his friend.

The man in Riker's arms went limp, and he released the rear naked choke hold. He glanced at the other man on the ground. The color had drained from his face, and he wheezed each time he took a breath. He wasn't getting up anytime soon.

Riker turned back to the last man standing and let out an involuntary snarl. He lunged, wrapping his arms around the man and dragging him to the ground in a second. The man was so surprised, he barely reacted. In an instant, Riker had an arm wrapped around his neck, and ten seconds later he was lying unconscious next to his friend.

Riker picked up the two guns—Glock 19s, just like the first two. He held them in his hand for a moment, thinking how easy it would be to end these three men. When an enemy came at you, it was your responsibility to make sure they couldn't come after you again. Don't hurt the enemy. Don't leave them unconscious. Finish the job. It was the only way to ensure your safety. That was what his training had drilled into him again and again.

But he wasn't that man anymore.

He popped the magazines and the chambered rounds out of the weapons and tossed them into the water trough that ran along the edge of the barn. He threw the empty guns in the garbage can outside the door.

When he reached the bathroom, he was relieved to find the door still locked and intact. He pounded on it with the heel of his hand, five quick bangs. *Thump thump thump thump thump.*

"It's me, Helen."

After a moment, the door opened a crack, and Helen peaked out. Li stood next to her, looking better than she had a few minutes ago, and a wide smile crossed her face when she saw Riker.

"Are they gone?" Helen asked.

"For the moment. Come on, let's go."

"What about waiting for the police?"

"New plan. We're getting out of here."

He led them toward the south entrance of the fairground, not bothering to take the less-traveled route, opting for the shortest path to the parking lot.

"My car's the other way," Helen said.

"They might have seen your car. We're taking mine."

Helen looked surprised by that, but she didn't argue. Riker scanned the growing crowd as they moved through the fair, eyes searching for polo shirts and windbreakers, but he didn't spot any. When they reached Riker's beat-up old pickup truck, Helen gave it a skeptical look. From the jewelry to her make-up and clothes, it was clear she was used to the finer things in life.

"Hope you don't mind slumming it," Riker said with a smile as he opened the door.

"You kidding? I'd ride a donkey if it got me away from those guys."

"Let's hope it doesn't come to that."

They climbed into the truck and Riker started the vehicle. Helen held Li on her lap, which Riker was fairly certain was illegal. On the other hand, he'd welcome a ticket if it meant the cops had shown up.

As they reached the end of the parking lot and turned onto the road, Helen touched Riker's arm.

"Thank you. For everything. If you hadn't been there, I'm not sure what would have happened."

Riker didn't reply. He'd barely even heard. His eyes were fixed on the rearview mirror and what he saw there—a car following them, with two men inside wearing polo shirts and windbreakers.

## 3

ROCKS AND DUST spit out from under the tires of the old F-150 as Riker pulled out of the lot. He gave it all the gas he could without losing control on the gravel road. The interior of the old truck was worn but clean. There were no screens or electronic readouts in the 1985 vehicle. Even the windows had cranks.

The black BMW behind them stood out in stark contrast to the old truck. Though the F-150 ran well, it was no match for the horsepower of the other car. This was a race Riker could not win. He'd have to play it another way.

"Helen, what time is it?"

"What? Why?"

He glanced at Helen, waiting for her answer.

"It's 8:15."

"Perfect. We should be able to make it in time."

Riker kept his foot on the floor, sending a plume of dust behind them. The two-lane road was narrow and curvy, with no shoulder on either side. He kept the truck in the center of the road, making it impossible for the sedan to get past. If the car pulled alongside them, it might be able to force them off the road.

The BMW driver apparently had the same idea. He tried to pass on the left, but he nearly lost control when one tire hit the soft dirt on the side of the road.

Pulling back behind the truck, the car's window rolled down and the passenger leaned out with a gun in his hand. He didn't stay there long. The dust from the truck's tires forced him back in the car. Riker could see him coughing and wiping his eyes when he ducked back inside. The car backed off a hundred yards and kept a steady distance behind them.

"Hold on to Li and stay low. This next part will be a little risky."

Helen wrapped both arms around her daughter and crouched over her, keeping their heads low.

The gravel road hit a wider, paved road in a t-intersection. Riker took the turn as fast as he dared. The old truck groaned as the tires gripped the pavement. Even with his foot mashing down on the gas the truck's speed climbed slowly after the turn.

The black sedan hugged the road, smoothly gliding through the turn. Riker grimaced as he watched the car cut the distance between them. He kept the truck near the center of the road, swerving first into one lane, and then into the other to keep the BMW from getting around them. The handling and power of the car were so much better than his truck he knew he couldn't keep it up for long. They'd get around him soon.

He searched the road ahead for his escape.

Soybean fields stood on both sides of the road. Riker knew the property well. The Johnsons had a dirt path between two of their fields. Calling it a road would have been generous, and that was what made it perfect. He just hoped they could make it that far.

The BMW made another attempt to get around the truck on the right. Riker swerved into the lane, blocking them. The driver knew what he was doing. He immediately cut left and accelerated. Before Riker could get the top heavy truck into the other lane, the sedan slid next to them. Riker knew that he would spin out if he slammed into the car with the back of his truck. In the rearview mirror he saw the passenger ready his pistol.

"Hold on!"

The car came up on the left and Riker kept his head as low as he dared, expecting a bullet to crash through the back of his skull at any moment. He slammed on the brakes and turned right hard. The truck lurched to the left, and for a moment he thought it was going to roll. Helen let out a yelp as the momentum of the turn whipped the top half of her body into Riker's right arm. He almost lost control of the wheel when she hit him.

The BMW skidded to a stop just past the turn. The car quickly backed up and followed the F-150 onto the farming road.

Riker gave the truck as much gas as he could. Soybean fields whipped past on either side of the narrow lane. The truck bounced over the large ruts and divots, but Riker kept them speeding forward. What the old truck lacked in horsepower, it made up in ground clearance and four-wheel drive. The BMW on the other hand moved at a snail's pace. Riker could see them struggling to avoid bottoming out and getting hung up on the high mounds of dirt.

Helen held Li tightly as the two of them bounced up and

down on the old bench seat. Li laughed when she launched into the air and came crashing down on Helen's lap. Riker focused on the road. Despite the truck's ground clearance, he knew he was risking a broken axle by traveling at this speed. Still, the distance between the two vehicles grew. Riker hoped they would have enough of a lead for the second half of the plan.

At the end of the dirt road, Riker turned left, heading toward town. He relaxed his grip on the wheel as the tires rolled along the smooth pavement. The blood returned to his knuckles and the white color disappeared. Glancing back, he saw the BMW was still making progress.

Riker turned to the girls. "Are you all right?"

"I'm fine," Helen said.

Li bounced up and down on her lap, giggling.

"Are we safe?" Helen asked.

"Almost. There's help ahead."

Riker pushed the truck to full speed, which was about ninety miles an hour. Houses started to appear in place of the fields on either side of them as they approached town. Riker glanced in the rearview mirror and spotted the black car. It still looked small, but it was quickly gaining ground. As he climbed the road toward the top of a hill, Riker took his foot off the gas and touched the brake, slowing the truck down to the posted speed limit of twenty-five miles per hour.

"What are you doing?" Helen asked. "They're going to catch us!"

"No, they aren't," Riker said with a smile.

As the truck crested the hill, it entered a school zone. A police car sat on the side of the road. Every local knew that the Henderson County Sheriff Department made half its budget from that speed trap. Riker saw that it was Jerry Kingsley sitting in the car today, his radar gun trained on each passing vehicle.

Riker made it another quarter mile before the BMW reached the top of the hill. It zoomed through the speed trap going at least sixty. The red and blue lights flashed on immediately and the sheriff's car took off after the BMW. Riker continued to watch as the car slowed, but it didn't pull over. Doubt flashed in his mind. He didn't think these men would be foolish enough to shoot a cop, but if he was wrong, it could be the end of Jerry Kingsley.

After a few minutes the BMW pulled over. Riker breathed a sigh of relief as the police lights disappeared in the distance. His risky maneuver had paid off. The danger had passed.

He made two left turns and headed back toward the center of town.

"Why are we going back?" Helen asked.

"Because that's where the police station is. I'll drop you and Li off there. The cops can help you get this straightened out. I would appreciate it if you told them that you hitched a ride with some old local."

Helen sat in silence, looking from Li to Riker. Then she said, "Don't take us to the police. I just need to get somewhere safe."

Riker snapped his head towards her. "Why wouldn't you go to the police?"

"My husband was involved in something. Something illegal." She took a deep breath. "If the police find out, I'm afraid they will take Li away from me."

Riker shook his head. Her logic seemed flawed, but his better instincts told him to keep quiet and stay out of her business. What did it matter to him if she didn't want to go to the police?

He thought for a moment. "I understand. I'll get you to a safe place, and then you can figure out what you need to do."

## 4

RIKER DROVE IN SILENCE, letting his mind wash over the events of the morning. He was already in much deeper than he wanted to be. Part of him was mad that he'd gotten involved at all. The other part felt he was a monster for considering leaving a woman and child in trouble.

"I'm going to drive you to a hotel." Riker said.

She thought a moment before answering. "I don't think the hotel is necessary. I'm renting a house on Lake Braydon. It's got deadbolts, a security system, and big thick doors. I'd rather go there than to some shady motel."

"I'll tell you something I learned a long time ago. The best security is not letting your enemies find you."

Helen sighed, but she gave him a warm look. "Fine. The hotel it is."

Li shifted on Helen's lap and let out a little whine.

"Sorry," Helen said. "This morning's been a lot. For her too."

"Can't say I blame her. I think there's a comic book in the glove compartment. It'll give her something to look at while we drive."

Helen opened the glove box and pulled out an issue of *The Incredible Hulk.* Li's eyes widened as she took the comic.

"Yīngxióng," the girl said.

Riker let out a chuckle. He knew the word. Yīngxióng was Mandarin for hero.

"Do you like superheroes?" he asked in Mandarin.

Both Helen and Li looked at him in surprise.

"Shì," Li answered. *Yes.*

"You speak Mandarin?" Helen asked.

Riker shrugged. "What can I say? I'm full of surprises."

A strange look crossed Helen's face, a mix of confusion, worry, and something else. Hope, maybe? The expression was gone as quickly as it came, but Riker filed it away.

Li flipped the pages of the comic book, quickly losing herself in its four-color world.

As much as Riker didn't want to get involved, he'd have to learn a little more if he really wanted to help them stay safe. He had no idea what they were up against. If he knew that, he might be able to give them some tips that could keep them alive.

"Tell me why those guys are after you."

Helen stared out the window as she answered. "I wish I could. I honestly do. I have some information. Pieces. But it doesn't fit together into any sort of sense."

"Try me."

Helen took a deep breath. "I've known for a long time that I couldn't have children. Biological children, I mean. My husband ran a little bookkeeping business. This was up in New York City, where we live. The business paid the bills, but only just. And adoption is expensive. He would have done anything to make it happen for us. He was a good man."

Riker noticed the past tense, but he kept quiet, letting her continue.

"Then he got a new job. He was working with some shady characters. I guess I knew that right from the beginning. He kept the details from me, but suddenly we had money. Enough to pay the bills and then some. Enough to make our dream come true."

She paused, touching Li's hair. The girl was staring at the comic book, studying each panel, before turning the page.

"We brought Li home three months ago, and for a few weeks everything seemed perfect. Exactly like we'd always imagined. And then one day he didn't come home from work. They found him in the office the next morning. Suicide, they said."

"I'm sorry," Riker said.

Helen didn't reply.

"You didn't buy that it was suicide?"

"No. It didn't make sense. Two months after bringing home Li? He was happier than I'd ever seen him. No way did he shoot himself in the head." She let out a humorless laugh. "I told the police my concerns, of course, but they weren't eager to believe the grieving widow. They said it was a cut and dried case. For all I know, the killers paid them off."

Riker gripped the steering wheel and stared at the road past the windshield. He was taking them to a little motel in Hanover, the next town over. Better to put a little space between Helen and the men looking for her.

"When the men tried to grab you, did they ask for anything? Were they looking for something?"

"No. I was in my house for six weeks after Ted died. We rented a house down here to get away from the city for a few days, and now they decide it's time to come after us? Why?"

Riker frowned. It didn't make sense to him either. "Is there anything else you can tell me? Maybe something your husband said? Anything about these guys and what they might want from you?"

She thought for a moment, then shook her head.

"I'm sorry. Believe me; I'd like nothing more than to be able to tell you what's going on. I've been wracking my brain. I'd never seen those men before today at the fair when they attacked me. For all I know, it doesn't even have anything to do with my husband. But I can't imagine why else they would resort to that type of violence."

Riker drove in silence for a few minutes. They were almost to the Hanover exit.

"This will be a safe place to wait. I'll give it a little while to be sure there is no one left at the fair. Then I'll drive your car back here."

She thought about that for a moment, then nodded slowly. "Thanks. I appreciate that."

As they pulled up to the motel, Riker turned to Helen.

"Do you have cash?"

"Yeah. A couple hundred."

"Good. Use it. I doubt they're tracking your cards, but let's be on the safe side."

She looked at him for a long moment. "I can't wait to get back to New York. No offense, but I've had enough of your state."

"Understandable."

"This is going to sound crazy but... would you come with us? Drive us back, I mean. For protection."

Riker was so caught off guard by the request that he didn't know how to respond.

"I'd pay you, of course. Like I said, Ted was bringing in a lot of money. I can afford to overpay for something like this."

Riker actually considered it for a moment before his better senses prevailed.

"Honestly, I'm not worth it. The car will drive just as fast whether I'm in it or not."

She looked at him as if she were disappointed, but not surprised.

"Do me a favor," she said. "Think about it. Don't give me a final answer until you get back."

"Deal." He thought for a moment. "Let me have your car keys. Once I'm sure no one is watching the car, I'll bring it back here. Then I'll get out of your hair."

"Or you'll come with us to New York."

He couldn't help but smile. "Or I'll come with you to New York."

Helen opened the passenger side door and tapped Li on the shoulder. She spoke in rudimentary Mandarin. "Time to give back the book."

"It's okay," Riker said. "She can keep it."

He stayed with them until they were checked into room 212. Then he instructed Helen to keep the door locked and to stay inside. He tussled Li's hair and said goodbye to both of them before returning to his truck. He decided to drive home for a bit. The men had seen his truck and he wanted to be sure they were gone before he went for Helen's car.

Riker was lost in thought on the drive home. He pulled up to his long driveway twenty-five minutes later. Now that the excitement was over and the adrenaline was fading, he felt tired and stiff. His muscles ached and he noticed three long scratches on his left forearm. When he'd gotten the injury, he had no idea.

He always left the grass a bit longer near the road, and

he didn't pull the weeds growing up around his mailbox. This was all by design. He didn't want the property to feel too welcoming. As he drove up the curvy driveway, he rounded a stand of trees and spotted his small, ranch-style home. The lawn was more carefully manicured here.

His eyes drifted to a small stick standing near the edge of the drive. He kept a piece of fishing line attached to the stick stretched across the driveway so that any vehicle coming up the drive would knock the stick down. He pulled his truck to a stop just in front of the fishing line, opting to walk the final twenty feet to the house. He did this partly to avoid having to reset the stick, but also because the walk to the house gave him time to observe the situation and detect anything amiss.

Today, everything looked normal. He unlocked his door and stepped into the house.

Riker prided himself on living a minimalist lifestyle. He didn't have more than he needed, and what he needed was very little. The walls were bare, and there were no magnets on the refrigerator. His furniture was sparse, inexpensive, and functional. He poured himself a glass of water and downed it in a single go. Then he headed to the shed out back.

Tending to his beehives was his favorite part of his job. He only did it once every ten days—disrupting the colonies too often could have negative impacts on their production. There was a meditative quality to the work. Every hive was its own little world with thousands of complex creatures living strange and beautiful lives. Riker had twenty bee colonies, which meant somewhere in the neighborhood of four hundred thousand bees. He took care of them, and their honey kept Riker fed. The simple symmetry of their relationship pleased Riker. Inside the shed, he lit his smoker and donned his bee suit. Then he headed out to the hives.

He followed a simple routine at each hive box. He pumped smoke around the box for a minute before slowly removing the cover. The smoke served a dual purpose. It both masked the panic pheromones released by the guard bees, stopping the rest of the colony from coming to the hive's defense, and it also caused the bees to prepare for the possibility of fire. They began consuming the honey in preparation to flee, and they ignored the man messing with their hive. Riker worked slowly and carefully, smoking each section of the hive. Next, he inspected the frames where the bees built their honeycombs.

He spotted the queen immediately. Her long, slim body was different from the rest of the colony. Then he checked for beetles, mites, or any parasites. He made sure the frames weren't getting close to being drawn out with honeycombs, and he checked for eggs and larvae. When he was satisfied everything was in good shape, he put it all back together, replaced the cover, and went on to the next hive box.

The whole process took just over two hours. He added additional frames to one hive box, but that was all that required his attention. When the work was finished, he felt the familiar combination of satisfaction that all was right with his hives and disappointment that he needed to leave them alone for another ten days.

After he went inside, he checked the time. It was unlikely that the men were still hanging around Helen's car. He grabbed the keys to his truck and thought of Li and her fascination with *The Incredible Hulk* comic book.

Riker went to a cabinet near the foot of his bed and pulled out a stack of comics.

He'd picked up the habit in the Navy. One of his buddies

had been obsessed with comic books. After hearing the guy go on and on about the various plot developments in the latest issues for weeks on end, Riker read one and was surprised by how much he liked it. These days, his weekly supply of comics was one of the few luxuries he allowed himself. He usually donated the comics after he read them, but he decided that this week he'd give them to Li instead. Maybe it would give her something to do on the long drive back to New York.

He went through the stack, pulling out the issues too violent for three-year-old eyes, then headed outside, the stack of comics wedged under his arm. He smiled at the thought of adding another superhero fan to the ranks.

Riker arrived at the fairgrounds five minutes later. He walked the perimeter of the lot before making his way to Helen's car. As far as he could tell, there was no one watching the vehicle. Even still, he drove around until he was confident no one was following him before heading to the motel.

He parked the car and left the comics on the passenger seat. He figured it would be a nice surprise for Li when she got in. Helen could drop Riker off at his house, they'd say their goodbyes, and that would be that.

He was still down the hall from room 212 when he realized something was very wrong. The door to the room stood wide open. He hustled over, heart suddenly pounding loudly in his chest. When he reached the room, he let out a curse at what he saw.

The frame around the door was badly splintered, as if someone had kicked it in.

"Helen?" he said as he slowly stepped into the room.

But there was no answer. Helen and Li were gone.

## 5

RIKER KNEW from experience that time was always the enemy when tracking someone. Memories faded, evidence was lost, and distances grew farther. If you couldn't find someone quickly, you probably couldn't find them at all. He fully intended to find Helen and Li.

His first clue was the lack of hotel staff or police in the room. Helen and Li must have been taken recently. Even a guest walking by would notice the kicked-in door and alert the hotel staff.

Inside the room, the sheets had been flung off one of the beds. Helen and Li must have been napping when the intruders forced their way inside. The rest of the room didn't give up any real information.

Riker stepped outside and looked down at the nearly empty parking lot below. He went down the stairs and turned his attention to the businesses across the street. The dingy strip mall featured a pawnshop, liquor store, nail salon and a Quick Mart.

He jogged across the street and stopped in front of the pawn shop, spotting a security camera on the exterior. The ancient device was angled toward the door, presumably to capture the face of each person entering the store. There was no chance it would catch any action from across the street. The liquor store was a different story. It had two exterior cameras, both newer models with wide lenses.

Riker went in and nodded to the old man behind the counter.

"Can I help you?" The clerk moved one hand under the counter and stood ramrod straight, casting a wary gaze on Riker. The man must have lived through a few robberies. People who came in fast and made a beeline for the counter were not generally checking for sales.

Riker moved both hands away from his sides, spreading his fingers to show the man that he wasn't holding a weapon. "I hope so. This might sound a little strange, but I need to see your security footage for the last hour. Sorry to be so direct, but time is of the essence."

The clerk looked Riker up and down for a moment, still holding his hand under the counter. "Two hundred."

Riker hesitated. "You want two hundred dollars for the footage?"

"Yep, that's what I charge. You're a P.I., right? I've owned this store for thirty years. I can spot you fellas the minute you step through the door. You always come in wanting to see footage of the hotel. I used to haggle on the price, but two hundred seems to be the most you guys will pay and it's the least I'll accept."

Riker liked this guy. The world would run a lot smoother if everyone just said what they meant. He walked over to the ATM next to the counter and got the money. He handed two hundred to the store owner.

The man pulled up a tablet from under the counter. He opened an app and brought up the footage from the exterior cameras. Riker was shocked at the quality of the footage. Fifteen years ago, video equipment with this level of detail would have cost a fortune. Now you could pick up a 4k system from any electronics store. He scrubbed through the footage until he found what he was looking for.

Thirty-five minutes ago, two black sedans had pulled up to the hotel. Three men jumped out of each car. They ran up the stairs, heading straight to Helen's room. Less than a minute later, they came out with Helen and Li. Li clung to Helen as a man with a gun walked them to the car. The entire kidnapping only took two and a half minutes.

Riker recognized three of the men in the footage from the day before. The others were new. He paused the video in a few spots and sent the still images to his phone. He got the license plates and pictures of the men's faces. Riker made note of which car held Helen and Li. He scrolled frame by frame when the cars pulled out of the parking lot. Both had something hanging from their rearview mirrors. He zoomed in until he could clearly see they were parking passes. He couldn't make out the words printed there, but he recognized the logo of Super 8 Motel.

Riker thanked the old man and left. Climbing into Helen's car, he felt a renewed sense of purpose. The only Super 8 in the area was about fifteen miles away.

Twenty minutes later, Riker pulled into the Super 8 parking lot and spotted one of the cars from the footage. He checked his notes; it wasn't the car that had taken Helen. Riker parked and watched the sedan. It wasn't long before three of the men from the footage walked up and began loading bags into the car.

Riker considered his options. He needed information, and he needed it quickly. Helen and Li were most likely in grave danger. He could go in fighting and try to beat the information out of them, but that would take time. Information obtained that way was also notoriously unreliable. He decided to go for the second option. He was going to get captured.

Riker walked up to the men loading the car. He held his hands at his sides with his palms facing the men. "Hey, guys."

The men stopped what they were doing and looked up in surprise.

"I think we have a situation that we need to work out. I ran into your friends at the fair. It got a little heated, but I'm hoping we can work something out in a more civilized manner."

Two of the guys pulled guns from inside their coats. One was a brute. He must have been six foot four and pushing three hundred pounds. The second guy was short and skinny. Both of them held Glock 19s. The third guy was dressed sharper and didn't draw a weapon.

Riker put his hands in the air. "Whoa! I'm just here to talk. You don't need guns."

One of the guys circled around behind Riker while the other two stayed in front.

"You are one dumb son of a bitch," said the unarmed man. "Louie, keep your gun on him. If he so much as sneezes, shoot him."

The three walked Riker through the side entrance and into their room on the first floor. They patted him down, but there was nothing on him. They sat him in the room's only chair. Louie kept a gun pointed at him and the other two relaxed a little.

The leader looked Riker up and down. "You've got balls walking in here, kid. Who are you with?"

"I'm not with anyone," Riker responded. "I'm just a local guy. I'm not looking for any trouble."

The man tilted his head. "I didn't think you would be local."

"What did you expect?"

"I thought you were one of the New York guys. Clearly you're not. So who are you?"

"I'm Matthew. I'm just a farmer over in Henderson County. Would you mind telling Louie to put the gun down?"

"The gun stays where it is, and I call bullshit. No farmer takes out four armed guys. Who do you work for?"

"I don't work for anyone. I just happened to see a woman and child in trouble and decided to help out. Speaking of Helen and her daughter, are they okay?"

A look of confusion crossed the boss's face, but it quickly faded. "They're fine. And they will continue to be that way as long as they cooperate. This isn't about them. It's about you. This is the last time I'm going to ask nice. Who are you?"

"I told you. I'm a farmer who was in the wrong place at the wrong time. If you want to get specific, I'm a beekeeper. Now I just want to help Helen get back home."

Louie laughed. "Oh, she's probably already back at her place by now. I doubt that's where she wants to be."

The boss shot Louie a look. "Shut your stupid mouth, Louie."

"Sorry, Tony," Louie said sheepishly.

"Why would you take her back to her place?" Riker asked.

"You don't ask the questions. I ask the questions, and I'm tired of asking nice," Tony said. He nodded at the third guy.

The big man took a step forward and gave Riker a right hook to the face.

Riker moved his head with the punch. The impact still hurt, but the smack of fist on skin sounded worse than it felt.

"I get it," Riker said, letting a little panic slip into his voice. "You guys have some issues with Helen. I can see that it doesn't concern me. Just let me go, and you'll never hear from me again."

Tony glared at him. "I still think you're full of shit. You're not leaving until I get the truth out of you."

Tony nodded at the brute who drew back his fist for another right hook. Riker waited to move until the momentum of the punch was at full speed. His hands shot up, grabbing the brute's arm. He sprang to his feet, knocking the chair backward. Riker felt the hulking meat of the arm as he spun his body, using the force of the blow against his attacker.

Louie flinched at the sudden burst of motion, and he squeezed the trigger of his 9mm. The gun went off, sending a round into the back of the man attacking Riker. The brute screamed and dropped to the ground.

Tony grabbed at the gun in a holster by his side. In his panic, he grabbed his suit coat as well and was unable to pull the gun free.

Louie's eyes were wide and his mouth gaped open. He stared at the blood coming out of the man he just shot.

Riker didn't need to think. His body did what it was trained to do. It was like his conscious mind was just along for the ride watching the scene play out. He worked the same way a master musician did. They no longer thought about the chords and placement of their hands, the music just flowed out. Riker was playing his song.

He did two quick kicks. The first knocked the gun out of Louie's hand. The second crashed into Louie's stomach. Louie's body bent where the kick landed, and he gasped for air. Tony was still fumbling with his gun as Riker took a step towards him. His arm shot out in a jab so quick it was a blur. He angled his fist down so the middle knuckle was extended forward and hit Tony in the throat.

A gruesome sucking sound escaped Tony's lips, and his hands shot to his throat. His eyes went red and tears streamed from the corners. The sucking sound continued, and Tony dropped to his knees. Riker hit him again. This time in the corner of his jaw. Tony went limp and fell to the floor.

Riker's heart pounded in his chest. Adrenaline pumped into his system and everything seemed perfectly clear. In that moment, he realized that he missed this. He looked around and saw the brute bleeding out and Tony lying on the ground. He pushed that thought away and got back to business.

Riker grabbed Louie. The man was still trying to catch his breath as he recovered from the kick. Riker wrapped an arm around his neck and forced him to look at his friends. "Your buddies don't have long to live without medical attention. You have one shot to save them."

Louie answered in a quiet voice. "What do you want?"

"Give me the address where they took Helen. Then you can get help for your friends. If you don't, I'm going to choke you out. When you wake up, both of them will be dead. I'd like to get moving, so you need to decide now."

Louie only stared at his friends for a moment before he gave Riker the address.

"Thanks, Louie. Sorry, but I'm only going to keep half my promise. I don't want you to warn the other guys that I'm coming." Riker squeezed hard with the arm that was wrapped around Louie's neck. He went limp after a few moments.

After quickly wiping down everything he had touched in the room, Riker picked up the phone on the desk and dialed 911. He told that operator someone had been shot and needed immediate medical attention.

He typed the address Louie had given him into his phone as he walked to his car. The house was over an hour away. Riker hoped that Helen and Li would still be alive when he got there.

# 6

RIKER STARTED Helen's Lexus and drove toward the house, mentally going over what he knew. The closer he got to his destination, the more he realized how little he had to go on. An unknown number of men were holding Helen and Li captive at their rental home for an unknown reason. Riker didn't know how the men had found them at the motel that he'd picked almost at random. He didn't know what they wanted from Helen, or why they'd inexplicably taken her back to her rental house. He didn't know how long they'd stay there or what they intended to do next.

He suppressed his mounting frustration. He'd certainly been in more dangerous situations back in the days before he came to North Carolina, but in almost all of them, he'd had some sort of intelligence, some morsel of information that gave him an edge. Here, he was flying blind.

For a moment, he considered heading back home to research and gear up. He didn't have much equipment from the old days—hell, he didn't even own a gun anymore—but there were a few useful items tucked away, just in case he ever needed them. Of course, he'd always assumed the items would be used against people coming for him, not people hunting a woman and child he barely knew. But retrieving those items meant giving the kidnappers more time to escape.

No, that couldn't happen. He had to act now. He only wished he had more information. Hell, he didn't even have his truck. Granted, the Lexus was comfortable and far more responsive than his F-150, but it just served as another reminder of how out of his element he really was.

The negative thoughts were spiraling; if he wanted to have any chance of saving Helen and Li, he needed to focus. His mind went where it always did when he needed a quick dose of tough love—to his mentor and former commanding officer, Edgar Morrison. He knew exactly what Morrison would say.

*Sure, Riker, you're in a tough spot. There's a lot you don't know. You're outnumbered. You're going in without all the information. Well boo-fucking-hoo. Don't tell me all the dollars Uncle Sam poured into training you were for nothing. Not to mention the years I wasted coddling your ass.*

Riker couldn't help but smile as he heard Morrison's gruff voice in his head. As far as Riker knew, the man had never smoked, yet somehow he had the voice of a pack-a-day eighty-year-old.

*Here's what you're going to do, numbnuts. You're going to concentrate on the advantages you do have. You're going to make a list and check it twice, like your Kristopher goddamn Kringle himself, you read me? It might not be a long list, but that's okay. Because you are a warrior. You're not looking to see who's naughty or nice—you're looking for your enemies' weakness. Somewhere on that list, you'll find one. When you do, you push on that weakness with everything you have. You press until your*

*enemy is begging for mercy, and then you press harder. That's
how you win.*

Riker sat up a bit straighter in his seat. He'd never had
that exact conversation with Morrison, but he'd had enough
similar ones that he knew that's pretty much what the old
guy would say. Of all the things he missed from the old life,
Morrison was near the top of the list.

Of course, Morrison was ultimately why he'd left the old
life. And if Morrison's bosses found out what Riker was up
to on this August morning, they would be less than happy.
There would be a price to pay.

Riker pushed that thought away and concentrated on
what the imaginary Morrison had told him. The list.

What did he know?

The men were from New York. Their presence here may
or may not have to do with the bookkeeping Helen's
husband was doing for them. Maybe her husband had
stumbled across something he wasn't supposed to see.
Maybe he had evidence of their crimes. Or maybe he'd
stolen money from them to pay for the adoption.

No, those weren't facts. They were speculation.

He knew Helen was afraid to involve the police. She
claimed that she was afraid of losing her child, but it felt as
if she wasn't telling him everything. He knew there were at
least four men he'd seen at the fair who were still unac-
counted for. And he knew these men were armed and he
was not.

So what were his advantages?

First, they didn't know he was coming. That was a big
one. It was hard to overestimate the importance of the
element of surprise. And they were in North Carolina.
These were New York guys. Outsiders. They were on Riker's
home turf.

As soon as the thought entered his mind, Riker knew that was his advantage. That was the weakness Morrison would have told him to press. He thought for a moment, then picked up his phone and opened the contacts list. He tapped the name 'Scott Riley.' The man answered on the second ring.

"Riker! How's it going, man?"

"Not bad, Scott. How are you?"

"Oh, you know, can't complain. Getting ready for the harvest."

Scott Riley owned a local farm. It was a small operation, but Riker got the feeling Scott's family was old money. He didn't do much hands-on farming, instead opting to run the business end of things and spend the rest of his time selling at local farmer's markets, which was how Riker knew him. Scott often stocked Riker's honey at his booths. When he wasn't working, he spent his time on his fishing boat, which was why Riker had thought of him. But he wanted to work up to that part of the conversation.

"Good crop this year?" Riker asked.

"Looks that way." Scott paused for a moment. "So, what's up?"

"Listen, you own a place up on Brayden Lake, don't you?"

"I sure do." The change in Scott's voice was immediate. This was his true passion, and he was clearly more than happy to discuss it. "Just about my favorite place on Earth. Why do you ask?"

"Well, I was thinking of maybe spending a week up there, just to unwind, get away from the day-to-day, you know? And I found this rental house online."

"You don't have to do that. If you're looking for a place to stay on the lake, my house sits empty most of the time. I'd be happy to have you stay there."

"That's very kind of you, but I couldn't put you out like that. I was more wondering if you knew anything about this rental house."

"Sure, what's the address?"

"2560 Mayflower Lane."

"Mayflower...that's not far from me. One sec, let me pull it up on Google." For a moment, the only sound was his fingers typing on a keyboard. "Ah, yes, I know it. Used to be the Thompsons' place, but they sold it to some folks from Charlotte, I think."

"You been inside?" Riker asked.

"Yeah, some time ago. I remember it has a beautiful second-floor balcony overlooking the lake. I imagine that sitting up there with your morning coffee would be mighty nice."

"That sounds perfect," Riker said, trying to keep the impatience out of his voice. "Anything else you remember about the house?"

Scott was quiet for a moment as he thought. "I remember a shed out back by the lake where Glen Thompson did his woodworking. Beautiful stuff. I thought about trying my hand at some woodworking after he showed me that place. Then my wife pointed out I have too many hobbies already. As usual, she was right."

Riker forced out a chuckle. "That sounds like just the sort of place I'm looking for. I appreciate your help."

After another couple minutes of small talk, Riker managed to untangle himself from the conversation and ended the call. Scott hadn't given him a lot of information, but his mental list had grown every-so-slightly. The beginnings of a plan were forming in his mind.

He reached Brayden Lake ten minutes later. He parked the Lexus three houses down from Helen's rental, leaving it in the shade of a large oak tree. This was the type of neighborhood where a strange car parked on the street was likely to raise the interest of the neighbors, but Riker hoped the fact that it was a luxury vehicle would be enough to keep anyone from getting too nosy. It looked like it belonged here.

Riker cut through the nearest yard and made his way down to the lake. He walked along the edge of the water until he spotted a house with a second-floor balcony. Riker had to admit, that did look like a nice place to enjoy a morning coffee.

The yard was flanked by two old-growth oak trees set wide enough apart that they didn't block the view of the lake from the house. The shed was set behind the farther tree. Riker silently thanked Scott Riley. If he hadn't mentioned the shed, Riker might not have noticed it.

He took a long look at the house. From where he stood, Riker couldn't detect any movement. The balcony was empty, and all the windows he could see were dark. He cautiously made his way across the yard.

The inside of the shed was a bit of a letdown after Scott's description. Whatever woodworking equipment had once stood here must have departed with the Thompsons. Now the shed was dominated by yard equipment. The workbench held only a single small toolbox.

That was all right. Riker didn't need much. He opened the toolbox and took out a flathead screwdriver. Then he headed for the house.

He reached the backdoor and carefully inspected the area. Peeking through the window in the door, he saw some sort of mudroom on the other side. Thankfully, it was

empty. At the far end of the mudroom, he saw the entrance
to what looked like a pantry.

Good. Chances of them holding Helen and Li in that
area were slim. Hopefully, that would allow Riker to get
inside without attracting their attention.

He tried the doorknob and found it was locked, just as
he'd expected. That was all right. A quick look at the lock
told him that wasn't going to be a problem. He reached into
his pocket and pulled out his keyring. On it was one of the
few items from the old days he hadn't been able to give up.
His bump key.

One of the strange realities of modern life was that
everyone locked their doors, and that few people realized
how little protection those locks really afforded them. There
were a dozen ways into any house. Windows could be
jimmied. Locks could be picked or even drilled. But Riker's
favorite method of entry was the bump key.

A bump key was simply a key with each tooth filed to
maximum depth. Insert the key into a lock, give the key a
firm tap while exerting a little pressure as if trying to turn
the key, and you could jolt the pins inside the lock into
place. Then you could freely turn the key. It was like having
a skeleton key to the world. Most locks, even quality deadbolts with solid protection against forced entry, had internal
cylinders that were susceptible to bumping. Riker had heard
estimates that over ninety percent of residential locks in the
United States were bumpable.

The thing that had shocked Riker was how easy
bumping was. Unlike actually picking a lock, bumping had
taken him all of five minutes to learn. And unlike a set of
lock-picking tools, a bump key didn't look any different from
a normal key to the untrained eye. Which meant all that
stood between ninety percent of Americans and an

unwanted intruder was a fifteen dollar key and ten minutes on YouTube.

Riker inserted his bump key into the deadbolt lock, put a little pressure on it, and tapped it with the back of the screwdriver. The noise was no louder than a finger snap, but it still seemed too loud to Riker. He turned the key, unlocking the deadbolt, then he waited to see if anyone had heard.

After thirty seconds, he was confident no one was coming. He inserted the key into the doorknob lock and repeated the process. Once again, the noise echoed loudly in Riker's ears. This time he waited a full minute before turning the knob and opening the door.

Silently, he went inside the house.

## 7

RIKER STEPPED QUIETLY through the door. The hardwood floors were beautiful, but they creaked when he put his weight on them. He paused at the first sound and removed his boots, placing them behind some bins in the corner. He crept across the room, spreading his weight across the entirety of his feet.

Opening the door at the end of the room, he entered the spare pantry. Nothing out of the ordinary, some two-liter bottles of soda, boxes of cereal and other snacks. The short hall next to the pantry led to the kitchen. Riker peered around the corner but didn't see anyone. His heart was beating quickly, his body's natural response to a fight-or-flight scenario. He took a deep breath and focused his mind. His heart rate slowed and he made his breathing shallow. Then he listened.

Riker had learned that people ignore most of the information their senses feed them. All that's required to gather that information is to pay attention. The tick of an old grandfather clock kept pace in a room nearby. Riker guessed it was in the living room on the other side of the wall from the kitchen. He heard the hum of air blowing through the vents, followed by the chime of a text alert from a phone. It was faint. He guessed it was upstairs and on the other side of the house. A few moments later he heard the murmur of voices. They were too quiet for him to understand the conversation, but he made out two distinct voices.

He heard the creaking of a mattress and the high-pitched sound of a little voice. Li was here. Hopefully, Helen was sitting next to her.

That put two men in a room with Helen and Li. Riker was sure there was a third man in the house. He had seen three people get into the car with Helen in the video footage. He continued listening but didn't hear anything else. He had to guess at the location of the last gangster. If two were watching their captives, the third one was most likely on the first floor. Probably watching the front of the house for him.

Riker slowly crept from the pantry into the kitchen. The sun cast a warm glow into the room. He could see the lake's reflection dancing off the pots and pans hanging from a rack above the kitchen island. He grabbed a cast-iron skillet.

He continued towards the opening that led to the room with the clock. He reached the corner and gripped the pan in one hand. Then he crouched and looked around the corner. The room was what he expected, a large living room with a fireplace, TV, and a grandfather clock. Except for the furniture, the room was empty.

Riker heard a toilet flush. The sound came from the hallway off the living room. He rushed over to the wall and pressed himself against it. The sink ran for a moment before the door opened. The floor creaked as a man walked down the hall. Riker gripped the frying pan with both hands, and his muscles tensed.

He swung hard as the man entered the room. The man caught the motion of the pan in his peripheral and tried to dodge. His reflexes were fast, but not fast enough to avoid the hit entirely. The pan struck high on his head as he moved away from it. The blow knocked him back. Riker saw a chunk of his hair flip up like a bad toupee. The pure white skull underneath flashed for a moment before the piece of scalp flapped back down. He let out a scream as he stumbled backward, using the wall to keep his balance. Riker swung the pan again, driving it into his diaphragm. The guy dropped to his knees, blood gushing from his head wound.

Footsteps echoed from upstairs, and a voice called out, "Jake, you, okay?"

Riker turned towards the sound and saw two men at the top of the open stairway. They pulled their guns, and Riker ran for the kitchen. Shots rang out and wood splintered around the entry to the kitchen as he dove back into the other room.

The shooters charged down the stairs, firing into the kitchen area. Bullets tore through the wall, shattering the glass faces of the cabinets. Riker dove behind the island. Glass and chunks of ceramic bowls and plates rained down on top of him.

The bullets stopped, and for a moment all was silent.

"You still alive?" a gruff voice asked.

Riker said nothing.

"Come out nice and slow, and we can work this out."

Riker heard them approaching the island from both sides. He picked up a large piece of a broken plate. He braced his foot against the cabinet and crouched, ready to pounce. In the blurry reflection on the stainless steel fridge, he saw one of the approaching gunmen. Just before the man rounded the corner of the island, Riker threw the plate across the room, breaking one of the large windows. Both men reacted to the sound and trained their weapons on the shattering glass. Riker pushed off the cabinet and dove over the island toward the man closest to the pantry.

The man tried to get off a shot, but Riker was only visible for a brief moment before the impact. His shoulder hit the guy in the chest and the momentum slammed him into the wall. Riker held onto him as they fell to the ground. The man landed on broken glass and screamed in pain as a shard tore into his upper leg. He tried to bring the gun around to Riker's head, but Riker grabbed his wrist with both hands. He gripped with all his strength and swung a leg over the top of the arm holding the gun. Riker thrust up with his hips and pulled back on the arm. There was a sound like a drumstick pulled from a turkey. The man's scream was so high pitched that he sounded like a child. The gun fell from his hand as a bullet struck the wall three inches from Riker's head.

Riker dove into the hall while the other gunman fired wildly in his direction. He felt a stinging pain and looked down to see blood dripping from the bottom of his right foot. A shard of broken glass protruded from the pad of his foot. He shook off the pain and looked around the room for anything useful. His eyes settled on a mop by the sink.

"He broke my fucking arm! Kill that son of a bitch, Henry."

"You get up and help me kill him," Henry yelled back. "Jake, get in here and help us."

A voice yelled back from the other room. "I'm bleeding bad. I can barely see a thing."

"Wipe your damn eyes and help us kill this guy. Once we're done with him, we can get you two patched up."

Riker waited until he heard the man with the broken

arm stand up. When he did, Riker shoved the mop head into the hallway that led to the mudroom. He shook it to make as much motion as possible. He also let out a scream, like the battle cry of an ancient warrior.

There was an instant volley of bullets. Followed by another scream.

"Holy shit, you shot me. Henry, you shot me!"

A smile formed at Riker's lips. These were the kind of guys who relied on intimidation. Their lack of actual combat skills was almost funny. Still, it only took one bullet to kill any man, and he reminded himself to focus.

"Oh man, I thought he was coming out. Are you okay?"

"No, I'm not okay. My arm is broken and I'm fucking shot."

Riker yelled, "There is no need for you to die. I just want to protect the woman and child. Leave now and you'll never see us again."

"We're not going to die. You are going to die!" Henry yelled back.

While Henry was speaking, Riker moved to the outer door and silently opened it. He slid through and out to the yard. He sprinted along the side of the house until he reached the shattered kitchen window. He peeked into the house and saw Henry and Jake approaching the mudroom. The third man slumped against the wall, he was limp and blood soaked his shirt and pooled on the floor.

Jake held his gun out in his right hand. He tried to wipe the blood out of his eyes with his left hand. Henry walked next to him, holding his weapon at the ready.

Riker grabbed a baseball-sized rock off the ground and waited for the two men to step into the hall leading to the mudroom. Then he hopped back inside through the window.

He ran towards the men from the kitchen, staying on the balls of his feet to keep from pushing the glass further into the sole of his foot. He needed to hit them hard while they were looking in the wrong direction.

Riker was in the hall with Jake and Henry before they realized what was happening. They turned in the tight space just in time to see Riker. Henry pointed his gun towards Riker, but it was too late. The rock smashed down on his wrist and the gun flew out of his hand.

Jake got off a shot that sounded ten times louder in the small space. The bullet struck the wall, and Riker grabbed his arm. Henry smashed a fist into Riker's side while he struggled with Jake for the gun. Jake and Henry pushed forward together and the three moved back faster and faster through the kitchen. Jake didn't drop his weapon, but Riker continued to control his wrist.

Morrison's voice echoed in Riker's head. *Kill clean and quick. The longer the encounter, the more that can go wrong.*

He was in a situation that required killing, but he had made a promise that couldn't be broken.

The three men tumbled to the ground as they passed the entrance to the living room. Riker saw a flash of color.

Jake landed on top of Riker and Henry was to his left. Jake managed to squeeze the trigger and get off another wild shot. Riker kept control of his arm, but the man had a surprising amount of strength and a strong will to live. Henry grabbed Riker's right arm and held it down.

"Kill him, Jake!" Henry yelled.

Jake used the weight of his body and both of his arms to fight against Riker. The gun moved towards Riker's head. Riker thrashed his pelvis upward to try to toss Jake off of him. It almost worked, but Jake stayed where he was and Henry made it impossible to use all of his strength. The gun was an inch to the left of Riker's head. Riker prepared to pull on Jake's wrist. He knew the change of force would throw him off balance.

A shot rang out, and a mist of blood and skull burst out of Jake's forehead. Jake went limp and fell onto Riker.

Henry stood up and two more shots echoed in the kitchen. Henry's body thumped to the floor next to his friend.

Riker pushed Jake off of him and sat up. He was shocked to see Helen holding a Glock. She looked at Riker and the two men she had just killed. She stood perfectly still for a moment. Then she put one hand to her mouth and screamed.

## 8

RIKER TOOK A STEP TOWARD HELEN, ignoring the shooting pain in his foot. His sock was wet with blood, but he didn't have time to worry about that now. He had a much greater concern—the shocked, shaking woman still holding a pistol in her hand.

"Helen, it's okay." He took another step toward her. "Why don't you give me the gun?"

On the ground, Henry let out a soft groan. The pistol in Helen's hand flashed two more times, and two rounds thudded into Henry's body.

Riker flinched as the report echoed through the room. He held his hands up, showing them open to Helen. He didn't like the distant, panicked look in her eyes. She was a frightened animal, all higher thought gone from her mind. There was no telling what she'd do. She might perceive him as a threat and fire before she even fully realized who he was.

"Helen, you did well. You saved me. Thank you." His words weren't entirely accurate, but he needed to calm her.

She blinked hard and looked at him as if seeing him for

the first time. "Matthew. Jesus. What the hell? These guys... they grabbed us at the motel."

"I know. I saw."

She looked at him strangely, as if not understanding. "You saw? Why didn't you help?"

"I saw the security footage. Are you all right? Does anything hurt?" It was an old trick Riker had learned a long time ago. Helen was mentally outside her body, quickly moving into the numbness of shock. By asking her if anything hurt, he was forcing her to once again be aware of her body. He could see the effect almost immediately. A bit of light came back into her eyes.

"I'm okay. They didn't hurt me. Not physically. How the hell did you find us?"

"I got the information from their friends. Is Li okay?"

Helen nodded slowly. "She's upstairs. Coloring, I think. The men didn't hurt her. I hate to say it, but she's sort of used to being passed around and carted to various locations at this point. She snaps back fast. Ted and I had hoped to bring a little stability to her life, but I'm not doing a very good job of that so far, am I?" She let out a weak laugh.

"I think you're doing fine." He took another step forward and held out his hand. "Why don't you give me the gun?"

She looked down at her hand and her eyes widened as if she'd forgotten the weapon was there. "Oh God. Yeah, of course."

She handed him the weapon. Riker ejected the round from the chamber, popped the magazine out of the pistol, and set it on the counter.

"Matthew, we're in real trouble here."

Riker looked at the bodies on the floor. He couldn't argue with her assessment.

"The men...they called their boss and gave him the address. They know where we are."

"Then we can't stay here long," Riker said.

Helen took one last look at the bodies on the floor and turned away. "I can't deal with this right now. I need to check on Li."

Riker followed her into the living room. She was walking quickly and with confidence. She was certainly still in shock, but at least she was starting to exert a little control of the situation.

"Helen, hold up."

She stopped and turned toward him, the pain clear in her eyes.

"What did they want? They held you here for a couple hours. They must have questioned you. Did they ask you for something?"

"Ted's laptop." She put a hand on the banister and let out a sigh. "I don't know what's on it or why they want it so badly, but they're clearly willing to kill to get it. They said they already searched our house back in New York. During the funeral. Pretty classy, huh?"

"Jesus," Riker muttered.

"I guess they've been watching me, waiting for me to go somewhere else. They thought he might have hidden it. I told them this place is just a rental. I've never been here before this week, but they didn't believe me. One of them held me at gunpoint while the others searched the house. They didn't find anything, since there isn't anything to find. Then they called their boss."

Riker looked at the bodies one more time. They were running out of options. Calling the police wasn't what Helen wanted, but what was the alternative? If Helen and Li went home, it didn't seem logical that the men would leave her alone. They probably had more manpower in New York than they did here, if that really was their home base. And then there was the issue of the bodies. Helen had rented this place, so it wouldn't exactly be difficult for the police to connect it to her once the bodies were discovered. The more Riker thought about it, the fewer options he saw. Going to the police was the only way.

But something else was bothering Riker, working at his mind like a seed stuck in his tooth.

"How is it possible they found you at that motel?" he asked.

Helen shook her head. "I've been thinking about that ever since they busted down our door. I can only think of one possibility. I made a call to a friend in New York. I might have mentioned to him where we were staying. Is it possible they somehow tracked my phone?"

"I don't know." Riker had been out of the game for six years. While it didn't feel that long, six years was an eternity when it came to technology. He really didn't know what was or wasn't possible now. "This friend... You think he might have turned on you? Given these guys your location?"

"No way," Helen said quickly. "He was Ted's best friend, and he's the only person other than me who believes Ted's death wasn't a suicide. There's no way he'd work with them." She thought a moment. "This friend, Dobbs is his name, he's a criminal lawyer. A good one. He might know what to do here."

"Okay," Riker said. "Call him."

Helen started to take out her phone, but Riker held up a hand.

"Use mine." He unlocked his phone and tossed it to her. He waited as she dialed.

"Dobbs, it's Helen. I'm using a friend's phone." She

paused, listening. "We're okay. But this morning some men broke into our room and took us. They brought us back to the rental house. And then... I don't even know where to start. Things got very bad."

Riker heard the sound of a child humming in the bedroom. He turned and went toward it, leaving Helen talking to her friend.

Despite Helen's words, Riker expected to find Li's face streaked with tears like it had been when he'd first seen her at the fair. But she looked...not happy exactly, but not concerned either. She lay on the floor, drawing with crayons. She looked up and smiled when she spotted Riker.

"Zǎoshang hǎo," Riker said. *Good morning.*

"Hi," she replied in Mandarin.

He walked over and crouched down next to her. He hoped his Mandarin was good enough to hold a slightly longer conversation. One way to find out.

"Did you hear the loud noises?"

She nodded, then turned back to her coloring.

"Are you alright?"

"Yes," she said. She looked up again and tears stood in her eyes. "I want my mommy."

In the distance, Riker could still hear Helen explaining the situation to her friend.

"She'll be in here soon, Li."

Li frowned as if she didn't believe him and turned back to her drawing.

"I'm sure this is all a little scary. You're a brave girl."

"I know," she said.

He cracked a smile at that, the first genuine one he'd felt since discovering the door kicked in at the motel. He looked down at the paper and tried to interpret her drawing. Riker hadn't spent much time with kids—he was the youngest in his family—and he had no idea about the drawing skill level of the average three-year-old, but this one was an indecipherable mess of lines and squiggles. He wasn't even positive which way was up.

"What are you drawing?" he asked.

"Yīngxióng." *Hero.*

Riker smiled again at that, suddenly remembering the stack of comic books on his passenger seat. Li would get a kick out of them, he was sure of it. Now that he squinted at the paper, he thought he could almost make out a human form. The too-long purple lines were legs and the messy green circle was the head.

"Is it the Hulk?" he asked in Mandarin.

"No."

"Then what hero is it?"

"Nín," she answered. *You.*

Riker felt a lump rising in his throat. Before he could muster a response, Helen stepped into the room. She looked back and forth between Riker and Li for a moment as if trying to figure out what they were up to.

"Everything okay in here?" she asked.

"Yeah. Li was just telling me about her drawing." Riker pushed himself to his feet. "What did your friend say?"

"He wants me to come to him. He can protect me in New York."

"In a legal sense?"

"And in the physical one. He has some private security on his firm's payroll. Once I'm safe, he'll call the police here and tell them what happened. He thinks he can make a case as to why I fled the scene. He said I should expect some legal problems for the foreseeable future, but it beats being dead."

Riker couldn't argue with that. "Okay, then we'd better

get moving. Get your stuff together. Essentials only. Leave your phone here just in case they are tracking it."

She nodded, then she looked at him oddly. "You never answered my question."

"What question?"

"About driving us to New York."

Riker frowned. He'd honestly forgotten about his promise to consider her offer. In his mind, he'd already turned it down. What he'd told her before still held true— the car wouldn't drive any faster with him in it. Yet, he knew a little more about these guys than he had earlier today. He knew about their seemingly uncanny ability to find Helen and Li anywhere, and the lengths they'd go to in order to capture them. If the men found them in the motel, who was to say they weren't going to find them again on the highways between North Carolina and New York?

And then there were the legal issues to consider. He didn't want to attract attention, but he'd pretty much failed in that regard. Too many people had seen him with Helen. Once it came out that three dead guys had been found in her rental house, it wouldn't be long before the police came knocking on his door.

"Dobbs can protect you, too," Helen said, as if reading his mind. "He said he was more than happy to act as your lawyer too if it comes to that. Pro bono. All you have to do is help us reach New York."

Riker didn't reply. He didn't like the sound of being in debt to some lawyer, but he couldn't afford to be arrested. A sure and sudden death lay at the end of the road.

He felt a tap on his leg and looked down.

Li smiled up at him. She held out her drawing.

"Lǐpǐn," she said. *A gift.*

Riker took the piece of paper and looked at it. He could

clearly see the form of the person in the drawing now. The hero. Him.

He thought about how he'd first seen Helen and Li running through the fair. He thought about how hard these men were fighting to capture them. He thought about Li's drawing.

Then he gave Helen his answer.

## 9

RIKER SAT down at the dining room table. He removed his bloody sock and saw a small shard of glass poking out of the bottom of his foot. He had found a bottle of peroxide in one of the bathrooms and a small tube of superglue in a kitchen drawer. Everything a redneck medic needed. He pinched hard on the glass and pulled. It came out a bit but his fingers slipped off the bloody glass. He winced and took one long breath. He tried again and this time was able to remove the quarter-inch shard of glass from his foot. Once the wound was disinfected and sealed, he put his shoes on and got to work.

Riker grabbed a towel and a jug of bleach from the mudroom. He raced through the house wiping down every-thing that he had touched while Helen and Li gathered their things upstairs. He poured a healthy amount of bleach over any bloody track he had left in the house. He wanted to get rid of any physical evidence that could tie him to the scene.

Riker wasn't thrilled with the quality of his cleanup job, but the clock was ticking. He walked back to Helen's car. Every other step reminded him that there was a wound in the bottom of his foot. Most people would curse the pain, but Riker was glad it was there. It reminded him that he needed to focus. He had kept up his physical training over the years, but he felt he had lost a bit of his edge without living the ethos every day.

Riker pulled Helen's car into the driveway and went inside for the girls. Helen was sitting on the bed staring blankly at Li, who continued to color and babble about imaginary worlds.

"It's time to go," he said. "Do you have what you need?"

"Yes, we're ready. Did you clean up the mess in the kitchen?"

"No, there isn't time."

"I don't want Li to see any of that."

Riker got it. From the stairs, pools of blood and cold dead legs were visible in the kitchen. He wasn't used to worrying about people's feelings. He normally focused on results and nothing else.

Helen grabbed a sheet off the bed and spoke to Li in Mandarin. "Li, we are going to play a hide and seek game. Are you ready for some fun?"

Li stood up and clapped her hands. "You hide. I am the best seeker."

"This is a special game. I will carry you while you hide."

"I know this game. Will we be somewhere else when I can see again?"

"Yes. We will see if Matthew can find us."

Riker watched Helen scoop up Li. The child was still innocent even in this messed-up world. He hadn't seen this part of life in years. In fact, he wasn't sure he had ever really seen it. With a blanket over Li, Helen carried her down to the car.

Riker backed out of the drive and headed down the

street. They'd driven half a mile when he heard a small voice from under the blanket. "Do you think he will find me?"

Riker laughed and looked in the rearview mirror. Helen sat next to Li in the back. She leaned down next to her covered head and spoke in a whisper. "You are very good at this game. I don't know if he will find you."

Helen looked at Riker in the rearview mirror and winked. She smiled for the first time that morning, and Riker realized just how beautiful she was.

"Helen, I can't find Li," he said in Mandarin. "Have you seen her?"

Li pulled the blanket off and put her arms in the air. "Chijing!" *Surprise.*

Riker smiled. "Oh my gosh, I couldn't find you. You are very good at that game."

Five minutes later, he looked back and saw that Li was asleep. She slumped forward in her seat, her head at an angle that made Riker question if she had any bones in her neck. Helen leaned against the window, staring at the countryside rolling by.

Neither of them spoke for nearly an hour. Helen finally lifted her head when Riker pulled off the highway at an exit marked Charlotte Douglas International Airport.

"Why are we stopping?" she asked.

"We need to switch vehicles. Whoever is after you obviously knows a lot about you. They know what you drive and probably know that you will head to New York City. So far they have been one step ahead, and I'd like to be sure we get you home without any more incidents."

"So we're renting a car?"

"Not exactly. Renting a car leaves records. We need something a little more off the books."

Riker pulled the car into the airport's long term parking lot. He did a few laps and watched other cars come and go. He eventually found what he was looking for—an old Cutlass. Riker watched it park. A young man got out and headed off with his bags. Riker pulled into a space five spots down from the vehicle.

He grabbed a coat hanger and screwdriver that he'd taken from the house. Unfortunately, a bump key wouldn't work on a car. He would have to use the coat hanger without drawing attention. He walked up to the 1993 Oldsmobile Cutlass and did a quick check of the lot to be sure that no one was too close. Then he bent the hanger and jammed it in the door frame. After a moment of jiggling it around, he felt it catch and pulled up. The push lock inside the window popped up.

Climbing into the driver's seat, he pulled off the plastic guard under the steering column and exposed the starter wires. A moment later, the car fired right up.

They were back on the highway fifteen minutes after they had pulled off the ramp. This time, Helen was sitting shotgun. Li was once again sleeping in the back.

"So who are you really?" she asked.

"I'm a beekeeper. In my opinion, I'm a very good one."

"Do you need to steal a lot of cars to make the honey? I can tell that wasn't the first time you've done it. I would imagine that most professional car thieves can't do it as fast as you just did."

"Well, there is a lot of downtime in the beekeeping world. I study a lot of different things to keep myself occupied."

"Things like how to disarm two men at a time? Or how to keep your cool in a firefight?"

"The kind of studies that I don't like to talk about." Riker met her gaze, and she got the message that the conversation was over.

After a brief awkward silence Riker asked, "How are you doing? Things got pretty bad back there. That can be hard to deal with."

"Honestly I'm not really sure how I'm doing. I haven't really processed it yet. Any time I start to think about it, my mind goes somewhere else. Part of me wishes that I hadn't done it."

"The part of me that's still alive is pretty glad that you did. It's good that you realize how serious it is to take a life, but those guys were murderers and kidnappers. They aren't worth your guilt or tears. Though I was hoping we would have a chance to interrogate one of them. There are so many unanswered questions."

"I'm sorry. I just wanted to make sure that they stopped. I didn't really believe that I could kill them." She paused for a second. "That sounds so stupid when I say it out loud. I don't know what else you can expect when you shoot a gun at someone."

"Like I said, you have nothing to be sorry about. I just wish we knew what we're up against."

They sat in silence watching lines tick by as the world grew dark. Riker turned the knob on the radio, listening to a few different news reports. He expected to hear about a triple murder and possible abduction, but there was no mention of it. He hoped that it would be a few days before the bodies were found. There was a long shot that whatever organization those guys worked for would cover it up.

"It's funny how they never show the real parts in those adventure movies," Helen said.

"What do you mean?"

"I mean you see the Avengers get news of trouble

halfway around the world, but you never see them booking flights and sitting at the airport for hours. They never arrive in another country tired and jet lagged. If you look at all the places they go, most of their time would be spent in transit."

Riker chuckled. "Well, they do have the Quinjet."

"The what?" Helen asked.

"The Quinjet. They would never have to wait in an airport."

"What is a Quinjet?"

"You know, their plane. You see it in *Age of Ultron* and then again in *Ragnarok*. That thing can go over Mach 2 so getting around isn't as boring as it is in real life."

Helen laughed at Riker. "You know how fast a fictional plane can go? You said you liked comics, but I didn't realize that you *really* like comics."

Riker's cheeks turned a little red. "I know it sounds silly, but I'm telling you the comics they make now are not just for kids. The stories are great, and they do a good job with lots of movies. They do kind of bastardize the story lines, but the MCU still puts on a good show."

"I was starting to think you were a master criminal, but maybe you are just a beekeeper from rural North Carolina."

"Hey, good entertainment is good entertainment."

"I'll take your word for it. Chances are slim to none that I pick up a comic book."

"Fair enough. What do you like to do for fun?"

Helen looked out the window long enough for Riker to think she hadn't heard the question. He was about to ask again, but she answered before he did.

"Honestly, I don't do anything for fun anymore. Before Ted died, we spent our time working the adoption process, and then we got Li. Now I'm a single mom. Doing things for fun hasn't been part of my life for a long time.

"You should change that. Once you get through this mess. Enjoy your life. Do some fun things. It can end in the blink of an eye. I've seen it happen a lot."

She gave him a soft smile. "Okay. If I make it through this, I promise I'll make some time for myself."

Riker nodded, silently promising himself that he'd give her the chance.

## 10

THEY'D BEEN on the road for a few hours when Riker suggested they stop for dinner. Li was getting antsy, and he knew they could all use some food in their bellies.

"Is that a good idea?" Helen asked. "Maybe we should wait until later when fewer people will be at the restaurant."

Riker considered that a moment, then shook his head. "If we eat now, we'll just be three more faces in the crowd. Waitstaff and other customers probably won't even remember seeing us. But if we stop at ten at night, we might be the only people in the restaurant. We'll certainly be the only ones with a three-year-old kid. Pretty tough to blend into the crowd in that scenario."

He pulled off the highway at the next exit and drove past Applebee's and Denny's, dismissing them outright. He'd seen the name of a local diner on the sign before the exit. A place like that was less likely to have security cameras, which made it a more appealing option.

When they stepped into the Lighthouse Diner, Riker knew he'd made the right call. The place looked like it hadn't been updated since the seventies, which put the odds of modern surveillance equipment pretty low. Even better, the restaurant was hopping. From the cars in the parking lot, Riker could tell the crowd was a good mix of locals and travelers. The waitresses were doing all they could just to keep up, which meant they'd be paying less attention to each customer, a very good thing in Riker's mind.

When they were seated, Riker selected a chair with a view of the entrance and the door to the kitchen. He kept both in his periphery as they settled in.

The waitress came by to take their orders. She was a woman in her fifties who had a look in her eyes that said she'd seen it all and would be taking exactly zero crap. But her eyes brightened when she saw Helen's shoes. "Hey, I love your Jimmy Choos."

"Thanks." Helen gave her a warm smile. "You've got a good eye."

Helen ordered a sandwich for herself and chicken fingers for Li. Riker went with the Salisbury steak. A risky order, perhaps, but it would come with a steak knife which meant he'd have a weapon at the table, one that wouldn't raise any suspicions.

After the waitress brought their drinks, Helen took a sip of her tea and leaned forward, a mischievous smile on her face. "Let's play a game."

Riker said nothing. He watched as a couple in their twenties walked in. The woman exclaimed loudly about how cute the restaurant was.

"Since you don't want to tell me about your past, I'm going to guess. And if I get it right, you have to tell me."

"Okay," Riker said.

Li was once again drawing with crayons, this time on the back of a paper placemat. She'd slept for most of the ride, but she'd spent every waking moment carefully paging through the comics Riker had brought for her. It looked like she was drawing some sort of battle scene now, maybe inspired by something she'd seen in those pages.

Helen gave Riker a long, pointed look, as if she were attempting to read his mind.

"You grew up in a small town," she began. "Somewhere out west, let's say. You did well in school, probably got accepted to a few good colleges after your mother made you apply. But you had other plans. You were patriotic, and you couldn't wait to serve Uncle Sam. So you joined up with the Army. How am I doing?"

Riker said nothing. His lips curled up in a slight smile.

"No comment? Okay, then I'll keep going. The Army wasn't quite what you expected. You got deployed quickly and spent the next few years in the Middle East. Somewhere along the way, you started to get disillusioned. Your boyish patriotism got all mixed up by actual reality. By your third or fourth tour, you weren't even sure what we were doing over there. You left the Army when your time was up, and you went back home. But home seemed different now, and you couldn't quite fit in. It was tough to shake all you'd been through, so you decided to start over. You bought a bee farm in rural North Carolina, and you've been there ever since. Until the day you bumped into us."

Riker's face betrayed nothing.

"How'd I do? Remember, you have to tell me. Am I right?"

"Nope," Riker said.

The waitress brought their food a few minutes later. The Salisbury steak was passible. Riker ate fast, keeping the steak knife gripped in his left hand as he took big bites, always with one eye on the entrance.

Li picked at her chicken fingers, still clutching a crayon

as tightly as Riker was holding the knife. They ate mostly in silence. When Riker finished eating, he set down his fork, but he slid the knife under the table, holding it down by his leg in case he needed it.

"So this Dobbs guy we're going to see," Riker said. "Does he work for a big firm?"

"No, but it's prestigious. He takes high-profile cases. Did you see that thing on the news last year about the stock-broker accused of killing his wife?"

Riker shook his head.

"Well, that was Dobbs' case. He figured out there was no way the guy could have done it due to a delay on his subway line that day. It was brilliant."

"And you're confident he can protect you?"

"If he can't, I'm not sure who can. It's the best option we have."

Riker didn't argue with that.

The bell over the entrance chimed as the door opened and a man walked in. Riker sat up a bit straighter, alarm bells going off in his head. The man was average height, but he was broad and looked solid. He wore a loose-fitting jacket. In late August, a jacket certainly wasn't necessary for warmth. Though if you were trying to conceal something—a shoulder holster for example—it might come in handy.

The man had a hard look in his eye as he scanned the diner. When his gaze reached Riker's table, he hesitated for just a millisecond before moving on, as if he were looking for something else. He reached into his pocket and he started walking toward their table.

Riker turned, angling his body and leaning forward so he'd be able to spring at the guy the moment he made a move. He was suddenly very glad they'd been seated at a table rather than a booth. In the booth, he would have been trapped. Here, he could jump up and lunge at the guy in one swift motion.

"Helen," Riker said softly, not taking his eyes off the man stalking toward him. "When I move, you duck. Grab Li and run to the bathroom, got it?"

"What?" Helen stared at him in confusion.

There was no time to explain further. Riker pushed back his chair ever-so-slightly and leaned forward on the balls of his feet. He'd have to get the timing exactly right. He could see a bulge in the man's jacket now. The hand was gripping something. Riker got ready as the man began to pull his hand out of the pocket. The hand cleared the jacket, gripping something that caught a reflection of the light.

Riker started to rise, but stopped himself at the last moment when he realized what the man was holding—a cellphone.

The man smiled as he made his way past them and to another table. He joined a woman and two kids.

Riker let out a breath and unclenched his jaw. His heart thudded loudly in his chest.

"What was that?" Helen asked.

"Nothing. False alarm." Riker loosened his grip on the knife. It had been a long time since he'd overreacted to the presence of a stranger like that. He supposed the events of the last couple of days had reawakened something inside him, something not entirely pleasant.

"All finished?" Helen asked Li in Mandarin.

"Yes," Li answered. She'd set down her crayon and was looking vacantly around the restaurant.

Riker reached into his pocket and pulled out a quarter. He held it in his hand a moment, tossing it gently until he was sure he had Li's attention. Then he held the quarter between the thumb and index finger of his right hand. He brought his left hand over as if to grab the quarter. As the hand closed around the coin, he executed a French Drop, letting the quarter fall into the open palm of his right hand even as he appeared to grab it with his left. It was a simple sleight-of-hand move, but a very deceptive one.

Li's gaze followed his empty left fist as his right hand disappeared beneath the table. He slowly opened the fist, finger by finger, revealing it was empty. Li's eyes widened.

"How'd you do that?" she asked in Mandarin.

"Magician's secret." He paused. "Unless you want to become a magician too. Then I'll show you."

She nodded eagerly.

Knowing the quarter would be too large to hide in her small hand, Riker fished a penny out of his pocket and handed it to her. He showed her how to hold it between her thumb and first two fingers, and how to release the pressure with the thumb just as the other hand started to close around the coin. The first time she tried it, the penny clattered to the table, and she looked disappointed.

"Practice," Riker said. "It will take a long time, but you'll eventually get it right. Think you can do that?"

She nodded solemnly and tried again.

Helen smiled. "Okay, I'm going to revise my guess at your history. Now I think you ran away from home and joined the circus. You were raised by an old magician who taught you the ways of the coin."

Riker chuckled. "Much closer."

"You're going to tell me someday."

"Okay," Riker said. "You want to know?"

Helen leaned forward in her seat.

"I did well in school. You were right about that. But the rest you got wrong. I was accepted to Cornell on a trombone scholarship, but I studied mathematics. My junior year, the

FBI recruited me. I spent the next ten years hunting serial killers. I used my math skills to create a profiling algorithm. I was a rising star until the day I encountered Randall Jeffrey Stokes, a killer who liked to burn people alive. He murdered my partner, and I went rogue. After I took him down, I retired to my family's bee farm and vowed to never hunt a serial killer again."

Helen stared at him for a long moment. "Liar."

Riker grinned. "Was it the trombone scholarship that gave me away?"

"Too many details," Helen said. "You can always tell someone's lying when they include so many details."

"Duly noted. My next lie will be far more vague."

Li was still practicing the French Drop. The penny seemed large in her tiny hand, and it was obvious she wasn't really grabbing it. But at least she wasn't dropping it anymore. It was a start.

"If we hit the road now, we'll be in New York in five hours," Riker said.

"Then let's get to it," Helen replied.

They paid the bill and headed back to the car. As they pulled back onto the highway, Riker felt a twinge of hope. Maybe this was all going to work out after all.

It wasn't long before all hell broke loose.

## 11

THE CAR WAS quiet after dinner. The hum of the highway passing beneath them put Li to sleep. Helen stared out the passenger window in silence. As the lines on the road sped past, Riker's mind wandered back decades. His conversation with Helen had brought up memories that he rarely visited.

Long ago, Coach Kane had changed the trajectory of his life with a simple question.

Early in his freshman year of high school, Riker found himself in the office. It was the first month of school and his third time sitting in a hard plastic chair in front of the door that read *Principal*. His face was swollen, and blood oozed from one split lip. He wondered if he would be expelled. Leaving school didn't seem like a big deal to him, but the thought of his father's reaction scared him.

Then Coach Kane walked by. If he had kept walking Riker probably would have been expelled, that day or one in the not so distant future. Instead, he stopped, looking Riker up and down.

"You're that kid that likes to fight. I've heard about you."

Riker didn't respond. He just sat with his eyes on the

floor.

"How would you like to fight without getting in trouble?"

Riker's eyes shot up to meet Coach Kane's. The man had his full attention.

Instead of expulsion, Riker was given a suspension, and Coach Kane took him under his wing. It may have been because he wanted to help a kid that needed it, or it may have been because he'd heard Riker took on four kids at once and held his own. Kane had helped him hone his aggressive, instinctive fighting style into a formidable wrestling technique.

Riker's life changed drastically because a middle-aged teacher took two seconds out of his day. Riker wasn't sure whether it meant much to Ed Kane, but that little moment made had all the difference for him.

Riker snapped back from the memory when he saw a Cadillac Escalade coming up fast behind him. It weaved around a few cars. Then it slowed and took a spot in the right lane. Riker thought of the guy with the phone in the restaurant. This might just be a driver who was about to get off on an exit, but Riker would rather err on the side of caution.

He sped up and passed a few cars. In the rearview mirror, he watched the SUV match his pace but keep its distance. He gradually slowed down and eased into the right lane. Cars passed him, but the SUV stayed back. That confirmed it—they were being followed.

Riker couldn't believe it. Somehow the men had found them again. He looked at Helen and then down at the purse at her feet. They had placed a tracker on her. It was the only explanation that he could think of. There was no other way they could have found them on the highway in a random car.

"Is Li secured well?" Riker asked Helen.

"What? She's in her car seat, so yes. But why?"

"Do you see the headlights four cars back? They are following us."

Helen turned her head and looked back. "I doubt that. There is no way they could have found us. I powered down my phone and haven't turned it on since the house."

"There is a tracker on you or something you are carrying. First I'm going to lose these guys then we will ditch your things and get you to safety."

"How are you going to ditch them if they can track us?"

"I've got an idea, but it will be a little bumpy."

Riker drove at a steady speed until he saw an exit that he liked. The sign indicated a truck stop and nothing else. He sped up and watched the other car keep pace. At the last moment, he took the exit and went down the ramp as fast as he could. The Escalade took the ramp, but when they reached the bottom, the top-heavy vehicle had to take it slow.

Riker turned left and floored it past the gas station. The road was lined with cornfields on either side. There were no lights other than the beams cast by the car. He could see the Escalade coming up behind them. Riker got the old car up to ninety miles an hour. The interior rattled and the engine roared, but he needed the Escalade to have a lot of momentum for his plan to work.

Riker stayed in his lane as the SUV started to come around on their left. A street sign up ahead indicated an intersection. The Escalade's passenger window slid down and the barrel of an assault rifle poked out. Riker waited as long as he dared.

"Hold on!" he shouted at Helen, and he slammed on the brakes.

The car skidded and he pumped the brakes, fighting to keep it on the road. The Cutlass threatened to spin out of control, but Riker kept it straight as his seatbelt bit into his chest. The Escalade hit their brakes and Riker saw the passenger shoot forward. The gun flew out of his hand and hit the inside of the windshield. Helen placed one hand on the dashboard and held the grab-handle with the other. Riker turned hard right when they reached the crossroad.

The car drifted, and for a moment Riker thought that he had taken the turn too fast. Their tires squealed and the car slid toward the shoulder. Just before the car hit the dirt, the tires gripped. Riker smashed the pedal to the floor, took one last look at the road in front of him, and turned off the lights.

Under the light of the moon, Riker could see a silhouette of the road. He hoped the grid structure of straight lines in the field would continue. If there was a sudden turn, he would not have time to react to it. He kept glancing back, watching for the glow of the SUV headlights.

Riker saw a break in the corn and slammed on the brakes. A slim, dirt access road led between two sections of the field. He threw the car into reverse and backed into it, rolling along the dirt until the car was hidden behind rows of corn. He put the car in drive and kept the engine running.

"Should we get out?" Helen asked.

"No. Stay put."

Riker rolled down his window. The sound of the large Cadillac engine roared as it approached. Riker could hear the gears shift as the vehicle accelerated. The headlights grew brighter and brighter as they came down the road.

Riker's heart pounded, and he waited with his foot floating over the accelerator. This was a game of milliseconds, and he needed his timing to be perfect. He had to judge the distance and speed of the SUV by the sound of the engine and the brightness of the lights.

Just before the Escalade was in view, he slammed his foot down on the gas. The car lurched forward out toward the road. The front of the SUV flew by, and adrenaline surged in his body before the moment of impact. For a moment, Riker thought he was going to miss his target, but then the crunch of metal filled his ears. In his peripheral, he saw Helen's head whip forward. Her hair danced past the front of her face.

The Cutlass clipped the back panel of the Escalade, and the SUV's back end slid on impact. The vehicle tilted, and its driver's side wheels left the pavement. The world seemed to move in slow motion. Riker hoped to see the SUV tip and then tumble down the road. Instead, the driver managed to keep it from flipping, but there was no way to keep it on the road.

The SUV hit the small drainage ditch on the far side of the pavement. It went down two feet and then back up, hitting at an angle. A smaller car would have crashed the bumper into the far side of the ditch, but they had enough clearance to avoid the impact. They were going fast enough to send the Escalade two feet into the air when it came out of the ditch. The SUV bucked up and down in the rutted cornfield, spraying dirt and crops into the air. It came to a stop fifty yards into the field.

For a moment that seemed to last forever, everything was still. Li whimpered in the back seat, a sound that soon grew into a full-on sob. Helen shook her head to clear it and unbuckled her seat belt. She jumped into the backseat to check on the child.

Riker flipped on the headlights. The light on the driver's side stayed dark, but the other still functioned. Riker could see some bent metal, but the hood wasn't buckled. The engine was still purring. It had been protected by old fashioned American steel.

The SUV didn't move. Smoke rose from the large vehicle's hood.

"Is Li okay?" Riker asked.

"I don't know. She's not bleeding, and her seat looks intact. I don't see any injuries."

Riker took a deep breath and tried to put the sobbing child out of his mind for the moment. "We've got to keep moving. Stay back there with Li."

Riker shifted the car into reverse. It let out a high-pitched squeal the moment his foot touched the accelerator.

"Shit!" Riker hopped out and ran to look at the front of the car. One side of the bumper hung down, touching the pavement. A piece of bent siding was pressed against one of the tires. He grabbed it and pulled as hard as he could, but the metal didn't give.

A noise came from the direction of the other car. Riker looked over and saw one of the men stumble out of the passenger side. He looked at Riker and fumbled for his gun. Riker ducked behind the Cutlass just as a shot rang out.

The SUV started to move slowly. The passenger side door was still open and the shooter climbed back into the moving vehicle.

Riker jumped back behind the wheel and stepped on the gas, this time ignoring the horrible sound of metal scraping asphalt. The car pulled hard to the right and smoke rose from the wheel.

Helen watched out the back window as the SUV pulled out of the ditch and onto the road. "They're still coming."

"I know. This is going to get messy."

## 12

RIKER GRIPPED THE WHEEL HARD, angry at his own stupidity. All of this could have been avoided. The men had found Helen and Li. Twice. They'd found them leaving the fair. They'd found them at the motel. And still Riker had just assumed the men were tracking them via Helen's phone.

The truth was, the tracker could be anywhere. If only he'd taken the time to stop and locate it definitively before hitting the road. Instead, he'd run like an idiot just hoping they wouldn't find him.

The last six years had made him dull. Granted, he could still win a fight—at least against guys with no real training. That had been ingrained in him by everyone from Coach Kane to Captain Morrison and three dozen people in between. His evasion skills were another story. He'd grown too comfortable. He was like his bees when he tended them, their senses dulled by the smoke to the point where they gorged themselves on honey rather than attacking the giant creature messing with their hive.

"What are we going to do?" Helen asked. The panic was

clear in her voice. It was understandable, but it was doing nothing to help the situation.

"For the moment, we're going to concentrate on staying on the road."

The car pulled hard to the right, fighting Riker every foot of the way down the state highway. To his left, the interstate ran parallel to this road. There was an onramp up ahead. He glanced down at the speedometer and saw he was going forty-eight miles-per-hour. Between the smoke pouring from the engine and the way the metal was rubbing against the tire, he wasn't sure he could push it much higher than that.

He glanced in the rearview and saw approaching headlights.

"Matthew!" Helen said.

"I see it."

The SUV appeared to be in worse shape than their Cutlass, but the damage must have been superficial. The big vehicle closed the distance between them fast.

Riker's mind raced as he tried to think through the problem. There was no room for error here. He couldn't mess up again as he had with the tracker. If he pushed the car too fast, the tire would blow. If he pulled over, they'd be sitting ducks for however many armed men were loaded into the SUV. If he stayed the course, they'd either ram him or start shooting. There didn't appear to be a good option.

He drew a deep breath. For the first time in years, he beckoned the voice inside his head, the one he usually fought to quiet. The voice of the warrior.

*You can do this. This isn't the first no-win scenario you've faced. It's not even the worst.*

As the smoke clouded his vision, his mind flashed back to another time there hadn't appeared to be a way out. He'd been driving a damaged vehicle then too, but instead of darkness outside his windows, there'd been the blinding desert sun. Explosions had rung in the distance as he raced through the war-torn city. Everything had been falling apart. His enemies were in pursuit, and he'd known he wouldn't be able to run forever. In the passenger seat, Chapman sat groaning, hands pressed to the wounds in his chest and stomach. From the wheezing noise when he breathed, Riker knew the man had a punctured lung. Without medical attention, Chapman wouldn't last long.

He'd managed to keep laser-focused, guiding the Army Jeep through the narrow streets, somehow recalling the map of the city and overlaying it on the chaotic scene. He'd dodged people, vehicles, and enemy combatants as he weaved through the city. Every time a bomb went off somewhere in the distance, the panic grew and he became more aware of the ticking clock between him and safety. Yet he'd managed to keep his cool when everyone around him was losing theirs.

*You made it through that day*, the voice reminded him.

Yes. But Chapman didn't. He couldn't stomach a similar outcome here. He couldn't allow Helen to die, and he sure as hell wasn't going to let anything happen to Li. He stifled a shout of frustration. This was a no-win situation.

*Then change the situation*, the voice whispered.

He gritted his teeth. The voice was right. This was no time to feel sorry for himself. That wasn't the path to victory, not on the wrestling mat, the battlefield, or some dark highway in rural Pennsylvania. He checked the road up ahead. Not far in the distance, he saw neon lights glowing.

"Okay, I know what we need to do," he said. "It's not going to be easy, and I need you to follow my instructions exactly. Can you do that?"

"Yes," Helen said.

"See that exit a half-mile up ahead?"

"We're not taking this hunk of junk back on the interstate, are we? I can't see where that would improve our situation."

"No, we're not heading for the interstate. We're headed for the truck stop."

"Can we make it that far?"

"Definitely." Riker hoped he sounded more confident than he felt. He changed over to Mandarin. "Li, are you all right back there?"

The only answer was a soft whimper. It was better than no response at all, he supposed.

In the rearview, the SUV was only ten feet behind them now and closing fast.

"When we get to the parking lot, I'm going to get us as close to the door as I can. When I say the word, you grab Li and run inside. Sprint to the bathroom and lock the door. Can you do that?"

There was a long pause. "Yes. What are you going to do?"

"I'm going to do my best to keep us alive."

They were less than a quarter-mile from the gas station now. Through the darkness, Riker could see other businesses along the road to their right. The SUV was so close now that Riker couldn't see their headlights. Apparently the men inside had abandoned the idea of shooting at the Cutlass and were either planning to ram it or force it off the road.

"Hang on," Riker said.

Helen tensed, grabbing the door handle and the armrest hard. Riker supposed she was learning that when he told her to hang on, he meant it.

The car lurched as the SUV kissed its bumper. Riker

kept his eyes locked on the parking lot ahead. He just needed to make it through one more intersection.

"Come on," Riker muttered.

The SUV bumped them again, and the car threatened to spin out of control. Riker kept his iron grip on the steering wheel, fighting to keep it on the road. As they passed through the intersection, Riker angled the car to the right. The tires thumped over the curb as he drove into the parking lot. His single remaining headlight illuminated the building next to the truck stop. It was an old motel with a vacancy sign blinking on and off.

He was relieved to see the SUV still on the road to his left, driving parallel to them now. The passenger window rolled down, and a man leaned out, pistol clutched in his hand.

"Head down!" Riker shouted.

Helen slid down in her seat, still gripping the door handle. Even in the dim car, Riker could see that the blood had drained from her face. Li whimpered again in the backseat.

Riker kept the car angled toward the gas station. Cutting through the parking lot gave them a direct line toward it, while the SUV would have to take a slightly longer route if they continued along the road. It would only buy them seconds, but Riker hoped it would be enough.

There was only one parking lot between them and the truck stop now. As they drove through it, he heard a loud pop. For an instant, Riker thought it was gunfire. But then he realized it was something else maybe just as bad. The car had been fighting him, trying to pull right ever since the cornfield, but now it was pulling much harder in that direction. Sparks flew up from the right front corner of the vehicle. The tire had finally blown.

"Shit!" Riker yelled as he fought to keep them headed toward the gas station. This car wasn't going to get them much farther, but they didn't need it to. If he could keep them going for another fifty feet, they had a chance.

Bright headlights blasted through the driver's side window, threatening to blind him. The SUV had turned off the road and was entering the parking lot.

"You ready?" Riker asked.

"Yeah," Helen answered, her voice anything but confident.

Riker kept his eyes locked on the entrance. He was pleased to see the lot was nearly empty. The fewer people around, the less likely it was that innocent bystanders would get hurt. The door was thirty feet away now. Twenty. Ten.

He let off the gas and stepped on the brakes, bringing them to a messy, grinding halt in front of the door. The car stopped nearly sideways, parallel to the entrance. Riker shifted into Park and threw open his door.

"Let's go!"

Helen hopped out and pulled Li out of the backseat.

The SUV screeched to a stop, and all four doors flew open.

Riker grabbed Helen's arm and guided her toward the truck stop, staying between her and the SUV. He saw shoes hitting blacktop as he pulled the door open and rushed inside.

"Go!" Riker shouted.

Helen ran through the truck stop, Li clutched to her chest, as Riker scanned their surroundings. The place was smaller than he would have expected from the exterior, but there were positives to the location. For one, it was all but empty. The only other people Riker saw were a burly, confused-looking bearded man standing behind the counter and two truckers sitting in a booth, a plate of food in front of each of them. There were rows and rows of items for sale, each partition standing about chest height. Plenty of places to take cover.

The burly man blinked in confusion at the sight of the woman and child rushing through the store toward the back bathroom. The door flew open again, and four men rushed in, Glocks in their hands.

"Get down!" Riker shouted at Helen. She hadn't made it to the bathroom yet, and she dropped down behind a stand of snack cakes.

"The hell is this?" one of the truckers asked. He reached into his coat and pulled out his own pistol.

Riker looked at the men stalking toward him, pistols drawn. This was going from bad to worse very quickly.

He heard the unmistakable sound of a shotgun raking. Turning, he saw the clerk behind the counter clutching a pump-action shotgun.

"Somebody better tell me what the hell's going on, and do it fast," the clerk said in a deep voice.

The four men didn't reply. Instead, they raised their weapons and prepared to fire.

## 13

Riker put his hands in the air. He wanted to be sure the civilians kept their guns pointed at the gangsters. Carefully, he tracked each weapon. Two of the men from the SUV had their guns trained on the cook holding the shotgun. The other two were aiming at the truckers. The shotgun was pointed at the center of the group of four men. The two truckers crouched in their booth, each armed with a pistol. One held his in a steady two-handed grip, but the other shook visibly. Riker could see that the thin wood of their booth wouldn't stop a bullet.

Riker's mind was in overdrive as he scanned the room for any advantage. The center of the room was filled with aisles of shelves. There were lots of junk food, single-serving personal items, poor quality souvenir clothes and an isle of small auto service items.

The other side of the room had the counter with the armed clerk behind it. He was a big guy, and he wore an apron that told Riker he served as cook as well as clerk. Past him was a small kitchen. Riker could see a skillet with food cooking on the gas stove. The area was packed with cooking supplies and ingredients. In the back was the shiny door of a walk-in cooler.

The four men stood just inside the truck stop entrance. One of them looked like a kid to Riker. He might have been in his early twenties, if that. Two of the guys looked hard. One had letters tattooed across his knuckles—probably prison ink. The man next to him was a tall redhead. He had a smile at the corner of his lips. The look on his face told Riker how this was going to turn out.

The last man was the oldest. Gray peppered his hair. From the way the kid kept looking at him, it was clear that he led this crew.

"This is a private matter between us and them," the older man said, nodding toward Riker. "There is no reason anyone needs to get hurt."

The guy behind the counter responded, "You made it my business when you busted in here with guns. Put them down and turn—"

He never finished the sentence. The redhead fired a shot into his chest. The cook was knocked back and fell to the ground without getting a shot off.

Riker sprang into motion diving behind the shelf with the auto supplies, keeping his eyes on the four men as long as he could. The kid turned his head in the direction of the cook when the gun went off. He should have taken a shot at the truckers. His head jerked back and a small red dot appeared just above his right eye. A large spray of blood came out the other side, covering the prison-inked guy in a bloody mess.

The silver-haired leader kept his cool and unloaded on the truckers. His first shot landed in one man's chests. The other guy ducked, but the man kept firing into the booth. Prison Ink followed his lead. Wood and stuffing flew as the bullets tore the bench apart. Neither of the truckers had a chance.

The redhead moved toward Riker. He went quickly, holding his gun in both hands. His smile was wider than before. He came around the end of the aisle, ready to shoot Riker, but the aisle was empty.

When the redhead stepped into the next aisle, Riker was ready. He popped out next to the man, a can of WD-40 in his hand. He shot a thick spray of the fluid into the smiling man's eyes. The man screamed, pressing both hands to his face. Riker shifted the target of the spray to the man's hands and the gun he was holding.

The scream drew the other guys' attention. Riker saw them turn, and dove over the counter to the kitchen. He landed on a tile floor covered in old grease.

The clerk sat on the floor leaning his back on a cabinet, his apron soaked with blood. One hand pushed against the wound in his chest while the other clutched the shotgun. He tried to raise the weapon, angling it toward Riker.

"I'm on your side," Riker told him.

He nodded weakly, letting the weapon clatter back to the floor. His face was pale, and Riker could see that he wouldn't last long without help.

The redhead was still screaming. "I can't see shit!"

"You'll be fine, Connor. We've almost got them."

"The only thing you guys have is small dicks," Riker yelled. "Especially you, Connor. You can't even take out an unarmed man."

Connor pointed his gun in the direction of Riker's voice. He squinted his burning eyes and shot one round toward the kitchen.

As the gun fired, the WD-40 soaking the gun burst into flames. His friends watched as the fire raced up his arm and to his face. Connor screamed and slapped at his face with his hands. He ran wildly, crashing into the shelves around him and knocking items to the floor. After a moment, he fell onto his stomach, screaming and thrashing. The putrid smell of burnt hair and flesh filled the air.

The leader ran over to Connor and slapped at his head and arms with his jacket. The flames lasted until there was no hair on Connor's head left to burn. He lay still on the floor, moaning. Smoke drifted from his head and clothes. The fire alarm started to sing out its high-pitched song and strobe lights flashed over the doors.

Riker grabbed a pan from one of the shelves. He dipped it into the deep fryer next to the stove. Scalding hot grease dripped off the side of the pan and onto the floor. He gripped the pan with both hands and stayed low against the back of the counter.

"Connor, are you ok?" Prison Ink shouted.

The only response was a series of groans.

"We'll take care of him after we finish that bastard off," the leader said. "We've got to do this quickly before the cops and fire department get here."

Prison Ink fired into the counter. The bullets tore through the kitchen and ricocheted off the floor. Riker stayed low, gripping the pan. The blind shots missed their mark. The man walked towards the counter, squeezing off a round with every step. Riker watched the man's blurry reflection in the freezer door. When he was close to the counter, Riker swung the pan hard. The pan stopped at the height of its arch, but the grease it contained sprayed out in the direction of the gunman.

Splatters of grease covered the man like water from a burst balloon. Only a few stray drops hit his face. The bulk of it splashed onto his chest. He screamed as it soaked into his shirt. The fabric held the hot liquid against his skin. Under that shirt, skin bubbled and flaked.

Riker jumped over the counter, still holding the pan. The scalded man was tougher than most; he stayed upright and kept hold of his gun. His face was scrunched up and his lips were drawn back, clearly fueled by rage.

Riker swung the pan hard. The iron cracked against the man's hands and the weapon they were holding, resulting in the gong-like sound of metal on metal and the crunching of bone. Somehow the tattooed man held onto his gun. Riker brought the pan around for another hit. Before he swung, the flash of a muzzle came from his left. Prison Ink flew backward with a large hole in his chest.

The clerk wobbled behind the counter holding his shotgun. A small tendril of smoke drifted up from its barrel. He looked satisfied, but his moment of revenge was short-lived. The leader of the group opened fire and two bullets struck the man's upper body. The shotgun clattered on the floor and the clerk fell forward over the counter. His upper body balanced on the counter for a moment before sliding backward, leaving a bloody smear.

Riker dove behind some shelves and the remaining opponent continued to fire. The 9mm rattled off shots. Bags of food burst open around Riker while he crouched and moved from one aisle to another. It was hard to hear over the fire alarm, but he concentrated, listening for one specific sound. Then he heard it. The release of a magazine and the sound it made falling to the ground.

The last man reached into his back pocket for a magazine, and Riker charged. With his eyes on Riker, he slammed the magazine into the Glock, but before he could pull the slide back. Riker's shoulder crashed into his chest. The man was knocked backward, the metal shelves behind him dug into the meat of his back as bags of candy fell to the floor. Riker slammed one hand against the inside of the man's hand and the other against the barrel of the pistol. Something in the man's wrist cracked and the gun flew out of his hand.

The two men bounced off the shelves and landed on the floor. Riker tried to stand, but lost his footing, slipping on a bag of M&Ms. The candy shot out from under his shoe, and he fell to his knees. The man stood and reached to his belt. He pulled out a black knife with a five-inch blade. Riker could see the trigger finger on his right hand was broken, a common side effect of disarming a man. It angled up in an odd direction, away from the rest of his fist. It forced him to hold the knife with an awkward grip.

Riker got to his feet and found his stance. He kept his weight on the balls of his feet, and he held his hands by the side of his face. He tensed, ready to move, and watched the man's eyes. The eyes always gave away the strike. Just before an attack, the mind wanted to see the target. Riker waited.

The gunman's eyes flashed a moment before he lunged. Riker stepped to the side and grabbed the man's arm, twisting it and pulling down hard. At the same time, he brought his knee up, connecting with the elbow. The opposing movements caused the arm to hyperextend at the elbow. The knife clattered to the floor.

Riker didn't let go of the arm. He continued to twist and pull it towards his back. The man dropped to his knees in pain. Riker pulled down on his arm one more time and brought his knee to the corner of the man's jaw. When the knee connected with the jaw, Riker felt an unnatural shift. The bottom half of the man's face moved a quarter inch, and he dropped to the ground motionless.

Riker's heart was racing, and he could feel the tension in

his muscles. He took a deep breath to calm himself. The room was complete chaos. Five men were dead and two were seriously injured. Smoke hung in the air as the emergency lights and alarms flashed.

"Helen, are you and Li okay?" He scanned the room for them.

"Is it safe?" The muted voice came from behind a bathroom door.

"Yes, but don't come out yet."

Riker ran over to a rack of clothes and grabbed a few random T-shirts and some sweatpants. He opened the bathroom door a few inches and handed the clothes to Helen.

"Take off all your clothes, and I mean everything. I want you and Li to put these on. Hurry, we need to get out of here fast. Make sure to play the hiding game with Li when you come out."

While they changed, Riker searched the four gunmen for cash. He didn't consider himself a thief, but he wasn't going to lose any sleep over taking money from these guys. The first three had less than a hundred dollars each. When he checked the leader he found a roll of cash. There was a little over a thousand dollars in it.

A few minutes later Riker, Helen, and Li ran out of the store with the sound of sirens approaching in the distance.

**14**

---

THE THREE OF them hurried through the parking lot, Riker leading the way past the sparsely populated car parking area and to the motel next door. He spotted a line of semi-trucks parked alongside the motel. In the distance, sirens cut through the air. It wouldn't be long before this place was crawling with police and EMTs. They had to be gone before that happened. The old gears in Riker's head were spinning faster now, as if lubricated by blood and violence. He felt like he'd completed a mission and was moving on to the escape and evasion phase.

"What are we going to do?" Helen asked.

"We're going to hide." Riker's voice was distant as he scanned the semis.

"In a truck?"

"Yes, in a truck." He paused as they reached the first semi in a row of a dozen or so. He took a long look at the vehicle, then moved on.

"Why not that one?" Helen asked.

"We're looking for a dry truck."

"A what?"

"That one's refrigerated. I'd rather not spend the next twelve hours in sub-freezing temperatures. We're looking for the other kind. They call it a dry truck."

He paused at the next vehicle. It looked like it would do. He quickly picked the lock, then lifted the handle on one of the doors on the back of the trailer, rotating it to the left. Opening the door a few inches, he shined the light from his cellphone inside. What he saw made him frown. The trailer was nearly full, and the way the load was secured didn't fill him with confidence. It would be no use hiding from the cops only to be crushed by shifting cargo when the truck started moving.

He shut the door, closed the latch, and replaced the lock. "Let's keep going."

This time, Helen didn't bother asking what was wrong with that truck. The sirens were getting closer now, and she knew as well as he did that their time was short. She didn't waste it with words. Maybe she was beginning to trust Riker's instincts.

The next vehicle was a fifty-three-foot dry truck, the most common type of semi on the road. Riker once again picked the lock and lifted and rotated the handle. When he peered inside, he liked what he saw much better this time. The trailer was only two-thirds full, and the pallets inside were nicely secured by two rows of straps attached to either wall. He climbed inside and tested the straps. When he was confident they were up to muster, he went back to the door and held a hand out to Helen.

"This is the one. Come on."

She handed Li to him. The girl squirmed in his arms, restless and confused. Despite Helen's earlier assurances that she was used to being carted around, the chaos of the last two days was clearly getting to her. Riker worried that spending the next half-a-day in the back of a semi-trailer wasn't likely to help the situation. But Li's comfort fell below her survival on the hierarchy of needs. He promised himself he'd try to make it up to her when this was all over. Setting Li down on the rough wooden floor, he went back to the door and helped Helen inside.

The door to the semi was designed so a person couldn't lock themselves inside the trailer. Riker looked at that latch that needed to be pulled towards the outside of the truck in order to slide the bar into place. He took the laces out of both of his shoes and tied them together to get all the length he could. Next, he made a loop on one end. He placed it over the metal handle that pointed up. He ran the other end of the laces through the gap at the hinges of the door. Then he got back in the truck and held the end of the string. He pulled the door shut and tugged on the string. He felt the handle turn to the side and the bar slide into place. When the handle turned parallel to the ground, the loop from the laces slid off. He pulled the laces through the seam of the truck door.

Everything would look normal from the outside of the truck. Riker wasn't sure how he would get the door back open, but that was a problem for another time.

"What now?" Helen asked in a soft voice.

"We wait." He grabbed the trailer door and hesitated for a moment.

Li let out a little whimper as darkness enveloped them.

"It's okay," Helen whispered in Mandarin. "Go to sleep."

That sounded like a mighty fine idea to Riker. He could hear the sound of the approaching sirens even through the closed trailer door now. The police might find them hiding back there, but worrying about it wouldn't change their odds. They'd made their decision, and now it was time to wait it out.

"How do we know where this truck's headed?" Helen asked.

"We don't. But anywhere's better than here, right?"

There was a long pause before she spoke again.

"So this guy might be headed south. Directly away from New York City. Maybe even back to North Carolina."

"Entirely possible," Riker admitted. He crawled his way over to the trailer wall and leaned his back against it. "Listen, I need to apologize. Not checking you guys for trackers was dumb. I shouldn't have been so careless."

"You couldn't have known." She moved next to him. Their shoulders lightly brushed against each other as she settled in.

"I could have and I should have. I'll be more careful from here on out. With your clothes, cellphone, and purse all back at the truck stop, I gotta believe we've ditched the tracker."

"Matthew, if it wasn't for you, they'd have us by now. And once they find whatever it is they're looking for on Ted's laptop, I don't imagine they'll let us go."

Riker said nothing.

"You've saved our lives. A number of times now. Do I love hiding out in the darkness in the back of a truck? No. I feel like a sitting duck back here. I keep imagining that at any moment, someone's going to open those doors and either drag us off to prison or shoot us in the head. But I trust you."

"I appreciate that." He paused for a moment, listening. He could make out at least two distinct sirens very close by.

Probably in the parking lot. "Listen, this trucker probably won't be out here until morning. And who knows how long he's going to drive before his next stop. We might as well settle in and get some sleep."

Helen let out a soft laugh. "After what we just went through? I've got so much adrenaline pumping through me that I won't be able to sleep for a week."

"You might be surprised. Your body needs rest, and it will take the opportunity even in less than ideal circumstances. Let it do its thing."

"Okay. I'll try."

Within a few minutes, both Helen and Li's slow, rhythmic breathing told Riker they were asleep. The human body was truly a marvel. As Helen fell into a deeper slumber, she leaned against Riker, instinctively snuggling up against him. He didn't fight it. He didn't dwell on it either. It was time for him to take his own advice and get some sleep.

He ran through the routine he'd used in the old days when he needed to sleep rough. He'd found long ago that the more aware he was of his own body and its needs, the easier it was to turn off his mind. Starting with his feet, he concentrated on each muscle, consciously relaxing it, letting the tension go. He worked his way up to his legs, his torso, his hands and arms. By the time he reached the muscles in his face, he found himself drifting away.

He slept hard, lost in a mercifully dreamless slumber. The world was gone for Riker. Though he was leaning against a metal wall and sitting on a cold wooden floor, he slept better than he did on his mattress at home.

When he finally opened his eyes, light was peeking through the cracks in the trailer doors. It was morning, which meant he'd slept for at least seven hours. He felt stiffness in his back and shoulders, but his mind was immediately alert. The weariness of the previous night was gone.

Helen and Li were still sleeping. Helen was pressed tight against Riker, her head on his shoulder. The intoxicating smell of her hair filled his nose. Li lay curled up on the floor a few feet away from the two of them.

The truck was moving now, and sounds of the highway cast a hypnotic spell. As Riker sat there, alone with his thoughts for the first time since finding Helen and Li at the rental house, he played the events of the last two days over in his mind. Some things didn't add up, and things that pointed in directions he didn't want to let his mind go. The constant rush of escape was lifted for the moment, and it brought clarity for Riker.

He looked at Li, the way her chest slowly rose and fell as she slept. She'd been through a time of almost unimaginable change and that had to bring fear and confusion with it. Yet, she still had the innocent optimism of a three-year-old. Riker vowed to himself that he'd protect that. He'd protect *her*. No matter what.

He didn't want to wake Helen, but he needed to move. Seven hours in a cramped, half-seated position wasn't doing his back any favors. He shifted ever so slightly, and he felt Helen stir. She drew a deep breath, not pulling away as he'd expected, but snuggling even closer for just a moment. Then she sat up.

"Where are we?" she asked.

Riker slipped the SIM card back into his phone and checked their location on his navigation app. "Massachusetts."

Helen let out a soft chuckle. "All the time trying to get to New York, and we drove right past it as we slept."

As far as Riker was concerned, it wasn't the worst news

in the world. Yes, they were north of the city now, but it seemed unlikely their pursuers would be looking for them in Massachusetts. Once the truck stopped, they'd start heading back toward New York, and this time they wouldn't have goons in an Escalade chasing them. "Let's just hope this guy stops for fuel before we hit Maine."

Helen stretched. "Maine's not so bad. You ever been?"

"A time or two."

"I've only been there once, but it was a memorable trip. Ted and I took our honeymoon there."

"Yeah?"

"We were so broke it was pathetic, but he insisted we have a proper honeymoon. He found this cabin online. According to the website, it was on a beautiful lake. We couldn't believe it was in our price range. Then we saw it in person."

"It didn't live up to the hype?"

"Let's just say the beautiful lake was more like a glorified swamp. This was the middle of summer, and the air conditioning didn't work in the cabin. And somehow, no matter what we did, bugs kept getting inside. I don't mean mosquitos, either. I'm talking black flies. When they bit you, it hurt. Not to mention that our only neighbor was this pervy guy in his seventies who kept creeping around. Ted was convinced he was trying to peek in our windows and get a glimpse of the honeymoon festivities."

Riker smiled. "Sounds like the cabin from hell."

"It was. And yet, we still had a great time. I'll never forget that trip, especially now that he's gone. I'll treasure those memories forever." She put a hand on Riker's arm and gave it a gentle squeeze. "I guess it just goes to show that good things can come out of bad circumstances."

They rode on in silence for the next three hours, Li

asleep on the floor, Helen nodding in and out, and Riker lost in his own thoughts. By the time the truck finally stopped, Riker felt he had his mind wrapped around the situation a little better. He was ready to head to the city. He just hoped there was safety waiting for them there.

# 15

RIKER FELT the truck maneuver through the stop-and-go traffic of a city. The driver was not just getting off for a food break; he was reaching his destination. He told Helen and Li to get ready to move.

"How do we get out of here?" Helen asked. "There is no way to open the door from the inside."

"There's always a way to get through a door."

Four bolts secured the locking mechanism on the door latch. Riker removed one of the ratcheting straps securing the freight and went to work on the rivets. He pried space between the edges of the rivets and the paneling of the back door. Then he wrapped the strap around the rivets. Once he was confident that it was secure, he hooked the other end of the strap to the support bar on the side of the trailer. Satisfied, he started to tighten the strap.

The door began to creak and bulge near the rivets. As Riker continued to tighten the strap, the latch locks slowly broke through the door, leaving a hole large enough to fit Riker's hand. He reached through and lifted the pole that locked the door.

They waited until the truck came to a stop, and Riker swung the door open. The day seemed incredibly bright after the dim interior of the trailer and it took a moment for their eyes to adjust.

Riker checked his surroundings. They were stopped at a light on a city street. Riker didn't recognize it, but it had the feel of a smaller city. Certainly not New York. He glanced at the nearest street sign, which read 4th Avenue. No help there.

The driver in the car behind them had a very confused look on his face. The three hopped out of the truck, shut the door and walked down the sidewalk as if it were a normal day. Riker glanced back at the truck. He wondered what the driver would think when he found his door broken from the inside and all the goods still in place.

Li started to talk quickly and jumped up and down. Even if he hadn't been able to speak Mandarin, Riker would have known she needed to go to the bathroom.

The three walked into the first diner they found. The hostess was on her phone when they came in. She looked up and started to laugh. She quickly regained her compose and asked if they wanted a booth or table.

Riker didn't understand why she was laughing. Then he truly looked at his companions in the light for the first time.

Helen's T-shirt hung down almost to her knees. The front had an image of a flying eagle and a waving American flag with the words "Trucker for Life" printed underneath. She wore blue sweat pants that were so baggy and long they completely hid her feet. That was a good thing since she wasn't wearing any socks or shoes.

Li's outfit wasn't much better. Her long T-shirt looked more like a dress. The words "Guns don't kill people, I kill people" were printed in camouflage on the front.

Riker suppressed a laugh and asked for a table at the back of the diner.

Li was completely unruly while they ate. She would not sit still and made loud noises. Riker tried to quiet her down but she smashed her silverware on the table and continued to draw attention.

"What is wrong with her?" Riker asked. "Why won't she calm down?"

"You really haven't spent much time with children, have you?" Helen shook her head. "First of all, she's three. She doesn't care about other people that much. Every three year old thinks the world revolves around them. Second, she's been stuck in cars or trucks for the last day. She needs to burn off some energy."

"Can't we just explain that she needs to focus now, and she can play later?"

Helen laughed. "Give it a shot. I want to see how this goes."

Li was smashing her fork up and down into a stack of pancakes. Riker spoke to her in Mandarin.

"Li, you need to be quiet. We don't want to cause a scene right now." Riker spoke in a low calm voice.

"Look, a dragon is attacking the mountain." She continued to smash the fork up and down. "Oh no, another dragon." She grabbed her butter knife and smashed it into the fork.

"That's great Li, but can they fight quietly?"

Li looked up at Riker and let out a very quiet roar in her high-pitched voice. She started to giggle and went back to attacking the pancakes.

Helen smiled. "You did better than I thought you would. In fact, you seem like a natural. I'm surprised that you don't have kids of your own."

"Not in this life."

The smile faded from Helen's face. "Family is important. You should consider it."

The two sat in silence for a moment while Li continued to play.

"What's the plan now?" Helen asked.

"First, we need to get the two of you some shoes. I suppose we can pick up clothes that fit a little better as well."

"Are you suggesting that I don't look good in my designer shirt?" Helen puffed out her chest. The silhouette of her breasts pressed through the fabric. Even in her ridiculous clothes, her beauty was undeniable.

Riker smiled. "You two look great. Especially our little gun-toting killer over there. I just think we need something that doesn't leave such an impression on anyone who sees you."

"Fair enough. What do we do after that?"

"We need a car. That will be a little tougher to get than the clothes."

"I'm starting to realize that you are pretty good at solving tough problems."

Once breakfast was over, they made a quick trip to a department store to acquire clothing and shoes for the girls. Helen shopped quickly, selecting a simple T-shirt and jeans for herself and an outfit for Li. Riker picked up a backpack and a few items he thought might come in handy on their journey. They were in and out in ten minutes.

After that, Riker found a small park. It was nothing fancy, but it had swings and playground equipment. Just what Li needed to burn off a little energy.

"Stay here while I get us a car. It shouldn't take long, and

I need you to be ready to go once I get it." Riker started to walk off in search of a car, but he felt a tug on his hand.

"Come play with me," Li said in her foreign tongue.

"Sorry kid, I have work to do. Stay with your mom."

"No. Play with me." She tightened her grip on his fingers and stomped one foot.

"I can't. I have work to do." Riker gently pulled his hand back, but Li held on.

"I think you should play with her," Helen said. "The more energy she uses, the smoother the rest of the trip will be. Besides, it might be nice to take a moment before fleeing in another stolen vehicle."

"We should get you somewhere safe. I don't think we should waste time here."

"No one has any idea where we are right now. They are going to be looking for me when I get back home. This might be the last time I can relax for a while. Can we just take a minute and enjoy the park?"

Riker didn't like it, but she had a point. They were in a random location with no worries. This might not happen again for Helen and Li. He sighed and let Li pull him toward the playground.

Li ran all over the park. She asked Riker to push her on the swings, watch her go down the slide, and play hero and princess with her. Riker kept a watchful eye on their surroundings while they played. He took note of everyone who happened to walk by and assessed every mom and child on the playground.

Then something happened that he didn't know was possible—he started to have fun. He entered Li's imaginary world and helped her escape from a dragon. She clapped when Riker scaled the play set and stood on top of the slide. He grabbed onto the support poles of the structure and lifted his body parallel to the ground holding the flag position just to show off.

Li laughed and told him he didn't know how to climb right. She jumped up on the slide to show him how it was done. Riker watched her go down the slide and caught her at the end.

He saw a mom out of the corner of his eye. He realized that he hadn't noticed her entering the park. Snapping himself back to an aware state, he silently scolded himself. A lack of focus could get them all killed. He put Li down and walked over to Helen. "We've played long enough. It's time to get moving. Watch Li and be ready when I get back."

He didn't wait for a reply before walking away.

He moved quickly but casually along the street looking for a car to target. Morrison's voice filled his head.

*Once you lose focus, death quickly follows. Distraction means death.*

Riker shook off his lapse in the park and promised himself that it would not happen again. He walked until he spotted an old car parked on the side of the road. One tire was low and it was covered with grime. It looked like it had been parked there for at least a week.

He checked the street and didn't see anyone. Reaching in his backpack, he pulled out what he needed. He quickly jimmied the lock of the old car and hopped inside. The engine cranked a few times and eventually started.

After a quick stop at the gas station to top off and fill the tire, he picked up the girls from the park. Their journey to New York was back on track.

Helen and Li sat in the back seat on the drive. Helen kept Li occupied and Riker focused on getting them to their destination. He kept the car at five miles an hour over the speed limit and obeyed every traffic law. Hours and miles ticked by, and before long the city came into view.

Riker looked in the rearview mirror and saw Helen and Li were asleep. "Helen, wake up. I'm going to need you to navigate."

She rubbed her eyes and looked at the sprawl of homes around them. They were only a few miles from the city.

"I can't wait to get back home," she said through a yawn.

Riker's body felt stiff from the hours of driving without a break. He looked forward to getting out of the car. He glanced in the mirror and caught some motion behind her.

At first, he figured he was just being paranoid, but he was sure the same car had been behind them for at least the last hour. Just to be safe, he took the next exit. He waited at the bottom of the ramp and saw that the other car took the exit as well. Then he got right back on the highway. The car followed them back on.

It seemed impossible but somehow their enemies had found Helen once again.

## 16

RIKER GRITTED his teeth and gripped the steering wheel hard. The car following them was a compact BMW, maybe the same model as the one that had followed them out of the fairgrounds a few days ago. It glided easily in and out of traffic as it cut the distance between itself and Riker's car. Riker had no illusions; the nineties Chrysler he was driving was no match for the BMW on the open road.

Getting off the highway and back on had been a necessary maneuver. He now knew for certain that they were being followed. The downside was that the person following them knew that he knew. They'd dropped all pretense of subtlety and were quickly approaching.

"Helen, I've got bad news," he said, glancing in the rearview mirror again.

Helen followed his eyes. After a moment, she spotted the BMW.

"You've got to be kidding me. That's impossible."

"I don't disagree," Riker said. "And yet, there they are."

Helen looked around for a moment. "We're close. Can I borrow your phone?"

Riker nodded. "You'll have to put the SIM card back in. Guess we don't have to worry about them tracking us now."

She grabbed his phone out of the middle console where he'd stowed it. As she replaced the SIM card, he watched the BWM. It was in the next lane over now and quickly approaching them. Riker wondered what the driver would do when he caught up to them. Would he risk shooting at them or trying to run them off the road on this crowded New York City highway?

Helen dialed a number and put the phone to her ear.

"It's me. Yeah, I'm using my friend's phone again. We're almost there, but we're in trouble. Somebody's following us. I think they might try to run us off the road." She listened for a moment, then spoke again. "Near the Bronx. We just passed Kingsbridge Heights." She listened again for a moment. "Yeah, I know the place. We'll get there as fast as we can. We're driving a red Chrysler LeBaron. Massachusetts plates. I really appreciate this, Dobbs." She pressed a button on the touchscreen, ending the call.

"What did he say?" Riker asked.

"He's got a guy nearby. He told me where to meet him. Take the next exit."

Riker didn't answer. He didn't like trusting this lawyer he'd never met with his life, especially since he already had his doubts about the guy. Helen seemed to trust him completely, but Riker was the suspicious type. It had kept him alive this long.

And yet, the thought of not being the person bearing the full responsibility of keeping them alive sounded mighty appealing. They needed help. A safe place to sleep. The end goal was in sight.

He waited until the last moment, doing everything he could to avoid revealing his intentions. Then he twisted the wheel and angled the car onto the exit. To his dismay, the BMW smoothly crossed two lanes weaving between trucks and followed them onto the exit.

"It's less than a mile," Helen said, the excitement clear in her voice. "We're almost safe."

Riker said nothing, not sharing in her optimism. A mile was no short distance on New York City streets, especially when you had gun-wielding madmen chasing behind you. And now that they weren't on the highway anymore, it seemed more likely they'd try to make a move. Riker drove hard, pushing the old Chrysler to the meager limits of its performance capacity. He weaved between two cars, earning a pair of middle fingers for his effort. The BWM quickly pulled up alongside him. Whoever was driving that thing knew how to work these city streets.

The BMW was right alongside them now. Out of the corner of his eye, Riker saw its passenger window begin to roll down.

Riker hit the brakes. The BWM raced ahead as the car behind Riker blared its angry horn at him. He turned right onto the next side street and cut over to the next road.

Helen looked at their surroundings. "Crap. I hope I can find the place. This isn't my part of the city."

Riker bit back the harsh reply he wanted to make. He was counting on Helen here. She was the only person in the car with any idea where they were going. Behind him, he saw the BMW glide onto the road. Riker took the next left, getting them back to the road they'd started on. He hoped that would help Helen orient herself.

"There!" she shouted on the next block. "That warehouse."

"Got it."

The large warehouse was surrounded by a fence lined

with barbed wire along the top. A tiny gap in the fence appeared to be the only entrance to the parking lot. Riker turned the wheel hard, not wanting to slow any more than he absolutely had to. The Chrysler groaned in protest as it slipped between the fence posts and into the lot.

"What now?" Riker asked.

"I don't know. He said his guy would be here."

Riker didn't love that answer, but he didn't bother complaining. He drove toward the warehouse up ahead. Behind them, the BMW entered the parking lot. Riker cursed silently, hoping they hadn't just trapped themselves. The only option left was to stay the course. He'd get to the warehouse and hope whoever Dobbs was sending was waiting there to help them.

The BMW was almost on top of them. Someone leaned out of the passenger window, gun in hand.

They'd almost reached the warehouse when a black Audi appeared, careening around the corner of the building. It charged into the space between the Chrysler and the BMW, putting itself sideways between the two vehicles.

The BMW slammed on its breaks, tires screeching to a stop, barely avoiding slamming into the Audi. The driver of the Audi threw open his door and stepped out. He charged toward the BWM, pistol in hand.

"That's him," Helen said. "That's Hendricks. Dobbs' guy."

"No kidding?" Riker said dryly.

The passenger door to the BMW opened, but Hendricks reached them before the passenger was able to get out. Hendricks raised his pistol and fired three quick rounds through the open window.

"Shit," Riker muttered. He didn't like the idea of going into battle with a person he'd never even met, but he had no choice here. There could be five guys in that BMW for all he knew, and he couldn't let this Hendricks guy face them alone. "Wait here."

"I have no problem with that," Helen said.

Riker threw open his door and started toward the BMW in a low crouch. The men in the vehicle were focused on Hendricks. That meant he might be able to sneak up undetected and—

"Look out!" Hendricks shouted.

A man was leaning out of the back passenger side of the BWM now, his pistol aimed at Riker.

Riker dove, rolling to his right as the gun went off. Tiny rocks flew into the air as the bullet hit the spot where Riker had been a moment before.

Hendricks was already in motion, diving into the car through the open passenger door. The man leaning out the window disappeared with a grunt as Hendricks dragged him back into the car. Two gunshots went off inside the vehicle.

The driver side door flew open, and the driver stumbled out. His attention was definitely on Hendricks as he looked back in horror at the interior of the car. Riker got to his feet and sprinted toward the guy, but Hendricks was faster. He leaped out of the driver's side of the car and slammed into the driver, taking him to the pavement in a perfect textbook tackle.

Though Riker didn't do it consciously, his mind was already taking notes on the way Hendricks moved. The way he'd approached the vehicle. The way he tackled the man.

*He was a football player once*, the voice in Riker's head whispered. *A linebacker, maybe.* That tackle had the practiced viciousness of a player who likes his job a little too much.

Now that Hendricks had the driver on the ground, he

flipped him over, pinning his arms to the ground with his knees. Then he raised the pistol, smashing it into the guy's head.

And the way he approached that car at the perfect angle. He's ex-military for sure. Maybe Special Forces. Not SEALs though. Army Ranger, maybe.

Riker trotted over. He looked inside the car and immediately wished he hadn't. Blood, hair, and brain matter were splattered all over the interior. Riker didn't have a weak stomach when it came to the aftermath of violence, but this was enough to give even him pause.

"Please. Stop!" the man on the ground shouted.

"How 'bout fuck you instead!" Hendricks shouted. He brought the gun down again driving it into the man's skull. This time when he raised the weapon, blood dripped from the barrel. "You come at me? At my people? And now you're saying stop?"

Riker stood frozen as Hendricks lowered the barrel of the gun. The man had a bloody gash in the back of his head. Hendricks put the barrel of the gun against the wound and pressed hard, pushing the metal a half-inch into the man's skull.

The man screamed in pain.

Hendricks wiggled the barrel up and down, a smile on his face. He pressed it in a bit further. He glanced over and saw Riker staring at him. His smile faded. He angled the gun down a bit and pulled the trigger, sending a bullet out through the top of the man's head.

Hendricks stood up, his eyes on the gore sprayed across the pavement. "You believe this shit? Look at this mess."

Now that the fighting was over, Riker had time to really observe the man. He had a messy shock of blond hair that was a little too long on the top. Whether it was unkempt because of the fight or it always looked that way remained to be seen. He was tall, having a good three inches on Riker, which put him at six-foot-four. He was broader than Riker too. He was muscular, but he didn't have that gym rat look. Clearly, he put in plenty of time at the weight bench, but he didn't live there. These were muscles that got put to use in the real world, as he had just aptly demonstrated.

Hendricks gave Riker a nod. "You must be Riker."

Riker nodded and held out his hand. Hendricks shook it, squeezing a little too hard, as if he had something to prove. Riker had to work to keep the grimace off his face.

"Thanks for your help," Riker said. "We've been running from these guys for days. Somehow they keep finding us."

Hendricks grinned. There was malevolence behind that smile. He was still riding high off the adrenaline of what had just happened, Riker knew. He couldn't blame the guy; he'd been there plenty of times himself. But he'd never taken such pleasure in the act of killing.

"Don't worry about it." Hendricks looked to the car where Helen and Li were still sitting. "It's us who should be thanking you. You brought our girls home." He waved toward the car.

Helen got out, waving back. She smiled at Hendricks, but there was a little hesitation there. She knew Hendricks, but maybe she didn't like him so much.

Hendricks popped the trunk and rummaged around inside for a moment. He came out with a black device not much bigger than a cellphone.

"What's that?" Riker asked.

"Well, they're tracking you somehow. This thing scans for GPS and RF signals. You mind?"

Riker shook his head and held out his arms as if he had

just been pulled out of the line for airport security. Hendricks ran the scanner over him.

"You're clean."

He checked Helen next. To Riker's surprise, she came back clean as well.

Hendricks nodded toward the car where Li was still sitting. "Let's do the kid."

Riker walked to the car and opened Li's door. She was huddled inside, hugging herself with her arms. Riker wondered how much of the violence she'd seen.

"You want to come out now?" Riker asked in Mandarin.

A nod was her only response. Riker helped her out of the backseat and walked her over to Hendricks. He ran the scanner over her without a word of greeting. It let out a small beep when it passed over the back of her neck.

"We have a winner," Hendricks said.

Riker tilted his head in surprise. "Hang on. There's a tracker in her neck?"

"Yep. Looks like somebody chipped her."

"How?" Helen said. "How is that possible?"

"Hell if I know," Hendricks said with a shrug. "No reason we have to figure it out in this parking lot, though. Let's get going. It's time to go see Dobbs."

## 17

BEFORE THEY LEFT THE WAREHOUSE, Riker and Hendricks cleaned up the site. Hendricks grabbed the spent shell casings from the ground, and Riker did a full wipe down of the Chrysler.

After they'd finished, Hendricks took a small black case out of the Audi's trunk. The sun glinted off some medical instruments inside as he opened it. Riker didn't get a good look, but he spotted some basic medical supplies, including a scalpel, bandages and disinfectants.

"Helen, hold the kid down," Hendricks said flatly. "I need to get that thing out of her."

Helen put Li on her lap in the backseat. Hendricks bent over them.

After a moment, the big man let out a grunt of frustration. "Hold her still. I don't want to jab the scalpel through her neck."

Li screamed, and a moment later Hendricks pulled a small chip from the back of her neck. He tossed the medical bag to Helen. "Clean her up. We don't want her getting an infection."

Riker gritted his teeth. He had known many men like Hendricks, men who capitalized on their lack of empathy by turning it into a career of violence. He forced himself to turn back to the task at hand. Once he was satisfied there were no prints left in the car, he parked it on the street and left the doors unlocked and the keys in the ignition. Hendricks tossed the chip into a sewer grate and the three headed out.

It took them over an hour to make it to the house. As they drove northeast through Brooklyn, the homes were packed tightly together, but things changed as they approached their destination. The lots grew bigger and mature trees gave each of the houses privacy.

The home surprised Riker. He expected a tight row home or penthouse condos. This was a large house on a lot that was over a third of an acre. An old Colonial with brown stucco and brick exterior stood before them. Riker noticed small cameras all over the exterior as they entered. He guessed that every inch of the grounds was covered by surveillance.

The home's interior was equally impressive. Eight-inch mahogany planks made up the floors. Pillars framed the entrance to the great room. Stained wood molding accented the tray ceilings.

Riker went over to the window and looked at the back yard. The perfectly manicured and landscaped lawn surrounded a magnificent fountain and outdoor kitchen. Riker was more interested in the window itself. It was triple-pane bulletproof glass.

Li clung to Helen and spoke in Mandarin. "I want to go home. You said we could go home."

Helen patted her head. "We will soon. The bad men aren't going to get us here."

Li lifted her head and looked at Hendricks. "Let's go. I want to go now."

Riker spoke softly in Mandarin. "It's okay, Li. No one is going to hurt you now."

Li buried her face into Helen's shoulder. Helen spoke in English. "I think she saw some things she shouldn't have. I'll try to get her to take a nap." She carried Li upstairs.

Riker waited until Helen was out of earshot, then turned to Hendricks. "What do you think all of this is about?"

Hendricks looked Riker up and down. "I think it doesn't concern you anymore. The only thing I don't understand is where you came from."

"North Carolina. Where I would still be if Helen and Li hadn't disrupted my life."

"Lots of guys in North Carolina speak fluent Mandarin?"

"Rosetta Stone had a package deal. North Carolina got the internet last month, so I was able to take the online version."

"Okay, smart ass. Who do you work for?"

"I work for myself. I'm a beekeeper."

Hendricks laughed. "A beekeeper? You expect me to believe that a beekeeper took out half a dozen gangsters? Unless those guys all died from bee allergies, I call bullshit."

"First off, I didn't kill any of them. Some of them died, but I didn't kill them. I would like to know who they were. You said gangsters. Are they part of the New York mob?"

"Like I said before, it doesn't concern you anymore. The door is right over there. Go home and tend to your bees."

"That's exactly what I intend to do. First, I need to be sure Helen and Li are safe. Then I'll get out of your hair."

Hendricks took a step towards Riker. "Then allow me to assure you. They're safe. I've got it from here."

"I think I'll wait until I meet this Dobbs. After the last few days, I'm not ready to trust anyone."

"Suit yourself. Dobbs will probably want to meet you, anyway."

Hendricks sat down in the living room and turned on the TV. Riker's legs were still stiff after spending the better part of two days driving. He had no desire to sit. Instead, he wandered through the house. He half expected Hendricks to tell him to stay put or to shadow him, but the big man didn't do either. Hendricks really didn't consider him a threat, and Riker was fine with that.

He walked through the house, becoming more uncomfortable with every step. This place was everything his wasn't. The design was for show, not practicality. The dining room was the size of half of Riker's house. Expensive-looking plates and glasses sat in perfect symmetry on top of the table. From the dining room Riker, could see the kitchen which held a table of its own. It seemed idiotic to Riker having two tables so close together.

The kitchen island was ten feet by eight feet with a solid granite top. The image of dinner guests unable to reach items in the center of it made Riker smile.

He found an office with French glass doors. A large wooden desk sat in the center of the room and the walls were lined with built-in shelves. Riker looked over the shelves. There were photos of a man standing next to various prominent figures. Riker assumed that was Dobbs. He saw the mayor and governor of New York, professional athletes, and a few world leaders, including the current president. The photos lined the shelves like trophies. Riker noticed another man in four of the photos. Dobbs stood front and center shaking hands with the famous person or wrapping an arm around their shoulder for the camera. The other man looked like he was trying to stay out of the frame.

Riker bent close and studied the images. That man in the background seemed to hold the attention of those around him. More eyes were on him than the famous faces.

Riker continued to explore the home. He created an internal map of the floorplan. He noted every bottleneck and entry point. During his walk, he noticed that there was a camera in every room. He had no doubt that he was being monitored remotely. Having a security system in a home like this was normal, but this one went above and beyond. Dobbs was either paranoid or his work put him in danger.

Once Riker felt comfortable with the layout, he made himself a sandwich in the kitchen. He felt a little odd eating a stranger's food, but he was hungry after the long drive.

Helen walked into the kitchen. She eyed the food that Riker had in front of him.

"How's Li doing?"

"She's asleep. I didn't think she would go down. I think she saw some things she shouldn't have today."

"I think we all saw some things we shouldn't have today. How are you holding up?"

"Better than I thought I would be at this point. I feel like all of this is just a dream. None of it has really set in yet." Helen grabbed some food out of the fridge as she spoke.

"It will set in over time, trust me. You might want to find someone to talk to. If you try to bury it, you might end up in a bad place."

"Noted. I'll be sure to take care of myself. How about you? Are you going to talk to someone about this?"

"I'll be fine. Time out in the country is all the therapy that I need."

Helen looked a little relieved by the answer. "Good. I would hate to think I screwed up your life."

"Like I said, I'll be fine. I am worried about you and Li. How would a tracking chip get into her neck?"

"I have no idea. It doesn't seem possible, but I saw Hendricks take it out. I've been going over everything in my mind. Li has been with me ever since we adopted her. The only thing that I can think of is the time after Ted died. There were days that I left her at daycare so I could make arrangements."

"What about Dobbs? Have you ever left her with him?"

Helen shook her head. "No. Dobbs is a great friend, but he is the last person who would babysit."

"I really want to help you and Li. Is there anything else that you can tell me about what's happening?"

She touched his hand and gave him a little smile. "You have helped us. We're safe now."

Riker locked eyes with her. He waited for her to say more, but she stayed silent. "There must be more, Helen. What else do you know?"

"I have no idea what's happening. I just know we're safe now."

"I think it's a little too soon to say that you are safe." Riker lowered his eyes and finished the last bite of his food. Morrison's voice came through.

*This is your last chance to get out. Leave them to their troubles, or you will have some real issues to deal with.*

Riker considered how to leave this behind him. The people after Li and Helen probably wouldn't bother tracking him down. To them, he would just seem like some hired muscle. If they never saw him again, they probably would not come looking.

He suspected that Dobbs would have Hendricks investigate his past. Depending on how deep they went, that could be a problem.

Riker thought that leaving this behind could work if he did it now. There was only one problem, the little girl sleeping upstairs. The little hand that had dragged him onto the playground earlier that day was so small. She didn't have any part in this, and she couldn't protect herself. Riker decided he would stay until he was sure she was safe.

Helen finished her food and grabbed both plates. She put a hand on Riker's shoulder. "You're a good man Matthew."

He watched as she took the plates to the sink. "The jury is still out on that. If you know me long enough, you might change your mind."

Riker heard Hendricks turn off the TV. He moved into the entryway and saw a man coming up the front walk. He was dressed in a tailored suit and carried a briefcase. His black shoes had a high shine and a large gold watch gleamed on his wrist. Riker had no doubt that this man's outfit was worth more than everything he owned.

Hendricks stepped into the hall, his posture straight and his eyes fixed on the middle distance. Riker knew a soldier standing at attention when he saw it. The door opened, and the man from the pictures in the office stepped inside.

His eyes immediately fixed on Riker. "Sorry, it took me so long to get here. I'm Paul Dobbs. You must be Matthew Riker."

## 18

HELEN RAN OVER TO DOBBS. "You have no idea how glad I am to see you."

"Not as glad as I am to see you." He held out his arms and she leaned in, giving him a quick, tight hug.

"You won't believe what we've been through."

"I want to hear every bit of it," Dobbs said. "Li's all right?"

Helen nodded. "Sleeping upstairs."

"Good. Thank God you're both okay."

"More like thank Matthew Riker."

Dobbs turned to Riker. "Well, since I can't shake God's hand, I'll have to settle for shaking yours."

He held out his hand, and Riker shook it.

Dobbs gave him an appraising look, scanning him head to toe once, and then again. Whatever Dobbs had expected from Helen's description, Riker didn't fit it. For a moment, Riker felt self-conscious in his dirty work pants, T-shirt, and hooded sweatshirt. His boots were sturdy, but nothing fancy, and they were scuffed from years of work. He quickly pushed the feeling away. He'd never been one to seek the approval of men like Dobbs, and he wasn't about to start now.

"Thanks for all your help," Riker said. "I appreciate you letting us come here."

"Don't worry about it." Dobbs paused. "So these men who were chasing you...any insight into who they might be?"

Riker was about to answer, but Hendricks took a step forward, subtly putting himself between Dobbs and Riker.

"Three white guys in a Beamer. They were armed, but nothing I couldn't handle."

"Okay," Dobbs said. "Did you, um, take care of them?"

"I handled things," Hendricks said.

"Good. Well, I'm just glad you all made it here safely."

There was finality to Dobb's tone that Riker didn't like. As if the problem were solved and there was nothing left to discuss.

"They won't be safe for long if those guys are still looking for them," Riker said. "Until we understand what they were after and why, Helen and Li will never be safe."

"Mr. Riker, I assure you that my home is well protected," Dobbs said with a smile.

"Damn straight," Hendricks muttered.

Riker wasn't so sure about that. Admittedly, the security system was impressive, and the locks would take more than a bump key to open. But in his brief time in the house, Riker had already located three vulnerable entry points. Granted, he wouldn't want to run into Hendricks in a darkened hallway, but if the intruder was stealthy, Hendricks might never know of their existence. The sheer volume of security cameras would be a problem, but there were ways around that too. The first step would be finding out whether someone was monitoring the footage in real time, and if so, whether they were onsite. Take that person down first, and the security footage would be playing to an audience of none.

Riker didn't mean to think that way. It wasn't as if he consciously plotted a plan of attack for any home he entered, but habits like that were hard to shake. Especially now, when he wasn't sure of his host's motives.

Still, he didn't think he'd win any friends by pointing out the gaps in Dobbs' security. Hendricks already didn't seem to like him, and there was no need to exacerbate that situation. He decided to try another tack.

"Helen and Li are safe while they're here, but are they supposed to stay in your house for the rest of their lives?"

"What are you suggesting, Mr. Riker?" Dobbs asked.

"I'm suggesting we figure out who those guys were."

Dobbs looked at him for a long moment before speaking again. "Hendricks, why don't you give Mr. Riker the grand tour? I'd like to speak to Helen for a few minutes."

"You got it, boss," Hendricks replied.

"Helen, if you would?" Dobbs gestured back toward the kitchen.

"Of course," Helen said.

Hendricks watched in silence as Dobbs and Helen left the room. He waited until they were gone, and he turned to Riker. "I saw you snooping around earlier. You really want a tour?"

"Not really, no."

"Good." Hendricks walked back to the great room and turned on the TV. He flipped the channels until he found a hockey game, then he pulled out his phone and opened a crossword puzzle app.

Riker wandered the room, taking in the fine detail on the built-in bookcases. Most were filled with elaborate editions of classics of literature. A single glance at the spines was enough to tell Riker they'd never been opened. He wondered if Dobbs bought them in bulk.

"Not in a TV watching mood?" Hendricks asked.

"Not really." Riker saw a cabinet in the corner and made his way over to it. Inside, he found a stack of board games. Most were unopened, just like the books. He spotted *Scrabble* and grabbed it off the shelf. He walked over and set it on the coffee table in front of Hendricks. "Want to play?"

Hendricks set down his phone and shrugged. "If you want to lose."

Riker dragged a chair from across the room and set it on the other side of the table from Hendricks.

"Did you serve?" Hendricks asked as they drew their tiles.

"Yeah," Riker said. He didn't elaborate.

"What branch?"

"Navy."

"Ah, you're a fucking squid." A slow smile crossed Hendricks' face. "See any action?"

"I don't recall," Riker said dryly. He arranged the tiles on his tray. Some military men loved talking about the old days, trading war stories like kids trade baseball cards. Riker wasn't one of them. From the way Hendricks was frowning, it was clear that he was.

"Look, man, I'm just making conversation. I'm trying to be friendly."

"You want to talk about your service record, I'm happy to listen. I'm just not big on sharing. It's a personal flaw of mine."

"I can never tell if you're messing with me or being dead serious," Hendricks said.

"Maybe that's a personal flaw of yours."

Hendricks just shook his head.

As they played, it became clear that Hendricks' vocabulary was limited at best. He spent long minutes considering his options before laying down his tiles, his face screwed up as if it were a physical effort. Then he'd play a word like *goat* for all of seven points.

Riker had come into the game with the intention of losing, but Hendricks was making the task difficult. Hendricks considered himself better than Riker, and Riker had hoped losing at *Scrabble* would cement the other man's low opinion of him. Losing against a guy like Hendricks took effort, but so far all was going according to plan.

Hendricks laid down j-o-k completing the word *joke* and setting up Riker to take advantage of a double word score box. Riker looked at his tray and sighed. He could play *jukebox*, scoring a cool fifty-two points. Instead, he played *job*.

"Dumb move, Riker," Hendricks said. "If you'd played one more letter, you could have gotten a double word score."

"I'll keep that in mind next time."

"Don't beat yourself up. I'm surprised a squid like you can spell at all." He was silent for nearly a minute as he thought about his next play. He laid down the word *cape*. "I was Army, myself. Did three tours in the desert. Was in more than my share of firefights. Walked away from every one of them, though I can't say the same for the sand monkeys who got in our way."

"That so?" Riker said. His attention was on the board. Hendricks had once again set him up, this time for a triple word score.

"My buddies and I were boots on the sand, saving democracy one bullet at a time, while you were getting a tan on the deck of some ship."

Riker tried to brush off the comment. He knew it was nothing more than the usual inter-branch ball-busting. Hendricks was probably genuinely trying to bond with him. Still, it irked him, the way Hendricks was jumping to conclusions about how he'd spent his military years.

Though he knew it probably wasn't a good idea, he couldn't help himself. He laid down the tiles r-w-t-h, building off the c in *cape*.

Hendricks stared blankly at the word for a long moment. "What the hell is that?"

"Crwth," Riker said, pronouncing it *cruwth*. "It's a Celtic musical instrument. Kinda like a violin. Don't forget to figure in my triple word score." He gestured to the notepad where Hendricks was keeping score.

"No way that's a real word. I'm raising the bullshit flag on that one."

"You're free to challenge."

Hendricks stared at him, fury in his eyes. Riker could practically see the wheels turning in the man's head as he tried to decide what to do. There were actual beads of sweat on his forehead.

Riker pretended to stifle a yawn as he waited.

"You know what your problem is, Riker?"

"I have a strange feeling you're about to tell me."

Before Hendricks could answer, Dobbs and Helen came back into the room. Both of them were all smiles. Riker realized this was the first time he'd seen Helen truly relaxed. She'd been on the run the entire time he'd known her. She looked different now. It suited her.

"My apologies, Mr. Riker," Dobbs said. "That took a bit longer than I thought."

"Not a problem. Hendricks kept me entertained."

"Excellent." He clapped his hands together. "I was

wondering if we might have a word alone. There's something I'd like to discuss with you."

Riker glanced at Helen, making sure she was all right being left alone with Hendricks. She gave him a little nod.

"Yeah, okay."

"Great. If you'll follow me."

He turned without waiting for a response, and Riker dutifully followed. As he exited, he saw Hendricks pick up his phone, no doubt to Google the word *crwth*.

Dobbs led him to the office behind the French doors. He gestured to one of the chairs in front of the desk. Riker took a seat.

"Can I offer you a scotch?" Dobbs said.

"No, thank you."

"Mind if I have one?"

"Not at all."

Dobbs poured himself a drink from an expensive-looking bottle on the drink cart and took a seat in the chair next to Riker. "Helen gave me the rundown on the events of the past few days. It sounds like you've had quite the adventure."

Adventure wasn't the word Riker would have used, but he kept silent.

"What did she tell you about me?" Dobbs asked.

"She said you were a lawyer. A friend of her husband's. She said you handle high-profile criminal cases."

"That's true. But, as you might have guessed, I do a bit more than simply try cases."

"Okay," Riker said, his face betraying nothing.

"My clients often require protection. Sometimes we have to dig up information to help with the cases. Hendricks and his team are helpful in both regards."

Riker waited, saying nothing.

"What you said before about Helen and Li not being safe until we know who was after them, there's a lot of truth there. I'm going to divert some resources into uncovering the truth of the situation."

"Good. I'm happy to hear that."

"My question for you, Mr. Riker, is what you plan to do next."

"What do you mean?"

"Well, it's clear you're fond of our girls. And who could blame you? I'm rather fond of them myself." He leaned forward, looking Riker in the eyes. "You've proven yourself capable. Are you ready to go back to your beehives? Or do you want to see this thing through?"

Riker didn't answer.

Dobbs took a sip of his Scotch before speaking again. "Mr. Riker, I'd like to offer you a job."

## 19

RIKER SAT UP A LITTLE STRAIGHTER, caught off guard by the offer. He had expected Dobbs to give him some money for his time and tell him to get lost. Rich guys always go for the money first. Dobbs had gone in a different direction.

"What's the job?" Riker asked.

"I'm always looking for driven, talented people. After hearing the tales of your adventure, I believe you are such a person. Still, I would need to confirm that for myself so this would be a trial position. Think of it as a contract job. If it goes well, there is a lot of room for advancement in my employment."

"And if it doesn't go well?"

"If either of us is unsatisfied with the arrangement, then we end our relationship and go our separate ways."

Riker nodded but said nothing. Dobbs sipped his drink waiting for him to start asking questions. When he didn't, Dobbs broke the silence.

"We'll need to investigate the men who have been following Helen. As you have seen, jobs like this straddle the line of the law. Judging by what Hendricks said and the resources that these men seem to possess they are likely tied to the mob. I don't know if you are familiar with the way things operate here in New York, but crime and politics often work hand in hand to make the city run. We need to know more about who we are dealing with before we bring in any law enforcement. Ideally, I would like this situation to be handled without involving the authorities."

Riker could tell that Dobbs wanted him to play a role in this conversation. He decided to let Dobbs maintain the illusion of control. "Why wouldn't you want to involve law enforcement? Assuming there aren't any inside guys."

"Helen's husband was involved in some activities that were not entirely legal. If there is any kind of investigation, Helen may find herself in a very difficult situation. Handling this ourselves will be better for everyone."

"You really think Tom was doing something illegal? Could he have been working for the wrong people without knowing the extent of his actions?" Riker watched Dobbs' reaction closely.

"I highly doubt that. Whenever the money is too good to be true, there is no question about where it comes from."

"And how about you? Any reason you'd want to avoid the police looking into your affairs?"

Dobbs swirled the brown liquid around the glass. If Riker's question angered Dobbs, it didn't show. "As I said, New York is a complicated city. The machine that runs it has many pieces. I intend to keep my part of the machine running smoothly."

"What do you want me to do?"

"You'll work with Hendricks. He will be leading this investigation. I need to check with some sources and see if we can find a place to start. Once I do, you and Hendricks will follow the leads until we find the source of this problem."

Riker scratched at his chin. "I appreciate the offer, but I had no intention of getting involved in any of this. I may stick around for a few days and dig around a little. Then I'll head back to North Carolina. It's probably not worth the trouble of bringing me on."

"That simply will not work. If you are running around the city performing your own investigation, it may interfere with the work we are doing." Dobbs paused. "I suggest you try working for me for one week. I can offer six thousand dollars for your time. My office will set you up as a contractor and the funds will be wired directly into your account from one of our subsidiaries. If you are really interested in helping Helen, this is the best way."

Dobbs' response spoke volumes to Riker. A powerful guy like this might want another lackey, but he wouldn't care enough to press the issue. Dobbs wanted Riker to stay close.

Riker sat silently for a moment, pretending to consider the offer. "That sounds like a fair deal. I'll take the job for the week."

"Wonderful. I'll make the arrangements for your payment. If you are as capable as I am led to believe, you'll do very well here." Dobbs stood and shook Riker's hand. "Now if you'll excuse me. I need to check with some contacts. Hendricks will give you instructions as soon as we have a plan."

"Thanks. I'll find a hotel room close by. Just give me a call when you need me."

"There is no need for that. I'll have my housekeeper set up one of the guest rooms. My house is your house for the week. If you decide to stay longer, we can work on getting you more permanent accommodations."

Riker went back into the TV room and found Hendricks still watching the game. "Looks like we're going to be working together."

Hendricks paused the TV and looked up at Riker. "What did you say?"

"I said that we are going to be working together. Dobbs just offered me a job. I'm going to help track down the guys who are after Helen."

"Bullshit. I don't need some dumb hick messing up the investigation."

"Hey, I'm just letting you know what I just agreed to with Dobbs. If you have a problem with it, talk to him."

"I think I'll do that." Hendricks pushed himself to his feet. "Don't get comfortable. I'll let him know that my team is full."

Riker shrugged. "He's in his office. Let me know how the conversation goes."

"I will, you arrogant prick." Hendricks made a beeline for the office.

Riker found Helen, a glass of red wine in her hand. She sat at the table watching the eternal spring of the fountain in the backyard. He took a seat next to her.

The large oak trees and bushes around the yard formed a barrier from the outside world. The perfectly manicured backyard looked like an oasis. It was as if there were nothing beyond it. Looking at the small peaceful world made the city and all its troubles seem like they were worlds away.

"It feels so good to be here." She turned to Riker and put a hand on his arm. "Thank you for everything you did. I really thought that I was going to die."

"Helen, I still don't think you're safe. I know how easy it is to slide into the wrong situation. One small step at a time and you can end up a million miles from where you wanted to be. I want to help you and Li get some real peace."

She looked down for a moment, then back up at him. A soft smile played on her lips. "You have helped us. Now that we're here, Dobbs will be able to take care of us. I'm hoping that you stay too."

"I guess he told you he was offering me a position."

Helen nodded.

"I've accepted. On a trial basis."

Helen looked relieved. "That's great. I'm really glad that you took the job. I'll feel better with you around."

"How well do you know Dobbs? Do you think I can trust him?"

"I trust him completely. I know that he can work outside of the lines, but he is really good at getting things done. He is incredibly loyal to the people who help him. Once you prove yourself to him, he is a great friend to have."

"I'm not planning on sticking around too long. I'll see things through with you and Li, but then I'm heading back to North Carolina."

Helen took a sip of her wine. "Do me a favor."

"What?"

"Keep an open mind about Dobbs. He employs a lot of people like you, and he treats them very well. You may find a place here. I know I'd like it if you did."

"Okay. But I want you to do me a favor, too."

"What?" she asked, raising an eyebrow.

"Think about getting out of this place. Whatever Dobbs is involved in, I don't want it to suck you in. Once we get you out of this mess, you may want to consider finding a little safety. Maybe start over somewhere besides New York."

She laughed. "Not in this life. I'm a city girl."

"I suppose I knew you would say that."

Helen finished her wine and put the glass by the sink. "I've had all the adventure I can take for a day. Good night, Matthew."

"Good night, Helen."

Riker walked through the house again. He looked out the windows checking for any signs of danger. There was a car parked in front of the house with tinted windows. Riker couldn't tell how many men were inside the vehicle.

Hendricks walked up, a grin on his face as he saw what Riker was looking at through the window. "No need to get scared. Those are our guys. In fact, the entire perimeter is covered. No one is getting in here."

"Good to know." Riker looked at Hendricks. "Did you straighten Dobbs out and tell him to get rid of me?"

Hendricks tightened his jaw. "Looks like I'm stuck with you for the week. I start the day early, so be ready. You are working under me, and I expect you to do as you're told. We've got a lot going on tomorrow. Don't fuck up my day."

Riker stood toe to toe with Hendricks. "Yes, sir."

"That's goddamn right. Your room is upstairs. Third door on the left. I suggest you get some sleep." Hendricks turned and marched out of the room.

Riker went upstairs to find his room. He noticed a light coming from one of the doors in the hallway and the soft sound of a child singing. He knocked lightly on the door. "Li?"

"Jin Lai," a high-pitched voice called out. *Come in.*

Riker entered the room. Li was lying on the bed with a comic book laid out in front of her. She looked back and saw Riker. She jumped up on the bed and said, "Look at my magic."

Li took a penny off of the nightstand. She held it in her right hand and moved her other hand in front of it. She fumbled it from right to left. Then she held out her empty right hand and shook it. Her left hand moved up and she stuck the penny in the back of her hair. She waved both hands with the fingers spread open.

"Ta-da! I am magic." She had a huge grin on her face.

"That's amazing! How did you do it?" Riker smiled. She was so proud of the trick.

"I am magic!"

"You should be asleep, little wizard."

"No, I'm not tired. We should play." She bounced up and down on the bed.

"Playtime is over today. I'm sure you will get to do lots of fun things tomorrow."

"Read me the story." She picked up the comic book off the bed and held it towards Riker.

"Will you go to sleep if I read it to you?"

"Yes!" She clapped her hands together and smiled.

Riker pulled back the covers and tucked Li under them. He sat on the side of the bed and read through the Hulk comic. After ten pages, he looked over and saw she was out cold. He tucked the blanket tight, turned off the light, and headed to his room.

She seemed so safe lying there in peaceful slumber. Riker knew that she was in mortal danger. He also knew he would do whatever it took to get her out of it. There would be time to sleep, but first, he needed to research.

## 20

RIKER WOKE up the next morning to the sound of footsteps outside his door. For a moment, he was disoriented, unsure of where he was. The overly soft mattress he was lying on, the way the window was situated on his right instead of his left like back home, even the subtle smell of whatever laundry detergent they'd used to wash his sheets—it was all unfamiliar. He was still trying to remember where he was when a heavy hand pounded on the door. The door opened and Hendricks stuck his head inside.

"Up and at 'em, Riker. We've got an assignment. Grab a quick shower, and I do mean quick. Then meet me downstairs." He shut the door and trudged away, his shoes clomping loudly on the hardwood floor.

Riker lay there for another moment, remembering everything now. Dobbs. Helen. Li. Hendricks was right; he had a job to do.

He got up, threw his clothes on, and walked across the hall to the bathroom. While he'd slept, someone had been kind enough to lay out a towel, washcloth, deodorant, toothpaste, and an unopened toothbrush. He tore open the toothbrush and cleaned his teeth. After that, he felt almost human.

It took him a few moments to figure out how to operate the shower. When he got it turned on, water cascaded at him from multiple directions. It wasn't an unpleasant experience, but it was another reminder of how far he was from home. While he showered, he went over the information he'd found on his phone the previous night.

The first thing he'd done was visit the website for Dobbs and Associates, his new boss's law firm. The website surprised him. He'd expected such a high-priced outfit to have a very professional, ultra-corporate website. Instead, he'd found a single page with only the firm's logo and nothing more. There wasn't even a phone number or email address. It was as if they'd decided anyone who wanted to contact them would already have their number, so there was no need to list it. Riker figured the only reason they had the website at all was to keep someone else from buying the domain name and using it to poach clients.

After looking at the website, he'd moved on to a more general search for information on Paul Dobbs. Sometimes it was difficult to find much information on a person, but Dobbs presented the opposite problem. There'd simply been too many search results to sift through. Most of them had been news articles on cases he'd been involved in or society pieces about charity events he'd sponsored or attended. Riker had read through five pages worth of that drivel without finding anything useful before he'd finally given up and gone to sleep.

After washing, Riker allowed himself thirty seconds to stand under the flow of the shower, enjoying the feel of the hot water against his skin. He reluctantly turned it off and got out. He put his dirty clothes back on, realizing he was on his third day of wearing them. Then he went downstairs.

He found Hendricks in the kitchen, finishing up a plate of eggs and a cup of coffee.

"Where can I get some of that coffee?" Riker asked.

"No time," Hendricks said, clearly taking pleasure in it. "You took too long in the shower. We gotta hit the road."

Riker pushed down his annoyance. "Okay. Let me at least say good morning to Li and Helen before we head out."

Hendricks stood up and brushed the crumbs off his sports jacket. "I don't know how they did things in the Navy, squid, but in the Army when it was time to head out on a mission, we dropped our cocks and grabbed our socks. They didn't give us time to kiss our mommies goodbye."

"So that's a no, then?"

"Follow me," Hendricks said with a frown.

Hendricks grabbed a bag off the counter and led Riker out a backdoor and down the winding path to the garage. As they walked, Hendricks looked him up and down. "If you're going to work for me, we're going to have to get you some new threads. I don't want people thinking I've got a homeless guy following me around."

"Sorry, my tailor's on vacation this week."

"I'll take you to my guy this afternoon. He'll get you sorted."

They entered the garage and walked past a Porsche on the way to the Audi Hendricks had driven the previous day.

"Dobbs' car?" Riker asked.

"One of them."

They got in the Audi, and Hendricks reached into the bag.

"You're going to need a sidearm. I'm partial to the Beretta M9 myself, and that's what most of my guys carry. But

Dobbs said he thought you'd be more comfortable with this. He had it delivered special last night."

Hendricks pulled out a pistol and handed it to Riker. It was a SIG Sauer P226, the model of service pistol that had been used by the Navy SEALs during Riker's years of service. Apparently, while Riker was researching Dobbs, Dobbs had been researching him right back. He wondered what kind of person could have a specific model of handgun delivered in the middle of the night. He supposed the same type of person who owned a six-bedroom house in Queens, had a Porsche in the garage, and a guest bedroom with a shower that sprayed water at you from five directions.

Riker held the pistol for a moment. It felt comfortable. Too comfortable. "I don't need a gun."

"You do if you're working for me. Part of your job is watching my back. I need you armed if shit goes sideways."

Riker looked at the pistol for a long moment. "Okay."

"I take it you know how to use that thing?" Hendricks reached back in the bag and handed him two more items: a concealed carry holster and a spare magazine.

"Yeah. It's just like a camera, right? Point and shoot."

"Well, just keep it in your pants unless I tell you otherwise. Last thing I need is a bullet in the back from a squid with no trigger discipline."

They drove in silence for a few minutes, making their way from the upper-class neighborhood to the commercial district. The traffic was even worse than it had been the previous evening. Hendricks was a tense driver, glaring at the other cars on the road as if they'd said something about his mama.

"So what's the job this morning?" Riker asked after a while.

"Simple delivery."

"Okay. What are we delivering?"

"Just dropping off a payment to some guys who did some subcontracting for Dobbs."

"And these subcontractors, does Dobbs usually send two armed guys to deliver their payments?"

"Listen, man, there's something you gotta understand. Mr. Dobbs has his fingers in a lot of pies. He deals with serious people on serious matters. Sometimes things cross over into what you might call unsavory territory, but it's all for a greater purpose. That man's done more for this city than any ten guys walking the straight and narrow. The homeless shelter on 223rd? The kids' rec center in South Brooklyn? The drug treatment facility on Lavender? None of it would exist without Mr. Dobbs."

"I wasn't questioning his ethics. I was just asking what we were walking in to."

"My point is, there are some things you're better off not knowing. Keep your head down, don't ask questions, and do as you're told."

"Got it. Don't question orders. I'll bet you were really popular in the Army. Your C.O.'s probably loved you."

Hendricks shot him a look but said nothing.

They drove in silence until they reached an apartment building on the south side of Queens. It looked high end to Riker. Not as high-end as Dobbs' neighborhood, but the monthly rent on one of the apartments would probably cost more than a year of Riker's mortgage payments back home.

Hendricks pulled into the parking garage and found a spot. Then turned off the car and glared at Riker. "Two rules in there. Keep your mouth shut and follow my lead."

"Okay," Riker said.

"I'm serious, man. These guys can be a little skittish. You

start running your smart mouth, things won't go so well. We could both end up with guns in our faces."

"I'll keep a lid on it."

"You'd better."

They got out, and Riker clipped the concealed carry holster inside the back of his pants. He followed Hendricks out of the parking garage. The doorman seemed to recognize Hendricks, and he let them right in. They walked to the elevator and Hendricks pressed the button for the twelfth floor. He clutched the bag to his chest as they rode up. If there was cash in that bag, Hendricks wasn't exactly being subtle about it.

When the elevator doors opened and they stepped out, Riker had a sinking feeling in his stomach.

"I don't love the set-up of this place," he said. "These long, narrow hallways. The fire exit is down at the far end. If these guys are as skittish as you say, maybe we should rethink this. Meet up with them somewhere public. More open."

Hendricks glared at him. "This is the opposite of keeping your mouth shut and following my lead. It's exactly why I didn't want you on my team."

"I'm just saying—"

"This meeting has been set up for days. These guys want their money. If I call them now and change the meeting spot, how is that going to look? They'd be way more suspicious then."

"I'll follow your lead," Riker said. "I'm just sharing my opinion. It's up to you what you do with it."

"Bend over and I'll show you what I'll do with it."

"Do we at least know how many guys are in there?"

"Why? You getting cold feet, Riker?" Hendricks smacked

him on the arm. "Don't worry. I'll protect you. No more questions. Let's get this over with."

Riker took a deep breath and followed Hendricks to apartment 1214, trying to push down the mounting concern rising up inside him. He'd accepted Dobbs' offer, and now it was time to do the job.

## 21

HENDRICKS POUNDED the door with the back of his fist three times. He took a step back, and the light disappeared from the peephole for a moment. The door opened, revealing a man dressed in slacks and a white T-shirt. His forearms were covered in black and grey tattoos. The only notable accessory was the gun hanging from his shoulder holster.

"I'm surprised that you showed up, Hendricks," the man said in a thick Russian accent. He stepped aside and waved an arm for the men to enter the room.

"This is the meeting time and place so I'm here," Hendricks said as he walked by.

Riker passed the man and went down a short hall. The condo had a large living room that was open to the kitchen. Old exposed bricks lined the walls and bricks of drugs lay on the table. Two men sat at the table packing the bricks into a small duffle bag.

A slender, clean-shaven man sipped on coffee in the kitchen. He stood in front of a plate of fresh-cut fruit. The knife was still next to the plate. He watched the room like the master of the world.

Riker already hated the situation. They were outnumbered two to one. One person was behind them, and another was out of reach with potential cover. The drugs made him nervous as well. It was rare to find a crew that dealt in the substance without one addict on the team. Guys like that were always an x-factor.

Hendricks stopped next to the table. "Good to see you, Igor. How's business?"

"It's better now if you have my payment in that bag," the man in the kitchen said. He casually leaned against the kitchen counter as he took another sip of coffee. He nodded toward Riker. "Who's this?"

"He's new to the crew. We'll see if he lasts."

Riker walked across the room to the kitchen. The two men at the table put their hands on their pistols. They didn't draw them, but they were ready to move. Riker extended one hand as he approached. Igor glared at him a moment, deciding how to react. Finally, he took Riker's hand and shook it.

"Nice to meet you, Igor. I'm Riker."

Igor looked at Riker's dirty clothes. "Where did you get this guy from, Hendricks? He seems like he should be shining my shoes, not doing a drop."

"Don't worry about him. He just doesn't know how to stand still and shut up yet. I'll teach him how things are done here."

"Who will teach you how things are done?" Igor said with a Cheshire cat grin.

"What's that supposed to mean?" Hendricks stood taller and puffed his chest as he spoke.

"I mean that our payment was due last week. We do not take deadlines lightly. How are you going to make up for that transgression?"

Riker moved to Igor's side, keeping his back to the wall while the men talked. He felt much more comfortable with all four men in his sightline. He hoped that things would go smoothly, but at least he would have a fighting chance if they didn't.

"How about you stay thankful that we are using your services?" Hendricks said. "Take your money when you get it and be happy."

Hendricks put the bag on the table in front of him, freeing up both hands. Then he turned to face Igor. Riker could tell that move was to get the guy behind him in his peripheral. It looked like Hendricks knew how to handle himself in these types of situations.

One of the men at the table spoke in Russian. Thankfully, it was one of the six languages that Riker spoke fluently.

"We should kick the shit out of both of these guys, boss. That will teach them not to be late."

The guy sitting next to him answered in Russian. "I agree. They talk to us like we are weak. We should teach them how strong we are."

Igor scowled. "Just sit there and keep your mouths shut. I will handle them. First, we will get our money. Afterward, we may teach them a lesson. Check the bag."

"What the hell did you just say?" Hendricks said in a loud voice that wasn't quite a yell. "I don't want to hear another word in Russian while I am here. English only. Do you understand?"

"I'll speak whatever language I want," the guy who'd started the conversation said. "It's not my fault you stupid Americans only understand English."

"Answer the question. What were you talking about?"

The man stood up and got inside Hendricks' personal

space. He was a few inches shorter than Hendricks, but he was big. His shoulders were broad enough to warrant a custom sports jacket. His arms stretched out the fabric in the biceps. Riker could tell he was a gym rat. Hendricks kept his ground when the man got in his face.

"I said it looks like you got a new boyfriend. We were all guessing who bends over and takes it and who gives it out. We all agree that you're the one getting it up the ass."

Hendricks' hand shot out in a blur. His fingers were wrapped around the back of the muscle-head's neck before he could react. With the other, he pushed his stomach back and then brought his face down hard on the table. It hit with enough force that the bag of drugs jumped up a few inches. The gym rat's face bounced off the table and he fell on his ass. Blood poured out of his nose and he lay there on the verge of passing out.

The other man at the table jumped up, reaching for his gun. Before he pulled it out Hendricks had his weapon drawn and trained at his face. The man behind Hendricks pulled his gun and pointed it at the back of Hendricks' head.

"Whoa! Everyone needs to calm down," Riker yelled in Russian.

Hendricks and the two men glanced toward the kitchen but kept their weapons aimed at each other.

Riker stepped behind Igor, wrapping an arm around his neck. Igor pried at the arm with his hands, but Riker had most of the airflow cut off. Igor's face was red and his eyes bulged. With his other hand, Riker grabbed the knife off the fruit tray and pressed the tip of the blade just under Igor's jaw, brushing against the skin of his neck.

Riker continued in Russian. "We are all professionals

here. There is a job to be done and no reason for good relationships to be ruined. Don't you agree, Igor?"

Riker let a small amount of pressure off of his neck. Igor croaked out, "Yes."

Riker switched back to English. "Why don't we all lower our weapons and act like civilized adults." No one moved.

"A little help here, Igor?" Riker let off a little more pressure.

"Yes," Igor croaked. "We are professionals. If Hendricks lowers his weapon, we will lower ours."

Hendricks didn't move.

"Hendricks, let's keep the boss happy and end this the easy way." Riker was ready for Hendricks to pull the trigger, but he slowly lowered his gun and put it back in its holster.

Igor spoke in Russian. "Lower your guns."

The two men in the living room lowered their weapons. Riker let go of Igor. He kept the knife at the ready.

"Sorry about the chokehold. I just wanted to keep everyone from losing their cool."

Igor rubbed his neck with one hand. He nodded to the man by the table. "Check the bag."

The man reached across the table for the bag. He watched Hendricks like a cobra ready to strike. Hendricks didn't move, and the man retrieved the object. He unzipped the bag and looked inside. He moved items around and stared at the contents.

"Is it all there?" Igor asked.

"Yeah, it's all here."

"Of course it's all there," Hendricks said. "We never welch on a deal."

"Great, then everyone is satisfied." Riker looked at Igor when he spoke. He knew he needed Igor to give the okay before they could leave without incident.

The other two Russians looked at Igor. They clearly were not satisfied. Their friend was starting to stand up. The front of his shirt was covered with blood, and he wobbled when he stood. His nose was almost sideways on his face.

"Hendricks, this can't stand. You laid a hand on my crew." Igor stood like a statue when he spoke. Riker could tell that he didn't want this to get out of control, but he couldn't look weak in front of his crew. He could see in Igor's eyes that he would risk death before he would lose face.

"Yes, Hendricks overreacted," Riker said. "He was insulted by your man. Both acted unprofessionally. Certainly, there is a solution that doesn't involve destroying a good business relationship."

Igor looked from Riker to his crew. "Damon, you were out of line. We don't speak to our business partners like that."

"Boss, he broke my fucking nose." Damon touched the mangled mess on the front of his face and winced.

"Yes, and that was out of line as well. What do you suggest Mr. Riker?"

Riker looked at Hendricks a moment. "One hit deserves another. One free shot from your man on Hendricks. Will that suffice?"

Igor smiled. "I think that will be enough."

Hendricks put his hand back on the butt of his gun. "Hell no. No one gets a free shot on me."

"You don't think you can take one punch?" Riker said. "I assume our boss wants this to end in a way that doesn't cause any headaches for him."

Hendricks thought for a moment. He slowly moved his hand away from the pistol and turned to face Damon.

"Fine. Give me your best shot, tough guy."

Damon spit a little blood onto the floor and cocked his right arm back. He threw a right cross that connected with Hendricks' cheek. Hendricks' head snapped to the side when the punch hit, but the rest of his body remained firmly planted. He whipped his head back towards Damon and looked him dead in the eyes.

"Do you feel better now, snowflake, or should we take this to the next level?" Hendricks asked.

Riker couldn't help but be impressed. That punch would have put most men on their backs. Hendricks didn't waiver.

"I think that is enough for one morning," Igor said. "Go back to Dobbs and tell him that we expect payment on time in the future. If not, things will not be so smooth."

"Make sure to keep your dogs on their leashes or things will not go smooth." Hendricks continued to stare at Damon.

"We will relay the message, Igor." Riker walked towards the door keeping an eye on the Russians.

"I'll see you around, Mr. Riker."

Riker and Hendricks walked in silence back to the car. When they got into the Audi, Hendricks broke the silence.

"You weren't completely worthless in there. You do need to get rid of the Mr. Rogers politeness. If you're not the alpha with these guys, you don't have their respect. If you don't have their respect, things get out of control."

"Sometimes playing nice keeps everyone from getting killed. I thought keeping everyone alive was part of this job."

"Like I said, you did good in there, but listen to me about the respect thing. Fear goes a long way with the guys we deal with."

Hendricks' phone beeped. He checked the message and started the car.

"Looks like Dobbs has a lead on the Helen thing. Let's see if you can prove it was more than luck in there."

The Audi sped away from the building towards Dobbs and the next mission of the day.

## 22

"I GUESS you've earned that cup of coffee now," Hendricks said when they got back to the house.

"What about Dobbs? It sounded somewhat urgent."

"One thing about Mr. Dobbs. You don't really want to interrupt him when he's working. He'll come find us when he's ready."

When they reached the kitchen, they found a wiry, balding man standing there, drinking coffee out of an over-sized thermos. The little hair that remained on his head was cropped close, and his arms were heavily tattooed. He gave Hendricks a friendly nod and looked warily at Riker.

"Who's the new guy?"

"I'm Riker." He held out his hand and they shook.

"This is Brennan," Hendricks said. "One of my top guys. You want to know what it takes to be successful in this organization, pay attention to him."

"You must be the guy who brought Helen and Li home."

"I didn't realize the news was out, but yeah, that's me," Riker said.

Hendricks grinned. "You kidding? These guys gossip

worse than old ladies. One of my guys in Queens sees you sneeze, a guy in Brooklyn will text, *Bless you*."

Riker rummaged around in the cupboards until he found a mug, and he poured himself some coffee.

"We're not that bad," Brennan said. "We just like to keep each other informed."

Riker took a sip of coffee, watching Brennan. "You Catholic?"

"What good Italian boy from the Bronx isn't?" he answered. "But how'd you know?"

"I spotted Our Lady of the Holy Ink," he said, nodding toward a tattoo of the Virgin Mary on Brennan's right forearm.

"Can you believe that shit?" Hendricks asked. "I have nothing but respect for the Holy Mother, but I'd like to be able to take a piss or jerk off without her staring at me, you know?"

"Luckily, I'm left-handed," Brennan replied.

Riker let out a laugh. Maybe it was the coffee, but he felt better than he had since that day at the fair. In a strange way, it felt good to be part of a team again. He'd missed the camaraderie. It was something that had been part of his life from his wrestling days all the way up until he'd left his old life behind and gone to North Carolina. He hadn't realized how much he missed it until he'd experienced a little taste of it again.

And yet, he couldn't let it distract him. He was here for a purpose, and it certainly wasn't to yuck it up with a couple wise guys in a rich lawyer's kitchen. He needed to stay focused.

"I think I'll go check in with Helen and Li. I'd like to say good morning to them before Dobbs is ready for us."

"You just missed them," a voice from behind Riker said.

He turned and saw Dobbs standing there, dressed in another suit, just as expensive-looking as the one he'd worn the previous evening.

"Helen thought Li deserved to have a little fun," he continued. "She took her to the Children's Museum for the day. I'm sure you'll see them tonight."

Riker nodded, suppressing the urge to question Dobbs further on the matter. His job today was to be a good soldier. "So, what's next?"

Hendricks shot him a look, the jolly attitude suddenly gone. Now that the boss was here, it was back to business, and he once again saw Riker as a rival. Dobbs didn't seem bothered by the question. He answered in a friendly tone.

"I've been thinking about Helen and Li's attackers. Only a limited number of people knew about Helen's vacation, and I trust most of them. There's one person in my employ I have a reason not to trust. It just so happens that he's the one who helped Helen book the vacation home in North Carolina."

Riker said nothing, though he was thinking this sounded like a long shot at best.

"Carter?" Hendricks asked.

Dobbs nodded.

"Son of a bitch," Hendricks said. "So we head over there? Shake him down?"

"Yes. I have reason to believe Carter recently came into a large amount of money. Money that didn't come from me. I think it's entirely possible he sold information on Helen and Li. If so, he can tell us who he sold it to."

Hendricks nodded along, clearly getting pumped for this job. Brennan's face was harder to read.

Dobbs looked at Riker. "This is going to be your true test. Things with Carter might get...let's just say messy. If you can handle this, I'll know you have the resolve to work in my organization."

Riker said nothing, but he wondered how helping beat up some untrustworthy employee was going to prove anything he hadn't already proven while getting Helen and Li back safely.

The drive to Carter's apartment took almost an hour. They once again took the Audi, Hendricks driving and Dobbs in the passenger seat. Riker and Brennan were shoved in the back. Riker had to admit the car had an impressive amount of legroom, but he had yet to encounter a backseat that wasn't at least a little uncomfortable. Brennan was a good three inches shorter than Riker, but he was sitting behind Hendricks who had his seat pushed all the way back and even leaned back a little, so he was just as cramped as Riker.

As they drove, Riker watched the city roll by. He'd been to New York City only once before, on a very different type of job. He hadn't stayed long, and his exit had been rather hasty. Now, despite the seriousness of the task at hand, he was grateful to have a little time to take it all in, even if it was from a cramped backseat.

He glanced over and saw Brennan wasn't looking out the window. His gaze was fixed on the two men in the front seat, taking in every word of the seemingly inane conversation.

"How long have you worked for Mr. Dobbs?" Riker asked him.

"About two years." His eyes were still on the men in the front seat.

"You like it?"

Brennan shrugged. "Yeah, I guess. The pay's good, and Mr. Dobbs treats us well."

"So you'd recommend I sign on long term?"

Brennan turned and looked at Riker. "That's a decision you'll have to make for yourself. The work...it takes its toll. Whether it's right for you isn't my call."

A few minutes later, they pulled up to an apartment building. This one seemed a little less upscale than the place they'd met with the Russians that morning. Still probably too expensive for Riker's tastes, but it didn't have that air that said if you don't have seven figures in your bank account, look elsewhere. Hendricks found parking on the street, and they piled out of the car and started toward the apartment.

"Anything I should know about this Carter guy?" Riker asked.

"He's a squirrelly bastard," Hendricks said. "He's liable to have a few guns stashed away, and he'll probably go for them once he realizes why we're here."

"He won't get to them, though," Brennan growled.

"Amen to that," Hendricks said.

They rode the elevator to the sixth floor, and Dobbs led the way to an apartment at the end of the hall. When they reached the door, Dobbs looked at Brennan and Riker.

"You two stand out of sight for now. No reason to let him know it's a party."

The two of them took a few steps to the left, so they'd be out of the sight of anyone looking through the peephole when Dobbs knocked.

They waited a few moments in silence. There was no answer, and Riker didn't hear any movement from inside the apartment. That didn't mean this Carter guy wasn't home, but these walls were thin. He heard a baby crying in an apartment halfway down the hall.

Dobbs knocked again, and they waited some more. Still no response and no sounds from inside.

"Either he's not home or he wants us to think he's not," Dobbs said.

"One way to find out." Hendricks took a step back. "Want me to break down the door?"

Dobbs nodded, then stepped out of the way.

"Hang on a second," Riker said.

Hendricks shot him a look. "Mr. Dobbs said we're going inside. Shut your mouth and give me some room."

"I'm not suggesting we don't go in. I'm just suggesting we don't call attention to ourselves by making a racket they'll hear in the penthouse." He reached into his pocket and pulled out his keyring. "Let me have a crack at it."

Hendricks rolled his eyes. "Oh, you're going to pick the lock? That shit ain't as easy as they make it look in the movies, Riker. Mr. Dobbs doesn't have all day to wait around while you try to prove you're some kind of badass."

Riker ignored the comment. He already had his bump key in the deadlock. He took out his pistol and used the butt of the gun to give the key a tap. It didn't catch on the first try, but on the second tap, the key turned freely.

"Holy shit," Brennan said, clearly impressed.

"You were saying, Hendricks?" Dobbs said with a smile.

Hendricks said nothing, but Riker could feel the man's eyes boring into the back of his neck as he moved to the lock on the doorknob. This one was easier, and it turned after the first tap.

Riker put his keys in his pocket. He started to put his gun away too, but Dobbs stopped him. "Better keep that out."

Riker nodded. Hendricks and Brennan drew their weapons too. Hendricks held his out in front of him, but Brennan carried his raised in a two-hand grip, pointed at the sky.

"Out of the way," Hendricks said. "Let me go first."

Riker figured he'd challenged Hendricks' authority enough for one morning, and he did as he was told.

Hendricks opened the door and peered into the dim apartment. "If you're in there, you better make yourself known right fucking now!"

There was no answer.

Hendricks went in first, and Riker and Brennan followed. The apartment was sparsely furnished and yet somehow still managed to be messy. The dirty dishes in the sink were at least a few days old, and wrinkled clothes were strewn all over the bedroom floor. The bathroom looked as if it hadn't seen the business end of a sponge in months.

When they'd checked the whole apartment, Hendricks called to Dobbs, and he came inside.

"That slippery son of a bitch must have seen us coming." Hendricks pointed to the coffee maker. It was still on with half a pot in it.

Brennan walked over to the small counter in the kitchen. He picked up a mug and held the sides. "It's still warm."

"Damn it," Dobbs said. "There might be something here we can use to find him. Look around."

Brennan started going through the kitchen while Hendricks went to work searching the bedroom. Riker stood in the center of the living room and turned a slow circle, taking it in.

"What are you doing?" Dobbs asked.

Riker didn't answer for a moment. He let his eyes wander. "I find that it's helpful to give yourself a moment to see the big picture. You can miss things if you dive right in."

He turned another half-circle before he noticed something. A tall bookshelf stood against one wall. It was only about half full, and most of the books were lying on their sides, as if they'd been tossed there haphazardly. Or they'd fallen.

Riker walked to the bookshelf and pulled it away from the wall. "Bingo."

He bent down, kneeling in front of a section of drywall a foot high that had been cut. There was a small hole near the left side. Riker stuck his finger in the hole and pulled. The section of drywall came away, revealing a hiding space behind the wall. He reached in and pulled out a duffle bag.

"Score one for the new guy," Brennan said.

Riker set the duffle bag on the kitchen table and unzipped it. Inside were five bricks of heroin and ten thousand dollars in cash.

## 23

THE FOUR LEFT the apartment and headed to the car. Hendricks threw the bag with the cash and drugs into a compartment in the trunk.

"Carter has been a busy boy," Dobbs said. "As I suspected, he's been playing both sides."

"I knew he was a slimy piece of shit, but I didn't think he was suicidal. He is going to get a lesson in what it means to be a traitor." Hendricks gripped the wheel of the car so hard his knuckles turned white.

"I want you to find him and bring him to me in one piece. I need to know exactly who he is working for and what information he gave them. After that, you can teach him any lesson you like."

Brennan shook his head sadly. "I shoulda known something was up. The guy's been acting weird the last few weeks."

"It won't take me long to find him," Hendricks said. "I know where his ex and his kid live. I bet if I ask them just right, Carter will come to us."

Dobbs grimaced. "I don't need to know the details. Just bring him in, and do it quickly."

"I'm not quite following all of this," Riker said. "I take it that he wasn't running heroin for you?"

"No," Dobbs said. "That substance has nothing to do with our business. He is working for someone else on the side."

"Maybe you should worry more about your business," Hendricks snapped, "which is doing what you're told and not asking questions."

Dobbs eyed Riker in the rearview mirror. "It's okay; he is just trying to get his bearings. You can't trust anyone that you don't know. I think it's time to get to know our mystery man a little better. Then we can form some trust." He turned to Hendricks. "Take us to Basta. If we're going to get to know each other we might as well do it over lunch."

Ten minutes later, they reached an unassuming brick building with a small sign that read *Basta*. Dobbs led them inside.

The moment Riker stepped through the door, he felt as if he had been teleported to a different world. The aromas hit him first. The blend of fresh herbs and homemade sauces made his mouth water. The street outside had been dingy and plain, but the interior of the restaurant was a beautiful blend of simple lines and small bursts of color. Soft lights and candles provided the only illumination; as far as Riker could see, there were no windows. This place was its own universe.

Dobbs walked to the hostess stand and was greeted with a smile.

"Mr. Dobbs, it's good to see you today. How many in your party?"

The four of them were ushered immediately into the

dining room. Dobbs walked tall making sure everyone noticed the special attention he received. A few people greeted him as he walked to the table.

Food seemed to float to the tables as waiters, busboys, and hostesses moved about the restaurant quickly and efficiently. The food resembled Italian fare, but he couldn't identify any dish for certain. There was no traditional lasagna or spaghetti and meatballs here. He had never cared much for overpriced food, but this place intrigued him.

Riker guessed there was no way he would have been let inside the building dressed as he was if he hadn't been with Dobbs. Once the four of them sat down a bottle of red wine was poured into a decanter on the table.

Brennan wore a big smile that had been there since the moment Dobbs had suggested the restaurant. He leaned toward Riker. "You are in for a treat. The food here is awesome."

"Just one of the many benefits of working for me," Dobbs said. He settled in for a moment before speaking again. "Tell me a little about where you came from, Matthew."

"The first thing I can tell you is that no one calls me Matthew. I've always gone by Riker. Second, I came from North Carolina, although I'm sure that's not what you meant."

"Well, Riker," Dobbs said, pausing to emphasize the name, "you are correct in assuming that I'm not asking about your current address. You clearly have been trained in more than farm management."

"I guess you know a little about that already. Hendricks gave me your gift. It was the same sidearm that I used in the SEALs. If you know about that, you probably found some information on my high school athletic career as well."

"Yes." A pleased smile crossed the man's face. "You were a gifted wrestler. It is a shame you weren't able to continue on to a college team."

Riker stared at Dobbs for a long moment. "So you know why I joined the military."

"I do. Those records weren't as easy to find, but I pride myself on having a good team for research."

"Wait, what happened that made you join the military?" Hendricks asked.

Dobbs ignored him. "What my team didn't find was any information on your life after the military. You left the SEALs, and five years later, you purchased a small plot of land in North Carolina. Care to fill in the gap?"

Riker took a sip of water before answering. "I worked as a contractor. Then I became a beekeeper. I've been doing that ever since."

Dobbs leaned forward, his eyes fixed on Riker. "I can tell that you don't like to talk about your past, which I appreciate, but I need to know a little more if I'm going to keep you around."

"I'll say this. The contract work that I did required discretion. I can tell this job requires the same. I don't kiss and tell, even after the job is done."

Dobbs stared at him for a long moment, his face unreadable. "Fair enough. We'll revisit this later, but for now, let's enjoy a meal together."

Food soon arrived at the table, and Riker quickly understood why Brennan was so excited about lunch. Every bite of food was a perfect blend of flavor and texture. The four men took in the masterful cuisine in silence.

"I do have a few questions of my own," Riker said between bites of food.

"What questions are those?" Dobbs asked.

Riker considered which question to ask first. He wanted to find out as much as he could, but he knew the wrong question would end the conversation. Small questions often led to big answers. So many secrets had been given to him just because people felt compelled to finish a thought or story.

"Will all the work be here in New York or is a lot of travel required?"

"Mostly here, but life is unpredictable. You never know when you will be sent to a rural area to rescue a woman and child."

"Fair enough." Riker lowered his voice to keep other patrons from hearing the next sentence. "One thing I need to be clear on is the drug situation. I don't need to know everything about your work, but I'm not going to be part of any drug operation."

Dobbs nodded thoughtfully. "I can't speak for everyone we associate with, but I make it a point to stay away from that type of business as well. At the same time, the world is not black and white. The important thing is that we make it a better place with the tools we have available."

"I'm not concerned about the world right now. I just want to help two people. Helen and Li. What do you know about her situation?"

"I'll know a lot more once we find Carter." Dobbs' phone rang and he looked at the screen. "Excuse me, I have to take this." He got up and walked to the back of the restaurant.

"So you were a SEAL," Hendricks said. "I'm surprised they didn't teach you to follow chain of command. Here's what you need to know. You answer to me, and you get a check once a week. Anything outside of that doesn't concern you."

"Jesus, give him a break," Brennan said as he stuffed

another bite into his mouth. "He's just trying to get his bearings. This is literally his first day on the job."

"First day, my ass. I saw how he handled himself this morning. This might be his first day with us, but he's not green."

"You're right," Riker said. "I'm not green, and I like to know what I'm getting myself into before I commit. So let me ask you two questions. First of all, how do you guys like being part of this crew?"

Hendricks locked eyes with him. "It's just this side of heaven. The pay is good. Dobbs is a professional and rewards loyalty. Besides, it's the only place guys like you and me can be who we are. I can see straight through your holier-than-thou attitude. You can tell yourself that you want to help people, but once you've seen action there is nothing like being in the shit. This is the only job for guys like us."

Riker held his stare and didn't say a word.

Brennan broke the silence. "Okay, Captain Intensity. He's right about the pay and Dobbs. It's the best gig in town. Personally, I like to avoid life and death shit. If you want to use your head instead of your fists, there is always a way around the violence." He paused for a second. "At least, almost always. The point is, it's a good job and I really think we can make the world a better place in our own little way."

"Like I said I'm not really interested in changing the world. A week ago I wasn't even interested in being part of it any more than I had to, but thanks for answering the question." Riker took a sip of water. "My other question is who do we work for?"

Hendricks and Brennan looked eyes for a moment. Then Hendricks turned back to Riker. "You work for me, and I work for Dobbs."

"Dobbs is a lawyer. The very nature of his job means that he works for other people. I need to know who I'm really working for."

"You are a smart one," Brennan said. "I worked for Dobbs for months before I even thought to ask that question."

"Shut your mouth, Brennan." Hendricks turned back to Riker. "I'm going to make sure Dobbs shows you the door. We don't need anyone on the crew that can't accept an order and make it happen. You ask too many damn questions."

"I agree with Hendricks in a way," Brennan said. "You don't seem like the kind of guy that normally works with us. If you think it isn't for you, then you should probably go back to farming or whatever it is you do."

Riker gave Brennan a nod. "Thanks for the advice. I'm really just here to finish what I started with Helen. Then I'll be heading out."

Dobbs walked back up to the table. He sat down and took a big sip of his wine. "Finish up. We are going to see Weaver."

Hendricks' head snapped in Dobbs direction. "Are we taking him?" He pointed a thumb at Riker.

"Yes. Mr. Weaver is interested in meeting the man without a past."

The side of Hendricks' mouth curled up in a slight smile. "All right, Riker. You wanted answers to your stupid questions? You're about to get them."

## 24

By the time they pulled up to the warehouse, Riker felt he was getting to know the backseat of the Audi pretty well. A little too well for his tastes, actually. But he was also getting to know his companions.

On the way to the previous two jobs, Hendricks had been full of bravado, much in the same way Riker and his fellow wrestlers had been on the way to a tournament in high school. Now he acted more subdued. Not nervous, exactly, but serious, as if he knew he wasn't going to be the cock of the walk in whatever situation they were about to walk into. Brennan was just as quiet as he'd been on the way to the other job, but Riker sensed more tension in him. He was sitting up straighter as they pulled into the warehouse parking lot. Even Dobbs seemed different. For the first time since Riker had met him, he didn't exude the confidence of a man who owned everything around him.

To Riker, this all meant one thing—they were going to see the boss.

There were at least a dozen other cars in the warehouse's parking lot. Riker wondered how many of them belonged to people doing actual warehouse work and how many belonged to those who served the mysterious Mr. Weaver in other ways.

The warehouse was a large building, at least fifty thousand square feet. It butted right up against the bay at the south end of New Jersey. They had gone past the port and Riker saw nothing but more warehouses with nothing in particular to distinguish them. Just a seemingly endless row of ugly buildings whose job was to store things until they were ready to be moved elsewhere. In the distance, he heard the beeping of a truck backing up and the sound of the water lapping against a boat.

As they walked to the warehouse, Hendricks sidled up next to Riker.

"You need to be on your best behavior now, understand me?"

Riker shot him a look of mock surprise. "Me? When have I ever not been on my best behavior?"

"I'm serious. Weaver doesn't appreciate smart comments."

"Then he must love you."

Dobbs chuckled at that, and Hendricks' face turned a deep shade of red.

"What Hendricks is saying in his less than elegant way," Dobbs said, "is that Mr. Weaver has many wonderful qualities, but a robust sense of humor isn't one of them. You'd do well to limit the number of jokes you tell to zero."

Riker nodded. "Remember, I was a SEAL. I'm all too familiar with guys without a sense of humor. I'll keep my mouth shut."

They reached the door, and Dobbs pressed the button next to it. There was no buzz or bell, but the button lit up green. As they waited. Riker saw the camera mounted over the door, and couldn't resist looking directly into it, as if he'd be able to see whoever was waiting beyond it, watching them. After a moment, there was a loud click. Dobbs grabbed the handle and pulled the door open. They walked in single file, Riker bringing up the rear.

Beyond the door was a long, narrow hallway. Just inside, there was a small room off to the right. A hard-looking man sat behind a bank of video monitors. Riker gave him a nod which the man did not return. That was okay. Riker was aware that friendliness was not the most important quality in a security guard.

As they reached the end of the hallway and stepped into the open area of the warehouse floor, Dobbs stopped and turned back to Riker. "Mr. Weaver's my oldest client. I've worked with him for decades. I actually got my start interning for him during law school. He's provided me with steady work ever since. My house, the cars, and everything that comes with it...none of it would have been possible without Mr. Weaver."

"He sounds like quite a guy," Riker said. He didn't mention the obvious question—what kind of businessman provides a criminal defense lawyer with steady work over the course of decades?

Riker scanned the room as they walked through it. There were at least a dozen men in the warehouse, all doing work that appeared at least somewhat normal for a warehouse environment. A forklift buzzed toward a stack of pallets on the west end of the room. Yet, for the size of the warehouse, they didn't seem to be storing a lot of wares here.

He spotted four exits other than the one they'd entered through. One was a small door at the other end of the warehouse. There were cargo bay doors to his left, and a single large bay door as well as a smaller door on his right, in the direction of the river. They walked past a large bank of three electrical panels on the wall as they approached an office on the east end of the warehouse. Through the glass wall, Riker spotted a tall, thin man working behind a desk, hunched over a laptop. He immediately recognized him as the man in the background of many of the pictures in Dobbs' office.

A beefy guard stood at the office door. He gave Dobbs a familiar nod as he approached and rapped on the office door before they even reached it. He opened the door and stuck his head through. "Dobbs is here, sir."

"Ah, good," a rich, baritone voice answered. "Send him in."

The guard stepped aside, and Dobbs, Hendricks, Brennan, and Riker all filed into the well-appointed office.

The man closed his laptop and stood up. He held out his hand to Riker. "You must be Matthew. I'm Jeff Weaver."

Riker shook his hand, not bothering to tell him he preferred to go by Riker. He didn't seem to be the type of man who would respond well to being corrected. "Pleased to meet you, Mr. Weaver."

Weaver let go of his hand and turned to Dobbs. "Tell me about the situation with Carter."

"Not much to tell, I'm afraid," Dobbs said. "He left his apartment in a hurry. Didn't even take his stash with him. He must have known we were on to him."

"The only question is how he knew." Weaver let out a weary sigh. "You trust people, give them every chance in the world, and this is how they repay you. It's a shame what the world has come to these days."

"Indeed it is," Dobbs agreed.

Watching Weaver, Riker understood what Dobbs had said about him. There was absolutely no humor in his eyes.

When he smiled, it was only with his mouth. The rest of his face remained emotionless. Riker had met some serious people in his time, guys who could order the deaths of hundreds of people with nothing more than a word. They all had that same look in their eyes. The knowledge that you controlled the existence of so many people changed a person. Whatever Weaver was involved in, he'd been at it for a long time, and it had left his eyes cold.

"Carter's stash. You have it with you?"

"In the car," Dobbs said.

Weaver just looked at him for a long moment.

Dobbs turned to Riker and Brennan. "Get the bag out of the car."

Riker nodded, then turned to Hendricks.

"What?" Hendricks asked.

"I need the keys."

"Oh, right." Hendricks fished them out of his pocket and tossed them to Riker. Riker and Brennan headed back out into the warehouse.

As they walked, Riker turned to Brennan. "I take it you've met Weaver before?"

"Yeah. A few times."

"Is he always so bubbly and warm?"

Brennan cracked a smile at that. "Actually, this is him in a good mood."

They walked in silence. Riker waited until they were outside before he spoke again. "So why do you think they really wanted to get rid of us?"

"Who knows," Brennan said with a shrug. "Some things are above our paygrade. Personally, I'm glad I don't have to hear everything that goes on. I'd rather just do my job."

Riker opened the trunk with the key fob and grabbed the bag. When they got back inside, he once again gave the security guard a friendly nod, and he received the same cool lack of response for his effort.

"This place is a real laugh riot," Riker said. "They should make a sitcom."

Brennan chuckled at that.

When they got back to the office, Riker saw there were two more guys in there now. Weaver spotted Riker and Brennan through the glass wall and waved them inside.

"Set it on my desk," he said.

Riker did as he was told. Weaver unzipped it and dug around inside for a moment. Then he looked up at Dobbs.

"Okay, enough fooling around. Let's have the conversation."

Dobbs nodded toward Hendricks.

Riker was suddenly aware of his mistake. In having him set the bag on the desk, Weaver had forced him to the middle of the room. Hendricks was behind him, and the two new arrivals stood on either side, flanking him.

He felt Hendricks' beefy hand on his shoulder. "Have a seat, Riker."

The men on either side of him had pistols in their hands now. With a sinking feeling, he realized he'd lost the fight before it had even started. He couldn't see any way out of this without taking a bullet or two. He needed to stay calm and see where this was going. He gave in to the pressure from Hendricks' hand and sank into the chair in front of Weaver's desk.

"What is this?" he asked.

"Take it easy," Weaver said. "We just want to talk."

Riker nodded toward the men on either side of him. "They need their guns out to talk?"

"A precaution. I've heard you're a bit excitable."

"Yeah? Who told you that?"

A figure moved past the glass wall, answering Riker's question. The door behind him opened, and someone new entered the room.

Weaver smiled at the new arrival, and this time there was actual joy in his eyes.

Helen walked past Riker and moved to Weaver's side. She looked so different that Riker barely recognized her. Her hair was styled, her makeup was perfect, and she wore a beautiful red dress. It was a far cry from the disheveled woman Riker had seen running through the fair or the one who'd slept on his shoulder in the back of the semi-trailer.

"There you are." Weaver stood up and put an arm around her, leaning in for a quick kiss. "It's been far too long since I've seen my girl."

## 25

RIKER PRESSED his palms against the arms of the chair. He could feel the smooth wood, worn down by a hundred hands that had been in the same position. The cushion under him was a thin compressed layer that no longer added any comfort. Focusing on a simple object was a trick Riker used when his mind was racing too fast. The technique worked, and he made a mental map of his situation.

A man stood on either side of him, each of whom had a gun pointed at the back of his head. Hendricks, Brennan and Dobbs were behind him, waiting for instructions. A large glass window to his left revealed the warehouse floor and at least a dozen men working. Weaver had the kind of power that allowed him to hold a man at gunpoint with his employees watching. Helen stood next to Weaver across the desk from Riker.

Her red dress hugged the curves of her hips, and the neckline dipped low, showing off ample cleavage. The fading bruise on her face was covered by makeup now, and her skin looked flawless. Ruby red lipstick matched her dress. Men would kill to be with a woman like this, but somehow it sickened Riker.

"Hey Helen, nice dress," Riker said. "Somehow I think you looked better in your trucker T."

"I don't believe that for a second." She inched one leg forward, sliding it through the slit that went ten inches past her knee. "Matthew, you need to be smart right now. No one appreciates what you did for me more than Jeff here. You could find a home here with us." She kept her arm around Weaver and her body tight to him when she spoke.

"Where's Li?" Riker knew that he wasn't going to get an answer to that one. He just hoped for a hint of shame in Helen's eyes.

"She'll be fine for as long as we have her. After that, she'll be gone."

The indifference in her voice made Riker want to wrap his hands around her neck and choke the life from her body. He gripped the arms of the chair hard and forced himself to stay calm. "So that's it? She was nothing but a job to you? Is there anything real about you?"

"Plenty. For example, my name is Helen Wilborn, and I do think you would make a great addition to the crew."

"That's a shame, Helen. I really thought that there was some good in you. The gun pointed at the back of my head tells me I was wrong about that."

Helen sighed. "I really do hope things work out okay for you. Just be honest with Jeff, and it will."

"Helen has spoken highly of you," Weaver said. "I'm grateful for everything you did for her, which is why you made it this far. If you are going to make it any further I need to know who you work for."

"I know you don't believe it, but the story that I told Helen is true. I wish I could say the same about what she told me." He locked eyes with her. "I knew something was off almost from the beginning."

"What are you talking about?" she asked.

"A lot of little things didn't add up. It started with the story about your husband. You said it yourself; if a story has too many details, it's probably not true. Those shoes the waitress at the diner commented on, the Jimmy Choos. I Googled them. They cost three grand. No one who just came into money leaves three thousand dollar shoes behind in a truck stop without even commenting on it. However you got your money, you've had it for a while."

"So then why help us?"

"Because you were in trouble. I knew that much was real. And it wasn't until I got to New York that I confirmed the truth."

"What truth?" Helen asked.

"Li isn't your daughter. Adopted or otherwise. I thought it was odd that you never showed me a picture of her, or talked about all her small achievements. You never told me any of the stories that every new parent can't stop talking about. But the chip in her neck confirmed it. The rest of the pieces fell into place pretty easily after that. Dobbs confirmed your story about Ted was a complete fiction. When I called your 'husband' Tom instead of Ted, he didn't even flinch."

"If you figured it out when Hendricks took out the chip, why didn't you leave?"

"Unlike you, I actually care about what happens to Li. I needed to stay and find out a little more information to make sure she would be okay."

"Good job on that, numbnuts," Hendricks said. "Now you're just an idiot with a gun to his head."

"I have to admit I didn't think the man behind the

curtain would be this cautious. I hoped to have a little more time to figure out what was going on here. I guess this conversation is just going to happen a little sooner than I expected."

Helen looked from Weaver to Riker. "I really do appreciate what you did for me. You saved my life and got me back home. This may not be the world you're used to, but tell Jeff what he needs to know and you'll be fine." She couldn't hold eye contact with the last lie.

Weaver stared hard at Riker for a long moment, as if trying to decipher a difficult equation. Finally, he appeared to come to a decision. "Brennan, take Helen back to my place and wait for me there. This conversation might take a while, and I don't want to bore her with business."

"You got it, boss."

Weaver drew Helen in for another kiss. He reached around and grabbed her ass when their lips touched. "Leave that dress on until I get home. I want to be the one to take it off of you."

Helen glanced at Riker one more time as she walked out of the office. "I hope I'll see you around."

As soon as the door closed, the joy left Weaver's eyes. "Who do you work for, Matthew?"

"It's Riker."

"What?"

"Call me Riker. I really hate it when people call me Matthew."

Weaver nodded at Hendricks. The big man stepped around in front of Riker, drew back his fist and smashed a hard right into Riker's stomach. The air rushed out of Riker's lungs, and he doubled over in pain.

"I'll call you whatever I want. I can tell that you have been in difficult situations before, so I'm not going to sugar-coat this. You're not going to make it out of this one. You can either give me the information that I want and die quickly, or you can spend the next few days being tortured and die in agony. I know neither of those options sounds great, but trust me, the first is much better than the second."

Riker drew a painful breath and forced himself to sit upright, meeting Weaver's gaze. "Thanks for the honesty. What happened to the option of joining your crew?"

"I would love a guy with your skills on my crew, but you asked Helen about Li. That tells me everything I need to know. Some guys get a chip on their shoulder and never let it go. I can tell you are one of those guys."

"Guilty as charged," Riker said. "What are you going to do with her?"

"It really doesn't concern you." Weaver sat down at his desk. He took out a bottle of Scotch and poured himself a drink. "Enough stalling. Answer the question. Who do you work for?"

"I went over this with Dobbs and Helen already. I work for myself. I'm a beekeeper in North Carolina."

Weaver gave Hendricks another nod. This time Hendricks slammed a right hook into the side of Riker's head. Riker moved with the punch, but Hendricks knew what he was doing. Stars filled his vision.

Weaver continued. "Someone within our organization has been feeding information to the police. I find it impossible to believe that you just happened to be in the right place to find Helen and Li when they were in trouble. Plus there is no real record of you. Just an address. No social media, no employment history after the military. Basically no proof you exist in the modern world. That leads me to believe that you don't. Helen told me that you went out of your way to avoid killing the men who were trying to kill you. Nobody hesitates to kill a guy that is coming after him with a gun. Matthew Riker is just a persona created for your undercover work. How's that for detective work? So who do you work for? Are you federal or local?"

Riker moved his head, trying to clear his vision and the ringing in his ears. "Sorry you have a cop in your crew, but that's nothing to do with me. It was dumb luck I happened to meet Helen when I did. I don't give a shit about the drugs or whatever else you're into here. The only thing I care about is Li's safety. Give her to me and I'll be on my way."

"Holy hell, you've got some balls," Hendricks said. He turned to Weaver. "Let's just put a bullet in him and get this over with."

"I appreciate your enthusiasm, but I need answers," Weaver said. "If he really is just some country boy who wants to play hero, no one will notice him missing. If he's a Fed and we are about to get raided, I need to know it. So we are going to be damn sure about what he is before we'd 'put a bullet in him'."

Riker looked up at Hendricks. "I knew you were an idiot when I met you, but I never thought you were a pedophile. It sickens me that any serviceman could be that kind of evil."

Hendricks glared at him. "What the hell are you talking about? I'm no pedophile."

"So you just kidnap little girls for fun? I'm on my way out. You can come clean with me, you sick fuck."

"I don't have anything to do with the girls. That's Helen's business. And I'd never even think of touching a kid."

Weaver shot Hendricks a look. "Shut up. We're here to get answers, not give them." He turned to Riker. "How did you find Helen at that fair?"

"You're not getting it. I was already there dropping off

honey." Riker continued quickly before Weaver could signal another punch. "I don't understand why she was there alone. If Li was chipped, that means someone wanted to verify her authenticity. She wasn't some random girl. Why send Helen alone without protection?"

"We're not stupid," Hendricks said. "She had protection. Four guys. They just got themselves killed before the exchange."

Weaver's eyes grew narrow and his face flushed a red hue. "What did I just say about not giving information?"

Hendricks' eyes went to the floor. "Sorry, Boss."

"So that's how it happened. Helen and her guys were attacked that morning by whoever was trying to get Li. She escaped and tried to save herself by heading for a public location. But these guys didn't care about making a scene. Once they had her, they went back to the exchange location. That's what they were doing at the lake house." Riker watched the look on Hendricks' face. The man would never win a poker hand. It was clear Riker had hit the nail on the head. "How do you like that for detective work?"

Weaver's face was cold. "I'm not that impressed. You think you're clever, but you stayed with Dobbs and walked right into a setup."

"You've got me there, literally. I thought taking the job would help me figure out what was going on here and who was in charge. Looks like you just wanted to make sure I stuck around."

"I couldn't have someone with your knowledge of Helen and Li just run off. I needed to know who you were."

"So what makes Li so special? Why was a rival willing to sacrifice so much to get to her?"

Weaver took a long sip from his drink. "I'm sorry to say that you are going to die without ever knowing the answer to that question. I'm starting to believe that you are telling the truth about who you are. Just some guy who was in the wrong place at the wrong time. There are only two problems. First, I need to be one hundred percent sure. Second, I really don't like you. I can tell you think you're better than I am. But you're not. You're just another guy sitting in the chair across from me. Just another little man whose life was decided by a conversation. So Matthew, is there anything else you have to say before I ask hard?"

Riker leaned forward. One of the men next to him thumbed the hammer back on his revolver and pressed it to the back of his head. "I do think I'm better than you. I think that you're a worthless piece of shit who trades in children's lives. You'll never know who I work for or what I've done. I'm going to give you one last chance. Give me Li, and I'll forget all about you. If you don't, I'm going to kill you and destroy your entire operation. I know neither of those options sounds great for you, but trust me the first is much better than the second."

Everyone in the room was silent for a moment. Despite its impossibility, the force of Riker's threat was so strong that for one brief moment the glass in Weaver's hand shook.

He set the glass on the desk and once again met Riker's gaze. "You're right, Hendricks. He does have some balls. We can change that. Why don't you go grab the blowtorch?"

## 26

RIKER HAD BEEN in some rough spots in his life, but he was pretty sure this was the first time a six-foot-four former Army Ranger had come at him with a blowtorch. He glanced around the room, taking in his situation. Besides Hendricks and his blowtorch, there were the two other armed guys. One of them had put his gun in his shoulder holster and was currently tying Riker's left hand to the arm of the chair. The other held a pistol to Riker's head.

Weaver was still behind his desk, arms crossed as he watched, his expression eerily blank. Dobbs looked a bit pale. Apparently, he wasn't used to this type of wet work. He talked a big game, but maybe the thought of watching a guy get his testicles burned off with a blowtorch wasn't sitting well with him. Riker wasn't the only one to take notice.

"You can go, Dobbs," Weaver said.

"No, I'm okay," he said quickly.

"I insist. Go have a drink. You've done well."

Relief washed over Dobbs' face. "Yeah, okay. Call me if you need anything."

Riker waited until he was gone, then turned to Weaver.

"So Dobbs is more of a paperwork guy? He struck me as pretty hands-on."

Weaver said nothing. Apparently he was serious about the no more answering questions thing.

Riker wasn't quite ready to make his move yet, and his only way to buy more time was to get somebody talking. If it wasn't going to be the highest-ranking guy in the room, he'd have to settle for the dumbest. He turned to Hendricks. "I notice you didn't bother taking away my gun. It's still stuck in the back of my pants."

Hendricks grinned, revealing two uneven rows of teeth. "Wouldn't do you any good, even if you could get to it. You think I'd give a guy I just met a loaded weapon? The gun's empty."

"Yeah, I know. I knew the moment you handed it to me."

The smile faded from Hendricks' face. "Bullshit."

Riker shrugged. "Maybe if you hadn't given me a SIG Sauer P226. But I know the weight of that weapon. Loaded and not. I held it in my hands too many times on too many missions."

"Yeah, well, you're going to die with it in your pants."

"Remains to be seen," Riker said. "It might fall out when I'm wriggling around in pain, right? Don't make assumptions."

"How about I shove it up your ass? Should stay nice and snug up there."

It wasn't the wittiest retort Riker had ever heard, but he let it go without a response. Because the guy had finished tying his left wrist down and was moving on to the right one. In shifting around, he'd put himself directly between Riker and Hendricks.

Riker waited for the perfect moment. It was difficult. Every fiber of his being wanted to attack, to fight for life.

Weaver had been wrong in a lot of his assumptions about Riker, but he had gotten one thing right. Riker had worked hard not to kill anybody up to that point. It would bring too much unwanted attention his way. But things had changed. They'd taken Li to an unknown location, and he didn't know what they were planning to do with her. The only chance that poor little girl had was sitting in a warehouse by the Upper Bay, surrounded by enemies, with one hand tied to a chair.

The time for holding back was almost over.

The guy bent down and placed the rope over Riker's right wrist. At that moment, Riker stopped holding back.

His right hand shot upward, grabbing the guy's middle finger. He rotated his wrist hard, and the man's finger bent nearly to the back of his hand before it made an audible snap. Just as Riker had expected, the man let out a grunt of pain and yanked the hand away. As he did, he instinctively bent over in pain, bringing his chest—and the shoulder holster—much closer to Riker's free hand.

At the same time, Riker flung back his head. When you were pressing an object against something and you lost contact, your first instinct was to re-assert contact. Riker's hope was that the man with the gun to his head would instinctively try to once again press the barrel against his skull rather than just shooting him. It wouldn't buy him much time, but he only needed a couple seconds.

As soon as his head snapped back, he snaked out his right hand and grabbed the gun in the first man's holster. He pulled it free and glanced to his left. He could just see the reflection of the man standing behind him in the big window. He half-turned in his chair and fired, hitting the man in the middle of the forehead.

The man with the broken finger cried out in anger, but

Riker was already turning again. He leveled the pistol and shot the man twice in the head.

Riker swiveled as the man fell, intending to take out Hendricks with the next shot, but the big man was already in motion. He dove to his right, tackling Weaver to the floor, safely behind his desk.

*Damn it.* Riker hadn't expected Hendricks to react so quickly. Now Hendricks had the advantage of cover, while Riker still had one hand tied to a chair. This was not a winning position. He needed to change things up, and fast.

He looked at the large glass window, then to the wall just to the right of the window. He knew what was on the other side of the drywall. He dropped to a crouch in front of the chair and fired one round into the large window. The glass splintered out from the bullet hole, but it didn't shatter cleanly as Riker had hoped. There was no time to worry about that now. He adjusted his aim to the right of the window and fired a barrage of rounds into the drywall.

The warehouse went dark. Riker's bullets had found the electrical panel on the other side of the wall.

Before the others could react to the sudden blackout, he got to his feet, holding the chair in front of him, his left wrist still tied to its arm. He charged at the window.

The chair legs slammed into it hard, and the glass shattered on impact. Riker kept moving, diving through the opening where the glass had been only moments before. Most of the glass was gone, cleared away by the chair, but Riker felt one stubborn shard slice into his right leg. He hit the ground on the other side of the window and kept moving. It was impossible to tell how bad the cut was in the near darkness. He'd have to deal with it later.

He scurried his way across the floor, pushing the chair in front of him, ignoring the panicked shouts of the warehouse workers. They might be used to their boss pulling people into his office and torturing them, but they sure as hell weren't used to the victim turning the tables, shooting a couple of their coworkers, and plunging the warehouse into darkness. It was clear from their voices that many of them were close to panic.

Riker stopped when he figured he was about halfway across the warehouse. He put the gun on the seat of the chair, and he set about freeing his left hand. It was no easy task in the darkness. His fingers were slick with blood; whether it was from some wound on his own body or from one of the men he'd shot he did not know. Wet fingers made it nearly impossible to get a grip on the slick nylon cordage. After struggling for what felt like minutes, he finally managed to loosen one strand of the knot. He pulled a little more, and his wrist was almost free.

A blue light illuminated the darkness ten feet in front of him. The blowtorch.

Riker let go of the rope and snatched the gun off the chair. He brought it up in one smooth motion and fired. Two things happened at once: a loud grunt told him his bullet had hit something, and the way his gun's slide stayed back told him his weapon was empty.

He had expected to make contact, but the fact that his pistol was empty surprised him. A Beretta M9 holds fifteen rounds. He'd shot the first guy once and the second guy twice. Plus, one through the window. Had he really fired eleven shots into the wall? Or had the guy he'd stolen the gun from not been carrying a full magazine? He didn't know and it didn't matter now.

He dropped the gun and his fingers went back to the rope. It took him a moment to find the strand he'd been pulling. Up ahead, the light from the blowtorch started moving toward him again, first slowly, then quickly as it picked up steam.

He gave the rope one last tug, giving himself enough slack to pull his wrist free.

As he stood up, a gun went off, and Riker felt something bite into his shoulder. He staggered backward but managed to keep his feet. Hendricks careened into him.

The big man had the blowtorch in one hand and a pistol in the other. As he fell, Riker reached up, grabbing the gun hand and twisting it. The pistol fell free, clattering to the cement floor and skidding out of reach. Hendricks barely seemed to notice. He was more focused on the blowtorch.

Riker's back hit the cement, sending a jolt of pain through his body. Hendricks was on top of him in a moment, crouching over him, bringing the blowtorch down toward his face.

"I got him, guys!" Hendricks called to the others. Blood seeped from a wound on his arm. It looked like Riker's shot had grazed him. "Over here!"

The blowtorch was almost to Riker's face now, but he saw his opening. His arm shot out, grabbing Hendricks' right leg. He twisted, driving his hip into Hendricks' right side, the one farthest from the blowtorch. Riker rotated his body, pressing his back into Hendricks and downward in an instant. Hendricks landed on his back with an *ooff*. It was a classic switch reversal. Coach Kane would have been proud.

Hendricks cried out in anger, shoving the blowtorch upward, but Riker was ready. He hooked Hendricks' left arm and shoved the blowtorch toward the big man's body. In an instant, his sleeve was on fire.

The flames raced up Hendricks' arm, and he began to flail. The fire spread, catching Hendricks' hair and Riker's shirt.

Riker leaped to his feet, tearing the shirt off and throwing it to the ground as he stood. Out of his peripherals, he could see men approaching from nearly every angle. The fire was drawing them, and it wouldn't be long before he was surrounded.

He took one last look at Hendricks on the floor, wishing he had just a few more moments to end the man, before he took off running for the far side of the warehouse. Though it was still dark, he knew what waited for him there: pallets stacked high, all the way to the window thirty feet up the wall.

When he reached the pallets, he scurried up, not daring to look back. His shoulder and his leg were both screaming out to him in pain, and he knew he was losing blood. He pushed all that away. The only thing that mattered was escape.

The shouts below him were reaching a fever pitch as he hauled himself to the top of the pallets. He didn't pause or give himself time to second guess his next move. He pushed the window open and dove through.

There was a moment of weightlessness as he fell through the air before he splashed down into the chilly waters of the bay.

## 27

THE ICY WATER of the bay gave Riker a moment's relief from the painful burn on his left arm. He stayed under water and swam with the current of the river. His shoulder sang out in agony with every stroke, but it functioned just fine. He knew that the shot in his shoulder hadn't hit bone or tendon.

Most people might panic in dark, icy water, but to Riker it felt like home. His BUD/S training for the SEALs stayed with him. Hell Week was mostly cold water, pain and lack of sleep. He had endured that, and he knew that he could endure a cold swim with a wounded arm.

The pain and cold focused his mind. His body did what it needed to and his mind ran through the events at the warehouse. Especially the look in Helens' eyes when she told him there was no point in trying to save her. She wasn't trapped in a system; she was part of it. Everything she had said to him over the last few days had been a lie.

Weaver was the key. Even if he could find Li, she would never be safe while Weaver was still breathing. It felt good to know his enemy.

He swam through the dark water until his lungs burned

before he broke the surface. After one quick breath, he dove back under and repeated the process. He kept his eyes closed and went with the flow of the water. Seeing through the filthy water was an impossible task. He thought about that water on his open wounds and quickly pushed it out of his mind. Right now he needed to focus on escape. He would deal with his injuries later.

After twenty minutes, he swam over to the concrete on the edge of the river and found the nearest ladder. He peeked over the concrete piling, scanning the shore, listening for any sign of people looking for him. Once he was confident there was no one close by he climbed out and started walking towards the center of the city.

The sun had set, but the streetlights illuminated his way. The wind blew, making him feel colder than he had in the river as the water evaporated off his skin. He took deep breaths and focused to keep from shaking. He inspected his body as he walked. The gunshot wound was bleeding, but it didn't look bad. It had hit the outer meat, just clipping him. He thought he felt blood trickling down the front of his calf, but his pants were soaked and in the darkness, it was hard to see how much blood was on his wet jeans. Pain washed over him with every step.

Riker pushed the pain away, prioritizing his tasks. He decided getting clothes was first. A bloody, shirtless man would draw attention, even in New York City. He walked close to the buildings, staying in the shadows until he found a small park. It was poorly lit and contained only a few people. Three homeless people lay on the ground covered by papers and old clothes. One man stood in the shadow of a tree. Riker watched until he saw another person walk up to the man. There was a short conversation followed by an exchange. That was all Riker needed to see.

The dealer was a hard-looking man in his early thirties. He wore a bulky hoodie that would conceal any weapon under it. Riker approached him head-on, stumbling as if he were drunk or high.

"Hey man, do you have any H?" Riker asked as he approached.

The man looked at Riker, his expression steady. A shirtless wet man with a gunshot wound was not the strangest thing the dealer had seen. "Beat it. I don't work on credit."

Riker continued to approach. "I've got money, what can I get for fifty bucks?"

"I know you don't have shit. Now buzz off."

Riker reached into his pocket as if he were going to pull out some cash. The dealer looked at his hand, watching for the money. Riker's other hand shot out a jab that slammed into the man's Adam's apple. He grabbed his throat and the man dropped to his knees. Riker moved around him in one smooth motion. Riker choked the man out in moments.

Riker relieved the dealer of his hoodie, three hundred dollars, and his Glock 19. He tucked the small sidearm into the back of his belt. The hoodie was large enough to cover any signs of the weapon.

He felt weaker as he left the park. The rate of blood loss had slowed, but his wounds needed attention. The bullet that missed his vital organs could still kill him if the wound became infected.

Riker noted his supplies. The water had destroyed his phone, so he tossed it into a trash can. At some point in the fight or the swim, he lost his Sig. Between the money left from his trip and that from the drug dealer, he had eleven hundred dollars. His final tool was the Glock 19 with one full magazine.

Riker walked along the street until he saw a cab. He hailed it and asked to go to the nearest Walgreens.

Riker went through the aisles quickly gathering supplies. Each time his hoodie brushed against his burnt arm a fresh wave of pain surged through his body. He grabbed bandages, gauze wrap, ointment for the burn, a sewing kit, and a large bottle of Extra-Strength Tylenol. He tossed a power drink and snacks into the cart.

The clerk stared cautiously at Riker while he rang up the items. In the bright fluorescent lights of the Walgreens, it was easy to see how bad he looked. His jeans were still soaked and the front of his right leg was dark crimson.

When Riker pulled a wad of cash from his pocket blood dripped down his hand. A large drop of the red liquid splashed on the counter when he handed over his payment.

"Oh my god. Are you ok?" the young clerk asked.

Riker smiled and gave a little laugh. "I'm fine, but you wouldn't believe the night I'm having. It has been a doozy!" He wiped up the blood on the counter with the sleeve. "Sorry about that mess."

The clerk gave an uneasy smile and handed him the change. "Well take care of yourself."

Riker slammed the Gatorade and a Snickers bar while he waited for another cab. The driver was an older black man and his cab was loaded with trinkets along the dash. "I need a cheap motel in a crappy part of town. Get as far from this part of the city as you can."

"You want a place that rents by the hour or by the night?" the cabbie asked without a pause.

"By the night. I'll be paying in cash."

"I got you."

The city flashed by Riker on the twenty-minute drive. The cabbie knew exactly what Riker was looking for. They began to pass prostitutes walking in front of liquor stores and pawn shops. Drugs were sold on the corners and people stumbled out of dimly lit bars. This was the kind of area where people were not noticed. Everyone kept their eyes down to avoid being seen and avoid seeing others.

The cab stopped in front of a hotel with trash littering its small parking lot. The green light of the neon Vacancy sign pulsed. Each green flash made it look like the place was covered in puke.

"Is this crappy enough for you?" the cabbie asked.

"It's perfect." Riker handed him twenty bucks for the fare. He pulled out another hundred. "If anyone asks, you didn't take anyone to a motel tonight."

The cabbie reached out and grabbed the bill. "What motel? I took two millennials to some yuppie store that sold expensive toast."

"Thanks, man. Have a good night."

At the front desk, Riker paid for four days upfront in cash. He signed in with a fake name and told the guy at the desk that he didn't need any maid service.

The room was exactly what he'd expected—an old bed, a TV and a bathroom. Riker wasted no time. He wanted a shower, and he wanted it immediately. When he tried to remove the jeans, he found they were stuck to the drying wound in his leg. He pulled hard and they gave way. A fresh stream of blood flowed from the wound. The cut on his shin was five inches long.

He got in the shower and rinsed the blood and grime from his body. As the water washed away the blood, he saw that the cut wasn't deep. His left arm didn't look great, but there were only a few blisters on it. Mostly red skin and first-degree burns. He cleaned the wounds with an antibacterial soap. The soap hurt, but he knew the next step would feel worse.

After stepping out of the shower, he pulled the sewing set from his bag and started working on his leg. He concentrated on the task as the small needle poked in and out of his flesh. He kept the stitches tight so that they would be harder to break. Occasionally, he poured hydrogen peroxide over the area to wash the blood away. Once he was finished with the stitches, he wrapped the wound with gauze.

Next, he went to work on the burn. The salve that he'd picked up felt soothing as he spread it over the red skin. Wrapping the bandages over it reminded him how sensitive the exposed nerves were.

When he finished, he stood up and walked over to the mirror. His vision was filled with spots. He wavered for a moment and put a hand against the wall to balance. Once the light-headedness had passed, he grabbed the needle and thread. Working on the wound in his shoulder proved to be the most difficult. He had to use his left hand while reaching across his body. He finished the entry wound with sloppy uneven stitches. Last was the exit wound. He turned his shoulder to see it in the mirror. Stitching this one was almost comical. He poked into his shoulder several times without hitting anywhere close to the right spot. After a frustrating thirty minutes, he finally completed the task. The skin was pulled tight with a crisscrossing section of misaligned stitches.

A bead of sweat stood on Riker's forehead. His heart raced from the pain and concentration. He looked in the mirror and saw a ghost white reflection. Stumbling over to the bed, he grabbed his bag. His body wanted to fade into oblivion, but he forced down another candy bar and drained another Gatorade. He also swallowed four extra-strength pain killers.

He lay on the bed and looked at his field dressed body. It wasn't the best work he had done, but it would suffice. His mentor's voice filled his head.

*If you're hurt, that means you're not dead. If you're not dead, you keep fighting. You can stop when all of your enemies are dead or when you are. Not a second before.*

An image filled his mind—Hendricks, Dobbs and Weaver standing in the office. Their time would come. Soon.

That was the last thought before sleep took him.

## 28

For a blissful moment after Riker opened his eyes, there was no pain. Then he tried to move. The aches hit him hard, every injury he'd suffered the previous night calling out to him all at once, as if they were fighting for his attention. There was the bullet wound in his shoulder, of course, and the burn on his arm. The cut on his leg made its voice heard. But there were also some new singers joining in the chorus. His lower back felt frozen, and his head throbbed with pain. Apparently throwing himself out of a thirty-foot-high window and into a river had jarred his body in some new and exciting ways. Or maybe it had been the fight before that. Or the effort not to drown after.

Whatever the cause, he was feeling the after-effects now. He fought the urge to lie there unmoving, to close his eyes and let sleep claim him once again. Maybe he'd feel better after a few more hours of rest. Isn't that what his body needed?

Sighing, he suppressed that instinct and threw back the covers. From the nightstand clock, he could see he'd slept for almost eight hours. It had been necessary, but it had also been enough. Any more sleep would just be a waste of the precious hours he should be using to find Li.

He climbed out of bed and waddled his way to the bathroom. Each step brought pain, but it also brought added mobility. By the time he reached the sink, he was walking almost normally. Looking in the mirror, he inspected his handiwork from the previous night. The stitches looked even uglier in the harsh light of day. He'd have a handful of new scars as a souvenir from yesterday's festivities, but that didn't bother him. There were plenty of old scars to keep them company.

Even though he'd showered just before bed, he decided to take another one. The hot water would help loosen his tight muscles. Steam filled the room as the heat of the shower did its magic. When he was done, he felt nearly human again. There was still pain, of course, but he was moving normally now. He was confident his body would be able to handle whatever he needed it to do.

His pants still hung on the chair where he'd left them the previous night. He ignored the smell of river water that they carried. Reaching in the pocket, he pulled out the money, intending to count it, but he found something else there along with the cash—a soggy piece of paper.

He unfolded the paper, set it on the dresser, and stared at it for a long moment. He could make out the figure clearly now, drawn in brown crayon, its fist pulled back to punch a bad guy. It was the drawing Li had given him. The drawing of her yīngxióng. Her hero. Riker swallowed hard and looked away. Where was Li now? Was she alone, locked in some room, frightened and wondering when her yīngxióng would come save her? Or was she somewhere even worse?

He pushed away the terrible images that sprang into his mind. Such thoughts weren't helpful. What was helpful was the process. The clues. He needed to consider what he knew and formulate a plan of what to do next.

He thought back to when he'd first met Helen and Li at the fair. There had been five men after them. Then three more at their hotel and three at the house. Another half dozen had pursued them on their way back to New York. That meant a minimum of seventeen guys had been sent to retrieve Li. There were two conclusions Riker could draw from that. One, Li was extremely valuable. This wasn't just some normal child trafficking situation. Bad men were willing to fight and die to claim possession of her. Two, Helen had been completely unprepared for such a show of force from her enemies. If she'd brought men along to protect her, they'd died before Riker had entered the picture. That meant that Helen and her team hadn't expected there to be trouble, at least not trouble of that magnitude.

Someone had tipped off the rival gang that Helen and Li would be in rural North Carolina. Riker had a pretty good idea who that snitch might be. Carter.

If he could get to Carter before Weaver's men did, he might be able to get more information on this rival gang. Maybe Carter could even tell him why Li was so valuable to these people.

He suddenly wished he had his phone. It would be nice to be able to search the Chinese news sites looking for any headlines about a prominent child who was missing. Maybe he'd swing by a public library later and use one of their computers.

A terrible thought suddenly struck Riker. What if the men Helen had been running from had been trying to save Li? Trying to take her back to her family? What if Riker had aided Helen in stealing the child? That would mean all the injured men he'd left strewn between New York and North Carolina were the good guys here.

He only considered the thought for a moment before deciding it didn't fit. After all, the men had actually had Li in their possession, and rather than taking her home, they'd taken both her and Helen back to the rental house. They had to be part of a rival gang.

A plan was forming in Riker's mind, and the first step of that plan was finding Carter. It would take some doing, but he thought he knew where to start. And Carter wasn't the only weak spot in Weaver's armor. Riker thought he might be able to make use of Brennan too. The man seemed to fill an odd role in Weaver's organization. He'd deferred to Hendricks as if he were under him, but in Weaver's office, Brennan had been Weaver's first choice to take Helen home. Brennan certainly came off as smarter than Hendricks. Riker thought there might be a way to use him in this plan.

But first, he needed to get to Carter.

He walked to the bedside table and opened the drawer. The Glock he'd stolen from the drug dealer lay there, waiting for him to grab it. He stared at it for a long while, thinking back to another hotel room he'd been in six years ago. The memory came back so vividly it was as if it were playing out again in front of him.

*Riker sits on the bed. It squeaks every time he shifts his body. His back sings with pain from the hundreds of small wounds from where the buckshot hit him a few days earlier, but he ignores the pain. His focus is on the man sitting in the chair across from the bed. Captain Morrison. The light reflects off his shaved bald head, and he wears a stern expression.*

*"What you're suggesting isn't advisable," Morrison says, his voice low and deadly serious.*

"I'm not asking if it's advisable," Riker says. "I'm asking if it's possible."

There is a long pause before Morrison answers. "Theoretically."

Riker feels something he hasn't felt in a long time—hope.

"I spoke to leadership about your request."

Riker's eyebrows shoot up in surprise at that. He wasn't expecting Morrison to bring this to their attention already.

"They aren't exactly comfortable with the idea," Morrison continues. "They know about the information you have, and they'd prefer to keep you close. They want you in the game."

"And what if I don't want to play anymore?"

"Then they'd rather have you as a friendly retiree rather than an active enemy." He pauses a moment. "However, they have conditions."

Riker expected no less. He waits to hear the terms.

"First, you forfeit any outstanding money they owe you."

Riker frowns at that. "They owe me for the last two jobs."

"Not anymore they don't. Not if you walk away. You go with nothing but what you have stashed away."

Riker thinks a moment, then nods. "What else?"

"You keep them apprised of your whereabouts. You get to retire, but that doesn't mean they aren't going to be keeping an eye on you. Anytime you move or even go on vacation, you let them know where you'll be. If they lose sight of you, they'll assume you're working for someone else, and they won't be happy."

"I can do that. What else?"

"This is the big one. Whatever you do next, it's gotta have nothing to do with what we do here. And I don't mean just soldiering. Security. Bounty hunting. Private investigation. You gotta stay the hell away from anything with even a whiff of violence to it."

"*I think you just listed every skill I have in the world,*" Riker says.

"*Yeah, well, get some new skills. Starting over means really starting over. You gotta keep your nose beyond clean. If you so much as get pulled in on a misdemeanor, leadership is going to assume you're back to your old life, and they are going to take action.*"

"*Let me guess? That action involves sending you and my old teammates to visit.*"

Morrison scowls at that. "*Just make sure it never happens. If they send me to kill you, you know I'll get the job done, even if I am fond of your stupid ass.*"

Riker knows the truth of those words. He also knows that if Morrison and his team came after him, he'd have zero chance of survival.

"*So are we agreed?*" Morrison asks. "*They let you walk away, and in return you never so much as touch a weapon again.*"

Riker considers how his life is about to change. "*We're agreed.*"

The memory was so vivid that Riker could almost smell Morrison's distinctive aftershave. He didn't miss the old life, but he did miss his mentor and his teammates sometimes. He also hoped to God he never saw them again. Because if he did, that meant he was about to get a bullet in the head.

He stared at the Glock for another moment. Eventually, he turned and looked at Li's drawing on the dresser. Yīngxióng. He'd been a lot of things in his time. A wrestler. A SEAL. A killer. Could he really be a hero for that little girl?

But there was really no choice, was there? He might not be hero material, but he was her only chance. There was no one else.

He reached into the drawer and picked up the weapon.

## 29

---

CAMOUFLAGE WAS important in every environment, and Riker knew that the city was no exception. Walking around in blood-stained, foul-smelling clothes would get him noticed. With the right attitude and attire, a person could become invisible in a city. That was what he needed to accomplish.

He walked to a bus stop and bought a week's pass out of a Metrocard vending machine. He also grabbed a map of the routes. On the front was a code you could scan with a phone to get an app with the map and times. Riker thought of all the topographical maps, city maps, and terrain markers he had used to find his way around the world. He wondered if future generations would be lost without a phone and GPS system.

While he waited for the bus, he studied the map. He started big, learning where each borough intersected with the others. Next, he studied the major roads, followed by important landmarks and buildings. After he built his internal overview he started to fill in the smaller roads. He couldn't learn every one, but he could memorize the strange layout of changing grids that make up New York City. By the time the bus came, he had a better knowledge of the city layout than half the people who lived there.

A few people stared when he entered the bus. His clothes stunk and his pant leg was crusted in dried blood. He got off at the first clothing store he saw and purchased the blandest outfit he could find. A dark blue zip-up hoodie, a gray T-shirt and blue jeans. There were no graphics or bright colors to draw the eye. He wore the clothes out of the store and tossed the old ones in the trash. Now he was part of the city's white noise.

Riker hopped on another bus and headed towards Carter's place. He studied the map on the ride, learning the city and the bus routes better and better.

Three blocks from Carter's place, he got off. He walked casually, glancing at the people and buildings around him. It was unlikely that Weaver's men would be looking for him here. They probably assumed he would flee the city or go after Dobbs. He still checked the area for any signs of an ambush as he approached. When he was convinced that the area was clear, he went to Carter's place.

He entered with the bump key. Nothing had changed since the previous day; neither Carter nor Dobbs' crew had come back. This gave Riker time to do a more thorough search. He started in the bedroom. The first thing he found was a small wooden box under the bed. Inside was a lighter, syringe, spoon and a bag of heroin. The box was only half-way under the bed which meant Carter was getting really sloppy. New users went out of their way to hide their problems from everyone, including themselves. Carter must have been at the point where he knew what he was.

Riker checked the closet next. There was a shoebox under a mess of clothes on the top shelf. Inside was a photo of a man standing next to a boy. They were in front of a lake and both of them held fishing rods. Riker stuck the photo in his pocket. There was also an envelope with a letter in it. Riker skimmed the letter. The recipient was Dad and it was signed by Jimmy. The letter was brief. Jimmy told his dad about a soccer game he'd won and asked if he would ever come back home. Riker tossed the letter back in the box but kept the envelope with the return address.

In the drawer next to the bed was a tablet. Riker powered it up, but it was protected by a password. He considered trying to crack the code, but he wanted the device as much as the information contained in its drives. He held the buttons down and did a factory reset. After finishing the setup process he had internet access again.

There were surprisingly few personal items in the small apartment. No pictures hung on the wall and the only things on the tables were junk mail mixed with old fast-food wrappers. Judging from his belongings, Carter didn't have much of a life. Riker emptied the contents of the trash can onto the kitchen floor. There were a dozen empty packs of cigarettes and dozens of losing tickets from off-track betting. That was the last clue Riker needed.

Riker took the tablet and searched for off-track betting locations. He was glad to see that there were not a lot of them around the city. Four were located in areas surrounded by pawnshops and liquor stores. The rest were in nicer areas far from the city center.

He looked up the address on the envelope and checked it against the map of the betting locations. One was close. The location had everything Carter could want. Access to his addictions of heroin and gambling, and he could try to keep an eye on his family who he knew would be in danger.

There were three shitty motels within walking distance

of the betting location. Riker saved a screenshot of the map with the motels on it and headed out to grab a bus.

The first motel that Riker went to looked as if it had been recently renovated. The paint was nice and exterior cameras and floodlights surrounded the building. He could see the desk clerk through the floor to ceiling windows of the lobby. He looked alert and polite. Riker knew that one was a miss. He pulled up his map and walked to the second location five blocks away.

The second place looked as if it hadn't changed in sixty years. The old brick building had two floors. A railing and walkway went around the second floor giving access to the rooms. Trash scurried across the parking lot in the wind. A woman in a short leopard print skirt stood on the sidewalk on the edge of the parking lot. When Riker walked by, she asked him if he needed a friend. Riker liked the odds of finding Carter here.

He went into the lobby and found a woman behind the desk. It was hard to judge her age, but she had a fair number of wrinkles around her eyes and a bit of grey in her hair. She could have passed for fifty-five, but Riker guessed she was closer to forty-five. The wrinkles and the sad look of her eyes were likely the product of a hard-lived life. She read a book with a shirtless man on the cover and didn't bother to look up when he walked in. Riker saw a picture of her standing next to a young man in a graduation photo. He noticed that she wasn't wearing a wedding ring.

She spoke without looking up from her book. "We've got a room if you want one. No hourly rates."

He walked over to the desk and leaned up against it. "I don't need any hourly rates, or a room for that matter."

She set her book down and looked up at him. "Then you're in the wrong place. I'm not buying anything so I don't need to hear a word out of your mouth. You know where the door is."

Riker gave her a casual smile. "I'm not selling anything either. I'm just trying to help out a single mom."

The woman behind the desk looked confused. This clearly wasn't what she expected to hear. "What do you mean?"

Riker reached his hand across the desk. "I'm Matthew."

She cautiously reached out and shook his hand. "Carla."

"Nice to meet you, Carla. I'm trying to track down this guy who skipped out on his child support. He hasn't paid in a year and a half. I've got to serve him so the judge can dock his paycheck. I know none of this is your problem, but I could use some help."

Carla stared at him for a long moment, then stood up with a sigh. "Goddamn deadbeat dads. I've got one of those running around out there. I was lucky if I got any child support at all. I'd go months without a dime and then when I threatened to get him into a courtroom I'd get a couple of bucks. I'm sure you know how that goes."

"Yep, those guys can really take advantage of people."

"They sure can. They don't care about anyone but themselves. Mine was named Fred. He left me with our kid. Didn't raise him and didn't pay for a damn thing."

"Sorry to hear that, Carla. The one I'm looking for is called Steve Carter. I'm sure he's using a fake name, but I've got a picture." Riker pulled the photo out of his pocket. He had it folded in half to show only Carter. "He probably checked in yesterday. I went to his place to serve him and the chicken ran out the fire escape."

Carla looked at the photo. She squinted at the image and then scoffed.

"Yep, he's here." She was a little somber when she spoke.

"What's the problem?"

"The guy that checked in isn't exactly the same as the guy in the photo."

"How so?"

"That looks like a guy that has a job. The one who checked in here is a strung-out mess. A judge might order him to make some payments, but honey, no one is going to see a dime from him."

"That's a shame." Riker paused for a little drama. "I'd like to try all the same. Could you tell me what room he's in?"

"You didn't hear it from me, but he's in 108."

"Thanks, Carla." He shook her hand again. "You're one of the good ones."

She smiled at him as he left. Riker was always shocked at how easily security systems were broken by exploiting the people in the systems. From simple motels to complex government buildings, making friends with the right person almost always brought the system to its knees.

Riker walked outside and around the exterior of the motel until he reached room 108. The curtains were pulled shut, but he could see the glow of the lights from inside. He knocked on the door and stood back so Carter would be able to see him through the peephole. Riker waited and watched for the spot of light in the peephole to be blocked by an observing eye, but it didn't happen. He put his ear to the door and listened. It was completely silent.

There were two likely scenarios. Carter wasn't there, or he was sitting on the bed with a gun pointed at the door. Both were problematic. If Carter was gone, Riker would have to wait until he came back. That could take hours if he came back at all. Since the clock was ticking on Li, Riker decided he needed to risk the second scenario.

The door used a key card, but the lock was an old one. He pulled his driver's license out of his wallet and slid it along the seam of the old door frame. Once he felt the top of the latch bolt, he wiggled the card until it slid behind it. Riker stood to the side of the door while he worked on the bolt. He was ready for a bullet to punch a hole in the door at any moment. Once the bolt was disengaged, he pressed against the brick wall and swung the door open.

No sound came from inside the room. Riker called out Carter's name, but there was no response. He edged around the door frame and realized that there was a third scenario.

Riker stepped inside the room and closed the door behind him. Carter was lying on top of the bed. He didn't move a muscle when Riker entered. On the stand next to the bed were a needle, spoon and lighter.

## 30

CARTER DIDN'T WAKE up when Riker said his name. A light slap didn't do the trick either. An ice bucket of cold water dumped on his head woke him up. Even then, his eyes opened slowly, and he looked dazed for a few moments as the rest of his mind, the part that was theoretically supposed to be doing the higher levels of thinking, slowly came back to Earth.

Riker stood there saying nothing, waiting until the man was able to talk to him. He didn't relish getting information from a heroin addict who still had the drug in his system, but it was his best lead at the moment.

Carter stared at Riker for a long moment, and a series of emotions crossed his face. Surprise and panic came first, but they were quickly replaced by confusion, and then sullen acceptance. Nearly a full minute after he'd opened his eyes, he finally spoke.

"I can't believe Weaver only sent one guy. Is that how little he thinks of me?"

"I don't work for Weaver," Riker said.

"Sure. Of all the rooms in all the shitty motels in the city, you just happened to break into mine. Forgive me if I don't believe you."

"Weaver wants you dead, yes?" Riker said.

Carter frowned. "Yeah, I gotta assume that's the case."

"Then if I worked for him, wouldn't I have put a bullet through your head while you were passed out rather than going to the trouble of waking you up?"

"You have a point." He pushed himself to a sitting position, a process that appeared far more difficult than it should have been. "So who are you?"

"First dry off," Riker said, tossing him a towel. "Then we'll talk."

Carter's reflexes were still less than stellar, and the towel hit him in the face before he could get his hand up to catch it. Riker walked to the desk across from the bed and took a seat in the office chair. In truth, he didn't care if Carter was wet or dry, but he did want to give him another minute or two for his drug-addled brain to clear the cobwebs before they talked. Carter dried his face and hair. He shifted around until he was sitting on the edge of the bed, facing Riker.

Riker was suddenly struck by how their positions mirrored his and Morrison's on that long-ago day when Morrison had told him the conditions for starting a new life.

"Okay, I'm good," Carter said. "You wanna tell me what you're doing here?"

Riker looked into his eyes, and he had to admit Carter did look more alert now. Probably as alert as he was going to get. "As I said, I don't work for Weaver. In fact, I'm trying to take him down. I'd say that puts you and me on the same side, wouldn't you?"

"I guess." Carter hesitated. "Or maybe I turn you in to Weaver and they forgive my misdeeds."

Riker shifted his expression slightly, going with the dead-eyed, dangerous stare he'd given his wrestling opponents during weigh-ins back in the day. It had worked then and it worked now. Carter's bravado withered under that stare.

"Weaver doesn't seem like the forgiving type. Neither am I. You strike me as a guy who doesn't have a lot of friends right now. If you did, you'd probably be crashing at one of their houses instead of this dump. I'm offering to be a friend, but if you want to go the other way with it, we can do that too."

"No," Carter said quickly. He sounded as if he was on the verge of tears. "You're right. I could use a friend. Everything's so fucked up. I never meant for all this to happen."

"How did it happen? How'd you get mixed up with Weaver's organization?"

Carter stared at the floor. For a moment, it seemed as if he wasn't going to answer, but he eventually met Riker's eyes. "Believe it or not, I used to be a working man. I did right by my family most of the time. Yeah, I partied a little on the weekends, but I kept a roof over our heads, you know? Then a couple years back I lost my job. My cousin told me about this opportunity with Weaver. That's what he called it. An opportunity. I started out working in the warehouse. Weaver runs a legitimate import business, mostly bringing in chemical products from Russia. I knew right away that there was some less than legal stuff going on."

"And yet, you stayed," Riker said with a growl.

"Look, man, yeah I knew Weaver was shady, but I figured it was just drugs or something," Carter said. His eyes pleaded for absolution. "I didn't know about the other stuff. The women. The...the kids." His voice hitched as he said it.

"Human trafficking," Riker said, his eyes hard.

Carter nodded. "But I swear, I didn't know. By the time they moved me from the warehouse to the main office and I started seeing what was really going on, I was in too deep. I couldn't just walk away."

"Let me tell you something I've learned from experience. You can always walk away. It may not be easy, but it's always possible."

"I tried, man. I swear to God, I tried. That's why I contacted Glen Paddock. He runs a rival organization. I thought if I got him some information, he'd be able to protect me. He said he would. And I kept my part of the bargain. But as soon as he had what he needed from me, he stopped returning my calls." He gestured to the room around him. "I tried to get out, like you said, and this is the result. I'm cowering in this motel room, hiding, fearing for my life."

"Don't forget shooting up," Riker said. He couldn't help it. He felt no sympathy for Carter. The man had knowingly been involved in a human trafficking operation. Instead of going to the cops, he'd tried to switch to another criminal operation. "And the bag of heroin and cash I found in your apartment? Were those part of your scheme to go straight too?"

Carter's eyes fell, and he stared at the floor. "So I've got my share of problems. And yeah, maybe I didn't always do the right thing. Maybe I've earned whatever's coming to me. I guess I'm at peace with that. But I know Weaver. He's not going to stop with me. He'll come for my family."

Riker thought back to Dobbs saying as much when they'd found Carter's empty apartment.

"My ex...honestly, she deserves as bad as me. She's the one who got me using in the first place. But Ethan, my son, he's innocent in all this. I tried to warn them, but Cindy won't take my calls. She's got a restraining order out on me. I sent a bunch of emails too, but I think she's deleting them unread."

Carter was close to panic now. Riker knew it was time to shift to the good cop routine. Or at least the less angry cop.

"I can't make any guarantees about your safety," he said, "but I can help your family. I'll make sure they get out of town."

"You'd do that?" Carter said, his eyes hopeful for the first time.

Riker nodded. "But only if you do something for me in return. I need you to help me take Weaver down."

Carter thought for a moment, then nodded. "What do you want to know?"

"The organization. How's it work?"

"Like I said, Weaver runs a legitimate import business as a front. It's called Dynamic Chemical Solutions. But he really makes his money importing people and selling them like cattle."

"How involved is Weaver in the criminal side of things?"

"Very." Carter leaned forward, getting into it now. "He's an old school gangster at heart. He can't help but be hands-on. If he was smart, he'd put some buffer between him and the illegal stuff, but the legitimate business just doesn't hold his interest."

"How about Dobbs?" Riker asked.

"He's involved too, but only as much as he has to be. I get the sense he doesn't have the stomach for the real implications of what they do. But he's a brilliant lawyer. He's managed to keep Weaver's operation under the radar and out of the view of law enforcement for decades."

Riker grimaced. He didn't like what he was hearing, but it all tracked with what he'd seen so far. There was one more person he needed to ask about. "Tell me about Helen's role."

Carter shook his head. "Man, she's a cold one. Her job is human resources, so to speak. Once the people are brought into New York, she gains their trust and keeps them under control until they are sold off. She facilitates that too."

A chill ran through Riker. He thought back to the way she'd rested her head on his shoulder in the back of the semi-trailer. He supposed she'd been working as hard to manipulate him as she did with her victims.

"There's a little girl," Riker said. "Li."

Carter nodded. "Oh yeah. That's the big job. The one Weaver and Helen have been working to set up for months."

"Why? What's so special about that girl?"

"I don't know. They kept the details a secret, but I know they have a client who's willing to pay very handsomely for that kid. I'm talking seven figures."

Riker pushed down the sick feeling in his stomach at the thought of Li being sold off to some "client." "They said you helped Helen pick out the house in North Carolina. I assume that means you also tipped off this Glen Paddock that Helen would be there."

Carter nodded. "I'd been in touch with Paddock for a while, but hadn't provided him anything useful enough to earn his protection. He somehow caught wind of this Li situation and told me to find out what I could. Turns out, I found out a lot."

"Tell me," Riker said.

"Helen picked the little girl up in Miami. The plan was for her to drive her to this house in North Carolina where she would meet the client and trade the girl for the cash. Easy peasy."

"Did Helen go to Miami alone?"

"No. She took four guys with her."

Riker grimaced. The guys must have been killed before he got involved. "And you told Paddock about the rendezvous?"

Carter nodded.

It was all starting to make sense to Riker. That was why Paddock's guys had taken Helen back to her rental house after grabbing her at the hotel. They'd probably kept Helen alive in case the client would only do business with her.

"Listen man, I don't even know your name," Carter said. "But I'm trusting you to keep your word. Please protect my family."

"It's Riker," he said, holding out his hand. "And I promise to do everything I can to keep them safe."

They shook, and Carter seemed to relax a little.

"I'm glad it was you standing over my bed when I woke up and not Hendricks. That guy is scary."

The burn on Riker's arm itched as if in response to Hendricks' name. "I take it you can still get in touch with Paddock?"

Carter nodded. "He's more secretive than Weaver. He gives me a new number each time. But I can get in touch with him."

"Good. Then for now, I just need two things from you. Give me your wife's address, and tell me where you think they are keeping Li."

## 31

RIKER STOOD under the shadows of a tree half a block away from the address Carter had given him. The neighborhood was in Queens, and it felt more suburban than any part of the city Riker had seen so far. The glow of streetlights revealed mist drifting to the ground. He watched the house for any signs of movement, but the windows remained dark.

He thought of Li and hoped that they weren't moving her while he spent time on an unrelated task. It crossed his mind to tell Carter that his family was safe without helping them, but he had given his word. Now he was here in front of their house. He thought about knocking on the door and having a conversation with Jill, Carter's ex, but he realized that he needed to deliver a message that she couldn't ignore. There was no time to come back again or spend hours convincing her to flee.

Riker hopped the fence and went to the back of the house. A light by the garage door illuminated the yard, which was mostly made up of dead patches of grass. He didn't see any sign of a dog. Before he picked the lock to the back door, Riker peeked in the window off the kitchen. The room was empty but he saw the magnetic strips of a home security system.

Riker checked a window on the side of the attached garage. Just as he suspected there was no sensor. He took off his hoodie and pressed it against the glass. He gave it a quick hit with his elbow. The cloth muffled the sound of the glass breaking and also protected him from any shards of glass as he climbed inside. He quickly found a panel in the ceiling that gave him access to the attic. He climbed onto the car and hoisted himself into the attic. After crawling around for a few minutes, he found the interior access point. He dropped into a hallway, bypassing the alarm.

Riker went to the master bedroom at the end of the hall. His stomach churned at the thought of what he was about to do, but he needed to be sure Jill would get the message. He quickly opened the door and saw Jill sleeping alone in the bed. He crept over and bent down next to her.

In a single, quick motion, he put one hand over her mouth and pointed his gun at her face with the other. Her eyes shot open, and she stared up at the gun and the big man pointing it at her. She tried to scream, but Riker put the weight of his body into the hand on her mouth. She made a small muffled noise and hit his wrist with her hands.

"Shut up and don't move if you want to keep your son alive," Riker spoke in a cold whisper.

She looked at the gun and stopped struggling. Her eyes darted to Riker in the dimly lit room.

"Jill, I'm not here to kill you, but men are coming here to do just that. Your ex, Steve, messed up bad. His mistakes are going to cost you and your son your lives." Riker paused so she could take in his words.

Her eyes were filled with fear and anger. She tried to

speak, but Riker's hand still covered her mouth. He felt her spit on his palm.

"You know that your ex was into some bad stuff. I didn't want to deliver this message, but I need you to hear me. You and your son will die if you don't get out of town right now. I don't mean in the morning, or after you have a chance to figure things out. I mean you leave now and don't tell anyone where you are going. Nod if you understand what I'm saying."

She did her best to nod.

"Good. Do you believe me that you are in mortal danger?"

A tear escaped from the corner of her eye and she looked at the gun in her face. She nodded again.

"I'm going to take my hand away from your mouth. Can you stay calm if I do?" Riker wiggled the gun menacingly.

She nodded again. He slowly moved his hand away from her mouth.

"What did Steve do?" she asked in a whisper.

"He crossed the wrong guys in a big way. They want him dead and they are going to use you to find him. They are not going to want any loose ends. They will kill all three of you. The more you know, the worse it will be for you. Just get your son and go somewhere where no one will look."

"Who are you?"

"I'm the guy trying to get Steve out of this mess. I promised him that I would make sure you are safe. I've dealt with the guys who are coming for you. Trust me, you don't want them to find you. Sorry to deliver the message in such an intrusive way, but I couldn't risk you not taking it seriously."

She rubbed her jaw and stared at Riker. "Fuck you. I hope they kill Carter."

"Fair enough. They probably will. They will torture you and your son if they think it will help find him."

Jill turned pale. Understanding dawned in her eyes, and she looked at the floor.

Riker left the house in silence. While he was leaving through the front door, lights turned on inside of the home. He hid in the shadows of an alley across from the house. He watched for fifteen minutes and then the garage opened and Jill drove off. Carter's family was as safe as they could be. It was time to move onto the next part of the plan.

Carter had told Riker about an office that most of Weaver's operations ran through. It was the home base for Hendricks and Brennan. It was also where most of the people they trafficked were kept. Riker realized that he needed a car. Getting there by bus would be okay, but escaping with a girl would have to involve a car.

Jill's neighborhood was filled with old shitty cars, and he quickly found one that would work. He grabbed a late 80s Ford Escort. It was easy to steal and one of the most unassuming cars on the road.

He reached the address that Carter had given him just after midnight. The streets were wet from the steady drizzle. Riker drove by the front of the building. It was an old four-story brick building. The lights in the third and fourth floors shined out onto the street below. Several cars were parked in front. One of them was Hendricks' Audi.

Riker turned the corner at the end of the block and parked the car. He went down an alley behind the buildings across the street from his target. He climbed the fire escape on the back side of the building. The top landing of the fire escape was fifteen feet below the roof.

Riker stood on the metal railing next to the building. The metal was cold and slick from the rain. He put one hand on the cold stone of the structure for balance. The edge of the roof was a foot higher than he could reach while standing on the railing. He looked down and saw the alley forty feet below him. Riker dried his hands on his clothes. He focused on the ledge of the building and jumped.

His hands caught the top of the ledge and he pulled himself up as hard as he could the second they made contact. He kept his momentum going and pressed himself up. He bent his waist over the edge and swung one leg over. The second leg followed, and Riker found himself standing on top of the roof.

He crouched while moving across the roof. He doubted that anyone was watching the top of this building, but fortune favors the cautious. He looked over the ledge on the other side of the roof.

From his vantage point, he could see into the rooms of the fourth floor of Weaver's building. As he expected, Hendricks was there. Riker smiled when he saw white bandages wrapped around the top of Hendricks' head. Riker's arm somehow felt better when he saw that the top of Hendricks' head was worse off.

Hendricks was in an office with Brennan. The two were having a conversation that looked civil to Riker. He counted six other men in the building. Riker stayed low and watched for any sign of Helen and Li.

After an hour he was soaked from the mist and had to concentrate to keep from shaking. There had been no sign of anyone coming or going into the building. Riker didn't see Helen, Weaver, or Dobbs. None of the men held their weapons at the ready and all of them seemed relaxed. Riker was fairly sure that Li was somewhere else.

Hendricks got a call and had a brief conversation. Riker couldn't tell much about the call from his position. After he hung up, Hendricks grabbed two other guys and went out of sight. A moment later the three walked out of the front door and got into Hendricks' car.

Brennan stayed in the office and made a phone call of his own. A little after one thirty in the morning Brennan shut off the light to his office. When he did, Riker moved back over to the fire escape. He hung and dropped back onto the top landing. He sprinted down the escape and back to the car. He kept the lights off as he turned around to the street Weaver's building was on. He made it just in time to see Brennan get into his car.

Riker followed him, staying a few blocks back. Brennan's car was a new Dodge Challenger. The oval tail lights stood out and made it easy for Riker to stay with him. Even at two in the morning, there was enough traffic in the city for Riker to stay out of sight.

Brennan pulled up in front of a brick row home. He got out and went inside.

Riker parked his car a block away. On the walk to the building, he replayed the time he had spent with Brennan in his head. He was ninety percent sure that he was making the right play. As long as he was correct, the odds of saving Li were going to go way up. If he was wrong, he would probably die.

He climbed the steps to the front door and rang the bell. He took a few steps back and held his hands at his sides, palms open and facing the door. Brennan checked the peephole and the door swung open.

Brennan held his pistol with two hands. He kept it trained on Riker's head. Riker stayed perfectly still with his arms away from his sides. He looked Brennan straight in the eyes.

"Holy shit, you must be crazy," Brennan said, holding the gun on Riker.

"At the moment, I'm just cold. Can I come inside before I freeze to death?"

Brennan looked confused. He just stood there with the gun pointed at Riker.

"Seriously, I'm soaked. Besides, I would like to get inside before anyone sees me here, or notices you holding a person at gunpoint."

"What makes you think I'm not going to shoot you right here?"

Riker slowly raised his hands above his head. He walked slowly towards Brennan. Brennan walked backward keeping his distance from Riker.

"Because cops aren't supposed to shoot unarmed men," Riker responded. "Now can I put my arms down so we can talk?"

## 32

BRENNAN STARED at Riker for a long moment, his eyes cold, gun still trained on his chest. "Is that supposed to be some kind of joke?"

"No. I suspected it five minutes after we met, but I knew for sure by the time we searched Carter's apartment."

They stared at each other for a solid ten seconds, neither saying anything. Finally, Brennan seemed to deflate. He lowered the weapon. "Get the hell in here."

Riker stepped inside and took in the apartment. It was smallish, but nice. As Riker had expected, there was an air of blandness to it. There were no family pictures on the wall. No mementos. Not even a bowling trophy. Brennan had clearly lived here for a while, but he'd never made the place his own.

Brennan eased the door shut and turned to face Riker.

"It's up to you how we play this," Riker said. "If you want, we can do the thing where you deny it, tell me I didn't see what I saw. But that would be a waste of time for both of us, don't you think?"

Brennan moved past Riker, saying nothing. He went to the couch and sank into it.

"You did a hell of a number on Weaver's people at the warehouse. Two men dead. Hendricks spent the night in the hospital."

"Couldn't have happened to a nicer guy."

"How'd you know? About me, I mean."

"There were quite a few clues at Carter's place. The way you held your weapon. The way you cleared the room. It was professional. You've had training."

"Could be I was in the military," Brennan said.

"I don't think so. Hendricks was explaining military terms to you, and if you were ex-military, he probably would have been busting your balls, making sure I knew whatever division you served in wasn't as cool as his."

"Seems like a stretch."

"When we went into Carter's apartment, I saw you touch your shoulder. Then you got a look on your face like you'd been caught peeking in your hot neighbor's window, and you ran your hand through your hair to cover up the move. You were reaching for your call radio, weren't you? Old habits die hard."

"Big assumption."

"Maybe. And I wouldn't be making it if it wasn't for that." He pointed at Brennan's forearm.

"The Holy Mother? So all Catholics are cops now?"

"No. But the Virgin Mary's torso isn't usually shaped just like the NYPD crest. You got the cover-up tattoo when you went undercover, didn't you?"

Brennan said nothing for a long time. Then he uttered a single word. "Shit."

Riker watched the other man carefully. An undercover operative who is found out has only two real options. Either they try to get the person who knows the truth on their side, or they try to eliminate them. Riker doubted an NYPD cop would kill him to protect his cover, but on the other hand, it seemed Brennan had been embedded with Weaver's crew for quite some time. To him, it probably felt as if his world was falling apart. Desperate people did desperate things. It was possible he'd try to make a move. Riker's best bet to keep Brennan's mind from taking him in that dangerous direction was to connect with him.

"Listen to me," Riker said. "I know a little something about being embedded with the enemy."

"That so?"

"I'm not going to go into details, but let's just say I've spent some time in hostile territory, pretending to be something I'm not."

Brennan shifted in his seat, the shock on his face shifting into another emotion Riker couldn't quite identify.

"Let me ask you something, Riker. Back in this mysterious past of yours, what was the longest you were ever embedding with the enemy?"

For a moment, Riker's mind flashed back there, and he could almost smell the rain forest and hear the motors of the skiffs that had carried him and the others up and down the river. And he couldn't help thinking about how it all ended—in blood and fire, with most of the village burned to the ground.

"Four months," he said.

"Yeah? And that four months. Did it feel long?"

"Longest four months of my life," Riker said, meeting Brennan's hard gaze. In truth, it had felt endless, a hellish existence where he was under constant stress that he hadn't been sure he'd ever escape.

Brennan leaned forward. The anger was clear in his

voice when he spoke again. "I've been undercover with Weaver for over two years."

"Two years?" Riker's own anger was rising now. "How the hell do you stand by for two years, watching as Weaver and his people traffic women and children, trading them like fucking baseball cards to the scum of the earth? What do you do when they get a new shipment of terrified women? Do you file a report while they get turned out? Is there a special form where you mark down how many kids got stolen this week?"

"Don't you get self-righteous with me, Riker. You think I didn't want to put an end to this? You think I haven't wanted to put a bullet through Weaver's head a hundred times while my bosses kept telling me they need more evidence? That the DA's office needs me to hold my position just a little longer while they finish building their case?"

"I'm sure your mental anguish is a great comfort to the kids who were trafficked two years ago. Assuming they are still alive."

"Fuck you," Brennan said, but there was no emotion behind it. He looked defeated.

They sat in silence, both staring at the floor.

Riker knew this was a precarious situation. Brennan could still be an ally in this fight, assuming he wasn't so straight-laced that he wasn't willing to help someone working outside the law. Being undercover for even a short time was terribly lonely. Your closest friends, the ones you're spending all your time with, are actually your enemies and they don't even know it. It can mess with your head something awful. And Brennan had been living that life for two years.

"Listen to me," Riker said. "I don't have time to wait for

your DA to finally make a move. Li will be long gone when that happens. I'm taking action now."

"Really?" Brennan said with a chuckle. "You're taking down Weaver? All by your lonesome?"

"I'd prefer it not be alone. My priority is Li. I want to help her, and if I have to take Weaver down to do it, then that's what I'll do."

"You've got a pair of balls on you, Riker."

"And so do you if you've been undercover this long." He paused. "How about you use them to help me?"

Brennan didn't answer for a long moment.

Riker knew he was asking a lot. He was asking Brennan to throw away the case he'd spent so long building. He was asking him to work outside the law and probably put his career at risk.

"The DA tells me they're almost ready to make their move," he said. "But they've been saying that shit for five months. I'm done waiting. Prison is too good for Weaver. You want help? I'm your guy. Where do we start?"

Riker couldn't suppress the smile that appeared on his face. It felt good not to be alone.

"First things first. Do you know where they're holding Li?"

Brennan shook his head. "That girl's not like their usual imports. Weaver and Helen are playing this one close to the chest. I'd normally know, but I'm out of the loop on this one."

Damn it. Riker was starting to realize he needed to figure out why Li was so valuable to Weaver and his client. If he had that information, at least he'd be able to level the playing field a little.

"Riker, there's something you have to understand. I'm all for taking down Weaver, but the timing is piss-poor. This other gang, the one Gary Paddock runs, they are making a serious play for Weaver's business. Both crews are on high alert. They're preparing for all-out war."

"Then I'd say our timing is pretty damn good," Riker said with a smile. "They'll be paranoid and looking for enemies in every shadow. We can use that."

"There's also Hendricks to consider. You severely pissed him off at the warehouse."

"Really?" Riker said dryly.

"Listen, you've only known Hendricks a couple days. The guy's brutal."

"I kinda figured that out."

Brennan paused. "It's not just that. Weaver's in it for the money. The people he sells might as well be laptops or bushels of wheat or whatever. He sees them as commodities. Hendricks is different."

"How?" Riker asked, not sure he wanted to know.

"The kids, the women... Hendricks gets off on it. It's a power thing. He actually enjoys what they're doing."

Riker tried to push down the disgust he felt. He needed to stay focused. "If we do our jobs, Hendricks will pay. Same as Weaver."

"Okay," Brennan said, his voice skeptical. "So what's our first move?"

Riker considered that a moment. It felt good to have a partner in this, but he'd only known Brennan a couple days. It would be foolish to trust him completely at this point. Besides, if Brennan was completely on the up-and-up, he was a valuable asset. A weapon to be used strategically, no different from the Glock in Riker's waistband. It was a cold way to look at the world, but it was also an effective one.

"For now, I need you to hold the line. Do your job and keep gathering information."

"Maybe you're not that different from the DA after all," Brennan said with a scowl.

"The difference is I'll only keep you waiting for a day or two. At the most. We have to move fast."

"And what will you be doing?"

"I'm not going to tell you that."

"So I'm supposed to trust you, and yet you can't trust me?"

"It's not that." That was a lie, but a necessary one. "It's better you don't know everything, just in case Weaver discovers who you are."

"You think they're going to suddenly spot me after two years?"

"You said it yourself. Things are different now. They're gearing up for war."

Brennan nodded. "Fine. I don't like it, but I understand it. How do I get ahold of you if I need you?"

"You don't. Sorry, but I don't even have a phone right now."

"So far you're not making it easy to be your partner." He got up with a sigh and walked to the kitchen. He came back with a notebook and a pen, and he sat back down and started writing. He tore out the sheet of paper and handed it to Riker. "Here's my number. If a call comes in from a number I don't recognize while I'm around Weaver's people, I won't answer."

"Good," Riker said. "Thank you."

"You realize this is life and death, right? For both of us. We can't afford to screw up from here on out."

"The thought had crossed my mind," Riker said. Then he made a split-second decision. "I'm thinking of going after Dobbs first. He knows where all the bodies are buried, and I'm thinking he would be the easiest to crack. He left the warehouse just after you did. Couldn't stand to stick around and watch me bleed, I guess."

"That's smart," Brennan agreed.

"It'll be tough to take him in his home. I'd rather catch him in public. Any thoughts?"

Brennan considered that a moment, then smiled. "Yeah, actually. Dobbs is a creature of habit, and I know exactly where his habits are going to take him tonight."

## 33

THE NATURE of man has always been predictable. From world leaders to pimple-faced high schoolers, guys just want to get laid. Riker wasn't surprised to learn that Dobbs had a weakness for a certain brothel in Manhattan. The building was near the financial district. Stockbrokers and hedge fund managers could sneak over during lunch or after the office closed.

Brennan told him, with a little embarrassment, that he had been there with Dobbs. The place was high-end and security was tight. Dobbs went there every week according to Brennan; it was one appointment he never missed. Two bodyguards drove him in a black Mercedes 550s. The guards got him to the entrance and waiting outside. He would arrive at three am and leave by five.

Riker parked his car a block away and walked over to the address that Brennan had given him. Even in the glow of the streetlights, the subtle beauty of old New York architecture stood out. Old stone arches accented large, blank-tinted windows. Riker didn't see a single external camera. Discretion would be a major concern for the clients of this establishment.

He saw a Lincoln Navigator pull down the ramp to the parking garage. The driver of the car handed a pass to the guard in the booth outside the rolling metal door. After a moment he handed it back and allowed the car to enter.

Two doormen stood near the front door. Riker guessed their only job was to tell people the building was closed. It seemed everyone entered or left through the garage.

Riker checked his watch. It was two fifty. He watched the building from across the street. Ten minutes later a black Mercedes entered the garage. Riker saw two people in the front of the car, but the back windows were tinted too dark to make out a shape.

He hurried across the street and walked along the side of the building until he found the garage's emergency exit door. Even criminal enterprises had to follow city code. Riker put his bump key into the door and tapped the pins into position. He knew that unlocking and opening the door would still set off the alarm. The bypass was simple. Most emergency exits had a built-in disarm. He simply turned the key clockwise, counterclockwise, and then clockwise again. The door pulled open in silence.

As he stepped inside, the Mercedes was driving slowly through the garage. It passed empty spaces and circled down the ramp. Riker waited until it was out of sight and moved quickly to catch up. The car continued its descent. He followed it to the lowest level of the garage. There were several cars parked on this level, but it wasn't close to full. The car parked ten feet from an elevator.

Riker moved fast along the wall. He wanted to get Dobbs the moment he stepped out of the car. He drew his pistol and watched the front doors of the car. He intended to use the element of surprise to be sure the guards never saw what was coming.

When Riker was halfway to the car, tires squealed around the curve of the ramp. He glanced back and saw the Navigator. The car stopped at the bottom of the ramp, boxing him in. Riker cursed himself for blindly walking into a trap. The doors to the SUV burst open and four men jumped out with assault rifles. Riker caught a flash of the passenger in the back of the SUV. It was Dobbs.

Riker was ready with his Glock and put one round into the driver's chest. He dove behind a car and gunfire exploded in the garage.

Glass shattered and sprayed over Riker. He was crouched low next to the passenger side front wheel. The engine block stopped the bullets from reaching him, but chips of concrete shot out from the wall behind him, stinging the back of his neck. The sound of gunfire echoed around the garage in a deafening clatter. It took Riker a moment to realize that shots were coming from the direction of the Mercedes as well. He was pinned down and had five men approaching his position.

These were not amateurs. They fired in shifts while the others moved in. A non-stop barrage of bullets hit the vehicle that shielded Riker. He knew that it wouldn't take long before one of them reached an angle that gave them a shot at him.

He looked up, scanning his surroundings for anything that might give him a chance at surviving this. After a moment, his eyes settled on the fire sprinkler heads lining the garage. He shot one round into the closest head. The fire safety system sprang into action. Water poured down and emergency lights flashed along with a blaring siren. There was a moment's pause in the gunfire.

Riker stuck his head up and fired through the blown-out car windows. He hit a second attacker in the chest. Then he ducked back down as bullets riddled the car. He inched around to the front of the car and lay down, spotting a gunman's legs. He put a bullet into the man's shin just above the ankle. He dropped to the ground, and Riker finished him with a shot to the top of the head. Blood mixed with the water streaming across the concrete.

The rest of the men unloaded their weapons toward Riker. Bullets ripped holes through the side of the car. He kept his position tight against the front of the car protected by the steel of the engine block. After a few seconds, the shooting stopped.

As the three shooters paused to load fresh magazines, Riker stood and ran towards the Navigator. He fired at the man between him and the Lincoln. He was moving full speed and the first shot missed its mark, hitting high left in the shoulder. The man spun but stayed on his feet. Riker kept moving and put a second round into his heart from five feet away.

Dobbs had moved from the back of the vehicle to the driver's seat. Apparently, he wasn't confident in his trap now that four of his guys were dead. Riker heard the bolt slide into place in one of the weapons behind him. He knew that he didn't have enough time to reach Dobbs, and he ducked behind another car. The rattle of an assault rifle filled the garage. Riker was pinned down next to the driver's door of a sedan.

Dobbs slammed his foot on the gas, but the water and oils of the garage had made the ramp slippery and the tires spun. The car slid sideways and smashed into the sidewall. Dobbs had enough sense to put the car into four-wheel drive and try again. This time the large SUV went back up the ramp and out of sight.

Bullets continued to come at a steady rate. Riker checked his surroundings. There were six sets of fluorescent lights along the top of the garage. Riker had eleven bullets left. He fired six times and the only light left was the pulsing strobe of the fire alarm.

The two remaining gunmen took cover behind concrete pillars. Riker stuck his hand through the broken window of the car. He closed his eyes and turned on the brights. The gunmen fired a few shots at the headlights, hitting the front of the car. Then Riker turned off the lights.

Riker stood up and saw the two men leaning against the pillars, squinting into the darkness, their night vision ruined. Riker fired two shots and the two men fell to the ground.

Behind him, Riker heard the sound of the SUV speeding up the ramps towards the exit. He ran over to the men he just shot. He found the keys to the Mercedes in the first man's pocket and a pistol in his shoulder holster.

Wasting no time, Riker got in the car and headed after the SUV. He bounced up when the low riding car hit two of the bodies on its way to the ramp. The car raced around the last turn and he saw the door to the exit sliding up to free Dobbs. The Navigator took off before the door was completely up. The top of the vehicle scraped against the bottom of the door. He came up the ramp to street level and squealed the tires as he turned onto the street.

Riker had the faster car, and he sped up the ramp one moment behind Dobbs. The two cars raced down the empty street. Riker opened his window and put on the cruise control. He leaned out of the window, keeping one hand on the wheel and holding his Glock with the other. He held as steady as he could and shot at the rear tire of the car. The bullet sparked off the pavement an inch from his target. He focused and squeezed the trigger a second time. This bullet hit its mark.

The tire exploded in a puff of compressed air. Sparks flew when the rim scraped the ground and the car lurched to the right. Dobbs corrected with a hard left, and the car hopped the curb. Dobbs slammed on the brakes a moment before he collided with a light pole.

Riker slid back into the seat of the Mercedes and stopped next to the Lincoln. He got out and went over to the crashed Lincoln. He could see that the airbags deployed. The door opened and Dobbs stepped out unsteadily, using the door to support himself.

Riker sprinted and kicked the open door of the SUV. It slammed into Dobbs, smashing his head into the side of the car and crushing his legs between the door and the frame. The door bounced back open and Dobbs fell to the ground.

Dobbs groaned on the ground. He attempted to pull a gun out of his jacket, but Riker knocked his hand away from it.

"You idiot." Dobbs glared up at Riker from the ground. "You are going to die a slow and painful death."

"Maybe, but not tonight, and not at your hands." Riker reached into Dobbs' jacket and took his gun. He dragged him to the Mercedes. "Tonight, you and I are going to have a conversation."

"Don't waste your time. I'm not going to tell you anything. Weaver would kill me if I did. As you saw here tonight, he plans for every eventuality, even your dumb ass attacking me while I'm just trying to relax. My advice to you is to put a gun in your mouth and pull the trigger. That will be the best death you can hope for. If Weaver gets you alive, he will do things to you that you could never even imagine."

Riker opened the trunk of the car. "As you'll soon find out, I'm actually pretty imaginative myself. But you don't need to worry about me. You really need to worry about yourself."

Sirens screamed out in the distance. Riker looked back down the street and he could see people and cars leaving the building they had just come from.

"I'm not worried," Dobbs said. "I'm protected by the most powerful kind of men. If you hurt me, it will be the last mistake you make."

Riker hit Dobbs in the stomach. He doubled over and dropped to his knees. "You lawyers really do like to talk. Right now we need to find someplace more private."

He took off his hoodie and ripped both sleeves off of it. He used one to tie Dobbs' wrists behind his back and the other tied his ankles together. Then he threw him into the trunk.

Dobbs looked up at Riker with venom in his eyes. "You'll regret this."

"You talk tough, Dobbs. I'm about to find out how much of that is an act." Riker shoved another piece of fabric into his mouth. He closed the trunk and drove off into the night.

## 34

RIKER PULLED into the parking lot of the abandoned industrial building, backing his car up to the large bay door on the east side. He'd spotted the place earlier, on the way to Weaver's warehouse, and made note of it. The grass growing freely through the cracks in the pavement and the boards over the windows spoke to the fact that the building hadn't been used for quite some time. Seeing as this was New York City, it surely wouldn't be long before some enterprising young businessman came along and turned it into a dozen lofts that sold for a million dollars a piece or something. But for tonight, it was Riker's.

The abandoned location, the noise of the river nearby, and the late hour all made this place perfect for what he needed to do tonight. It wasn't going to be pretty, and it might get loud.

He walked around to the back of the car, whistling softly to himself. He didn't realize he was doing it until he recognized the tune. It was "The Ants Go Marching," the old nursery rhyme. He almost chuckled as he realized what it was. An old teammate, code-named Timber for both his towering height and his ability to take men out with brutal efficiency, had always whistled that tune when they were engaged in some serious black ops that didn't require silence. It had driven the others nuts, but Timber hadn't been able to stop. It was a weird, unconscious habit that morphed over time from being annoying to being endearing. It eventually got to the point where it felt strange if he wasn't whistling the tune in the lead up to a mission. He'd even whistled it once on a mission that *did* require silence; Morrison had reprimanded him so severely that he hadn't whistled at all for a month after that.

Riker had made fun of Timber mercilessly for the whistling habit, but apparently, he had picked it up himself. He didn't mind. It was like having a piece of his old friend here with him.

He made his way around the car and inspected the large door to the abandoned building. A padlock and chain secured it. He considered whether to try bumping it or using another method, but then he saw an easier way in. The window to the left of the door was boarded over. He managed to pry one board loose and saw most of the glass was gone. In less than three minutes, he'd removed all the boards, and he climbed inside.

He gave the building a quick inspection, kicking up dust with every step. He could actually hear the rats scurrying away as he approached. That was fine with him. It all added to the ambiance. The only light came through cracks in the boarded windows, making it hard to see, but it was enough. After a moment his eyes adjusted to the slivers of light. He spotted what he needed at the north end of the building—a chair and a few old desks. Grabbing the chair, he was about to head back toward the window, but he decided to go through the desk drawers. Most were empty, but a few held deteriorating file folders, which he pushed aside. In the third desk, he found a rusty old flathead screwdriver. He put it in his pocket and carried the chair over near the window. Then he went outside and opened the trunk.

Dobbs' eyes bulged with anger, and he wriggled wildly when Riker grabbed him and hauled him to his feet. His hands and feet were still bound with the sweatshirt sleeves. Riker pulled the one off of his mouth.

"Help!" Dobbs screamed.

Riker's right hand lashed out, catching Dobbs with a mean slap to the side of the head. Dobbs staggered back, but Riker caught him before he could fall.

"You'll probably want to save your voice," Riker said. "You're going to be doing a lot of screaming." Grabbing his arm, he dragged him to the open window. "Climb through."

Dobbs shook his head vehemently. "Oh no, if you think I'm going in there with you, you've got—"

"Fine, I'll do it." Riker grabbed him by the back of his belt and heaved him through the window. Dobbs landed on the floor with a thud. Riker climbed through after him.

He picked Dobbs off the floor and set him in the desk chair.

"What is this place?" Dobbs asked, his voice hoarse with fear.

Riker shrugged. "Beats me. It's pretty isolated though. You can scream all you want now."

Dobbs declined, staring at Riker with wary eyes.

"I'm going to ask you some questions now, Dobbs, and you're going to answer them."

"Like hell I am."

Riker sighed. "Still playing the tough guy, huh?" He reached into his pocket and pulled out the screwdriver. "Here's the thing about torture. It does work eventually, but it takes time. Usually the person lies for a while before they get to the truth. And it's messy work. I'm talking hard, physical labor. A lot of times, you accidentally kill the person, which is always embarrassing."

Dobbs said nothing, but the fear was evident in his eyes now.

"You know what always gets the person in the end?" Riker asked. "It's not the pain, although there will be pain, more than you've ever experienced. More than you would have thought possible. No, what always gets them to talk is the piece-by-piece destruction of their body before their eyes. It's the knowledge that they will never again be the same after this experience, and the longer they wait, the worse it's going to be."

He lifted the screwdriver, making it catch the light just so as Dobbs stared at it.

"Torture itself isn't complicated. Take this screwdriver for example. I could shove it under your fingernails. Flay the skin on your face. Use it to pop out an eyeball. All sorts of neat stuff. Granted, it's rusty, but if you make it to the point where tetanus is a problem that means you lived through this, so you won't have reason to complain. But you know what? I'm not going to start with this."

He slid the screwdriver back into his pocket and untied one of Dobbs' hands, securing the other to the back of the chair with the sweatshirt sleeve. Without warning, he took the pinky finger of Dobbs' free hand and bent it hard to the side, breaking it.

Dobbs cried out in pain and surprise, his eyes wide with terror now.

"Let's get started," Riker said. "These women and kids you bring in...do you usually get them in Miami, or is Li a special case?"

"No," Dobbs said. "We usually have them shipped into the Port of New York and New Jersey. The captains of the shipping vessels help us smuggle the imports in."

Riker fought to keep the smile off his face. A single broken finger and Dobbs was already cracking. Some tough guy. "The imports, huh? That's what you call the human beings who you traffic?"

"Humans? Barely. We're bringing them from one hellish existence in their home countries to another here in the US. At least they get a couple meals a day. Their lives are probably better here."

Riker broke Dobbs' ring finger.

"Ah! I answered, man!"

"Your answer pissed me off. How many have there been? How many women and kids have you helped Weaver smuggle into the country?"

"Total? I don't know. I don't have my records in front of me."

"Ballpark it."

"I don't know. Hundreds."

Riker bent Dobbs' middle finger viciously until it snapped. Dobbs screamed, staring in horror at his mangled hand.

"Let's talk about Li. I take it she's not your usual 'import'?"

"No," Dobbs said, his voice nearly a sob.

"Why Miami?"

"That's where she lived. Her family was visiting the States."

"Her family?" Riker couldn't help himself. He broke the index finger. He waited until the screaming stopped to continue. "I take it her family's some big deal. Is her dad a billionaire or something?"

"Yeah. He's this important guy in China."

"What's his name?"

"Zong Lingyu. Some people we work with on other imports tipped us off that he'd be in the country, and they helped us grab Li down in Florida. Helen went down to get her.

*Zong Lingyu.* Riker filed the name away to look up later.

"Where are they holding Li?"

"I don't know."

Riker gave Dobbs' damaged hand a hard shake. "Listen to me. This hand is never going to be the same. Don't make me ruin the other one too."

"I swear to God, I don't know. They keep me out of that stuff as much as possible. It's a plausible deniability thing."

Riker stared into the man's wide, frightened eyes. Dobbs was telling the truth. Which meant he'd have to play this another way. He reached into Dobbs' jacket pocket and pulled out his cellphone. He went to unlock it and saw it was set up with FaceID security. He held it up in front of Dobbs' face, and the phone unlocked. Going to the contacts, he scrolled until he found Weaver's number, and he pressed it. He waited as the phone rang three times.

"Where are you?" Weaver said. "We've got a problem."

"Yes, you do," Riker said.

There was a long pause.

"Is Dobbs alive?"

Riker grabbed Dobbs' injured index finger and squeezed. Dobbs screamed in pain.

"That answer your question?"

"What do you want?" Weaver asked.

"I think you know the answer to that. I want Li. I'll trade Dobbs for her, straight up."

"I didn't realize you had a thing for little girls, Mr. Riker."

Riker squeezed again, making Dobbs scream. "You're not doing your man any favors. This is a one-time offer. You get Dobbs, and I get Li. I'd highly recommend you accept. Meet me in one hour at the port you use to bring in your imports. We'll do the exchange there."

There was another long pause.

"I'll make the trade, but not there. Too many eyes. And I'll need a little more time to collect Li."

"When and where?" Riker growled.

"I own a property on Briarwood Drive. Dobbs knows the place. It's a new construction, so it'll be empty at night. Meet me there in two hours, and we'll make the trade."

"Agreed. But you try anything funny or you don't show, Dobbs gets a bullet in his head, and the NYPD gets every file on his computer. Understand?"

"Yes. I'll see you in two hours, Mr. Riker."

Riker kept the phone to his ear until he heard the click of the call disconnecting. He turned to Dobbs. "You know about this construction site on Briarwood Drive?"

Dobbs nodded weakly.

"Good." Riker untied his arm from the chair and then resecured his wrists together. Grabbing him by the collar, Riker hauled him to his feet. He had two hours before the meeting, and he had to make them count.

## 35

WITH DOBBS SECURED in the trunk of the car, Riker pulled out his new phone. After he first used the FaceID to unlock the phone, he changed the password and security settings. He now had a list of all the members of Weaver's team and their numbers. He gave Carter a call, but he didn't pick up. Riker worried that he was in a drug-induced coma, but considered that there was no way he would answer a call from Dobbs.

After a quick text explaining that he had Dobbs' phone, Carter picked up. Riker was formulating a plan that could take Weaver out, but he needed the help of his small team.

"How did you get Dobbs' phone?"

"I've got more than his phone. He's in the trunk of my car. I set up a trade for him with Weaver."

"Weaver is going to make a trade? I hate to be the one to tell you, but you'll be walking into a trap."

"No kidding. I have two hours to get things set up, and I need your help. I know Weaver will never bring Li, but I think I can find out where she is. I'm going to need a little more information about this rival gang."

Carter paused. "Before I help you anymore, I need to know that my son is safe."

"He's taken care of. They left town hours ago. I don't know where they went, so I couldn't tell anyone if I wanted to."

Carter started to speak, but his voice cracked. He took a breath and tried again. "Thanks, Riker."

Riker was surprised that Carter still cared so deeply about his son. He was a strung-out criminal of the worst sort, but he still wanted to protect his family. The thought was strange to Riker. He'd never had a real family. He felt connected to the men he served with, but off the battlefield, they could take care of themselves.

"You're welcome. Now let's get down to business. We don't have much time. I need to know where this other gang operates. Any of their buildings will do. It just needs to be important and protected."

"What are you going to do?"

"I'm going to get them pretty pissed off." Riker smirked when he thought about having two major organizations wanting him dead at the same time.

Carter gave him the address of a stash house that Paddock's guys used. It wasn't too far away.

"Great. You are going to get a call in about an hour from Paddock or one of his guys. They will want to know where Weaver is. Tell them that he is making a drop at the Briar-wood Drive location. Make sure that they know it is a big exchange so they will need a lot of guys."

"Holy shit, you're fueling a gang war? You're not actually going to be there, are you?"

"Don't worry about me. Just make sure you give them the information."

"Okay, I'll take care of it."

After hanging up, Riker considered calling Brennan. Calling him on Dobbs' phone was risky. If anyone went back and checked the records, they would see the call was made after Riker had taken Dobbs. It would be pretty obvious at that point that Brennan couldn't be trusted. Riker decided it was worth the risk. No one would have the time to check phone records for the next few days, and by then this was all going to be finished, one way or another.

Brennan answered right away.

"Dobbs?"

"Guess again," Riker said.

"Holy shit, it's true. You got Dobbs. Weaver is freaking out right now. He has everyone scrambling."

"Yep, I've got Dobbs. He's curled up nice and cozy in the trunk of the car. Weaver wants me to meet him to trade for Dobbs. He told me he was going to bring Li, but I'm guessing he is just going to bring a lot of guns. Are you supposed to go to Briarwood Drive?"

"No. I'm heading back to the main office. I'm one of the few guys who aren't going to be there. He's worried that you aren't going to show at the meeting, so he wants his other locations protected."

"Good. It's going to get messy, so I was hoping that you wouldn't be there. I'll be keeping Weaver busy until dawn. I need you to use the time to try and find out where they are keeping Li. Weaver will have as many guys as he can spare watching her. I also have a name I need you to look into. Zong Lingyu."

"Who is that?" Brennan asked.

"He's Li's dad. I'm guessing we will be able to put the pieces together once we figure out what makes him so important. Get all the info you can as fast as you can. I'll call you after the meetup with Weaver, if I'm still alive."

"I'm starting to think the odds are in your favor. Just watch yourself out there."

"You do the same. Weaver is too distracted to look for any leaks in the organization right now, but you still need to watch your back. I'm sure he's going to be unhinged enough to take out anyone he even suspects is working against him."

"I've been dodging suspicions for two years. I think I can do it for another week," Brennan said, and he ended the call.

Riker had just one more call to make on the stolen phone. He opened the contacts and touched Helen's name. She answered on the first ring.

"Where the hell are you, Dobbs?"

"Not Dobbs. Try again."

There was a long silence before she spoke. "Listen, Matthew. I'm sorry things went down the way they did. I truly am. You saved my life. I never meant for you to get hurt."

"And yet here we are," Riker said.

"I owe you one, so let me give you a piece of advice. Leave. Go back to your bees. Weaver's pissed at you, but he has way too much going on right now to waste resources on chasing you back to North Carolina."

"I think you know my answer to that. Not until Li is safe." He paused a moment. "I know you're trying to help me, so let me do the same for you. I know people, Helen. People who could get Li back to her parents and help you get clear of all this."

She barked out a bitter laugh. "How? By testifying? I'm in too deep for that, Riker. I've been in too deep for years."

"Helen, I know from experience that sometimes it feels like you can't start over. But you can. There's always a way out."

"Ah, so that's what this is. You're the prince who's going to save me from my tower and the mean Weaver who has me locked up there. Have you considered that maybe I like my position in life? I worked my ass off to get here, and I'm not giving it up. Certainly not because some country boy doesn't approve of my lifestyle."

"I'm sorry to hear that, Helen. I truly am." With that, he ended the call.

Riker stopped by a gas station on the way to the stash house. He got a portable gas container, three forty ounce beers, some shop rags, and lighters. Once he had his supplies, he headed to the address Carter had given him.

The house was in a bad area of town. The place didn't look like much from the outside, but Riker noticed six cameras when he drove by it. He assumed there were several more that he didn't see. There wasn't anyone in front of the house which would make this easier.

Riker parked down the street. He emptied out the beer from the bottles and filled them with gas. It only took him a few minutes to make three Molotov cocktails. Once they were prepared, he opened the trunk.

"Hey, Dobbs. You are going to take a walk with me."

Dobbs looked up from the trunk. The tough guy attitude was gone and he just lay there.

"Why would I go anywhere with you? You destroyed my hand."

"I think you realize that I am a serious guy, so listen to what I'm about to tell you. You are going to get out of the trunk and do exactly as I say. If you don't, I'll show you that I didn't destroy your hand, I just hurt it. I can always remove those broken fingers. Since I don't have a knife on me, it will take a lot of elbow grease to pop them off."

Dobbs stared up at him, eyes wide with terror. "You're a monster."

Riker laughed. "Guys who sell women and children are monsters. One of the side effects of creatures like you and Weaver are guys like me. Now, are you ready to follow my instructions?"

Dobbs got out of the trunk and stood next to Riker.

"Good boy. Now just stick by my side and keep a lookout. I want you watching high and low."

The two walked in front of the stash house. Dobbs did as he was told and marched next to Riker. When Riker was sure all the cameras had captured Dobbs, he lit the three bottles. He threw the first into the front door. The glass shattered and flames jumped up the front of the house. Dobbs and Riker were illuminated by the orange glow.

Riker quickly threw the next two bottles through the windows. He grabbed Dobbs by the shoulder and they ran back to the car. He could hear shouts from inside the house and he saw several people run out the front door. Their shoes and pant legs caught fire from the gas that burnt on the porch.

Riker threw Dobbs in the passenger seat and then started the car. A gunshot rang out from behind them. One of the men fired a few wild shots at the car. Riker sped off into the night, leaving the glow of the fire behind them.

"What the hell did you just do?" Dobbs asked. "That place had nothing to do with us. I don't even know what it was."

"Don't worry about it. It was just a stop I needed to make before the trade. I think you've had enough time in the front seat though."

He pulled over and tossed Dobbs back in the trunk. As soon as he had the car on the road again, his phone rang.

Carter's name was on the display.

"You succeeded in pissing them off. Paddock's guy called me up and wanted to know where he could find Weaver. He said that Dobbs torched his place."

"Great. Did you tell them where he would be?"

"Yep, I gave them the address. I've got to warn you, they didn't just see Dobbs. They were asking me about a guy that he was with. I think someone recognizes you."

"What did you tell them?"

"I said that I had no idea who Dobbs was with. There are a lot of guys and I don't know all of them. They pressed the issue for a while. I don't think that they believed me."

"Thanks for the heads up. I don't think that will matter by morning. I'm hoping these guys will be in shambles by the time this is over." Riker was about to hang up, but he thought about Carter's kid. "Carter, do me a favor and don't put any of that shit in your veins tonight. If things go the way I plan, you may be able to walk away from all of this. It's a chance most people don't get."

There was a long pause, and Riker wasn't sure they were still connected. Finally, Carter spoke again. "I swear that I'm finished with that shit." There was another short pause, and Riker heard a toilet flush. "I just got rid of the stuff I had. I'm not going to blow this chance."

"I hope that's true." Riker hung up the phone.

He knew that the odds of Carter getting clean were close to zero. Still, something in his voice almost convinced him that he would do it. Normally when guys like that talked about getting clean there was either overconfidence or a tremble that said they knew they couldn't. Riker didn't hear either of those things when Carter spoke. He heard acceptance and resolve. Riker actually found himself rooting for the guy. He hoped this was his bottom and that he could turn himself around.

He pushed the thought out of his mind. His mission wasn't to save a junkie. He looked at the clock and saw that he had fifty minutes to get to the meeting site. That meant that he could get there with enough time to scope out the area and set up. He knew the next few hours would be dark and bloody, but he wouldn't lose sleep over the death of anyone who trafficked in human life.

He thought about the promises that he had made to Morrison. He had already broken too many of those promises to think it would go unnoticed. He figured that his life was forfeited at this point. He wanted to make the time he had left count for something. If a little girl who loved superheroes got to live, that seemed like a fair trade.

## 36

RIKER ARRIVED at the construction site on Briarwood Drive a half-hour before the meeting was scheduled to start. He parked a block away and left Dobbs in the trunk while he went to check out the location.

He noticed a Mercedes parked across the street, lights off, with two dark figures inside. Weaver must have sent a couple guys ahead to watch for Riker's arrival. That was fine. They could watch him work. In the darkness, they'd have little if any idea what he was doing.

The building on the site was nothing more than a four-story skeletal structure. In the darkness, it looked like some ancient, unfinished temple rising toward the sky. Riker walked around the structure twice, making note of the blind spots and any good places for cover. He entered the structure itself, walking each floor and climbing the work ladders until he reached the top floor and took in the property from above. He made note of the crane mounted on top of the building, its hook attached to a steel beam on the ground, even climbing into the operator's seat to get a view of the area from that angle.

When he was satisfied he had a good handle on the layout, he returned to his car and got Dobbs out of the trunk. He dragged the whimpering man across the construction site, to a spot with a view of the property from three angles and a construction trailer at their backs. There they waited.

Weaver's people started showing up ten minutes before the meeting. The first car parked on the north side of the property, its headlights pointed toward the center. The second parked on the south side, bathing the yard with light from that angle. The third and final car parked on the west side. Most of the property was illuminated by headlights now, but Riker thought he could use that. The low angle of the light cast odd shadows, and men looking anywhere but east would have bright lights shining in their eyes.

As if responding to some unknown signal, all four cars, including the one across the street, opened their doors at once. Three men filed out of each car, except the one across the street, which held two. Eleven guys. Riker didn't like his odds. He'd have to play this very well and get the timing exactly right.

Riker spotted Weaver immediately, mostly by the protective way his men circled around him as they approached. Another familiar figure towered over the others—Hendricks. The light wasn't good enough for Riker to get a good read on his injuries, but he had to be hurting from the previous night.

To Riker's complete lack of surprise, there was no little girl with them.

Riker stood with his back to the trailer, Dobbs between him and the approaching men. He held his Glock 19 in his right hand. The magazine was full and Dobbs' gun was

tucked into the back of his belt. Two guns and two magazines for eleven guys—not great.

"Mr. Riker," Weaver said in a loud voice when they were
twenty feet away. "Are you ready to make the exchange?"

"I brought my guy," Riker answered, scanning the others,
waiting to see who would make the first move. He needed to
be ready. "Where's Li?"

"She's safe, for the moment."

"Weaver," Dobbs shouted, his voice close to panic, "this
guy's crazy! He broke my fingers. He—"

In the illumination of the headlights, Riker saw Weaver
nod to someone to his right. That was it, Riker knew. The
signal.

At the nod, Riker shoved Dobbs forward and ducked
down, diving to his left. At the same time, Hendricks raised
his weapon and fired. Dobbs jerked as the bullet struck him
in the head. Whatever caliber weapon Hendricks was using,
it was big enough to make one hell of an exit wound. Blood
and brain matter splattered onto the trailer behind Dobbs,
and onto Riker.

Riker ignored it, moving fast, disappearing into the
shadows on the far side of the trailer before Dobbs' body hit
the ground. He moved to his right, working along the edge
of the construction site, doing his best to stay in the shadows. He wanted the headlights behind him, so that anyone
shooting at him would have the lights in their eyes.

Weaver's men scanned the perimeter, searching for him.
He crouched down behind a pile of steel beams and waited.

"Dobbs worked for me for thirty years," Weaver said. "I
considered him a dear friend. As you can see, I'm taking this
situation rather seriously."

Hendricks crept along the edge of the site, moving near
the trailer, looking for Riker in the shadows.

"If I'm willing to do that to a friend, what do you think I'd do to Li?"

Riker waited, watching the others. They would spread out soon, he hoped, and he'd start taking them one-by-one. He didn't have to kill them all; he just needed to stall until the second part of his plan began.

"You should know that I left very specific instructions with the men guarding Li," Weaver said. "If I don't check in with them in thirty minutes, they put a bullet in her head."

This wasn't working. The men were staying clustered together. He needed to draw them out more. He turned, facing away from Weaver, hoping his voice would echo off the car to his left, making it difficult to pinpoint his location.

"Bullshit!" he shouted. "I heard that girl's worth seven figures. No way you'd give that up."

As soon as he finished speaking, he started moving, running in a low crouch toward another bit of cover up ahead.

"My life is worth considerably more than seven figures," Weaver answered. "If I'm dead, what do I need money for? And the men with Li have no understanding of her true value. They'll follow orders."

Riker gritted his teeth. He hated to admit it, but he believed Weaver. The man was egotistical enough to burn the world down in his own wake.

"Why don't you step into the light so we can have a civilized conversation?" Weaver asked.

But Riker was barely listening. His attention was focused on the four cars racing toward the construction site. As they skidded off the road and men poured out, Riker smiled. Paddock's gang had arrived.

In an instant, the construction site erupted in chaos. Weaver's men had no idea who these new arrivals were, but they knew they were shooting at them. Two men fell to Paddock's gang's bullets. Weaver's men herded him toward the trailer, trying to get him to safety.

Riker scanned the construction site, looking for Hendricks. The last thing he needed was that guy sneaking up behind him. He wouldn't want to face Hendricks in a fair fight, let alone be caught off guard by him.

"Riker, remember what I said!" Weaver shouted. "If I die, so does she!"

Riker cursed softly. Paddock had Weaver outnumbered fifteen to eleven. As much as Riker hated it, he was going to have to help Weaver get out of this alive. He glanced toward the center of the construction site, suddenly aware of what he needed to do.

Gunfire spat from every direction as he made his way across the site. He stuck to the shadows as much as possible, but the scene was total chaos. Odds of him catching a stray bullet were way too high for his liking.

Up ahead, he saw three of Paddock's men stalking toward the trailer where Weaver was huddled. He waited in the shadows until they were ten feet away and fired. His first shot caught the first man in the chest. His second hit another in almost the same spot. His last shot took the third man in the head. All three were down before they even fired a round. Normally, Riker would have put at least two bullets in each of them, but at this point, he cared more about getting to his target than ensuring they were dead. He paused just long enough to grab a magazine from one of their Glocks before moving on.

He'd just about reached the unfinished building when something struck a steel beam three feet from his head. He turned and saw Hendricks glaring at him, weapon raised. Half the hair on his head was gone, and his face displayed some nasty burns. Apparently, while the rest of the gang members were focused on killing each other as Riker had intended, Hendricks had a more pressing goal—revenge.

Riker raised his gun and fired back, putting three bullets into the empty space where Hendricks had just been. The big man moved surprisingly fast, diving back into the shadows. Riker considered whether to pursue him for a moment, then decided against it. He ran to the nearest work ladder and started up into the building.

When he reached the top floor, he paused, checking the scene below. Paddock's men had Weaver's crew nearly surrounded now. It wouldn't be long before they took him out. Riker needed to act fast.

He grabbed a cinder block off a stack near the corner of the building. Then ran to the crane and climbed into the operator's seat. He wasn't entirely sure he had a full understanding of the controls, but this was no time for indecision. He started the crane, grabbed the stick and pressed the right foot pedal. To his relief, the arm began to move. As soon as it did, every eye on the ground turned up toward him. Good. Their attention would buy him a moment.

He swung the crane arm out over Paddock's men gathering near the trailer, and he let the steel beam drop. Below, the men shouted as they attempted to dive out of the way. Two of them were crushed.

Both groups were shouting now, and Riker couldn't make out what they were saying. But then, as one, their attention turned from each other to the crane above. The men on both sides started shooting at him.

"Great," Riker muttered. "You try to help someone..."

From this distance, their pistols weren't likely to hit him, but he still didn't like the idea of being trapped on top of this building. He saw a handful of guys running toward the structure, no doubt planning on cornering him on the top floor. It was time to get moving.

First, he had one more weapon in his arsenal. Ignoring the bullets firing up at him, he began to work the controls again. He moved the hook, swinging it toward the building. On his first try, it caught nothing. But on the second try, the hook latched onto one of the steel girders that built the floor of the second story. Once he was sure it was securely hooked, Riker grabbed the cinder block he'd set next to him and held it over the right foot pedal. He took a deep breath and let it drop.

As the boom arm retracted, trying to raise the hook, Riker jumped out of the operator's seat and sprinted toward the back of the building. The crane let out a terrible whine as Riker reached the second set of ladders at the back of the building and started down. He was almost to the first floor by the time the crane pulled itself free of its base and tumbled to the ground, landing near where both gangs were gathered with a terrible crash.

Shouts of pain and panic filled the air as Riker reached the ground level, but he didn't bother looking back. He sprinted away from the scene, running toward his car parked a block away. He'd managed to do some damage to two gangs, but they would both be after him now.

He just hoped he'd bought Brennan enough time to find something they could use.

## 37

As the sun rose over the New York skyline, the city began to pulse with life. Riker's heart was finally slowing down to a normal pace as the adrenaline from the battle left his body. He had wanted to wipe out Weaver and his gang tonight. Now he found himself hoping that Weaver was still alive. If he died in the fight, Li was already dead.

He kept his eyes on his rearview mirror as he drove, watching for a tail, but he didn't see one. The construction site exchange had been a disaster, but if Brennan dug up Li's location it wouldn't be a total loss. Riker tapped Brennan's name on the screen of Dobbs' phone.

"Hey Bill, this isn't the best time," Brennan said in a rushed voice. "Can I give you a call later?"

"I take it you're not alone right now. Did Weaver live?"

"Yep."

"Did you find any information?" Riker knew that he shouldn't keep Brennan on the phone, but he didn't want to wait for any info.

"Yeah, but I gotta go. I'll call you later." Brennan hung up the phone.

Riker's mind felt foggy. No sleep and little food were taking their toll. No matter how much he wanted to keep working to save Li, he needed a clear head. Right now, there wasn't anything he could do without more information. He picked up some fast food on the way back to the hotel. Once the smell of the food hit his nose, his stomach screamed out for sustenance. The bag of food was empty within two blocks.

Riker parked the car around the block and walked to his hotel room. Once inside, he threw his clothes on the bed and inspected his wounds. Blood seeped through the bandages on his shoulder and the leg. Seeing the injuries made his mind pay attention to them again, and the pain came back stronger than before. Exhaustion was setting in, but he forced himself to re-dress the wounds. Once they were clean and cared for, he made one more call, promising himself he could sleep when it was done.

"I can't believe that you're still alive," Carter said when he picked up the phone.

"Honestly I'm a little surprised about it too. Things didn't go exactly as I planned. Have you heard from anyone?"

"Yeah. Paddock's guys really want to find you. They called me asking if I knew anything about you or where you were. I told them I had no idea who you were, but I could tell that they were pissed."

"Did they mention anything about Weaver? Did they get him?"

"They said that the attack tonight was a total cluster fuck. They didn't get Weaver and both sides lost a couple of guys. What are you going to do now?"

"I'm working on figuring out where Li is. After that, I'm going to get her. If you hear anything about where she is or get any useful information, let me know." Riker's eyelids felt heavy as he spoke.

"If I hear something, I'll let you know, but I may not be much use to you for a little while. I'm starting to feel like shit."

Riker could hear the fear in Carter's voice. He knew what was coming.

"All right. Just stay in your room and remember that it will pass. If I call, answer the phone." Riker didn't know what to say to a junkie who was about to go into withdrawal. That was the best he had.

"That's right. It will pass." Carter hung up the phone.

Riker made sure his phone was on full volume and set it on the stand next to the bed. Sleep overtook him moments after his head hit the pillow.

*Riker crouches in a basement, wiring up the last charge of C4. Two teammates watch the entrances, making sure he has time to work. Once the charges are set and concealed, the three go across the street and watch through the window of their room.*

*They are in Al Ghuta, an area that most Americans couldn't find on a map. Riker watches junk cars drive by the building through his binoculars. His two teammates sit in silence, waiting for his signal. The tension is always high in these moments. Some people wouldn't be able to keep their mouths shut, but these men have all lived through moments like this before. The things they are thinking about couldn't be put into words.*

*A car stops in front of the building across the street. Riker watches the men get out and walk inside.*

*"We have confirmation on target one," Riker reports to the men in the room.*

*"Roger that," Brown answers. He takes out a small black case and opens it up on the floor. Inside is a slot for a key and a switch covered by a white plastic tab.*

*A few minutes later a second car appears. Four men get out, and Riker watches their faces through the binoculars.*

*"Confirmation of target two," Riker says, his eyes fixed on the building.*

*"Roger that, target two." Brown sticks a key into the case and turns it. A red light starts to flash. He flips up the plastic cover to expose the switch.*

*A woman and a child approach on foot. Riker draws a sharp breath as they enter the building. "Hold. We have civilians inside."*

*Brown keeps his hand over the switch. "We have a go for collateral damage on this one. Can you confirm that both targets are inside?"*

*Riker looks from the building to his teammate. He opens his mouth but nothing comes out. The pulse of the red light gives an intermittent glow to Brown's face.*

*"Can you confirm?" Brown asks again.*

Riker's eyes opened and he sat up in bed. The phone was ringing on the nightstand next to him. He scooped it up and saw Brennan's name on the screen.

"Hey." Riker was still half in the dream and his own voice sounded distant.

"You awake enough to talk?" Brennan asked.

Riker looked at the phone. He had been asleep for five hours. "Yeah, I'm up. What do you have?"

"Lots. First off, Li is a really big deal. I guess not Li, but her dad. He's a major political figure in China. He's pushing a democratic agenda that the Communist Party really does not like. He has enough popularity that they can't kill him without unifying the people."

"But, they are hoping to get him to shut up," Riker guessed. "Holding his daughter captive would be a good way to do it."

"Exactly. Weaver doesn't give a shit about politics, but he does care about the money. Li isn't a seven-figure job. She's a nine-figure job."

"Holy shit."

"Yep, there is a lot of money and power in China right now and the people that have it don't want to give it up. They are paying one hundred million for that kid."

"No wonder Weaver and Paddock are willing to sacrifice so much for her."

"That brings me to the second piece of information. Apparently, a tentative truce formed after last night's events. Weaver and Paddock had a little sit-down and worked out some kind of deal. Apparently, that much money is enough to go around."

Riker thought about that for a moment. "I guess a chunk of a hundred million bucks is a good deal, but I can't believe they agreed to work together."

"Well, you had a little something to do with that. Weaver told them all about you. He said you set them up for last night by torching their safe house. He also let them know you were the guy that messed up their operation in North Carolina. Basically, he used the enemy of my enemy argument in combination with a lot of money."

"Damn it. I was hoping to pit them against each other, not bring them together."

"The good news just keeps coming. You ready for more?"

"Let's hear it."

"The trade for Li goes down tomorrow. If you want to save her, tonight is the night."

"Please tell me you have a lead on where she is."

"I did come through on that one. I talked to one of the crew this morning. He said that Helen was looking hotter than ever. She and Li are at Weaver's place in the city."

Riker sat up straight on the bed. "That's great. We can get in there and grab her."

"That's not great. Weaver is there with most of the crew. That place is a fortress on an average day. Right now, he is on full alert and fully armed. We're about twenty guys short of what we'd need to storm in and get her out."

"We've got the rest of the day to come up with a plan to even the odds. Can you meet up, or will they notice you leaving?"

"They gave me some time to get some rest. I don't have to see anyone until tonight."

"All right, I'll see you at your place."

Riker threw on his clothes and got ready to head out.

He called Carter to check in before he left, but there was no answer, even after three tries. He thought about Carter's motel. It was probably the worst place to leave a junkie. The area had as many dealers as liquor stores. Riker decided to grab him on the way to Brennan's. He told himself that a third guy may help, even if it was Carter. There might be a way to use him as a distraction. Riker knew that deep down he had a soft spot for the guy. He wasn't exactly sure why. Maybe it was because he had helped save his family. Maybe it was because if Carter could find redemption it was possible for anyone.

When he arrived at the motel, Riker spent a few minutes scoping out the area. When he was confident that it was safe, he headed to Carter's room. The door was locked and the lights were off, so Riker let himself in with the bump key. He assumed he would find Carter sleeping on the bed, or puking in the bathroom. When he turned on the light, he found a much more gruesome scene.

Carter's body was tied to a chair. His head was slumped forward and blood covered his clothes and the carpet around his feet. His right ear was missing, which gave his head a misshapen look. Riker walked over to him and touched his neck. The body was cold. They must have gotten to him shortly after his last phone call.

Riker looked at him for a moment and saw that there was something on his forehead. The word "Traitor" was carved into his skin in blocky lines.

Riker stared at the dead man. He could see by the blood that covered the damage that it had been done while he was still alive. Then a thought occurred to him.

Paddock must have given up Carter as a peace offering to Weaver. If Riker's actions had not united the gangs Carter would still be alive.

He forced himself to take another good look at the man in the chair. He inspected every cut and bruise. Rage built up inside of him. Riker swore that he would remember Carter when Weaver begged him for mercy.

Before, he had wanted nothing more than Li's safety. By the time he left the room, he had something much more destructive in mind.

## 38

THIRTY-MINUTES LATER, Riker knocked on Brennan's door. His knuckle left a little smudge of blood where he'd hit the wood. He didn't know whose blood it was—his, Carter's, or one of the many guys he'd made bleed in recent days—but seeing that dark red smudge brought him back to all the violence he'd seen over the years, from the first guy whose nose he'd bloodied on the playground to the last guy he'd killed for QS-4. He'd thought those days were over, but here he was again. Maybe they'd never be over. Maybe he didn't want them to be. The things he did weren't nice, but there was no denying he was good at them. Few people who could do what he could. He was in elite company when it came to dealing out death.

The thought sickened him. Over the past six years, he'd almost started to believe that maybe there was more to him than all that. That there was another life for him besides one spent performing acts of violence. But deep inside, he'd known. This was who he was.

The peephole darkened, then the door opened.

Brennan nodded hello. "Get in here before anyone sees you."

Riker trudged inside just far enough for Brennan to shut the door.

"You all right?" Brennan asked, looking him up and down.

"Fine." Riker didn't know which of his many injuries Brennan was referring to, and he didn't care. He was in some pain, mostly from the burn and the bullet wound, but he was fully functional. That was what mattered. He could do what needed to be done to get Li back. "Tell me about Weaver's house."

"You get right to business, don't you?" Brennan said with a smile.

"Sorry," Riker said. "How's the family? Are the kids good?"

Brennan shot him a look. "Fine, down to business. I think we can expect at least a dozen guys at Weaver's tonight. All packing and keeping an eye out for your ugly mug."

"Entrances?"

"Front door and back door. Both will be guarded, of course. There's roof access, but that'll be guarded too. Not to mention the security system. Cameras everywhere, monitored on-site. If you thought Dobbs' house was wired, you ain't seen nothing yet. There's no way you're getting in without them spotting you."

Riker thought for a moment. "You've been inside?"

Brennan nodded.

"Draw the layout for me?"

Brennan led Riker to the living room. The notebook where Brennan had written his number was still on the coffee table. He picked up the pen next to it and started drawing, taking Riker through the house room by room.

"This is where Li will be?" Riker asked when Brennan got to the third floor.

"Stands to reason. There are three guest bedrooms on that floor. I'll bet Weaver's got her in one of them. My guess would be it's the first one on the left as you come up the steps. That room only has one window. The others both have two."

Riker picked up the notebook and studied the diagrams Brennan had drawn, trying to picture the layout and cement it in his mind. If he somehow did manage to get inside, he wouldn't have time to wander around and get his bearings. He'd need to get to Li quickly. When he found her, he'd have to figure out a way to get a three-year-old kid out through a dozen gunmen and a barrage of flying bullets. Looking at the layout in black and white on paper, it looked like a dire situation. He didn't have long to come up with a solution either.

"How are you sitting for weapons?" Brennan asked.

"I've got two Glock 19s and four mags. One half empty."

Without a word, Brennan got up and went to the bedroom. He came back a moment later and set two more magazines on the table. "Better to have them and not need them."

"Thank you," Riker said, picking them up and putting them in his pocket. "That gives me seventy rounds if my count on the half mag is right. Lord help me if I need more than that. You wouldn't happen to have a knife, would you?"

"Only of the kitchen variety," Brennan said with a grin.

Riker thought for a moment, then shrugged. "I'll take it."

Brennan went to the kitchen and got a steak knife, which Riker stuck in his belt.

"I'll have about eighty rounds myself," Brennan said as he sat back down. "So between that and your arsenal of guns and kitchenware, we should be all set."

Riker raised an eyebrow.

"What?" Brennan said. "Like I'm not coming with you?"

"You'd do that? Come along on this suicide mission?"

Brennan shrugged. "I've lived under the near-constant threat of death for two years. I say, bring it."

Riker gave him a long look, trying to figure out if the guy was serious. He was. The more time Riker spent with Brennan, the more he was starting to like him. He hadn't expected to find a friend in New York, but he was damn glad he had.

"I appreciate the offer," Riker said, "but no."

"No?"

"Look, if I fail to get Li back, which is a very strong possibility, I need someone who knows what's going on and is still alive."

"Don't give me that shit."

"I'm serious, Brennan. There are not many people I trust, and you're starting to become one of them. I don't want you getting killed on some dumb suicide mission. I need you to promise to protect Li if I can't."

Brennan stared at Riker with hard eyes. He nodded. "Yeah, okay. I promise."

"Good." Riker glanced out the window and saw the sun had almost set. He looked at his watch. "We should head over there. You can drive me?"

"You got it."

They'd been driving a few blocks, Brennan behind the wheel and Riker in the passenger seat, when Brennan spoke again. "The stuff I told you about Li's father. How he's trying to spread democracy in China and all that. That has some big implications. If you save Li, it could potentially change the course of China's government."

"And if I don't save her?"

"Same thing, but the other way. All I'm saying is, it brings a lot more weight to this thing, doesn't it?"

Riker thought a moment, then sighed. "Honestly, man, that shit's all above my paygrade. I don't care if she's the next Dalai Lama or some homeless orphan. She's just a kid who's in trouble and she thinks I can help her. I don't want to prove her wrong."

Brennan smiled. "I knew you were good people the moment we met."

"Must be rare meeting good people, especially as a cop, even before you were undercover."

"Not really. I mean, on the one hand, yeah, you've got Weaver and his crew. They're the worst of the worst. Absolute scum. But they're the exception. In my experience, the vast majority of people are out there just trying to do their best. They may not always get it right, but they're trying hard. That's why I do what I do—to protect the regular good people from the outliers like Weaver."

Riker let out a chuckle. "Wow, Brennan, I'm surprised to hear such a positive worldview from a New York City cop. Especially one undercover with Weaver. I gotta imagine you've seen some things that would have most people changing their minds."

Brennan's expression grew serious. For a long moment, he didn't answer. When he did, his voice was thick with emotion. "I have. If there's worse out there than the things I've seen, I don't even want to know about it. But I made myself a promise early on. I vowed that no matter what happened, I wouldn't let it change me. Not the core of me, who I really am. That positive worldview. It's the one thing they can never take away from me. If I start seeing the world the way they see it, then I've lost everything. I'd be a shell of a man. There's no way I want to live like that."

Riker stared out the windshield, watching the buildings roll by. How long had it been since he'd seen the world the way Brennan saw it? His SEAL days? High school? Before? He'd always told himself that his cynical worldview was some sort of hard-won wisdom. But here was a man who'd seen the absolute worst, just like Riker, and he still thought people had good at their core. Not just three-year-old girls, either. All of them.

Did that make Riker a shell of a man?

Brennan glanced over and saw the expression on Riker's face. "Oh hey, look man, I didn't mean anything about you."

"No, I know," Riker said.

"Everyone's got their own way of handling things. You cope with stuff in the way that works for you." He hesitated, as if not sure whether to continue. "All I'm saying is that one of the few things you control in life is the way you see the world. Why not look at it in a positive light? Funny thing about people—they can be sons of bitches sometimes, but they're worth it."

They drove in silence the rest of the way. After about fifteen minutes, Brennan pulled over, parking under a large oak tree. He pointed to a house half a block down and across the street.

"That's the one. I figured it might be dangerous to get any closer. They might recognize my car."

"Good call," Riker said. "Remember what we talked about."

Brennan nodded. "I'll be a good little boy and wait in the car."

Riker stared at the house for a long moment, trying to

line the windows up in his mind with the layout Brennan had drawn in his notebook. Even from this distance, he could see a large man standing near the door, arms crossed.

Brennan reached under his car seat and pulled out a pair of binoculars. When he saw Riker's surprised expression, he said, "Never leave home without them."

"Very cop-like of you."

Brennan held the binoculars to his eyes for a moment, then offered them to Riker. He took them and peered through. After a moment of adjustment, he could see the house as clearly as if he were standing in front of it.

"These things are powerful," he said.

"Only the best for the NYPD's finest."

Riker took a closer look at the large, stoic man standing in front of the door. He looked tough enough to at least raise the alarm before Riker took him down. Not that Riker had ever planned to go in through the front door.

He angled the binoculars upward, intending to check out the situation on the roof, but he paused when he saw something in the third-floor window. Hendricks stood peering out at the street, his large frame filling the entire window. Riker could see him much more clearly now than he had the previous night. At least a quarter of his hair was burned away, and his scalp and the left side of his face were covered with blisters. The surly expression on his face spoke to the pain Riker knew he must be feeling. All the while, his eyes scanned the street searching. Looking for Riker.

Suddenly, Hendricks turned, as if someone had spoken to him. He glanced back at the street once more and reluctantly stepped away.

Riker kept watching the window, though he wasn't sure why. After a moment, a much smaller figure appeared.

It was Li.

## 39

THE SUN WENT DOWN on the city as Riker went over his plan one last time in his mind. He needed to take out at least twelve guys while keeping a small girl alive. It was a long shot, but he had faced long odds before. He checked his gear, said goodbye to Brennan, and headed across the street.

While Riker appreciated the detail and architecture of the brownstone homes, he didn't care about the looks, just the functionality. The stone structures and outcroppings made them easy to climb. He scaled the side of a home eight houses down from Weaver's.

The high-end homes all had rooftop decks. Riker crept from one to the next. Each had outdoor kitchens and gardens. He kept to the shadows and stayed low. Each area had high side walls giving it privacy from the neighbors. He went over each one until he came to the home next to Weaver's.

Riker crouched behind the six-foot wall and heard voices on the other side. He listened and made out two distinct male voices.

"You do not want to be around Hendricks right now. I

heard he broke Charley's nose just because he said that the burns don't look that bad. The guy shouldn't be working right now. He's out of control."

"You'd be out of control too if your head was all burnt up. I'd hate to be the guy that did that to Hendricks. He's going to kill him slowly."

Riker moved to the edge of the building and looked around the end of the wall. He saw the two men sitting on outdoor chairs. Each one had an assault rifle lying across their laps. They were smoking and they shared an ashtray on a small table between them. Neither was taking the job of guarding the roof seriously. That was all the advantage Riker needed.

A brick wall was the only thing separating the two men from Riker. He moved to their position and got out his knife. The anticipation of battle filled his body. His heart quickened and his senses seemed to come alive. Two men sat one foot away from him, and in seconds they would be dead. Or he would be. His grip on the knife's handle tightened, and he took a step back, every muscle in his body tightening.

He sprang into motion, putting one hand on top of the wall and swinging his body over. He came down between the two seated men on the other side. The man to his right let out a single grunt when Riker slammed a blade through the side of his neck. He used so much force that the blade poked through the other side of the man's neck and his hand slammed against the puncture wound.

An expression of shock and confusion appeared on the other man's face. He grabbed at the rifle on his lap. Riker stepped on the weapon, pinning it to his legs and pressing the man down in his chair. He struggled against the weight, trying to free his weapon.

Riker yanked the knife out of the first man's neck. He put

pressure on it, slicing forward as he pulled. Blood sprayed from the wound the moment the blade came free. Riker spun his body and brought the knife into the second man's neck. His eyes went wide and he tried to scream, but the air passage to his lungs was blocked by a steel blade. Riker pulled the knife out and the man slumped forward, joining his friend face down on the roof. Two down.

Riker looked around the deck. It was just like Brennan had described. Double doors led into the house. A large hot tub and an outdoor kitchen stood next to them.

Riker took an assault rifle and a radio from one of the guards. He went over to the hot tub and found the electrical box on the wall next to it. He opened it and flipped the large breaker that controlled the electricity to the hot tub. A flexible metal conduit went from the breaker to the tub. He grabbed it and pulled as hard as he could until the wire came free from the tub. He stripped back the end of the electrical wire with his knife and laid it next to the doors.

Next, he found the water spigot on the side of the house. He put the hose near the electrical wire and turned it on full. While water flooded the deck, he took a plastic chair and put it next to the breaker and stood on top of it. Satisfied, he took the radio and pressed the call button.

He did his best to imitate the voice of one of the men he had killed and screamed into the radio. "He's here on the roof! We have him pinned down. Get your asses up here!"

As soon as he made the warning, he emptied half the assault rifle's magazine into the side of the hot tub. Water gushed onto the deck. He grabbed the breaker and waited.

A voice yelled out through the radio, "We're coming up. Did you get him?"

Riker fired another few shots into the tub and clicked the button. "Hurry up!"

The doors burst open and six guys stepped out. Water rushed around their feet and Riker flipped the switch.

The six men fell to the roof in unison. They convulsed for a moment before their muscles locked in place. Riker forced the breaker to hold the connection as smoke rose from the wires. He released the fuse, killing the power. Eight down.

Riker ran to the edge of the roof. He looked down and spotted the guard at the front of the house. He paused for a moment, then set the rifle down; he needed both hands for this. He flipped over the edge and started to scale down the front of the building.

As he descended, a voice called out on the radio. "What's going on up there? Is he dead?" It was Hendricks.

The guard below him looked up at the sound of the radio. Riker was still fifteen feet above him. He didn't hesitate, pushing off the side of the building and jumping towards the large man. The guard pulled his pistol and stepped to the side, moving out of the way, but not far enough. Riker was able to grab his arm as he landed. He bent his legs and kept his momentum going, leaning into the force of the fall. Both men tumbled down the front steps.

Riker tucked and rolled down the short flight of concrete stairs that led to the sidewalk. The edge of the old steps pounded into his sides and back, but he was ready and came to his feet once he reached the bottom. The guard was less acrobatic. He tumbled down, flailing and trying to grab onto anything he could. His arms smashed against the stairs and the gun clattered to the sidewalk when it flew from his hand.

Both men stood facing each other. Adrenaline hid the pain of any injuries they had taken from the fall. The guard had seemed big when Riker saw him from down the street.

Now that he stood toe-to-toe with the man, he looked like a monster. He was two inches taller than Riker and outweighed him by eighty pounds. Riker went for his gun but the big guy moved with surprising speed. He threw a jab, hitting Riker in the side of the face. The blow put him off balance and a second jab landed, knocking him back farther. If he would have thrown another few quick shots, Riker might have lost the fight. Instead he drew back a hook intended to end the fight.

The slower punch gave Riker enough time to get his footing. He could tell this guy had boxed before, or at least brawled a lot. When he threw the hard punch, Riker shot at his legs and took the fight to the ground. The big guy clearly wasn't used to anyone coming at him in a fight. He hit the ground hard from the takedown. Riker spun around to his back and slid an arm around the man's neck.

The guard grabbed Riker's arm with his hands, keeping some of the pressure off of his neck. He was strong as an ox and started to stand up with Riker on his back. Riker kicked out the back of his knee, and he fell forward like a cut tree. The guy never let go of Riker's arm, and his face bounced off the sidewalk.

His grip on Riker's arm relaxed as blood pooled around his head. Riker didn't take any chances and tightened his grip around the neck. After a few seconds, he was satisfied that the man was not getting back up. Nine down.

Riker stood and a wave of pain ran through him. Blood dripped down his arm, and he knew that the stitches in his shoulder had ripped open. He took a breath and focused. There would be time to deal with the pain later. He had a mission now. He took one of the Glocks from his belt and trudged to the door.

He swung the door open and stayed low. The sitting

room was empty and laid out exactly as Brennan had described. He moved quickly down the hall towards the stairs. With any luck, the remaining men would be on the roof trying to figure out what had happened and where he was. He could come up behind them and finish them off.

He reached the bottom of the stairs and saw movement from the room on his left. He stepped back and turned to see the flash of a gun barrel. If he hadn't caught the movement in his peripheral, he would have taken a bullet to the head. Instead, the small piece of lead hit the wall an inch from his face.

He dove blindly toward the shooter and grabbed the wrist holding the gun. Another shot fired, hitting the ceiling. His ears rang from the sound echoing in the small hallway. He looked at his attacker and saw Hendricks staring at him, hate in his eyes.

Hendricks brought his head down hard and smashed it into Riker's face. Riker saw stars and his legs went weak. His body wanted to fade to black, but he knew that would mean death. He focused on holding the wrist with the gun and used all his will to return strength to his legs.

Hendricks spun his body, trying to pull his wrist free. Riker held on and was spun with the arm. Hendricks swung his left fist into Riker's side, connecting with his rib cage. The pain helped him snap back from the edge of unconsciousness.

Riker twisted Hendricks' wrist and pulled down hard. He brought his knee up to meet the back of Hendricks' elbow. When the two connected, the arm bent an inch past the normal stopping point, and the gun dropped to the floor.

Hendricks yelled out in pain and brought up a knee of his own. It connected with Riker's stomach. The force was enough to lift him half an inch off the ground. Riker stumbled back half a foot and slammed into the wall behind him. He sucked in a breath and saw feet coming down the stairs. Hendricks threw a hard left hoping to finish Riker, but he ducked and the punch slammed into the wall.

Riker watched four men run down the stairs all with their weapons drawn. Hendricks saw them too and moved back by the stairs, away from Riker. Riker dove into the kitchen on the other side of the hallway as bullets flew behind him.

## 40

IF RIKER HAD one philosophy when it came to combat, it was this—never give your enemy a fair fight. Control as many factors as humanly possible to give yourself the best chance at survival. It had been true going all the way back in his time on the wrestling mat. There were rules, yes, but there were plenty of ways to turn the fight to your advantage that had nothing to do with wrestling moves. Everything from how you looked at the other guy at weigh-in to how you walked up to the mat; it all mattered. Back in the day, Riker had carefully orchestrated every moment to give himself slightly better odds than the other guy.

That rule was doubly true when facing multiple opponents. Real life wasn't like the movies—taking on two guys in a straight-up fight was an incredible challenge with very long odds, even for the most skilled fighters. That was why Riker did his best never to take on more than one person in a straight-forward manner. Whether it was a helium tank to the face or a current of electricity applied to a water-logged deck, he was always seeking the advantage.

And now here he was, cornering himself in a kitchen

with Hendricks and at least four other guys fast approaching. His odds were not great in this situation, and he still hadn't set eyes on Li. His mind raced, trying to find any advantage against the five armed men.

He pushed himself to his feet, starting toward the island in the center of the kitchen, hoping to grab a bit of cover. If he could hide behind it, he had a shot at taking out the men one-by-one as they passed through the doorway. He'd made it two steps before Hendricks surged into the room.

The big man's face was beet-red, even the parts that hadn't been burned. His eyes shone with a fury that was almost a living thing, and they locked on Riker like a magnet to steel. He charged, arms outstretched, a pistol in one hand.

Morrison's words came back to Riker like a flash of lightning. *You have any idea how many dollars Uncle Sam invested in training your sorry ass to be a killing machine? Your body is a goddamn supercar with nitro surging through its veins. Killing is programmed into its operating system. All you gotta do is put your foot on the gas.*

That was when Riker stopped thinking and allowed his body to react.

As Hendricks grabbed for him, Riker slid forward. In one fluid motion, he slipped between Hendricks' outstretched hands and threw his right arm around the big man's neck. He pulled with the arm at the same time he threw his right hip into Hendricks, executing a perfect headlock hip throw.

Hendricks had to weigh two-fifty, most of it solid muscle, and his momentum carried him forward. He flipped over Riker and landed flat on his back.

Riker hesitated for only a split-second, spotting the other men in the doorway, weapons drawn. He suddenly recognized his advantage—he didn't need to worry about friendly fire. They did.

Hendricks rolled onto his side, trying to raise his gun, but Riker was on top of him before he could. He dropped to the floor behind Hendricks, slamming an arm across his face with all the force he could muster. With his other arm, he reached under Hendricks' leg, grabbing it under the knee. He brought his hands together, clasping them and catching Hendricks in a cross-face cradle. It was a basic wrestling move, but one that would be tough for a non-wrestler to escape. Hendricks' arms and legs were both trapped, leaving him little ability to move.

Riker leaned back, putting Hendricks' body between him and the doorway. The four men were gathered in the entry, weapons raised, panicked looks on their faces.

"Don't shoot!" Hendricks shouted at them.

"Stay where you are or I'll snap his fucking neck," Riker said. There was no way for him to do that from his current position, but he was hoping these guys wouldn't know that.

The men stood frozen with indecision.

"Let me go, you piece of shit!" Hendricks said, his eyes bulging as he attempted to break free.

Riker concentrated on maintaining his grip as his mind raced. He'd bought himself a few moments by taking Hendricks to the floor, but no more than that. He couldn't hold Hendricks in the cradle forever, and the moment he let go, he was a dead man.

He took a deep breath—in through the nose and out through the mouth. Timing. The key was timing. He needed to use the element of surprise. If he could release Hendricks, grab his gun out of his belt, and be in motion before the men in the doorway reacted, he might survive.

Seemed like a long shot. Not the advantageous situation he'd been hoping for.

In the distance, he heard a small voice yelling.

"Yīngxióng! Yīngxióng!"

Li.

The sound of her frightened voice almost broke his heart. She must have spotted him at some point during the fight, either through the window or on the stairs.

As the surprise faded, his resolve grew. This was what he was fighting for. Long odds be damned. He needed to help Li.

He was about to release his hold and take his chances when a figure moved behind the four men.

"What the hell's going on here?" Brennan asked.

As the four men turned, Riker made his move. He released his hold and pushed off Hendricks, his hand going to his waistband and the gun stowed there. Hendricks rolled to his knees, surprised at his sudden freedom. But as Riker pulled his pistol free, one of the men in the doorway was already taking aim. There was no way for Riker to get off a clean shot. He dove behind the island as the man fired.

Once he was behind cover, he ducked to the edge of the island and peeked out, trying to draw a bead on everyone's position.

Hendricks got to his feet and began stalking toward the island. Through all the grappling, he'd managed to keep hold of his pistol, and he held it in front of him in a two-handed, approaching more cautiously this time.

The men weren't questioning Brennan's presence, too caught up in the battle at hand. And behind them, Brennan was raising his pistol, pointing it at Hendricks' back.

At the worst possible moment, one of the men glanced at Brennan.

"Look out!" he shouted.

Hendricks turned and spotted Brennan, weapon raised. He dove as Brennan fired. The shot clipped Hendricks, tearing through the flesh of his left arm.

This was Riker's chance. The men's attention was divided now. To his frustration, he didn't have a clear shot at Hendricks from his angle behind the island, but he did have the other four men in his field of vision. He fired at the one on the far left, putting a pair of bullets through his chest. As the man fell, Riker took aim at the second man. But a shot rang out from the kitchen, and Brennan staggered backward.

"No!" Riker shouted. He leaned around the island further and spotted Hendricks, his weapon aimed where Brennan had just been standing. Hendricks sprinted toward the man who had fired on him, joining the others in the doorway.

Hendricks fired at Brennan as he ran, and there was a grunt of pain.

Riker saw one of the other men move and ducked back just before bullets rained down on the island.

"Motherfucker, you shot me!" Hendricks said, pain clear in his voice. "Why the hell would you do that?"

There was no response from Brennan.

A new voice spoke, this one female. "Hendricks, there's no time for this. We have to go."

It was Helen.

A mix of anger and the sting of betrayal rose up in Riker at the sound of that voice. If he hadn't spotted her running through the fair that day—or if he had ignored her—he wouldn't be in this dire situation.

But then Li would have no chance. She'd have no yīngxióng to protect her.

Yeah, some job her hero was doing now. Getting his only friend shot and waiting to die behind a kitchen island.

"Like hell," Hendricks said. "I'm finishing this."

"You're not listening," Helen said. "If we don't leave now, we'll miss the meeting."

Riker leaned around the counter and fired. All the remaining men were in the hall on the other side of the door now. His shot hit nothing but drywall. That was all right. The goal had been to keep them from coming through at him. He had the kitchen now. The question was whether he could hold it.

"I'm not leaving 'til he's dead," Hendricks said.

Helen's voice was stern when she spoke again. "Don't be an idiot. Riker's pinned down. You've been shot."

"I'm fine."

"This little standoff is going to take time to resolve. Time we don't have. Weaver is waiting, and if we don't get the kid to the meet-up on time, there's going to be hell to pay. Do your job and come with me."

There was a long pause.

"Fine," Hendricks said, his voice bitter. "You assholes better finish this. I want to see Riker's head on a dinner platter by the time I get back."

Footsteps echoed as Helen and Hendricks walked away. Riker heard a little girl's voice call out one more time. "Yīngxióng! Jiùmìng!"

*Hero. Help.*

In the distance, a door closed.

Riker gritted his teeth in frustration. They were taking Li. This was his last chance to save her.

There were three men still out there, tasked with ending Riker's life. They had the luxury of time on their side. They could wait all day for him to peek around the island. But

Riker had only moments before Li was gone forever. Damn strategy and tactical advantage and everything else. He needed to act.

He drew a deep breath and exploded around the counter.

A head peeked out from behind the door frame, just enough to expose a single eye. Riker fired, and his round went through that eye and out the back of the man's head. As brains and bits of skull splattered the wall behind the man, Riker moved sideways, getting an angle and spotting the second man.

He fired again before the first man hit the ground. The shot hit the second man in the chest, and he staggered backward. Riker squeezed off another round, putting a bullet through the man's head. In less than three seconds, he'd ended two lives.

The last man was huddled behind the other side of the door. All that stood between him and Riker was a single wall. Riker ejected his magazine and slapped in a new one, listening to the man's frantic breathing.

He raised his weapon and fired ten rounds into the drywall between him and the man. He heard the man grunt in pain as at least one of the bullets struck home. Riker stepped around the doorframe and put a bullet in the man's head.

His eyes scanned his surroundings for a moment, checking for more enemies, but all they found was blood and carnage. Then they settled on Brennan.

He lay on his back, clutching a wound on the lower-right part of his chest. Another wound, this one in his stomach, was seeping black blood. His face was pale, and he stared up at Riker with wide eyes. He stretched out his hand, something dangling from it. Car keys.

"Brennan, we need—"

"There's no time," the police officer said weakly. "Go."

Riker hesitated for only a moment, then he nodded. He grabbed the keys and started running.

As he stepped out the front door, he saw a Mercedes pulling away from the curb. In the glow of the car's interior lights, he saw Hendricks behind the wheel, and Li's small face staring out at him from the backseat.

## 41

---

THE WIND PRESSED against Riker's face as he ran. His arms pumped and his strides were long. He pushed his body as hard as it could go to reach the car parked half a block away. Every breath—every heartbeat—meant Hendricks was farther away. Each tap of his foot on the pavement meant they could be lost to him forever.

He hit the button to unlock the car as he approached. He threw the door open and started the car before it was shut. He saw the Mercedes take a left two blocks up, and he slammed the car into drive. The car lurched forward and he was after them.

Riker's eyes darted to the left as he passed Weaver's place. Light from the open door spilled out onto the street. He wondered if Brennan was still alive. He wasn't going to let that sacrifice be for nothing.

The light at the corner turned red, but Riker didn't slow the car. He watched the cross streets and saw traffic start to move. He kept his foot on the gas pedal until the last possible moment. Then he pulled the emergency brake. He turned the wheel and the tires lost their grip on the pavement for a moment. He had to hold himself in place while the car drifted around the corner. His rear bumper almost clipped the cars moving across the intersection. Horns blared and profanities echoed out from the cars behind him.

The tires regained their traction, and he mashed the pedal again. The Mercedes was up ahead of him, weaving through traffic. Riker cut between two cars, almost clipping one when he changed lanes. The other cars that filled both lanes were going forty miles an hour slower than his car. There was no way between them. He smashed the horn and jumped the curb, taking the car onto the sidewalk. Sparks flew from the front of the car when it scraped the sidewalk. One man turned his head and dove out of the way when he heard the horn. Riker swerved to avoid him and clipped a newspaper dispenser. The box flew into the air, showering black and white pages across the street.

He cut hard left back onto the street and came out ahead of the cars that had blocked his way. His car fishtailed when it hit the road, but he kept it under control. The Mercedes took a quick right, and Riker followed. He accelerated and made up ground when the other car was slowed by traffic. Riker expected to see red and blue lights behind him at any moment, but none came.

Hendricks' car found an opening and sped up again, but Riker found an opportunity to get behind them. He squeezed between two cars directly behind his target.

Riker expected Hendricks to take evasive action, or open fire on his car. To his surprise the Mercedes slowed, keeping pace with the flow of traffic. Riker wasn't sure what Hendricks' plan was, but it gave him a moment to think.

An image flashed in his mind—Brennan lying on the floor, the blood draining from his body. Riker grabbed Dobbs' phone from his pocket and dialed 911.

As the phone rang, a memory burst into the front of his mind.

*Brown lay on the floor, the blood pooling around his body. Riker presses his hands against the hole in the man's chest, but the blood still gushes out from under his palm.*

*"Stay with me. You're going to make it!" Riker shouts.*

*Brown's breathing is quick and shallow. There are no heroic last words. He doesn't give Riker a message of love for his wife. His shallow breath just stops and his eyes gloss over. One of the toughest men that Riker ever met is nothing but a dead weight on the floor. The image of that last breath and the change to his scared eyes is burned into Riker's mind.*

*The moments that follow are a blurry mess, consumed by rage. They had been pinned down behind their overturned trans- port. He's aware of little more than the thump of his rifle and the screams of the other men. He is pretty sure he is screaming too. When he stops firing, everyone but Riker is dead.*

*He puts Brown over his shoulder and starts the long walk. He carries Brown over his shoulder. After three hours, he can feel his former brother-in-arms stiffen with rigor mortis. Riker's legs burn and his back aches, but he doesn't stop to rest. He puts one foot in front of the other until his shins feel as if they will crack. He still half-expects Brown to wake up. If anyone could tell death to fuck off, it would be him.*

*Two hours later, he reaches the extraction site. The day has come and gone on with him on his feet. His socks are wet with blood and pus. The muscles in his calves and back scream out in pain.*

*The relief hits him when he stands on top of the hill, and a tear wells in the corner of his eye. "We made it," he says, but there is no one to hear him. Brown is no more than a bunch of tissue already beginning to rot. Riker collapses on the ground and waits for the chopper. It isn't just Brown that dies that day; it is a part of Riker.*

"911, what's your emergency?" the operator asked for a second time.

"Officer down. He needs immediate assistance." He gave them Weaver's address and hung up the phone.

The car moved with traffic along the busy street. He was debating how to stop Hendricks' car when a phone rang. Riker hadn't noticed it before, but Brennan's phone was in its mount on the dash. The screen had a single letter on it— W. Riker hit the button on the wheel to answer the call.

He heard the click of the phone coming through the speakers, but it stayed silent for a moment. A familiar voice filled the car.

"You still alive Brennan?" Weaver asked.

"Maybe, but I'm not him."

There was a pause. "You really are a fucking cockroach."

"I'm sure lots of people would say the same about you. Although I think cockroach is a better title than you deserve."

"I expected more from you than playground insults, Matthew." Weaver emphasized his name when he spoke. "I thought you were a man of reason."

"I am a man of reason. I just don't trust anything that you say."

"Trust this. If you don't stop following that car, I'm going to have Hendricks put a bullet in that girl and throw her out onto the street so her tiny body goes under your tires."

"What makes you think I'm in a car?"

"I just spoke with Hendricks. He told me that you made a mess of my house. He also told me that Brennan betrayed me, and that you're in pursuit of him now. If you don't stop, I will have the girl killed."

"The girl's name is Li. And I highly doubt it."

"This is no bluff. She will not be the first child that I've had killed." Weaver spoke like he was talking about a round of golf. Killing children was a matter of casual conversation to him.

"Go ahead then if it's no big deal. Shoot her and toss her out of the car. I'm close enough that I'll see the flash through the tinted windows."

Riker's statement was met by silence.

"Li isn't just some random kid," he continued. "I'm guessing the people paying you don't respond well to failure. If you kill her, you might as well put a bullet in your own head."

"I'll be just fine no matter who I kill," Weaver said, but there was less confidence in his voice now. "So you know who the kid is. Are you working for the Chinese or for an American agency? I'm going to kill you either way, but I'm curious."

"I'll tell you, but not over the phone. I assume you will be wherever this car is going. I'm looking forward to having a face-to-face conversation."

"I respect you enough that I'll kill you quickly. No chair and torture, just a single bullet. That means this will be the last time we get to talk, and I would like to know. I may send your head to your bosses. I'm betting they will be pissed to lose an asset like you."

"You need to believe that I'm part of a bigger picture, don't you? The truth is your important, hardcore empire is on the verge of collapse because of one guy. I don't work for anyone, and I don't really give a shit about you. All of that power you hold is just a bunch of bullshit. Next week, I'll be selling honey at a farmer's market, and you will be a blip on local news. They probably aren't even going to mention your name. They'll just say some sick criminal who sold women and kids is dead."

Hendricks' car was still in front of Riker. They were getting farther and farther from the city center. There were fewer people around and those that were looked rough.

"Oh, my power isn't pretend. I build and destroy people's lives on a whim. If you really are just an ex-merc selling shit to farmers, then you should beg me to kill you. You're worse than dead already. Just walking around with no real purpose and nothing to show for anything you've done."

Riker didn't have a quick response. His mind was fixed on the vehicle in front of him, considering how to disable the vehicle without harming the passengers. Even if he was able to stop them, he would have to deal with Hendricks.

"No sharp remarks for that one. You know that you are worthless." The smile was clear in Weaver's voice.

"Doing honest simple work is better than trafficking women and children. My life might not mean a goddamn thing, but at least I know that. You don't even know what a piece of shit you are."

"I'll tell you two things that I do know, Matthew," Weaver said. "First, the girl is going to be sold to my client. After that I don't care whether she lives, dies, saves the world, or becomes a whore. I'll have more than enough money to rebuild everything that you destroyed."

"That isn't going to happen." Riker moved his car into the lane next to the Mercedes. An open parking lot was coming up to the left. He had a chance to side-swipe the back side of the car and force it off the road. The lot was big enough that they shouldn't crash. He rolled down the window and got his Glock ready. He wanted to put a bullet in Hendricks before he could regain control of the car.

"Don't you want to hear the second thing?" Weaver said in an almost gleeful tone.

"I'm a little busy right now."

The Mercedes stepped on the gas and pulled away before Riker could make his move. He accelerated to match their speed and considered shooting out the back tires.

"I know exactly where you are."

Riker focused on the rear tire of Hendricks' car. He caught a flash of lights from the corner of his eye. An instant later a vehicle smashed into the passenger side of his car.

## 42

THE WORLD SPUN and the screech of tires filled the air.
Something slammed against Riker's head. He may have lost
consciousness, he wasn't sure, but if so it was only for a
moment. He raised his head off the steering wheel and
touched a hand to it. It came away wet with blood. He
turned and saw the car that had slammed into him. Its doors
were still closed, and the two men inside looked as stunned
as Riker felt.

He threw open the door, staggering out onto the street.
The other car had smashed his passenger side pretty well,
but it looked like the vehicle would still be drivable. He
started toward the car that had hit him, but an SUV skidded
to a stop behind it, and three doors opened.

Riker clenched his fists. He didn't have time for this. He
could risk taking on two men, but five was too many. He'd
have to play this another way. He turned and sprinted away
from the cars, ducking down the nearest alley.

He wiped the blood from the cut above his eye with the
back of his hand as he scanned his surroundings, looking
for something he could use. He had his Glock, but he'd

prefer not to go that route if he could help it. They were in an upscale part of the city, the kind of area where gunshots get reported rather than ignored. The kind of place where cops respond in minutes.

To his left, there was a fire escape leading up three stories. It wasn't perfect, but Riker thought he could make it work. He quickly ascended the metal steps. When he reached the second level, he found what he was looking for —a low voltage wire strung across the wall. He gave it a hard yank, pulling one end free. Then he grabbed the knife out of his belt and cut through the other end, giving himself fifteen feet of cordage.

He glanced at the entrance to the alley. Still empty. He shouldn't have been surprised. These weren't Weaver's top-level guys. Those would all be either at the meet-up with the client or on their way there. These guys had heard about Riker by now and probably wanted to plan their attack before they charged into a dark alley after him. Understandable, but dumb. Giving him time to prepare wasn't a good move.

He quickly tied a makeshift noose in one end of the cord and fed it through the metal bars of the fire escape. Then he lowered the noose.

The first two men came into the alley slowly, their guns ready and their eyes scanning the ground for Riker. It was almost too easy. Riker centered the noose above the first man and dropped it another three feet. As soon as it slipped over the man's head, Riker pulled it tight. He jumped over the railing, holding the other end of the cord.

As Riker fell, the cord went taut. The metal railing formed a pulley, jerking the man violently upward and snapping his neck. Riker landed softly, his descent slowed by the man's weight. He had the knife in his hand. As the second man looked up at his friend in shock, Riker drove the blade into his throat.

Riker turned and saw the other three men approaching. As they entered the alley, Riker slipped behind the dumpster, peeking around the corner to keep them in view. As one, they spotted the other two men, one lying in a lifeless heap, a noose around his neck, and the other wriggling on the ground with a steak knife through his throat.

"Actually, you know what?" one of the men said. "Fuck this."

He turned and sprinted out of the alley.

Another one of the men glanced back, clearly considering running too, but the third guy glared at him.

"Don't pussy out on me, Nelson. He's cornered in this alley. We got this."

Nelson took another look at the two guys on the ground, then nodded, the lack of confidence clear on his face.

As the men started forward, Riker ducked down, considering his options. The number one factor here was time. Li was racing toward her destination, and if he didn't get to her soon, she'd be gone. He could charge these two guys—they didn't seem like the two most intimidating men on Weaver's roster. Yet, they were armed, so it was a risk. There was a chance one of them would get off a lucky shot.

The more Riker considered it, the more he realized he was going to have to use the Glock. That posed its own risks, but he'd move fast and be gone before the cops had any chance of showing up. He pulled the weapon out of his belt and slipped in a new magazine, well aware he only had two left after this. Back at Brennan's apartment, seventy rounds had seemed like a luxury. Excessive, even. But he was going through them much faster than he'd like.

He listened to the men's footsteps. They were

approaching slowly, cautiously. That was fine. He'd let them set their own pace, freaking themselves out, their heart rates jacked. It was better that they were close when he made his move. He only intended on shooting one of them.

They were almost on top of him. Riker squeezed his eyes shut and drew a deep breath, clearing his mind. Then he exploded out from behind the dumpster.

Riker had already selected his target. Not Nelson—he wanted Nelson alive. The other man was older than most of the individuals on Weaver's crew that Riker had met. A guy whose career had stalled out at middle management—you hated to see it. He reacted more quickly than Riker would have expected, drawing a bead on Riker, his pistol steady in his hands.

It didn't matter. His fate was a foregone conclusion. Riker squeezed off a quick double-tap, and two rounds hit the man in the chest. He fell backward onto his ass.

Nelson watched with wide eyes, his pistol lagging six inches behind his gaze. Riker shifted his own pistol to his left hand as he surged toward Nelson, drawing back his right hand. He let his fist fly, and it collided with Nelson's jaw. He felt the bone shift under his hand, and there was a loud crack. Nelson staggered back, his jaw now sitting at an unnatural angle to the rest of his face.

Riker reached out and grabbed Nelson's pistol, giving it a hard twist, yanking it from the man's hand. Nelson barely even resisted the move. Riker shoved the gun into his belt and snaked out his hand again, this time grabbing Nelson's leg, sending him sprawling to the ground.

Nelson stared up at him like a cornered animal.

"You should have split like your buddy," Riker said.

"Listen, man," Nelson said, his words slurred as he spoke through his broken jaw. "I'm telling you this for your own good. Weaver's going to kill you. But he's busy with the thing with the kid right now. This is your chance. Take your own advice. Run."

Riker grimaced, feeling the anger rising up inside him. This guy might look like a recruit who didn't know his asshole from his elbow, but he knew what Weaver's operation was really up to. He knew about Li. Despite his skittish nature, he was willingly working for an organization that sold vulnerable human beings into the worst lives imaginable. Any pity Riker might have felt for the man drifted away like smoke.

"People keep telling me that," Riker said. "That Weaver's going to kill me. Strange thing is I'm still alive. Most of them aren't. The rest won't be for very long."

"I don't know about any of that. I'm just doing my job."

"That's the difference between you and me," Riker said. He crouched down next to Nelson and put on his more sadistic smile. "You're just doing your job. I do this shit for fun."

Nelson stared up at him, eyes wide, saying nothing. He was sufficiently freaked out, Riker decided. Time to get this over with.

"I'm going to ask you a question, and you are going to want to answer honestly the first time I ask. Understand?"

Nelson said nothing.

"Good." Riker leaned forward. "Where are they taking Li?"

"I can't," the man said, his voice breaking. "They'll kill me. Or they'll let Hendricks have me, which is worse."

Riker didn't respond. Instead, he moved his gaze to Nelson's hands. He found injuring a man's hands to be very motivational. People experienced much of the world through their hands and fingers. Seeing them broken caused them to re-evaluate their situation. It had worked with Dobbs.

Yet, unlike with Dobbs, time was incredibly short here. It was very possible someone had called the cops after hearing the gunshots. Riker didn't have time for big, intimidating speeches or slow applications of pain. He needed this over quickly.

"Nelson, that was not the answer I was looking for."

He grabbed Nelson's right hand, holding it firmly. With his other hand, he gripped Nelson's pinky finger and gave it a hard snap, breaking the bone near the joint.

Nelson cried out in pain, but Riker was just getting started.

Keeping his grip on the finger, Riker began to twist. He rotated the finger ninety degrees. One hundred eighty degrees. Three hundred sixty degrees.

Nelson was screaming now as bone ground against bone. Riker twisted the finger in the other direction, rotating it a full seven hundred twenty degrees. He released the finger for a moment, letting it dangle loosely, so he was sure he'd completely disconnected the finger bone from the rest of the hand. Then he grabbed it again and began to pull.

Nelson howled in pain. Riker ignored it, pulling harder and harder. He'd never actually done this before. He wasn't even sure if it was possible. He pulled with all his strength, watching the skin stretch, but not break. After thirty seconds of pulling, he decided he needed to rethink his approach.

"Excuse me for a second." He got up and walked over to the man he'd stabbed. He wasn't surprised to see that the man was dead now. Riker pulled the knife out of his throat and walked back over to Nelson.

Nelson was cradling his injured hand, trying to get to his

feet. Riker put a foot on his shoulder, shoving him back down. He grabbed Nelson's pinky finger once again and made two quick cuts with the steak knife, one on the left side of the pinky, and one on the right. Tightening his grip on the pinky, he pulled as hard as he could.

This time, the finger came off in a single try. The skin near where Riker had sliced broke cleanly, but the skin on the other parts of the finger was stretched and torn.

Riker slammed a hand against Nelson's mouth, stifling his screams. With his other hand, he held the finger up in front of Nelson's shocked face, letting him see the severed digit and ragged skin dangling from it.

Riker tossed the finger over his shoulder and spoke in a quiet voice.

"I'm only going to ask nine more times. Where are they taking Li?"

## 43

RIKER DROVE his newly acquired SUV with one hand on the wheel and the other keeping pressure on the cut to his forehead. Besides providing answers to where they were taking Li, Nelson had gladly handed over the keys to his vehicle. In exchange, Riker had allowed him to live, albeit tied up in the trunk of a car. He'd be found eventually. Riker had even applied a tourniquet to make sure he didn't bleed out before that happened.

Riker thought about the information he'd been given. Weaver was making the exchange at a private airfield with a warehouse an hour outside of the city. One thing was certain. Riker was not prepared for this fight. The location was big, fortified, and loaded with armed men. He played the scenario in his head. To do this properly he should perform boots on the ground surveillance, have a team of at least six highly trained guys, a few assault rifles, a couple RPGs, and a high powered sniper rifle. A little air support would be nice, but he could do without it in a pinch. Then he looked at his bloody face in the mirror to bring himself back to reality.

He had a Glock, an extra magazine, an SUV, and an open wound on his head. He focused his mind, visualizing the attack. He was past long odds; this was suicide. He needed more firepower. There was no way for him to get more guns quickly, but he knew the world was full of weapons. Sometimes you just had to think a little outside of the box. He had learned that lesson fighting in the Middle East. The US troops had factory made guns and computer-enhanced targeting systems. But Riker had seen armored vehicles that cost hundreds of thousands of dollars destroyed by materials you could get from local stores. He had learned that traps and ambush beat superior firepower nine out of ten times.

Riker used Dobbs' phone to find a big box hardware store on the way to the airfield. He grabbed a cart when he walked through the doors. A young employee stood with his mouth open, staring as Riker walked in. Riker looked down at himself. Blood splattered his clothes, and he imagined his face looked even worse.

"Oh, my God," the young man said. "Do you need help?"

"Nope, I know my way around the store. Thanks."

The guy stood staring at Riker. "I mean, do you need medical attention?"

"For this little cut? I'm fine. I smacked my head while I was working. It looks way worse than it is." He walked off before the guy had a chance to respond.

He moved as quickly as he could through the store. He wanted to run, but he couldn't risk attracting any more attention than he was already getting. He grabbed super glue, electrical tape and some shop towels and went into the bathroom. Five minutes later he had the wound closed and dressed. After washing the blood off his face, he looked a little less as if he had just been in a car crash and killed some guys.

Time ticked by but Riker forced himself to plan. He pulled out Dobbs' phone and used Google Maps to see an overhead satellite image of the airfield. He had a good idea of what he needed to do, but seeing the layout of the buildings helped finalize the plan.

While he worked through the details of his attack, he made a mental list of items he needed. Once he was satisfied with the plan, he raced through the store.

The cart filled quickly while Riker darted from aisle to aisle. He picked up buckets of screws, tanks of MAPP gas, a bolt cutter, metal braided rope, nylon rope and copper wire. He grabbed a timer and an A/C adaptor plug for the SUV. He picked up a few knives a backpack.

When Riker made it to the checkout area, he saw the snack food, and he suddenly realized how hungry he was. He threw an entire box of Snickers bars into the cart along with a six pack of Gatorade.

After checking out, he tossed everything into the back of the SUV and hit the road. The stop hadn't taken long, but he feared he had squandered what precious little time he had. The exchange was going to happen soon, and if Li got on the plane that was coming for her Riker would never see her again.

Some of the color returned to his face while he ate candy bars and drank glorified sugar water. He'd lost a fair amount of blood from the head wound and the sugar helped his body recover. He kept the car nine miles over the speed limit. He knew that being pulled over for speeding would be the end of Li. It took everything he had to keep from smashing the pedal to the floor.

A world of pavement started to give way to trees and grass. He could see the skyline in his rearview mirror. A huge cemetery passed by on the right. The open space reminded him of his little piece of land in the country. It was such a simple place where nothing happened. He had left QS-4 with a lot of conditions. He had to stay off-grid and away from any kind of action. That was okay with Riker. He didn't want to interact with anyone or anything. That hatred of the world was the reason he'd gotten his first beehive. A kid had come by his house selling newspaper subscriptions. Riker put a beehive between his house and the road a week later. He figured most normal people would stay away from a house swarming with bees. Riker assumed he would get a lot of bee stings, but he knew he could handle much worse pain. To his surprise, he was never stung coming or going from his home. The lack of attacks was the first thing that caught his attention. He would walk by the hive every day. Thousands of bees came in and out. They would buzz by him but he was never stung.

He started to sit on the lawn and watch the colony and its constant motion. The bees weren't bothered by his presence. The continual work of the hive was beautiful to him. Bees didn't complain, they didn't take the day off, and they didn't fight with each other. They were all armed, but none of them attacked unless they were attacked first.

The simple deterrent for his home became an obsession. He studied bees. He learned how to maintain a healthy hive and harvest the honey. Riker came to think of them as a superior species. None of them ever tried to overthrow the queen or carried out an attack on another hive.

The world Riker lived in was nothing but hostile aggression. He had killed so many and looking back he wasn't even sure why. He'd followed orders and assumed it was for the greater good. By the time he got out, he wasn't sure there was any good left to protect.

He thought of his hives and realized the simple truth. They would continue their peaceful existence and never be aware if he didn't make it out of this situation. His death was irrelevant to them. In fact, his death would be irrelevant to everyone.

His thoughts circled back to the task at hand. There was one person that his life mattered to. A small girl had her life in the balance. That was not irrelevant.

Riker pulled his SUV off the road in a wooded area a half-mile from the entrance. He grabbed Brennan's binoculars and double-timed it through the woods. Once he found a good vantage point, he lay on the ground and observed.

The first thing he checked was the landing strip. He was relieved to see there was no plane on it. That was the only positive. The perimeter of the property was protected by a twelve-foot fence. A razor wire spiraled along the top of it. Floodlights illuminated patches of land and created pockets of darkness.

The building inside was a large warehouse with a flat roof. Riker could see three men on that roof. There was only one road in. That road was blocked by a sliding barricade and had a guard gate with two men inside. The entry to the warehouse was one hundred feet past the gate. Two men guarded that door. Riker didn't see anyone else on the exterior of the building but he did see cars parked out front.

He counted nine vehicles including the Mercedes that Hendricks had been driving. He guessed that meant between eighteen and thirty-six guys total. Considering how much trouble he had already caused and the value of the transaction the number was likely to be closer to thirty-six.

He snuck back to the SUV and prepared. He lined the back of the truck with tanks of MAPP gas. Ten boxes of screws got dumped on top of them. Each box contained one thousand five hundred screws for a grand total of fifteen thousand. He hooked the timer and adaptor into the outlet in the car. Then he ran an extension cord to the back. He wrapped the copper wire around one tank of gas in the center creating a coil. Next, he connected one end to the hot and one to the neutral end of the power cord. Copper doesn't melt until it hits 1981 degrees Fahrenheit. The steel that made up the tank had a higher melting point, but the pressure from the heated gas inside along with the weakened metal would do the job.

The SUV was now a mobile bomb. One that had fifteen thousand projectiles. He rigged the steering wheel with the nylon rope to keep it from veering off the road. Riker found a windshield sun cover in the back of the car. He put it in place so that no one could see inside.

While he worked he constantly looked up and listened for the sound of a plane. He didn't know how long the exchange would take, but once the plane arrived he would be out of time.

He loaded the rest of the gear into his pack and checked the magazines for his pistol. He ran through his attack plan one last time.

The voice of Riker's CO from the SEALs filled his head. *You are the tip of the spear. Before the first platoon steps foot on the battlefield, you will disrupt the enemy in ways he does not understand. You will unravel their structure; you will unnerve their soldiers. Your brothers in arms will clean up the mess that you leave behind. They will receive the glory, but you will be the instrument of the enemies' defeat. Your units will have the power to win wars.*

The memory prepared him for what he was about to do. He went to check over the rig in the SUV one more time when he heard the engine of a small plane overhead.

## 44

RIKER CHECKED his pack one last time, knowing he couldn't linger near the SUV much longer. The sound of the plane growing louder, roaring as it approached the airfield, was like a ticking clock. He needed to move fast. Zipping the pack shut, he threw it over his shoulder. Anything he didn't have in the pack, he'd have to do without.

He stuck his head out of the vehicle, checked his angles one more time, then he started the engine. No turning back now. He shifted the SUV into drive and gently placed the brick on the gas pedal, letting gravity do the work. As the vehicle lurched forward, he eased the door shut, and trotted away from the approach road and into the darkness.

As he reached the chain-link fence around the perimeter of the airfield, Riker stopped, his eyes fixed on the small plane soaring low over his head. A moment later, it touched down gently and rolled down the runway, coming to a halt halfway between the fence and the hangar at the end of the runway.

Riker risked a glance toward the SUV still heading toward the gate. The weight of the brick kept the vehicle moving at a slow but steady pace of around fifteen miles an hour. Riker set his pack on the ground and opened it, pulling out a set of bolt cutters.

A man at the gate yelled toward the SUV. Riker couldn't quite hear the words, but he understood the message—stop or face the consequences. The vehicle just kept rolling on at fifteen miles per hour.

On the runway, the plane's door was already open, and Weaver and six of his guys were trotting toward the plane, apparently going to greet the client.

Everything was happening at once now. Riker needed to keep moving. He went to work on the fence with the bolt cutter, opening up a space large enough to squeeze through. As he was easing through the opening, gunshots rang out to his right.

The men at the gate were firing on the SUV. First a warning shot followed by a barrage of automatic fire. And still, the vehicle came.

Riker couldn't help but pause on the inside of the fence as ten men poured out of the small building near the gate and converged on the SUV, forming a half circle around it, weapons raised and pointed at the vehicle. The vehicle hit the gate, not going fast enough to break through the closed fence, but not stopping, just bumping against it.

The man nearest to the driver's side door took a step toward the SUV, his hand reached out to grab the handle.

That was when the wiring inside the vehicle reached the critical temperature. Though Riker couldn't see it, he knew what was happening inside the SUV. The heat caused the first MAPP gas tank to explode, sending a shower of screws into the rest of the gas tanks and setting off a deadly chain reaction.

Screws exploded in every direction, tearing into bodies

like thousands of bullets. From his position, Riker could clearly hear the men screaming as they fell. He could only imagine what it felt like to have dozens of screws tearing through your skin, your muscles, driving into your very bones. It must have been an absolutely terrible way to die.

He allowed himself to feel something like pity for the ten men who were currently lying on the pavement, dying from the shrapnel from his homemade bomb, but only a moment. He hardened his heart and refocused. They were his enemies, his targets, and now there were ten less of them. That was all that mattered.

He turned his attention to the hangar. A handful of men ran out at the sound of the explosion. They were scrambling now, trying to figure out who was attacking them.

Good. Just as Riker had planned. He'd hoped the explosion would draw them out of the hangar, giving him a better chance to slip into the building unseen. It was also allowing him to get a better look at their numbers. Four men were running out of the hangar, plus the six men with Weaver. The three guards on the hangar's roof moved to the front of the building. They focused on the explosion and the frontal attack.

"Wait!" The voice was low and impossibly loud, somehow bellowing all the way to Riker's ears.

For a moment, he didn't know who'd yelled. Then he saw Hendricks standing near the door to the hanger.

"We stay here. Defend this location. And help the boss!"

The six men near the plane closed ranks around Weaver, hustling him back toward the hangar. Three Chinese men hurried down the plane's steps, following at Weaver's heels.

Riker cursed under his breath. Once again, Hendricks had thrown a wrench into the well-considered machinery of his plan. He had a feeling he and Hendricks wouldn't both make it through this night. Maybe neither of them would.

Giving Weaver and Hendricks more time wouldn't help anything. Riker needed to keep moving, even though things weren't going exactly to plan. He trotted across the dark field, staying low, making his way to the now silent plane.

When he reached it, he scanned the airfield with his eyes. Other than the dead men near the gate, Riker was the only person not near the hangar. Just as Hendricks had ordered, most of them were now in the building. There were still three men on the roof with rifles. They worried Riker. He'd have to deal with them before he figured out a way to get inside the heavily defended building.

But first, he needed to deal with the plane.

He pulled a metal cable out of his pack. Reaching up, he jammed the cable inside the engine under the right wing, packing it inside tight. If anyone started the engine, the engine would immediately be destroyed.

He felt a moment of accomplishment. There was no way they were flying Li out of this airfield now. Granted, they could drive her out after they killed Riker. He'd just have to make sure that didn't happen.

Now that the plane was disabled, there was nothing left except to face the real target—the hangar. He paused for a moment, considering his best approach. Walking straight in that building would be suicide. He needed to draw the men out. He could think of only one way to do that. He needed to get to the roof.

A direct approach would only get him killed. For a moment, he considered trying to climb the building on the east side, but he decided against it. It would be difficult and risky. Even though it would take more time, he needed to work his way around the perimeter of the field, to get to the ladder on the south side of the building and get behind the men who were all facing north toward the gate.

He moved quickly through the dark, dropping his pack and leaving it near the fence. It wouldn't help him. It took him nearly five precious minutes to get around the back of the building, but it allowed him to move through the darkness until he was only ten yards from the building. He sprinted through the thin shaft of light near the wall, ignoring the pain singing through his body, and reached the ladder. He climbed quickly, not wanting to pause and consider what he was about to attempt.

When he reached the top of the ladder, he stopped with his hands on the top rung and let out a soft whistle.

"The hell was that?" a voice on the roof said.

Riker waited in silence as footsteps approached. There were three guys on that roof. He wasn't worried about the first one. But the second and third guys? Their positions would determine everything.

After a moment, someone leaned over the edge of the building, the barrel of their rifle pointing down toward Riker.

For a split second, time froze for Riker. It was as if his mind were grinding time itself to a halt to give itself one more instant to strategize.

Then time sped up and all hell broke loose.

He reached up and grabbed the barrel of the rifle in an iron grip, yanking it downward. The man tumbled over the edge of the building, letting out a surprised shout as he fell thirty feet to the pavement below.

Riker didn't have the luxury of affording that man another second's thought. He charged up the ladder, exploding off the top rung and onto the roof. As his feet touched the metal roof, he surged forward. He saw two men in front of him, twin dark silhouettes hunkering toward him. He charged at the shorter, broader man first.

The broad man held a rifle in his hands—a great weapon at a distance, but tough to bring around in time to shoot a target charging at you. The man did his best, but Riker reached him too quickly, grabbing the rifle with both hands and driving it back and up, slamming the butt into the man's chin.

The man managed to maintain his grip on the rifle as he staggered backward. Riker held fast as well. He snapped his right leg forward, kicking the man hard in the balls. The man let out a pathetic grunt, and he released the rifle as he fell.

Riker spun the weapon around, wedging the stock against his shoulder in an instant as he drew a bead on the second, taller man. He squeezed the trigger, sending a burst of three rounds into the thin man's chest. Then he turned back to the broad man and squeezed off another three rounds.

"What's going on up there?" a voice said through a radio clipped to the thin man's belt. Riker thought about picking it up and answering, but he didn't think that would serve much of a purpose.

He tried to steady his breath, just as he'd been trained to do, in through the nose and out through the mouth. He'd somehow survived this initial assault, but there were at least eleven more men in the hangar, not including the Chinese men and Weaver.

He stalked toward the edge of the building, considering his next move. He needed to draw out the men in the hangar. His first thought was to shoot down through the thin metal roof at them. It wasn't ideal—they might just fire back up at him—but then he saw something lying near the edge of the roof.

"Oh, hell yeah," he muttered. Finally a bit of good luck.

He picked up the RPG 7 and gave it a quick visual inspection. The rocket-propelled grenade was exactly the type of weapon he'd wished he had when preparing for this assault. Someone up there liked him.

He set up the weapon, took aim, and fired. The rocket whistled through the air and found its target, slamming into the body of the plane on the runway with a deafening boom. Riker allowed himself a quick smile as he dropped the RPG7 and picked up the automatic rifle.

Just as he'd hoped, the men poured out of the hangar, running around in a panic, confusion ruling their actions. Riker opened fire. He took out four of them in as many seconds. Adjusting his aim, he took out a fifth, leaving five more men, not including Hendricks, Weaver, and the Chinese men.

He prepared to fire again, but something sharp bit into his leg, and he let out a grunt of pain. The broad man stared up at him, his hand still holding the combat knife that had sliced through Riker's thigh, a sadistic smile on his bloody face. The bullet holes in the left side of his chest were seeping blood, but he didn't seem to notice.

The thin man reached up and snatched the rifle from Riker's surprised hands. In a moment, he had tossed it over the edge of the building. His foot lashed out, sending the RPG 7 cascading to the floor after it.

"That evens the odds a bit, doesn't it?" he said.

Riker blinked hard, pushing down the wave of pain that threatened to disorient him. All that existed in this world was him and the man with the knife.

"It really doesn't," he said.

He grabbed the wrist of the hand holding the knife with his left hand. With his right, he grabbed the man's throat. He squeezed viciously with both hands, as if his very life depended on it. Which it did. When the thin man finally went limp, he released him, letting him fall to the roof with a thump.

Riker breathed hard, trying to keep his bearings through the pain and nausea coursing through him. Blood poured from the knife wound in his leg, and it was all he could do to keep upright.

Then he saw it.

A man stood on the east side of the building, the one Riker had thought too risky to climb. His huge form cast a long shadow across the roof in the moonlight.

"Let's fucking finish this," Hendricks said.

Riker steadied himself and turned toward the bigger man.

"Yeah," he said. "Let's finish it."

## 45

A COLD WIND blew across the black tar roof. Shadows and light fought for space atop the building. Glowing lights around the building made Hendricks' face look pale and dead. The gauze around his head and the bandages on his neck completed the look of Frankenstein's monster.

Sixty feet of open, flat space separated the two men. Hendricks had his 9mm drawn. He squeezed the trigger, expecting to end the fight before it began. The crack of the gunshot seemed small on the open rooftop.

The part of Riker's brain that controlled conscious thought took a backseat to his instincts and training. He dropped to one knee and pulled up the body of the man he had just killed. One bullet went past them, and the second round hit the corpse. He sprang up, holding the body in front of him like a shield. If there was pain coming from the wound in his leg, Riker didn't feel it. He held the body high with his head tucked behind the shoulder. He tilted forward and sprinted, the weight of the body increasing his forward momentum.

Riker couldn't see past his shield. The crack of the 9mm

sounded like an automatic. He ran at full speed, and he felt the tap of small rounds hitting the dead man in his arms. Hendricks was well trained with the weapon, but part of that training was to shoot at center mass. The bullets fired at almost the same pace as Riker's feet hit the ground. In three seconds, the last shell ejected from the gun and Riker reached Hendricks.

The instant before Riker and the body that protected him made impact, Hendricks stepped to the side. Riker let go of the corpse and tried to stop, but his momentum kept him moving forward. He tumbled forward, arms reeling. The body flew over the edge of the roof, but Riker dropped to one knee, managed to stop a few inches from the edge. Hendricks pointed his gun at Riker's face pulling the trigger. The empty chamber didn't produce the result he'd expected.

Riker sprang to his feet as his hand shot out and grabbed Hendricks' wrist. He pulled hard and twisted his body, trying to throw the large man off the roof. Hendricks moved towards the edge, but he put one foot on the ledge and used the power of his leg to pull back in the opposite direction. Riker kept his grip, but the battle of strength went to Hendricks.

Riker felt his feet leave the ground and Hendricks tossed him away from the edge. He let go of the wrist and tucked a shoulder into the ground. He rolled and reached for the gun in his belt. He came to a stop with one knee on the ground and one foot on the roof. Hendricks didn't let up and raced towards Riker.

Riker's hand wrapped around the butt of the gun in his waistband and time slowed to a crawl. This game of milliseconds could end the fight. He brought the gun around and increased the pressure on the trigger. Hendricks kicked hard and a flash brightened their faces.

Hendricks' boot connected with the gun a moment before it fired. The bullet still hit the target, but not in the intended location. Hendricks' right arm swung backward as his foot connected with Riker's gun. The kick sent the gun flying across the roof.

Both men regained their balance, and they stood toe-to-toe. Blood seeped through Hendricks' shirt at his right forearm.

Riker threw a hard left hook and Hendricks instinctively blocked with his injured arm.

He screamed out in pain when the blow connected with the fresh wound. Most men would crumple when they felt pain like that, but Hendricks used it. He threw a left hook of his own and it connected with the side of Riker's face. A high-pitched ringing canceled out the sound of the world and white spots filled his vision as Riker staggered backward. Hendricks threw a right hook to finish him. Riker's arms didn't want to work, but his will to survive was stronger than the pain of the blow and his hands and forearms came high enough to block the blow. Hendricks was running on rage and another hard left came for Riker. This one was telegraphed enough that Riker ducked it and shot out for Hendricks' legs.

Riker shot forward, smashing his head into Hendricks' stomach. He grabbed the back of both knees with his hands and pushed forward into the big man. Hendricks fell backward, landing on his ass. In wrestling, the double leg take-down was a masterful move, but here on the roof, there were no rules governing the game. Hendricks grabbed Riker around the neck with both hands.

Riker felt the raw strength of Hendricks' large hands

choking the life from him. His thumbs crushed into Riker's larynx, and his fingers dug into the back of Riker's neck. Riker used his left hand to grab Hendricks' forearm. He slid his hand down the arm until he felt a hole in the sleeve. He hooked his thumb through the bullet hole, squeezing as tightly as he could and turning his wrist to force his thumb deep into the open wound.

Hendricks howled and released his grip. Riker did not. His thumb touched the flattened bullet inside the arm and he pressed harder. He straddled Hendricks and crashed hard punches into his face with his free right hand. Three fast hard hits landed on his eye socket. Hendricks lost all technique and resorted to instinct, bucking his body. He flailed and twisted with enough force that Riker was thrown off.

Riker got to his feet. The wound in his leg caused him to stagger. Blood trickled down his thigh. He took a deep breath. His injured throat made the air feel like hot smoke on the way to his lungs.

Hendricks stumbled to his feet. Riker saw his left eye was mostly closed from the bruised and beaten tissue. He held his right arm at his side. Blood dripped off of it in a steady stream. He reached to the back of his pants and his hand came back holding a knife.

Riker reached into his pocket and pulled out a folding knife. He flicked the blade into place with a click. For a moment the night was quiet as the two warriors stared at one another.

"Not bad for a squid," Hendricks said. He spit out a mouthful of blood. "I'm going to bring your head down to the kid after I take it off."

"Don't just talk about it. Let's see what you've got left." Riker motioned Hendricks toward him.

Hendricks moved in slowly. Riker shuffled to the left, trying to use the swollen eye to his advantage. Hendricks slashed out with the knife. The air hummed with the speed of the blade. Hendricks' reach was long and Riker had to take a step back to avoid the knife. The thin piece of metal narrowly missed Riker's neck.

Riker continued to circle left looking for his opening. Hendricks stayed with him and jabbed the knife at Riker's chest. Riker took a risk, turning his body sideways instead of moving back. The knife cut across his chest. The wound wasn't deep but it slid through his shirt and skin across the meat of his pectoral muscle.

The move left Hendricks exposed and Riker racked his knife down into Hendricks' left shoulder. The three-inch blade sunk into the joint and Hendricks' left arm went limp. His knife fell to the ground with a thud. Riker pulled his blade back out and blood sprayed from the wound. That bright red stream told Riker that Hendricks was finished. The arterial blood meant that he would bleed out in minutes. Riker drew back to strike a final blow.

His opponent might have been a walking dead man but he didn't know that. Hendricks drove his body into Riker, wrapping his right arm around him. His right shoulder dropped into Riker's sternum and he ran forward, lifting him off the ground. Riker's feet kicked with no results as Hendricks ran towards the edge of the building.

Riker was doubled over on Hendricks' shoulder. He had no leverage to stop the motion or free himself. He brought his knife down hard in the meat of Hendricks' back. The blade buried itself deep, but Hendricks didn't slow.

Riker could see the edge of the roof out of the corner of his eye. In a few seconds, the two fighters would fall to their deaths. Riker pulled the knife out and brought it down hard one more time, aiming for the center of the back. The blade found its mark and slid between two vertebrae in the thoracic spine. The gruesome sound of the blade scraping bone came through in a muffled vibration. The spinal cord behind the bones was sliced in half.

Hendricks' legs went limp and his weight collapsed onto the roof. Riker's lower body was smashed between Hendricks and the tar on the roof as they skidded to a stop. Hendricks' shoulder drove deep into Riker's guts, and he lost most of his air.

Hendricks let out a scream, and his right arm flailed wildly. Riker drew in a breath and pushed Hendricks off of him. He rolled to his knees and pushed himself up. His knife was still stuck in Hendricks' back and he raised his fist, turning to Hendricks.

Blood flowed from Hendricks' shoulder. It followed the drainage line of the roof and dripped off the building a foot from where they stopped. The screaming had stopped and his right arm moved less and less. Hendricks looked up at the sky with his eyes open. The color of his face went white, contrasting sharply with the black of the roof and the red of the blood. Then all movement stopped and a final gasp of air left Hendricks.

Riker looked around the roof and saw his gun. He walked toward it. His entire body sang out with a symphony of pain. He touched his wounded chest and looked down. There was no way to tell how much of the blood covering him was his own.

A voice in his head screamed at him to lie down. His body wanted him to stop. There was nothing more important than finding a safe place to rest. Riker pushed that small voice down so deep that it was silenced. He pushed the pain to that same place, telling himself that pain was just a reminder of how powerful he was.

That force of will filled him. He picked up his Glock and made sure that the magazine was full and a round was chambered. Somewhere in the hangar under his feet were a little girl that needed help and a man that needed to be put down.

## 46

RIKER THOUGHT he was in pain as he stood on the roof, but when he climbed down the ladder, he was reminded what real pain was all about. The ladder forced his body to stretch in ways that standing hadn't, and each of his many wounds cried out, letting its displeasure be known. He pushed it down. One way or another, the end was in sight.

By his count, there were at least five of Weaver's guys still inside the hangar, no doubt hunkered down and ready to defend their boss. Plus, he had to worry about Weaver and the three Chinese men who had apparently shown up to purchase Li from Weaver. And Helen. He couldn't forget about Helen.

After reaching the ground, he put a hand into his pocket, checking to make sure that the last of the magazines Brennan had given him hadn't fallen out during the fight. Gun held in a two-handed grip and pointed at the ground, Riker eased his way around the perimeter of the building. When he reached the main entrance, he kept his back against the bay door and peeked through the smaller glass door next to it. He saw a flash of motion inside the hangar and whipped his head back just as a shot rang out. A bullet shattered the glass.

Riker kept his back to the metal bay door, gun ready, listening.

For a moment, there was nothing.

Someone inside shouted, "We know you're out there, shithead! If you think—"

Riker pivoted around and spotted the man who was speaking twenty feet beyond the shattered glass door. Riker put two bullets in the man's chest and ducked back against the bay door. Once again, he waited.

All was silent inside the hangar.

Weaver hadn't taken Riker seriously enough before, but he was certainly taking him seriously now. Riker imagined him huddled in that building somewhere, frightened for his life. The thought made Riker happy.

After ten more seconds, another voice called out to him.

"Mr. Weaver suggests you stand down."

Riker pivoted around again, looking through the door, but this time the speaker was smart enough to stay out of sight. He took a tentative step inside. The bright fluorescent lighting filled the large empty space, but Riker didn't see anyone but the dead man fifteen feet in front of him. He hurried to his right and took cover behind a shipping crate. No one fired or even spoke.

Riker risked a look over the crate and into the large, open room. There were only a few places to hide in here. He spotted a desk at the far end of the room, and a stack of boxes to their right. There would surely be men hiding behind those. There was a doorway on the far end which presumably led to some offices of something. Riker was willing to bet that Weaver, Helen, and the clients would be cowering there.

And Li. That had to be where they were holding Li.

He shifted his weight to the balls of his feet, getting ready to move the moment he needed to. The enemies had seen him enter through the door. They knew his position. But he didn't know theirs, at least not for certain. He needed to get them talking.

"You said something about standing down. Why the hell would I do that?"

"You're outnumbered," a man answered. The voice came from behind the boxes on the far end of the room.

"Not as outnumbered as I was twenty minutes ago."

Another voice spoke, this one coming from somewhere near the desk. "We've got Hendricks. He's going to hurt you so bad that—"

"I already killed Hendricks." Riker inched to the right side of the crate, getting ready to charge.

There was a long pause.

"You shot Hendricks?" the man behind the desk finally said.

"Nope. Didn't need a gun. I killed him with my pocket knife."

Another long pause.

"Bullshit." There was a hint of something new in the man's voice now. He'd been scared of Riker before, but now he was terrified.

"Afraid not. Want to see how I did it?"

With that Riker sprang into motion. He sprinted across the room, firing his Glock as he charged across the fifty feet of open space. The shots hit the far wall, not coming close to any particular target. The purpose of the shots wasn't to kill —it was to provide him cover, to keep the frightened men in their hiding spots until Riker reached them.

He was still ten feet from the desk when he fired his

sixth shot and the slide of his Glock locked back. He ejected the magazine with one hand, grabbing his last magazine out of his pocket with the other. As his gunshots ceased, the man behind the boxes peeked his head out, looking for a clear shot of his own.

Riker went to the ground, covering the last six feet to the desk in a slide, like a ballplayer trying to beat a throw to second base. As he slid, he slammed the new magazine home and chambered a round. The moment he cleared the desk and spotted the man huddled behind it, he squeezed off two rounds, putting one in the man's head and one in his chest.

He rolled into a crouch behind the desk, pausing to see if the man behind the boxes would take a shot. When he didn't, Riker sprinted toward the boxes, keeping them between him and the other man. When he reached it, he ducked around the far side and exploded toward the man. He wrapped both arms around the man, forcing his gun down, and tackled him to the floor. Then he tore the pistol from the man's hand and shot him twice.

Riker crouched there over the dead man, catching his breath. He'd ended three lives in less than thirty seconds. But he wasn't done yet. The doorway to the back of the hangar stood ten feet away. It was open a crack, just far enough that Riker wasn't able to see anything beyond it but a shaft of light.

He'd have to be careful now. Li was back there some-where, and he wouldn't put it past Weaver to use the girl against him somehow. He moved toward the door, staying low, ready to fire. Using his foot, he pushed it open and waited, listening for movement. He heard nothing.

Taking a deep breath he stepped through into a hallway. As he did, the sound of something heavy hitting the floor came from his left. He almost started to turn, but a shadow to his right caught the corner of his eye. He spun to his right and saw a dark figure much too large to be a three-year-old girl. Riker fired, dropping the man.

Someone behind the falling man moved, ducking around a corner and into one of the offices. Riker charged forward. He stepped through the office doorway, pulling back just in time to avoid the bullet fired at him. Riker dropped to one knee and fired three shots, taking the man down.

Riker waited nearly a minute and heard nothing but silence. He left the office, which was now empty except for the dead body, and looked to his left where he'd heard the bang. He saw a large paperweight lying near the wall. The bastards had actually tried the trick of throwing a heavy object across the room to distract his attention away from them. Worse yet, it had almost worked.

There was only one other office. Riker stalked toward it. When he reached the door, he didn't hesitate. He threw it open and stepped inside.

Four terrified faces stared out at him.

The three "clients" stood on the left side of the room, each dressed in suits that probably cost more than Riker's truck. Their eyes were wide.

Directly in front of him, Weaver sat behind a shoddy old desk, his hands raised, showing them empty.

And to the right, sitting on a small couch, were Helen and Li.

"Nǐ hǎo, Li," Riker said.

"Nǐ hǎo," she whispered. *Hello*.

"Matthew," Weaver said, "you've proven yourself quite capable. I'll admit it—I underestimated you. I apologize."

"Helen," Riker said. "Play the hiding game. Cover her eyes."

"You've done a lot of damage to my organization," Weaver continued. "But all is not lost. With the money we're about to make, we can rebuild. A man like you in a city like this? There's no telling how high you could rise. How high *we* could rise. Together."

"Cover her eyes, Helen," Riker repeated.

Helen let out a sharp, joyless laugh. "No way. Whatever you're going to do, she's going to see it. She's going to see what you are. We'll see whether you're still her *Yīngxióng* after that."

"All that matters is her safety. You think I care what she thinks of me?"

"I think it's all you care about. You want someone to look at you like you're a hero. But you're not. You're nothing but a killer."

Riker couldn't argue with that. He spoke in Mandarin. "Li, play the hiding game. Cover your eyes."

The little girl solemnly nodded, and she put her hands over her face.

Riker slowly turned toward the three clients.

"Whoa, hang on," Weaver said. "You don't know who these men are. These are not the type of people you are allowed to shoot. If they die, you won't—"

Riker squeezed off six rounds, two into each man. Then he turned to Weaver.

Weaver drew a deep breath, and the friendly facade slipped away. "You stupid, stupid man. Do you have any idea what you've done? You've bought hell down on all of us!"

"Wouldn't be the first time." Riker pulled the trigger once again.

Weaver rocked back in his chair and lay still, a bullet

through the center of his forehead.

Riker turned to Helen.

"Here's what we're going to do," he said. "We're going to get in one of those cars outside, and I'm going to drive you to the police station. You'll confess everything. We'll get Li home."

She gave him a bitter smile. "I think we both know that's not going to happen."

"Helen, please," Riker said. His voice was soft, nearly pleading. "A life in prison is better than no life at all."

She sighed, and the fight seemed to go out of her. "I don't like it, but you're right. I agree to your terms. But only if you—"

Her hand jerked up from the couch cushion, and light reflected off something metal. It was a good move, but Riker was too fast for her. He fired his last two rounds before she even had the gun pointed at him.

She slumped back, her vacant eyes staring up at the fluorescent lights.

Li huddled on the far side of the couch, hands still pressed tightly against her face.

Riker went to her and crouched down in front of her. "Keep your eyes covered a little longer."

To Riker's surprise, she pulled her hands away from her face. Eyes still squeezed shut, she threw her arms around Riker's neck. She pulled him close, hugging him with all the strength in her three-year-old body.

Riker hugged her back. It was almost impossible to believe that he'd done it. He'd saved her. All the terrible things that had been done to him and that he'd done to others, they were all worth it now. Li was safe.

"Xiànzài huí jiā?" she whispered. *Go home now?*

"Shì," he answered. *Yes.*

## 47

RIKER FOUND a set of keys on one of the bodies in the warehouse. He carried Li out to the cars in front and hit the unlock button. He put her inside and told her he would be right back.

He went back to a bathroom by the offices. He glanced in the mirror and laughed to himself. He looked like shit. He rinsed the blood from his face and arms. His clothes were still soaked in blood, so he took the jacket off one of the dead guards in the warehouse. He still looked bad, but a glance he could pass for normal.

In the warehouse he found some fifty-gallon drums of fuel. He opened the top of two of them and tipped them over, rolling one of them from the wall next to the other barrels to the front door of the warehouse. A trail of fuel poured out along the route. Liquid continued to pour out in glugs from the barrel as Riker walked back to the car. He pressed the cigarette lighter in the car. When it was ready, he threw it into the puddle forming around the entrance of the building. The glow of the fire filled the night sky as they drove away.

They drove in silence for a little while. Then Li started to chatter in Mandarin.

"I think you need a Band-Aid. You have an owie on your face." She pointed to a place on her cheek that mirrored a cut on Riker's.

"I think you're right. I may need a few Band-Aids," Riker said in her native tongue.

"You should put ice on it too. That's what my mom does when I have an owie. Ice cream is good too. You will feel better with ice cream."

"I didn't know that Li. Are you a doctor?"

Li giggled. "No I'm a little girl. I don't have a job. Where are we going now?"

"I'm going to take you to some people that know your parents. They will take you to your mom and dad."

"Are you coming?"

"No, I need to get back to my home too."

"To see your family?" Li asked.

"I don't have a family. I do have a lot of bees."

Li smiled and held out her arms like wings. She made a buzzing sound. "Why don't you have a family?"

"I guess I just haven't gotten around to that yet." Riker wasn't used to the direct line of questions that came from a kid.

Li paused and thought. "Is it because you are busy saving people? Are you a hero like the Hulk?"

"No, I don't normally do that. It was special for you."

"You should save more people. You just need a costume. I think it should be pink. Pink and have a cape."

Riker laughed. It made his sides hurt, but it still felt good. "I think that would be a great costume. Maybe you should become a superhero. I think you would be good at it."

"Yes, I would be a great superhero. We could help people together. Did you know that plum blossoms are red and white?"

"I didn't know that."

"Yes. I know lots about flowers."

Riker listened to Li jabber in the back seat for the rest of the drive back into New York City. She jumped from topic to topic, speaking with the authority of a three-year-old. He mostly listened and answered the occasional question. He felt something he hadn't felt in a long time—a sense of peace.

Riker had executed hundreds of missions. They typically ended with death. If there was a benefit to any of it, he never really saw it. This was real. A little girl was alive. She would be reunited with her family. He didn't need to think about her family's political factions on a global stage. He just needed to listen to her talk about her pet cat to know he'd truly done the right thing.

An hour later, Riker parked the car on Broadway in lower Manhattan. Across the street was a large building that held the FBI office.

Riker turned to Li in the back seat who was singing a song she was making up. "Li, I need to go."

"When will you be back?" she asked.

"Some people are going to take you to your parents now. They are nice people who work for the FBI."

"Why can't you take me to my parents?"

"I wish I could, but I need to go get a Band-Aid for my owie."

"Ok," she said, a frown on her face.

"Wait right here in the car, Li. They will be here soon. Okay?"

"Okay, I will stay here."

Riker took a moment to wipe his prints from the steering wheel, console, and door. He stepped out and looked to the back seat one last time.

"Hug," Li said and stretched out her arms towards Riker.

The small gesture caught Riker off guard. He opened the door to the back seat and gently placed his arms around the small child. She squeezed back as hard as she could.

The pain, exhaustion and relief hit him all at once in that hug. His vision blurred and tears filled his eyes. One escaped and made its way down his cheek.

He pulled back from Li and her smile faded when she saw the tear. She reached out towards his face and mimicked grabbing something. She put her hands together and then opened one hand showing that there was nothing inside.

Riker recognized the coin vanishing trick, but he was confused. "What did you make disappear?"

Li smiled. "Your sadness."

Those words hit him harder than any punch that had been thrown at him. He just smiled at Li for a moment.

"Zàijiàn, Li," Riker said. *Goodbye, Li.*

"Zàijiàn, Yīngxióng." *Goodbye, Hero.*

Riker walked away from the car and pulled out Dobbs' phone. He called the FBI office and asked to speak to the first available agent. He was connected to a female agent a moment later. Riker told her that the daughter of Zong Lingyu was in a black SUV across from the office on Broadway. That got the agent's attention in a big way. She started to rattle off questions, but Riker just told her to go to the car and save the little girl.

He hung up the phone and continued walking down the street. He moved casually, keeping an eye on the car. When he was a block and a half away, he saw two agents approach the SUV. A moment later, they pulled Li out of the vehicle.

Riker turned the corner, tossed the phone into a trash can, and hopped onto a bus. He made a few transfers to cover his track. A few hours later he reached his motel room. He walked to the bed and collapsed. He slept for the next twenty-four hours.

Three days later, Riker walked into a hospital. His face was bruised and a bandage covered the cut on his forehead. He fit right in among the sick and injured. On the second floor he found the room he was looking for and slipped through the door.

The man in the hospital bed turned to see Riker enter.

"Hey, Brennan. It's good to see you alive."

Brennan took a second for the surprise to register. "I didn't think I'd see you again." He smiled. "You look like shit."

"Thanks, that's about how I feel too." Riker crossed the room and shook Brennan's hand. The man had an IV in his arm and several monitors connected to him.

"I assume that you came here to give me a new car. It's the right thing to do when you crash a man's Charger."

Riker laughed. "I've wrecked so many cars in the last week that I forgot one of them was yours. Besides, someone hit me. You'll have to get in touch with their insurance."

"That's got to be the strangest excuse I've ever heard."

"It was a pretty strange week. I haven't had one like it in a long time."

"Well I'm glad you did," Brennan said.

"What are you talking about? You are recovering from multiple gunshot wounds thanks to me."

"Okay, I'm not thrilled with that part, but I'll take it with everything else."

"Yeah, I'm glad we were able to get Li back to her parents."

"Me too, but it's a lot more than that. Weaver's entire organization is wiped out. One of the worst human traffickers in the US is completely gone. Even if we would have put our case together and put Weaver away, it would have taken years. There would have been enough time for someone else to take over. Hell, Weaver probably would have run the thing from prison if he ever went there. I'm not a fan of vigilante justice, but I think it worked out in this case."

"What are the guys in your department saying about this vigilante?"

A smile crept across Brennan's face. "I thought you probably hadn't come by just to wish me well. If you're wondering who's looking for you, the short answer is no one. I didn't mention you to anyone, and your name isn't going to come up in my report. The investigators on this don't have any clue what happened. They think that Weaver lost a gang war. We just don't have the resources to figure out exactly what went down. Since the end of the story is that a bunch of human traffickers are dead, the force doesn't want to spend the time and money to figure out what happened."

"What about the FBI? Have you heard anything about them? Did Li make it back to her family?"

"I know a little. They questioned me for a while. I told them that I didn't know who the kid was until the night I tried to save her. They are trying to figure out who dropped her off at the agency and what happened at an airstrip outside of the city. I didn't mention anything about you."

"Thanks. What about Li?"

"The people from the FBI wouldn't give me much information, but they said she was with her family and safe."

"How about you? You going to get out of New York after this?"

"Hell, no. I'm taking your credit for getting the kid home safely. I'll basically be able to go straight to detective. I'm looking forward to being a part of the force again."

"You're kidding. I figured you would want to get away from this cesspool."

"Hey, that's the best city in the world you're talking about. Not to mention it's my home."

Riker saw that Brennan meant it. New York was special to him. "Sorry, man. I'm just a country boy afraid of the big city."

"Don't worry about it. What are you going to do?"

"I'm going to head back to my quiet life. Nothing but lying low and avoiding trouble."

"That's it? You're just going to go hang out in the country?"

"Yep, that's it."

"Are you worried that someone will come for you? I get that there isn't much left of Weaver's organization, but Paddock is still out there."

"I don't mean to sound arrogant, but I'm not scared of Paddock. I think he will lie low after this, or he will try to fill the void that Weaver left. Either way, he'll have other things to deal with."

"You definitely sound arrogant. You shouldn't take organized crime lightly. These guys can hold a grudge."

"There are much more dangerous groups out there than New York City gangs."

"Yeah? How do you know?"

"I used to be part of one."

Riker walked to the door. He looked back one last time.

"Thanks for your help, Brennan. I'm sure you'll do great cleaning up the city."

"See you around, Riker."

# EPILOGUE

It took Riker three days to travel home, partly because he was taking it slow, giving himself time to heal and breathe a little after the trauma he'd just been through, but also because a part of him was afraid of what he might find when he arrived there. He rode the Greyhound for a few hours and spent a full day in Pennsylvania, walking the streets of some small town selected at random, enjoying his anonymity. He was still visibly bruised and the cut over his eye looked nasty, but no one commented on it. People left him alone, exchanging only a polite few words when the situation demanded it.

He tried not to think too much about the fallout of his actions. The only thing he let himself dwell on was the thought of Li reuniting with her parents. That thought brought him joy. He wondered how she'd explain him to them, or if she would even try. He wondered if she'd remember him.

After his second night in the Pennsylvania hotel, Riker walked to the bus station and bought a ticket for North Carolina. The thing that finally got him moving was the thought of his hives. It had been ten days since he'd tended to them. He needed to get home.

He slept hard on the bus, suppressing the part of his mind that was always cautious of danger. Paddock was still out there, possibly looking for him. Then there were the Chinese men, the ones Weaver warned him not to kill. Perhaps their colleagues were looking for Riker, too.

And of course, there was Morrison.

The bus dropped Riker off in Henderson. He walked the three miles home to his farm, though there were certainly people he could have called for a ride. He wanted to approach home slowly and on foot. When he reached it, he waited in a stand of trees fifty yards away and watched the house for a full hour. Finally satisfied there was no one inside, he walked to the front door, pulled out his keys, and let himself inside.

The house was just as he'd left it—clean, orderly, and perhaps a bit cold. It was eerily silent. Riker had expected to feel some great sense of comfort when he walked through those doors, but the bare walls and tidy closets brought him nothing of the sort. It was just another place, no different from the shady motel he'd stayed at in New York City.

He'd lived there six years. Perhaps, he thought, it was finally time to make it home.

His hives needed tending and the shower was calling to him, but there was something he wanted to do before he got to either of those things. He opened a kitchen drawer, rummaging through the spare batteries and pens until he found what he was looking for—a magnet.

He walked over to the fridge. It was a stainless steel, double-doored Whirlpool. Its interior was as well organized as everything else in the house, and its exterior was clean and empty, nothing but polished steel.

Riker reached into his back pocket and pulled out a wrinkled piece of paper. He unfolded it carefully. Li might not have a future as an artist, but every stroke of the crayon meant something to him. He put the piece of paper on the fridge door and stuck it in place with the magnet.

Riker stepped back and crossed his arms, smiling as he stared at the drawing.

He turned away, headed outside, and went to work.

---

IN A NONDESCRIPT CONFERENCE room in an unknown location somewhere on the Eastern Seaboard, Morrison silently read through the papers in front of him. Stone, the only other person in the room, waited patiently, letting his boss read and process the information.

Finally, after nearly ten minutes, Morrison set the folder on the table and sighed. "Are we sure it was him?"

Stone flipped through the pages in front of him. There were police reports, eye witness testimony gathered by their investigator, and photographs. It was the photos that most captured Stone's attention. Reports were one thing, but seeing the carnage in living color was something else entirely. There was a photo taken in a truck stop. One in an alley. One at a New York brownstone. And the pièce de résistance, the half-burned, corpse-ridden remains of a private airfield.

"Let's see," Stone said. "A kidnapped child returned to her family. A New York City criminal empire dismantled. Fifty-two people dead and a survivor who says his finger was pulled clean off of his hand. And by all accounts, it was the work of one man. Yeah, we're pretty sure it was Matthew Riker."

Morrison sighed again. "He was doing so well. It's been six years. Our investigators said he appeared to be happy with his new life."

"Come on, boss. You think a guy like Riker was ever going to be happy with the simple life? It was only a matter of time."

Morrison thought for a moment. "It's clear there were special circumstances here. Riker always had a strict moral code, even back in the old days. These people violated it, and they paid the price. Child trafficking...it's almost understandable what Riker did."

Stone pushed the papers aside and leaned forward, looking Morrison in the eyes. "Boss, I read the agreement he signed. It was crystal clear, and there was no exception for special circumstances. Don't tell me you're going to let this slide."

"No," Morrison said. "As much as I'd like to, we don't have a choice here."

"Good," Stone said with a nod. "So what's the move?"

"He broke the contract, and now he has to pay the penalty. We're going to North Carolina. It's time to pay Riker a visit."

# AUTHOR'S NOTE

Thanks so much for reading THE IMPORT. Matthew Riker has been living in my head for quite some a while. It was only a matter of time before he fought his way out onto the page.

I hope you enjoyed getting to know Riker. If you did, please consider leaving a review for the book.

Riker's next adventure is called GHOST AGENT, and I think you're going to love it. Say tuned… it will be out in July 2020.

Thanks again, and happy reading.

J.T. Baier

CPSIA information can be obtained
at www.ICGtesting.com
Printed in the USA
BVHW070820010321
601377BV00004B/347